THE REBEL DOC
WHO STOL
HER HEART

BY
SUSAN CARLISLE

MILLS
BOON
&

Born to a family that was always on the move, **Tina Beckett** learned to pack a suitcase almost before she knew how to tie her shoes. Fortunately she met a man who also loved to travel, and she snapped him right up. Married for over twenty years, Tina has three wonderful children and has lived in gorgeous places such as Portugal and Brazil.

Living where English reading material is difficult to find has its drawbacks, however. Tina had to come up with creative ways to satisfy her love for romance novels, so she picked up her pen and tried writing one. After her tenth book she realised she was hooked. She was officially a writer.

A three-times Golden Heart finalist, and fluent in Portuguese, Tina now divides her time between the United States and Brazil. She loves to use exotic locales as the backdrop for many of her stories. When she's not writing you can find her either on horseback or soldering stained glass panels for her home.

Tina loves to hear from readers. You can contact her through her website or 'friend' her on Facebook.

Susan Carlisle's love affair with books began when she made a bad grade in math in the sixth grade. Not allowed to watch TV until she'd brought the grade up, she filled her time with books and became a voracious romance reader. She has 'keepers' on the shelf to prove it. Because she loved the genre so much she decided to try her hand at creating her own romantic worlds. She still loves a good happily-ever-after-story.

When not writing Susan doubles as a high school substitute teacher, which she has been doing for sixteen years. Susan lives in Georgia with her husband of twenty-eight years and has four grown children. She loves castles, travelling, cross-stitching, hats, James Bond and hearing from her readers.

HER HARD TO RESIST HUSBAND

BY
TINA BECKETT

MILLS &
BOON

Published in Great Britain 2014
by Mills & Boon, an imprint of Harlequin (UK) Limited,
Eton House, 18-24 Paradise Road, Richmond, Surrey, TW9 1SR

© Tina Beckett 2014

ISBN: 978 0 263 90739 1

Harlequin (UK) Limited's policy is to use papers that are natural,
renewable and recyclable products and made from wood grown in
sustainable forests. The logging and manufacturing processes conform
to the legal environmental regulations of the country of origin.

Printed and bound in Spain
by Blackprint CPI, Barcelona

Dear Reader

There comes a time in our lives when we're confronted with tough challenges or painful decisions. When those decisions are of a life-changing nature there's a temptation to draw inward and isolate ourselves, locking out those who love us the most.

Tracy Hinton faces just such a situation. And at a time when she should lean on her husband the most she shuts him out completely, creating a rift that soon grows too wide to bridge.

That could have been the end of the story, but sometimes we're given a second chance—an opportunity to right the wrongs of the past. What we do with that chance will set the course for our future. Will we waste it? Or will we embrace it and accept the good things life has to offer?

Thank you for joining Ben and Tracy as they embark on a very special journey of healing and second chances. In confronting the mistakes of the past they rekindle a love that has never quite died. These two characters stayed with me long after I wrote 'The End'. I hope you enjoy reading their story as much as I enjoyed writing it.

Love

Tina Beckett

Dedication

To my husband, who stands beside me
through thick and thin.

And to my editor, Suzy,
for making me dig deeper than I ever thought I could.

Recent titles by Tina Beckett:

THE LONE WOLF'S CRAVING**
NYC ANGELS: FLIRTING WITH DANGER*
ONE NIGHT THAT CHANGED EVERYTHING
THE MAN WHO WOULDN'T MARRY
DOCTOR'S MILE-HIGH FLING
DOCTOR'S GUIDE TO DATING IN THE JUNGLE

*NYC Angels
**Men of Honour duet with Anne Fraser

**These books are also available in eBook format
from www.millsandboon.co.uk**

**Praise for
Tina Beckett:**

'…a tension-filled emotional story with just the
right amount of drama. The author's vivid description of
the Brazilian jungle and its people
make this story something special.'
—*RT Book Reviews* on
DOCTOR'S GUIDE TO DATING IN THE JUNGLE

'Medical Romance™ lovers will definitely like
NYC ANGELS: FLIRTING WITH DANGER
by Tina Beckett—for who doesn't like
a good forbidden romance…?'
—*HarlequinJunkie.com*

CHAPTER ONE

TRACY HINTON DIDN'T faint.

Her stomach squirmed and threatened to give way as the scent of death flooded her nostrils, but she somehow held it together. Calming herself with slow, controlled breaths was out of the question, because breathing was the last thing she wanted to do right now.

"How many are there?" She fitted the protective mask over her nose and mouth.

"Six deaths so far, but most of the town is affected." Pedro, one of her mobile clinic workers, nodded towards the simple clay-brick house to his left, where an eerily still figure was curled in a fetal position on the porch. Another body lay a few yards away on the ground. "They've been dead for a few days. Whatever it was, it hit fast. They didn't even try to make it to a hospital."

"They were probably too sick. Besides, the nearest hospital is twenty miles away."

Piauí, one of the poorest of the Brazilian states, was more vulnerable to catastrophic infections than the wealthier regions, and many of these outlying townships relied on bicycles or their own two feet for transportation. It was hard enough to make a twenty-mile trek even when one was young and healthy, which these poor souls had not been. And cars were a luxury most couldn't afford.

She wouldn't know for sure what had caused the deaths until she examined the bodies and gathered some specimens. The nearest diagnostic hospital was a good hundred miles from here. In any case, she'd have to report the possibility of an epidemic to the proper authorities.

Which meant she'd have to deal with Ben.

Pedro shook his head. "Dengue, you think?"

"Not this time. There's some blood on the front of the man's shirt, but nothing else that I can see from this distance." She stared at the crude corral where several pigs squealed out a protest at the lack of food. "I'm thinking lepto."

Pedro frowned. "Leptospirosis? Rainy season's already over."

The area around the house consisted of a few desiccated twigs and hard-packed clay, confirming her colleague's words. The sweltering heat sucked any remaining moisture from the air and squeezed around her, making her nausea that much worse. Situated close to the equator, the temperature of this part of Brazil rarely dipped below the hundred-degree mark during the dry season. The deadly heat would only grow worse, until the rains finally returned.

"They have pigs." She used her forearm to push sticky tendrils of hair from her forehead.

"I saw that, but lepto doesn't normally cause hemorrhaging."

"It did in *Bahia*."

Pedro's brows went up. "You think it's the pulmonary version?"

"I don't know. Maybe."

"Do you want to take samples? Or head for one of the other houses?"

Reaching into the back pocket of her jeans, she eased out her cellphone and glanced hopefully at the display. No bars. What worked in São Paulo obviously didn't work here. "Is your phone working?"

"Nope."

She sighed, trying to figure out what to do. "The tissue samples will have to wait until we come back, I don't want to risk contaminating any live patients. And maybe we'll come within range of a cellphone tower once we hit higher ground."

Benjamin Almeida pressed his eye to the lens of the microscope and twisted the fine focus until the image sharpened, making the pink stain clearly visible. Gram negative bacteria. Removing the slide, he ran it through the digital microscope and recorded the results.

"Um, Ben?" His assistant's hesitant voice came from the doorway.

He held up a finger as he waited for the computer to signal it had sent his report to the attending physician at the tropical disease institute of *Piauí*. The man's office was fifteen steps away in the main hospital building, but Ben couldn't take the time to walk over there right now. Dragging the latex gloves from his hands and flicking them into the garbage can to his right, he reached for the hand sanitizer and squirted a generous amount onto his palm.

"Yep, what is it?" He glanced up, his twelve-hour shift beginning to catch up with him. There were two more slides he needed to process before he could call it a day.

"Someone's here to see you." Mandy shifted out of the doorway, the apology in her cultured Portuguese tones unmistakable.

"If it's Dr. Mendosa, tell him I just emailed the report. It's a bacterial infection, not a parasite."

A woman appeared next to Mandy, and Ben couldn't stop his quick intake of breath. Shock wheeled through him, and he forced himself to remain seated on his stool, thankful his legs weren't in charge of supporting his weight at that moment.

Inky-dark hair, pulled back in its usual clip, exposed high cheekbones and a long slender neck. Green eyes—right now filled with worry—met his without hesitation, her chin tilting slightly higher as they stared at each other.

What the hell was *she* doing here?

The newcomer adjusted the strap of a blue insulated bag on her shoulder and took a small step closer. "Ben, I need your help."

His jaw tensed. Those were almost the exact words she'd used four years ago. Right before she'd walked out of his life. He gave a quick swallow, hoping his voice wouldn't betray his thoughts. "With what?"

"Something's happening in São João dos Rios." She patted the bag at her side, words tumbling out at breakneck speed. "I brought samples I need you to analyze. The sooner the better, because I have to know why people are suddenly—"

"Slow down. I have no idea what you're talking about."

She bit her lip, and he watched her try to collect her thoughts. "There's an outbreak in São João dos Rios. Six people are dead so far. The military police are already on their way to lock down the town." She held her hand out. "I wouldn't have come if this wasn't important. Really important."

That much he knew was true. The last time he'd seen her, she had been heading out the door of their house, never to return.

He shouldn't be surprised she was still roving the country, stamping out infectious fires wherever she went. Nothing had been able to stop her. Not him. Not the thought of a home and family. Not the life she'd carried inside her.

Against his better judgement, he yanked on a fresh pair of gloves. "Do I need a respirator?"

"I don't think so. We used surgical masks to collect the samples."

He nodded, pulling one on and handing another to her, grateful that its presence would hide those soft pink lips he'd never tired of kissing. Ben's attention swiveled back to her eyes, and he cursed the fact that the vivid green still had the power to make his pulse pound in his chest even after all this time.

He cleared his throat. "Symptoms?"

"The commonality seems to be pulmonary hemorrhage, maybe from some type of pneumonia." She passed him the bag. "The bodies have already been cremated, unfortunately."

"Without autopsies?" Something in his stomach twisted in warning.

"The military let me collect a few samples before they carted the bodies away, and the government took another set to do its own studies. I have to document that I've destroyed everything once you're done." She lowered her voice. "There's a guard in your reception area whose job it is to make sure that order is carried out. Help me out here. You're the best epidemiologist around these parts."

He glanced at the doorway, noting for the first time the armed member of the *Polícia Militar* leaning against the wall in the other room. "That wasn't one of my most endearing features, once upon a time."

He remembered all too well the heated arguments they'd had over which was more important: individual rights or the public good.

Biting her lip, she hesitated. "Because you went behind my back and used your job as a weapon against me."

Yes, he had. And not even that had stopped her.

His assistant, who'd been watching from the doorway, pulled on a mask and moved to stand beside him, her head tilting as she glanced nervously at the guard. Her English wasn't the best, and Ben wasn't sure how much of their conversation she'd grasped. "Is he going to let us leave?" she asked in Portuguese.

Tracy switched to the native language. "If it turns out the illness is just a common strain of pneumonia, it won't be a problem."

"And if it isn't?"

Ben's lips compressed as he contemplated spending an unknown amount of time confined to his tiny office.

With Tracy.

He had a foldable cot in a back closet, but it was narrow. Certainly not large enough for...

"If it isn't, then it looks like we might be here for a while." He went to the door and addressed the official. "We haven't opened the tissue samples yet. My assistant has a family. I'd like her to go home before we begin."

Ben had insisted his office be housed in a separate building from the main hospital for just this reason. It was small enough that the whole thing could be sealed off in the event of an airborne epidemic. And just like the microbial test he'd completed for a colleague moments earlier, any results could be sent off via computer.

Safety was his number-one priority. Mandy knew the risks of working for him, but she'd been exposed to nothing, as far as he could tell. Not like when Tracy had rushed headlong into a yellow fever epidemic four years ago that had forced him to call in the military authorities.

The guard in the doorway tapped his foot for a second, as if considering Ben's request. He then turned away and spoke to someone through his walkie-talkie. When he was done, he faced them. "We'll have someone escort her home, but she'll have to remain there until we know what the illness is. As for you two…" he motioned to Ben and Tracy "…once the samples are uncapped you'll have to stay in this building until we determine the risks."

Mandy sent Ben a panicked look. "Are you sure it's safe for me to leave? My baby…" She shut her eyes. "I need to call my husband."

"Have Sergio take the baby to your mother's house, where she'll be safe. just in case. I'll call you as soon as I know something, okay?"

His assistant nodded and left to make her call.

"I'm sorry." Tracy's face softened. "I thought you'd be alone in the lab. I didn't realize you'd gotten an assistant."

"It's not your fault. She's worried about the risks to her baby." His eyes came up to meet hers, and he couldn't resist the dig. "Just as any woman with children would be."

He mentally kicked himself when the compassion in Tracy's eyes dissolved, and anger took its place.

"I *was* concerned. But it was never enough for you, was it?" Her chest rose as she took a deep breath. "I'm heading back to São João dos Rios as soon as you give me some answers. If I'm going to be quarantined, I'm going to do it where I can make a difference. That doesn't include sitting in a lab, staring at rows of test tubes."

He knew he'd struck a nerve, but it didn't stop an old hurt from creeping up his spine. "Says the woman who came to *my* lab, asking for help," he said quietly.

"I didn't mean it like that."

"Sure you did."

They stared at each other then the corners of her eyes crinkled. She pulled down her mask, letting it dangle around her neck. "Okay, maybe I did…a little. But at least I admitted that I need you. That has to count for something."

It did. But that kind of need was a far cry from what

they'd once had together. Those days were long gone, and no matter how hard Ben had tried to hold onto her back then, she'd drifted further and further away, until the gulf between them had been too huge to span.

Bellyaching about the past won't get you anywhere.

Ben shook off the thoughts and set the insulated bag on an empty metal table. He nodded towards the aluminum glove dispenser hanging on the far wall. "Suit up and don't touch anything in the lab, just in case."

She dug into her handbag instead and pulled out her own box of gloves. "I came prepared."

Of course she had. It was part of who she was. This was a woman who was always on the move—who never took a weekend off. Tracy had thrown herself into her work without restraint…until there had been nothing left for herself. Or for him.

He'd thought she'd stop once the pregnancy tests went from blue to pink. She hadn't. And Ben hadn't been able to face any child of his going through what he had as a kid.

Gritting his teeth in frustration, he glanced around the lab, eyeing the centrifuges and other equipment. They'd have to work in the tiny glassed-off cubicle in the corner that he'd set up for occasions like this.

Keeping his day-to-day work space absolutely separate from Tracy's samples was not only smart, it was non-negotiable. If they weren't careful, the government could end up quarantining his whole lab, meaning years of work would be tossed into the incinerator. He tensed. Although if their findings turned up a microbe that was airborne, he'd willingly burn everything himself. He wouldn't risk setting loose an epidemic.

Not even for Tracy. She should know that by now.

"I have a clean room set up over there. Once we get things squared away with Mandy, we can start."

Tracy peered towards the door where the phone conversation between his assistant and her husband was growing more heated by the second. "I was really careful about keeping everything as sterile as I could. I don't think she's been exposed to anything."

"I'm sure it'll be fine. I'm going to take your bagged samples into the other area. Can you wipe down the table where they were with disinfectant?"

As soon as Ben picked up the insulated bag, the guard appeared, his hand resting on the butt of his gun. "Where are you going with that?"

Ben motioned towards the clean room. "The samples can't infect anyone else if they're kept enclosed. You can see everything we do from the reception doorway. It'll be safer if you keep your distance once we've started testing, though."

The guard backed up a couple of paces. "How long will it take? I have no wish to stay here any longer than I have to."

"I have no idea. It depends on what we're dealing with."

Putting the bag in the cubicle, he gathered the equipment he'd need and arranged it on the set of metal shelves perched above a stainless-steel table. He blew out a breath. The eight-by-eight-foot area was going to be cramped once he and Tracy were both inside.

An air handler filtered any particles floating in and out of the clean room, but there was no safe way to pump air-conditioning into the space. They'd have to rely on the wheezy window unit in the main lab and hope it kept them from baking. He could offer to send Tracy on her way before he got the results—but he was pretty sure he knew how that suggestion would be met, despite her waspish words earlier.

You couldn't coax—or force—Tracy to do anything she didn't want to do. He knew that from experience.

Mandy appeared in the doorway to the reception area just as Ben turned on the air filter and closed the door on the samples.

"It's all arranged. Sergio called my mom and asked if she'd care for the baby overnight. He's not happy about staying home from work, but he doesn't want me to stay here either."

"I don't blame him. But look on the bright side. At least you can go home." He smiled. "Tell Sergio he should count his lucky stars I haven't stolen you away from him."

Mandy laughed. "You've already told him that yourself. Many times."

Tracy spun away from them and stalked over to the metal table she'd previously sanitized and began scrubbing it all over again. She kept her head down, not looking at either of them.

"Is the guard going to take you home?" He forced the words to remain cheerful.

"They're sending another policeman. He should be here soon."

"Good." He had Mandy go back and wait in the reception area, so there'd be no question of her being anywhere near those samples. Returning to the sealed cubicle, he slid the insulated bag into a small refrigerator he kept for just this purpose. The air was already growing close inside the room, but he'd worked under worse conditions many times before. Both he and Tracy had.

He could still picture one such occasion—their very first meeting—Tracy had stepped off the *Projeto Vida* medical boat and stalked into the village he had been surveying, demanding to know what he was doing about the malaria outbreak twenty miles downriver. He'd been exhausted, and she'd looked like a gorgeous avenging angel, silky black hair flowing behind her in the breeze, ready to slay him if he said one wrong word.

They'd barely lasted two days before they'd fallen into bed together.

Something he'd rather not remember at the moment. Especially as he was trying to avoid any and all physical contact with her.

She might be immune, but he wasn't. Not judging from the way his heart had taken off at a sprint when he'd seen her standing in that doorway.

Tracy dumped her paper towel into the hazardous waste receptacle and crossed over to him. "I just want to say thank you for agreeing to help. You could have told me to get lost." She gave a hard laugh. "I wouldn't have blamed you if you had."

"I'm not always an ogre, you know."

Her teeth caught the right corner of her bottom lip in a way that made his chest tighten. "I know. And I'm sorry for dragging you into this, but I didn't know where else to go. The military didn't want me to take the samples out of São João dos Rios. They only agreed to let me come here because you've worked with them before…and even then they made me bring a guard. I honestly didn't think anyone else would be affected other than us."

"It's not your fault, Trace." He started to reach out to touch her cheek, but checked himself. "The government is probably right to keep this as contained as possible. If I thought there was any chance of contamination, I'd be the first one to say Mandy needs to stay here at the lab with us."

He smiled. "If I know you, though, not one microbe survived on that bag before you carried it out of that town."

"I hope not. There are still several ill people waiting on us for answers. I left a colleague behind to make sure the military didn't do anything rash, but he's not a doctor, and

I don't want to risk his health either." She blew out a breath. "Those people need help. But there's nothing I can do until I know what we're dealing with."

And then she'd be on her way to the next available crisis. Just like she always was.

His smile faded. "Let's get to work, then."

The guard stuck his head into the room. "They're sending someone for your friend. They'll keep her at home until the danger has passed."

Ben nodded. "I understand. Thank you."

When he went to the doorway to say goodbye to Mandy, she kissed his cheek, her arms circling his neck and hugging him close. When she finally let go, her eyes shimmered with unshed tears. "I'm so grateful. I can't imagine not being able to tuck my Jenny into bed tonight, but at least I'll be closer to her than I would be if I stayed here."

His heart clenched. Here was a woman whose baby meant the world to her—who didn't need to jet off to distant places to find fulfillment. Unlike his parents.

Unlike Tracy.

"We'll work as quickly as we can. Once things are clear, make sure you give her a kiss and a hug from her uncle Ben."

"I will." She wiped a spot of lipstick from his cheek with her thumb. "Be careful, okay? I've just gotten used to your crazy ways. I don't want to break someone else in."

Ben laughed and took off one of his latex gloves, laying his hand on her shoulder. "You're not getting rid of me any time soon, so go and enjoy your mini-vacation. You'll be back to the same old grind before you know it."

Mandy's escort arrived, and as soon as she exited the building, he turned back to find Tracy observing him with a puzzled frown.

"What?" he asked.

She shrugged. "Nothing. I'm just surprised you haven't found a woman who'd be thrilled to stick close to the house and give you all those kids you said you wanted."

"That would be impossible, given the circumstances."

"Oh?" Her brows arched. "And why is that?"

He laughed, the sound harsh in the quiet room. "Do you really have to ask?"

"I just did."

Grabbing her left hand, he held it up, forcing her eyes to the outline of the plain gold band visible beneath her latex glove. "For the same reason you're wearing this." He stared into her face. "Have you forgotten, *Mrs. Almeida*? You may not go by your married name any more, but in the eyes of the law…we're still husband and wife."

CHAPTER TWO

SHE'D FORGOTTEN NOTHING.

And she'd tried to see about getting a divorce, but being overseas made everything a hundred times more complicated. Both of the Brazilian lawyers she'd contacted had said that as an American citizen, she should return to the States and start the proceedings there, as she and Ben had been married in New York. But asking him to accompany her had been out of the question. Even if he'd been willing, she wasn't. She hadn't wanted to be anywhere near him, too raw from everything that had transpired in the month before she'd left *Teresina*—and him—for ever.

Staying married probably hadn't been the wisest move on her part but she'd thrown herself into her work afterwards, far too busy with *Projeto Vida*, her aid organization's floating clinic, to set the ugly wheels in motion. Besides, a wedding ring tended to scare away any man who ventured too close. Not that there'd been many. Her *caution-do-not-touch* vibes must be coming through loud and clear. She'd never get married again—to anyone—so keeping her wedding ring and her license made keeping that promise a whole lot easier.

Too bad she hadn't remembered to take the ring off before asking Ben for help.

She realized he was still waiting for a response so she

lifted her chin, praying he wouldn't notice the slight tremble. "We're not married any more. Not by any stretch of the imagination. You made sure of that."

"Right." Ben turned away and gathered a few more pieces of equipment.

Her thumb instinctively rubbed back and forth across the ring, a gesture she'd found oddly comforting during some of the tougher periods of her life—like now.

Strange how most of those times had found her wearing surgical gloves.

Studying Ben as he worked, Tracy was surprised by the slight dusting of grey in his thick brown hair. She gave herself a mental shake. The man was thirty-eight, and she hadn't set eyes on him in four years. Change was inevitable. What hadn't changed, however, were the electric blue eyes, compliments of his American mother, or how they provided the perfect counterpoint for tanned skin, high cheekbones and a straight, autocratic nose—all legacies from his Brazilian father. Neither had he lost any of that intense focus she'd once found so intimidating.

And irresistible.

Snap out of it, Tracy.

She donned the scrubs, booties and surgical gear Ben had left out for her and moved into the glassed-in cubicle where he was busy setting up.

"Close the door, please, so I can seal it off."

"Seal it off?" Swallowing hard, she hesitated then did as he asked.

"Just with this." He held up a roll of clear packing tape. "Is your claustrophobia going to be a problem?"

She hoped not, but feeling trapped had always set off a rolling sense of panic that could quickly snowball if she wasn't careful. It didn't matter whether the confinement was physical or emotional, the fear was the same. Glancing through the door to the reception area, she noted the exit to the outside world was plainly visible even from where she stood. "As long as I know there's a door right through there, I should be fine. The room being made of glass helps."

"Good."

Ben taped the edges of the door, before removing the insulated bag from the fridge and examining the labels on each tube inside. Selecting two of them, he put the rest back in cold storage.

"What do you want me to do?" Tracy asked.

"Set up some slides. We're going to work our way from simple to complex."

He turned one of the tubes to the side and read her label out loud. "Daniel, male, twelve years." He paused. "Living?"

"Yes." Her heart twisted when she thought of the preteen boy staring at her with terrified eyes. But at least he was alive. As was his younger sister Cleo. Their mother, however, hadn't been so lucky. Hers had been one of the first bodies they'd found in the village. "Febrile. No skin lesions visible."

"Signs of pneumonia?"

"Not yet, which is why this seemed so strange. Most of the dead had complained to relatives of coughs along with fever and malaise."

"Liver enlargement in the dead?"

She swallowed. "No autopsies, remember? The military destroyed everything." Her voice cracked.

Ben's gloved hand covered hers, and even through the layers of latex the familiar warmth of his touch comforted her in a way no one else ever could. "Why don't you get those slides ready, while I set up the centrifuge?"

Glad to have something to take her mind off the horrific scene she and Pedro had stumbled on in São João dos Rios, she pulled several clean slides from the box and spread them across the table. Then, carefully taking the cotton swab from Ben's outstretched hand, she smeared a thin layer of material on the smooth glass surface. "What are you looking for?"

"Anything. Everything." The tense muscle in his jaw made her wonder if he already had a theory. "You'll need to heat-set the slides as you smear them."

He lit a small burner and showed her how to pass the slide across the flame to dry it and affix the specimen to the glass.

The sound of a throat clearing in the outer doorway made them both look up. Their guard cupped his hands over his mouth and said in a loud voice, "Your assistant has arrived safely at her home."

Ben flashed a thumbs-up sign. "Thanks for letting me know."

Tracy's fingers tensed on the slide at the mention of Ben's assistant, which was ridiculous. Yes, the woman had kissed him, but Brazilians kissed everyone—it was a kind of unspoken rule in these parts. Besides, the woman had a family. A new baby.

Her throat tightened, a sense of loss sweeping over her. Ben had wanted children so badly. So had she. When she'd fallen pregnant, they'd both been elated. Until she'd had a devastating piece of news that had set her back on her heels. She'd thrown herself into her work, angering Ben, even as she'd tried to figure out a way to tell him.

That had all changed when he'd sent the military in to force her out of a stricken village during a yellow fever outbreak. She knew he'd been trying to protect her and the baby—not from the disease itself, as she'd already been vaccinated the previous year, but from anything that had taken her out of his sight. She hadn't need protecting, though. She'd needed to work. It had been her lifeline in a time of turmoil and confusion, and his interference had damaged her trust. She'd miscarried a week later, and the rift that had opened between them during their disagreement over the military had grown deeper, with accusations flying fast and furious on both sides.

In the end she'd opted to keep her secret to herself. Telling him would have changed nothing, not when she'd already decided to leave.

Work was still her number-one priority. Still her lifeline. And she needed to get her mind back on what she was doing.

Tracy took the long cotton swab and dipped it into another of her sample jars, laying a thin coating of the material on a second glass slide, heat-setting it, like she'd done with the first. "Do you need me to apply a stain?"

"Let's see what we've got on these first."

"There were pigs in a corral at one of the victims' homes. Could it be leptospirosis?"

"Possibly." He switched on the microscope's light. "If I can't find anything on the slides, we'll need to do some cultures. Lepto will show up there."

He didn't say it, but they both knew cultures would take several days, if not longer, to grow.

Tracy sent a nervous glance towards the reception area, where the guard lounged in a white plastic chair in full view. He twirled what looked like a toothpick between his thumb and forefinger. For the moment his attention wasn't focused on them. And he was far enough away that he shouldn't be able to hear soft voices through the glass partition.

"That could be a problem."

Ben turned toward her, watchful eyes moving over her face. "How so?"

"I told the military police you'd have an answer for them today."

"You did *what*?" His hand clenched on the edge of the table. "Of all the irresponsible—"

"I know, I know. I didn't have a choice. It was either that or leave São João dos Rios empty-handed."

He closed his eyes for a few seconds before looking at her again. "You're still hauling around that savior complex, aren't you, Tracy? Don't you get tired of being the one who swoops in to save the day?"

"I thought that was *your* role. Taking charge even when it's not your decision to make." She tossed her head. "Maybe if you'd stopped thinking about yourself for once…" As soon as the ugly words spurted out she gritted her teeth, staunching the flow. "I'm sorry. That was uncalled for."

"Yes. It was." He took the slide from her and set it down with an audible *crack*.

The guard was on his feet in an instant, his casual manner gone. *"O que foi?"*

Ben held up the slide. "Sorry. Just dropped it." Although he said the words loudly enough for the guard to hear them, he kept his tone calm and even. Even so, the tension in his white-knuckled grip was unmistakable.

The guard rolled his eyes, his face relaxing. "I'm going to the cafeteria. Do you want something?"

How exactly did the man expect to get the food past the sealed doorway? Besides, she wouldn't be able to eat if her life depended on it. "I'm good. Thanks."

"Same here," said Ben.

The guard shrugged and then checked the front door. He palmed the old-fashioned key he found in the lock before reinserting it again, this time on the outside of the door.

He meant to lock them in!

"No, wait!" Tracy stood, not exactly sure how she could stop him.

"Sorry, but I have my orders. Neither of you leaves until those samples are destroyed."

She started to argue further, but Ben touched her shoulder. "Don't," he said in a low voice.

Holding her tongue, she watched helplessly as the door swung shut, a menacing snick of the lock telling her the guard had indeed imprisoned them inside the room. A familiar sting of panic went up her spine. "What if he doesn't come back? What if we're trapped?"

Stripping off one of his gloves, he reached into his pocket. "I have a spare. I know you don't like being confined."

Sagging in relief, she managed a shaky laugh. "You learned that the hard way, didn't you?"

The vivid image of Ben playfully pinning her hands above her head while they'd tussled on the bed sprang to her mind. The love play had been fun. At first. Then a wave of terror had washed over her unexpectedly, and though she'd known her panic had been illogical, she'd begun to struggle in earnest.

A frightened plea had caught in her throat, and as hard as she'd tried to say something, her voice had seemed as frozen as her senses. Ben had only realized she was no longer playing when she succeeded in freeing one of her hands and raked her nails down his face. He'd reeled backwards, while she'd lain there, her chest heaving, tears of relief spilling from her eyes. Understanding had dawned on his face and he'd gathered her into his arms, murmuring how sorry he was. From that moment forward he'd been careful to avoid anything that might make her feel trapped.

A little too careful.

His lovemaking had become less intense and more controlled. Only it had been a different kind of control than what they'd previously enjoyed, when Ben's take-charge demeanor in the bedroom had been a huge turn-on. That had all changed. Tracy had mourned the loss of passion, even as she'd appreciated his reasons for keeping a little more space between them. Her inability to explain where the line between confinement and intimacy lay had driven the first wedge between them.

That wedge had widened later, when he'd tried to limit her movements during her pregnancy, giving rise to the same sensation of being suffocated. She'd clawed at him just as hard then, the marks invisible but causing just as much damage to their marriage.

The Ben of the present fingered the side of his face and gave her a smile. "No permanent damage done."

Yeah, there had been. And it seemed that one patch of bad luck had spiraled into another.

"I always felt terrible about that," she said.

"I should have realized you were scared."

"You couldn't have known."

Even her father hadn't realized their play sessions could change without warning. There'd always been laughter, but the sound of hers had often turned shrill with overtones of panic. A gentle soul, her father would have never hurt her in a million years. It didn't help that her older sister had been a tough-as-nails tomboy who'd feared nothing and had given as good as she'd got. Then Tracy had come along—always fearful, always more cautious. Her father had never quite known what to do with her.

She was still fearful. Still flinched away from situations that made her feel trapped and out of control.

And now her mom and her sister were both gone. Her mom, the victim of a menacing villain who'd stalked its prey relentlessly—turning the delicate strands of a person's DNA into the enemy. Passed from mother to daughter. Tracy had been running from its specter ever since.

Ben donned a fresh glove and picked up the slide he'd smacked against the table, checking it for cracks. Without glancing up at her, he said, "You look tired. I put the folding cot in the corner in case we needed to sleep in shifts. If I know you, you didn't get much rest last night."

"I'm okay." He was right. She was exhausted, but no way would she let him know how easily he could still read her. Or how the touch of concern in his voice made her heart skip a beat. "It's just warm in here."

"I know. The air-conditioner in the lab is ancient, and the filter doesn't let much of it through, anyway."

Even as he said it, a tiny trickle of sweat coursed down her back. "It's fine."

He pushed the slide beneath the viewer of the microscope and focused on the smear. "How old are the samples?"

"Just a couple of hours."

He swore softly as he continued to peer through the lens, evidently seeing something he didn't like. He took the second slide and repeated the process, his right hand shifting a knob on the side of the instrument repeatedly. Sitting up, he dabbed at perspiration that had gathered around his eye with the sleeve of his lab coat then leaned back in for another look.

"What is it?" She felt her own blood rushing through her ears as she awaited the verdict.

It didn't take long. He lifted his head and fastened his eyes on hers. "If I'm not mistaken, it's pneumonic plague, Tracy." Shifting his attention to the test tube in her hand, he continued, "And if you're the one who took these samples, you've already been exposed."

CHAPTER THREE

Tracy sagged and swallowed hard, trying to process what he'd said through her own fear. "Are you sure?"

"Here." He moved aside so she could look at the slide.

Putting her eye to the viewfinder, she squinted into the machine. "What am I looking for?"

"See the little dots grouped into chains?"

"Yes." There were several of them.

"That's what we're dealing with. I want to look at another sample and do a culture, just in case, but I'm sure. It's *Yersinia pestis*, the same bacterium that causes bubonic plague. I recognize the shape." He rolled his shoulders as if relieving an ache. "Bubonic plague normally spreads from infected rats through the bite of a flea, but if the bacteria migrate to a person's lungs, it becomes even more deadly, spreading rapidly from person to person by way of a cough or bodily fluids. When that happens, the disease no longer needs a flea. We'll want to put you on a strong dose of streptomycin immediately."

"What about you?"

"I'll start on them as well, but just as a precaution." Ben dripped a staining solution on another slide. "Most of the people who work in the lab are vaccinated against the plague, including Mandy. But I assume you haven't been."

"No, which means neither has… Oh, God." She rested

her head against Ben's shoulder for a second as a wave of nausea rolled over her. "That town. I have to get back there. They've all been exposed. So has Pedro."

"Pedro?"

"*My* assistant."

Just as he pushed the slide back under the microscope, the lock to the outer door clicked open before Tracy had a chance to figure out how to proceed.

The guard pushed his way inside, glancing from one to the other, his eyes narrowing in on her face. She sat up straighter.

"Problema?" he asked.

Instead of lunch, he only held a coffee cup in his hand.

A tug on the back of her shirt sent a warning Tracy read loud and clear, *Don't tell him anything until I've taken another look.* The gesture surprised her, as he'd always been buddy-buddy with the military, at least from what she'd seen over the course of their marriage.

Still holding one of the slides, he casually laid it on the table. "We need to run a few more tests before we know anything for sure."

"No need. Our doctors have isolated the infection and will take the appropriate containment measures."

Containment? What exactly did that mean?

Her brows lifted in challenge. "What is the illness, then?" Maybe he was bluffing.

"I'm not at liberty to say. But my commander would like to speak with Dr. Almeida over the phone." He gave Tracy a pointed stare. "Alone."

A shiver went over her. Alone. Why?

What if the government doctors had come to a different conclusion than Ben had? What if they were assuming it was something other than the plague? People could still die…still pass it on to neighboring towns. And São João dos Rios was poor. How many people would lose loved ones due to lack of information?

Just like she had. She knew the pain of that firsthand.

She'd lost her mother. Her grandmother. Her sister—although Vickie's illness hadn't been related to a genetic defect. The most devastating loss of all, however, had been her unborn child. Ben's baby.

All had died far too young. And Tracy had decided she wasn't going to waste a second of her time on earth waiting around for what-ifs. Movement, in her eyes, equaled life. So she'd lived that life with a ferocity that others couldn't begin to understand.

Including Ben.

Genetic code might not be written in stone, but its deadly possibility loomed in front of her, as did a decision she might someday choose to make. But until then she was determined to make a difference in the lives of those around her.

Or maybe you're simply running away.

Like she had with Ben? No, their break-up had been for entirely different reasons.

Had it?

She pushed the voice in her head aside. "Why does he want to talk to Dr. Almeida alone?"

"That's not for me to say." The guard nodded towards the bag. "Those samples must be destroyed."

"We'll take care of it." Her husband's voice was calm. Soothing. Just as Zen-like as ever. Just as she imagined it would have been had she told him about the life-changing decision she was wrestling with.

And his icy unflappability drove her just as crazy now as it had during their last fight.

How could he take everything in his stride?

Because it was part of who he was. He'd grown up in Brazil…was more Brazilian than American in a lot of ways.

As Ben stripped the tape from around the door and sanitized his hands before stepping into the hallway with the guard, Tracy sighed. She never knew what he was thinking. Even during their marriage he'd been tight-lipped about a lot of things. But as aloof as he'd been at times, she'd sensed something in him yearning for what he hadn't had when growing up: the closeness of a family.

It still hurt that she hadn't been able to give that to him. That even as she was driven to work harder and harder by the loss of her baby and by whatever time bomb might be ticking inside her, she was gradually becoming the very thing he despised in his parents.

Her sister had died never knowing whether or not she carried the defective gene. It hadn't been cancer that had claimed Vickie's life but dengue fever—a disease that was endemic in Brazil. She'd been pregnant at the time of her death. Her husband had been devastated at losing both of them. As had she. But at least Vickie had been spared the agonizing uncertainty over whether or not she'd passed a cancer gene down to her child.

As much as Tracy had feared doing just that during her pregnancy, she'd never in her weakest moments wished harm to come to her unborn child. And yet she'd lost the baby anyway, as if even the fates knew what a bad idea it was for her to reproduce.

Her vision suddenly went blurry, and she blinked in an effort to clear her head from those painful thoughts. As she did, she realized Ben and the guard had come back into the room and were now staring at her.

"What?" she asked, mentally daring him to say anything about her moist eyes.

Ben's gaze sharpened, but he said nothing. "I need to

leave for São João dos Rios. Do you want me to drop you off at the airport on my way out of town?"

"Excuse me?"

Why would she need to go to the airport? Unless…

No way!

Her hands went to her hips. "I'm going with you."

Both Ben and the guard spoke at once, their voices jumbled. She caught the gist of it, however. Evidently Ben had been invited to go but she hadn't been.

Outrage crowded her chest. "I'm the one who took the samples. I've already been out there."

"And exposed yourself to the plague in the process."

"Exactly." Her hands dropped back to her sides, palms out. "I've already been exposed. And I'm a doctor, Ben. I've spent my life fighting outbreaks like this one. I should be there."

His voice cooled. "It's not up to me this time."

"*This* time. Unlike the time you sent your goons into that village with orders to send me packing?" She almost spit the words at him. "My assistant is still in São João dos Rios. I am not leaving him out there alone."

Stepping around Ben, she focused on the guard. "I'd like to speak with your superior."

The man blinked several times, as if he couldn't believe she was daring to defy whatever orders he'd received. "I'm afraid that's not possible—"

Ben's fingers went around her upper arm and squeezed. "Let me talk to her for a minute."

Practically dragging her to the other side of the room, his stony gaze fastened on her face. "What are you doing?"

"I already told you. I'm doing my job."

"The military wants to handle this their way. They'll go in and treat those who aren't too far gone and make sure this doesn't spread beyond São João dos Rios."

"Those who aren't too far gone? My God, stop and listen to yourself for a minute. We're talking about human beings—about children like Daniel and Cleo, who are now orphans. They deserve someone there who will fight for them."

"You think I don't care about those children? I was the one who wanted you to slow down during your pregnancy, to…" He paused for several long seconds then lowered his voice. "I care just as much about those villagers as you do."

His surgeon's scalpel cut deep. She could guess what he'd been about to say before he'd checked himself. He still thought her actions had cost the life of their child. And the worst thing was that she couldn't say with any certainty that he was wrong. She'd worked herself harder than ever after she'd had the results back from the genetic testing—struggling to beat back the familiar sensation of being trapped. But that wasn't something she wanted to get into right now.

"Let me go with you." She twisted out of his grasp so she could turn and face him. "Please. You have pull with these guys, I know you do. Call the commander back, whoever he is, and tell him you need me."

He dragged a hand through his hair then shook his head. "I'm asking you to walk away, Tracy. Just this once. You don't know how bad things might get before it's over."

"I do know. That's why I need to be there. Those two kids have already lost their mother. I want to help make sure they don't lose their lives as well."

She was not going to let some government bureaucrat—or even Ben—decide they were a lost cause. "I'll take antibiotics while I'm there. I'll do whatever the government people tell me to do. Besides, like I said before, my assistant is still in the middle of it."

She couldn't explain to him that she really did need to be there. This was part of what being alive meant—fighting battles for others that she might not be able to fight for herself. She took a deep breath. "Please, don't make me beg."

A brief flicker of something went across his face then was gone. "Listen, I know—" Before he could finish the guard appeared in front of them, tapping his hat against his thigh, clearly impatient to be gone. "We need to leave."

Tracy kept her pleading gaze focused on Ben. *He had to let her go. He just had to.*

Ben swore and then broke eye contact. "Call General Gutierrez and tell him we're on our way. Both of us."

The man didn't bat an eyelid. "I'll let him know."

Exactly how much influence did Ben have with these officials? She knew his salary came from the government, but to say something like that and expect it to be accepted without question…

She swallowed. "Thank you."

Jaw tight, Ben ignored her and addressed the guard again. "We'll follow you out to the village once I've destroyed the samples. We need to use my four-wheel drive to haul some equipment."

The guard swept his hat onto his head before relaying the message to his superiors. When he finished the call, he said, "My commander will have someone meet you at the town square and direct you to the triage area they've set up. But you must hurry."

Ben nodded. "Tell them we'll be there within three hours."

"Vai com Deus."

The common "Go with God" farewell had an ominous ring to it—as if the man had crossed himself in an attempt to ward off evil. And pneumonic plague was all that and more. Its cousin had killed off large swaths of the world's population in the past.

Despite her misgivings about working with Ben again,

a couple of muscles in her stomach relaxed. At least she wouldn't have to fight this particular battle on her own.

Ben would be there with her.

And if he found out the truth about the genetic testing she'd had done before their separation?

Then she would deal with it. Just as she'd dealt with the loss of her baby and her own uncertain prognosis.

Alone.

As they hurried to finish loading his vehicle, a streak of lightning darted across the sky, pausing to lick the trunk of a nearby tree before sliding back into the clouds. The smell of singed wood reached Ben a few seconds later, followed by an ominous rumble that made the ground tremble.

Tracy, who stood beside him, shuddered. "Only in *Teresina*."

He smiled. "Remember the city's nickname? *Chapada do corisco:* flash-lightning flatlands. If ever lightning was going to strike twice in the same spot, it would be here." He shut the back of the grey four-wheel-drive vehicle. "I'd rather not put that theory to the test, though, so, if you're ready to go, hop in."

She climbed into the SUV and buckled in, staring in the direction the jagged flash had come from. "That poor tree looks like it's lightning's favorite prom date, judging from the color."

Scarred from multiple strikes over the years, it stubbornly clung to life, clusters of green leaves scattered along its massive branches. Ben had no idea how it had survived so many direct hits.

Their marriage certainly hadn't been as lucky.

He got behind the wheel and started the car. "It'll eventually have to come down."

"Through no fault of its own," she murmured. "It's sad."

Was she thinking of what had happened between them? It had taken every ounce of strength he'd had after she'd left, but he'd forced himself to keep living. In reality, though, she had been gone long before she'd actually moved out of the house. He'd accepted it and moved forward.

Right.

That's why he was on his way to São João dos Rios right now, with Tracy in tow. He should have just shut her down and said no. General Gutierrez would have backed him in his decision. So why hadn't he?

"You sure you want to do this? The airport is on our way. We could still have you on a flight to São Paulo in a jiffy."

She jerked in her seat, gripping the webbing of the seat belt before shifting to look at him. "I can't just turn my back on the town. That's not how I operate."

Really? It had seemed all too easy for her to turn her back on him. But saying so wouldn't help anyone.

They reached the entrance to the highway, and Ben sighed when he saw metal barricades stretched across its width.

The four-lane road—long under construction—was still not finished.

He coasted down a steep incline to reach the so-called official detour, which consisted of a narrow dirt track running parallel to the road. It looked more like a gully from water run-off than an actual street. As far as the eye could see, where the highway should have been there was now a long stretch of hard-packed orange clay that was impassable. At the moment trucks seemed to be the only vehicles braving the washboard tract Ben and Tracy were forced to use. Then again, there was no other option. Most things, including food, were moved from city to city via semi-tractor-trailers. And with the current conditions of the highway it was no wonder things were so expensive in northeastern Brazil.

"How long have they been working on this?" Tracy asked.

"Do you really need to ask?"

"No. But it *was* paved the last time I was here."

They'd spent most of their marriage in *Teresina*, the capital of the state of *Piaui*. He'd rearranged his job so he could stay in one place. Ben thought Tracy had been willing to do the same. How wrong he'd been.

She *had* come off the medical boat and put someone else in her place, but that was about the only concession she'd made to their marriage. By the time he'd realized she was never going to slow down, he'd lost more than just his wife.

"Yes, it was paved, after a fashion." He grimaced. "I think the shoulder we're on is in better shape than the highway was back then."

Ben slowed to navigate a particularly bad stretch where torrential rains had worn a deep channel into the dirt. "Well, some parts of it, anyway."

"My car would never survive the trip."

He smiled. "Are you still driving that little tin can?"

"Rhonda gets great gas mileage."

His gut twisted. He could still remember the laughter they'd shared over Tracy's insistence on keeping her ragamuffin car when they'd got married, despite the hazardous stretches of road in Teresina. To his surprise, the little vehicle had been sturdier than it had appeared, bumping along the worst of the cobblestone streets with little more than an occasional hiccup. Like the bumper she'd lost on a visit to one of the neighboring *aldéias*. She'd come back with the thing strapped to the roof. He smiled. When he'd suggested it was time to trade the vehicle in, she'd refused, patting the bonnet and saying the car had seen her through some tough spots.

His smile faded. Funny how her loyalty to her car hadn't been mirrored in her marriage.

He cast around for a different subject, but Tracy got there first.

"How's Marcelo doing?"

Ben's brother was the new chief of neurosurgery over at Teresina's main hospital. "He's fine. Still as opinionated as ever."

She smiled. "Translated to mean he's still single."

"Always will be, if he has his way." He glanced over at her. "What about you? How's *Projeto Vida* going?" The medical-aid ship that had brought them together was still Tracy's pet project.

"Wonderfully. Matt is back on the team and has a baby girl now."

Tracy's sister had died years ago, leaving her husband, Matt, heartbroken. "He remarried?"

"Yep. Two years ago." She paused. "Stevie…Stephani, actually, is great. She loves the job and fits right into the team."

"I'm glad. Matt seemed like a nice guy." Ben had met him on several occasions when they'd traveled to *Coari* to deliver supplies or check on the medical boat.

"He is. It's good to see him happy again."

Which was more than he could say about Tracy. Maybe it was the stress of what she'd been dealing with in São João dos Rios, but the dark circles under her green eyes worried him. He glanced to the side for a quick peek. The rest of her looked exactly as he remembered, though. Long, silky black hair that hung just below her shoulders. The soft fringe of bangs that fluttered whenever the flow from the air-conditioning vent caught the strands. Lean, tanned legs encased in khaki shorts.

And as much as he wished otherwise, being near her again made him long for family and normalcy all over again. He'd always thought she would bring stability to his life, help to counteract his tumultuous upbringing. His parents had drifted here and there, always searching for a new adventure while leaving their two young sons in the care of their housekeeper. In many ways, Ben had felt closer to Rosa than to his own mother, so much so that he'd kept her on at his house long after his parents had moved to the States on a permanent basis.

He'd thought life with Tracy would be different. That their children would have the close-knit family he'd always longed for as a kid. But Tracy, once the first blush of their marriage had faded, had started traveling again, always finding some new medical crisis to deal with, whether with *Projeto Vida* or somewhere else.

He could understand being married to your career— after all, he was pretty attached to his—but he'd learned to do it from one central location. Surely Tracy could have done the same.

Instead, with every month that had passed, the same feelings of abandonment he'd had as a kid had taken root and grown, as had his resentment. And once she'd fallen pregnant, she'd seemed more obsessed about work than ever, spending longer and longer periods away from home.

When he'd learned she was dealing with a yellow fever outbreak in one of the villages he'd finally snapped and called his old friend General Gutierrez—despite the fact that he knew Tracy been vaccinated against the disease. His ploy had worked. Tracy had come home. But their marriage had been over, even before she'd lost the baby.

So why hadn't he just settled down with someone else,

like Tracy had suggested a few hours earlier? Marriage wasn't exactly a requirement these days. And why hadn't Tracy finally asked for a divorce and been done with it?

Questions he was better off not asking.

"What's the time frame for pneumonic plague?"

Her question jolted him back to the present. "From exposure to presentation of symptoms? Two days, on average. Although death can take anywhere from thirty-six hours after exposure to a week or more. It depends on whether or not other organ systems besides the lungs have been compromised."

"Oh, no."

"Speaking of which, I've brought packets of antibiotics in that black gym bag I threw in the back. Go ahead and dig through it and take a dose before we get there."

Tracy unhooked her seat belt and twisted until she could reach the backseat. She then pulled out one of the boxes of medicine and popped a pill from the protective foil. She downed it with a swig from her water bottle then shoved a couple of strands of hair back from her temple. "You have no idea how glad I am that you were able figure it out so quickly."

"I think I do." Surely she realized he was just as relieved as she was. "Not everyone has the equipment we do."

"Or the backing of the military."

He ignored the bitterness that colored her words. "Part of the reality of living in a developing country. We'll catch up with the rest of the world, eventually. Marcelo's hospital is a great example of that. It's completely funded by sources outside the government."

"So is *Projeto Vida*." She paused when they hit another rough patch of road, her hand scrabbling for the grip attached to the ceiling. "Speaking of funding, we'll need to check with the nearest pharmacist to make sure they have enough antibiotics on hand. I'll pay for more, if need be."

"I was already planning to help with the costs." He glanced over and their eyes caught for a second. When he turned his attention back to the road, her fingers slid over the hand he had resting on the emergency brake before retreating.

"Thank you, Ben," she said. "For letting me come. And for caring about what happens to those people."

He swallowed, her words and the warmth of her fingers penetrating the icy wall he'd built up over the last four years.

It wasn't exactly the thing that peace treaties were made of, but he got the feeling that Tracy had just initiated talks.

And had thrown the ball squarely into his court.

CHAPTER FOUR

MILITARY VEHICLES BLOCKED the road to São João dos Rios—uniformed personnel, guns at the ready, stood beside the vehicles.

"They're not taking any chances," Ben muttered as he slowed the car on the dirt track.

"In this case, caution is probably a good thing." As much as Tracy worried about the presence of the Brazilian army, she also knew the country's military had helped ease Brazil's transition from a Portuguese colony to an independent nation. Not a drop of blood had been shed on either side. The two countries were still on good terms, in fact.

There was no reason to fear their presence. Not really. At least, that's what she told herself.

Ben powered down his window and flashed his residence card, identifying both of them. "General Gutierrez is expecting us."

The soldier checked a handwritten list on his clipboard and nodded. "You've been told what you're dealing with?"

No. They'd been told nothing other than Ben being asked to come, but Tracy wasn't sure how much this particular soldier knew. She didn't want to start a mass panic.

Ben nodded. "We're aware. We brought masks and equipment."

She didn't contradict him or try to add to his words. She

knew he'd done quite a bit of work for the military and he'd probably identified many other pathogens for them in the past. They had also taken the time to track her down and challenge her work four years ago, when Ben had asked them to, something that still had the power to make her hackles rise.

The soldier nodded. "I'll need to search your vehicle. General Gutierrez said there were to be no exceptions. So if you'll both step out, please."

Ben glanced her way, before putting the car in neutral—leaving the engine running and nodding at her to get out. He handed her a mask and donned one himself as he climbed from the vehicle.

The soldier looked in the backseat. He then gave the dizzying array of equipment they were carrying a cursory glance but didn't open any of the boxes. He seemed to be looking for stowaways more than anything, which seemed crazy. Who would want to sneak into a plague-infested area? Then again, she'd heard of crazier things, and nobody wanted this disease to get out of the village and into one of the bigger cities. *Teresina* wasn't all that far away, when you thought about it.

Ben came to stand next to her, and she noticed he was careful not to touch her. She swallowed. Not that she wanted him to. She'd had no idea they'd be thrown together in a situation like the one they were currently facing. But despite the pain that seeing him again brought, she couldn't have asked for a better, or more qualified, work partner.

She heard her name being called and turned towards the sound. Pedro hurried toward them, only to be stopped by another soldier about fifty yards before he reached them. The man's point came across loud and clear. Once she and Ben crossed this particular line, there'd be no going back until it was all over. Who knew how long that could be?

"Ben, are you sure you want to do this? You can drop me off and go back to Teresina. There's no reason to risk yourself and all your work."

A muscle spasmed in his jaw, his eyes on Pedro. "*My* name was the one on the dance card, remember?" He shoved his hands in his pockets. "Besides, this is part of my job. It's why I work at the institute."

"Yes, well…" She didn't know how to finish the statement, since her reasons for wanting him to go back to the safe confines of his office was nothing more than a bid to keep her distance. She'd used his invitation as a way to regain access to the town, but she was also smart enough to know they might need his expertise before this was all over. So she held her tongue.

She glanced back at the soldier, who was currently peering beneath the car at its chassis.

Really? The guy had been watching way too many TV shows.

"Can I go in while you keep looking? My assistant is motioning to me, and I want to start checking on the patients." Daniel and Cleo were in there somewhere.

The soldier waved her through, even as he switched on a flashlight and continued looking.

"Tracy…" Ben, forced to wait for his vehicle to pass inspection, gave her a warning growl, but she shrugged him off.

"I'll meet you once you get through the checkpoint. Don't let them confiscate the antibiotics."

And with that, she made her escape. Securing her mask and feeling guilty, she stepped around the line of military vehicles and met Pedro, pulling him a safe distance away from the soldier who'd stopped him.

"It's pneumonic plague," she whispered, switching to Portuguese while noting he was already wearing a mask. "You'll need to start on antibiotics immediately."

"I thought so. They're staying pretty tight-lipped about the whole thing, but they've set up a quarantine area. Those who are ill have been kept separate from those who still appear healthy—which aren't many at this point."

"Any more deaths? How are Daniel and Cleo?"

"Who?"

"The two kids we found in the field."

Daniel, the boy she'd taken samples from, had been lying in a grassy area, too weak to stand and walk. His sister, showing signs of the illness as well, had refused to leave his side. They'd carried them back to an empty house, just as the military had shown up and taken over.

"No change in the boy, although there have been two more deaths."

"And Cleo?"

"She's definitely got it, but now that we know what we're dealing with, we can start them both on treatment." Pedro slung his arm around her and squeezed. "Can I say how glad I am to see you? These soldier boys are some scary dudes."

He said the last line in English, using his best American accent, which made Tracy smile. She glanced over at Ben, who was still glowering at her, and her smile died.

The soldiers weren't the only scary dudes.

Pedro continued, "The military docs have IVs going on some of the patients, but they wouldn't tell me what they injected into the lines."

"Strange." She glanced at one of the houses, which currently had a small contingent of guards at the doors and windows. "Did they say anything about antibiotics?"

"I think they're still trying to get a handle on things."

Ben joined them on foot, and she frowned at him. "Where's your car?"

"They're going to drive it in and park it in front of one

of the houses. They've evidently got a research area already set up."

He glanced at Pedro, whose arm was still around her, obviously waiting for an introduction. Okay, this was going to be fun. She noticed Pedro also seemed to be assessing Ben, trying to figure out what his place was in all this. He'd never asked about her ring, and she'd never volunteered any information. Several people had assumed she was widowed, and she'd just let it ride. Maybe she could simply omit Ben's relationship to her.

Well, that would be easy enough, because there was no relationship.

"Ben, this is Pedro, my assistant." She hesitated. "Pedro, this is Ben, head epidemiologist at the *Centro de Doenças Tropicais* in Teresina. He's the one I went to see." Maybe no one would notice that she'd conveniently left out his last name. Not that she went by it any more.

Ben held out his hand. "Ben Almeida. Nice to meet you." He slid Tracy a smile that said he knew exactly what she'd done and why. "I also happen to be Tracy's husband."

The look of shock in her assistant's eyes was unmistakable, and he quickly removed his arm from around her shoulders. He shot her a look but dutifully shook hands and muttered something appropriate. She, on the other hand, sent Ben a death stare meant to cut him in two. Instead, he seemed totally unfazed by her ire.

Ben nodded. "I've heard Tracy's account of what happened here. Why don't you tell me what you've observed?"

It was said as if she was clueless. Pressure began building in the back of her head.

Her assistant knew better. "Well, she's probably told you more than I could. We've got about fifteen cases of… Tracy said it's pneumonic plague?"

"Yes." Ben's eyes followed the progress of some men

in hazard gear as they went from one building to another. "And judging from the way they're treating it, they know what they're dealing with. Are they still burning the bodies?"

"Yes. Two more in the last couple of hours," Pedro said.

"The boy whose sample I brought in—Daniel—is still alive, but he's pretty sick. His sister is as well."

She didn't need to say what else she knew: antibiotics needed to be started within twenty-four hours of the appearance of symptoms to be effective. Ben would already know that. The treatment window was narrow, but she wouldn't give up, no matter how sick the patient.

Tracy ached for the two children, their mother ripped from them without so much as a funeral service or a chance to say goodbye. Just thrown onto a flaming pyre to destroy any pathogens. How many other kids would watch helplessly as the same thing happened to their relatives? As much as she knew it had to be done, it still didn't make it any easier. How would she feel if the body being burned was Ben's?

No. Not Ben. She wouldn't let her mind go there.

"Where are they putting you up for the night?" she asked Pedro.

"They've got medical civilians in one house and military personnel in another. They post guards out front of both of them, though."

Ben's four-wheel drive pulled up beside them and the soldier poked his head out of the open window. "I'm taking your vehicle to the research center we've set up. Do you want a ride?"

"We'll follow on foot," Ben said. Tracy got the idea, he wanted to continue their conversation in private. "And if you could put Dr. Hinton in the same house as me, I'd appreciate it. I haven't seen my wife in quite a while and would like some alone time with her if possible." He quirked an eyebrow at the man, while reaching over and taking her hand in his and giving it a warning squeeze. The presumption of his move made the rising pressure in her head grow to dangerous levels.

Her poor assistant squirmed visibly.

If Pedro hadn't been beside them, she'd have made it plain how little contact—of any sort—she wanted with him. But she knew Ben well enough to know he didn't say or do anything without a good reason.

The driver grinned and promised to see what he could do.

But, oh, she was going to let Ben know she was *not* happy with that arrangement. She hadn't wanted anyone to know what their relationship was, and now everyone in town would be snickering behind their backs.

"Nice work," she hissed.

Pedro shifted from foot to foot. "I'm sorry, I had no idea you were… I just assumed you were…"

"Single?" Ben supplied, an edge to his voice.

Wow, was he actually doing this? He'd never expressed any hint of jealousy when they'd been together. And she didn't appreciate it now.

"No, not exactly. I just knew she didn't have anyone living with her."

Ben's brows lifted. "You knew that for a fact, did you?"

"Well, yes. W-we had staff meetings at her house on a regular basis."

Tracy took a closer look at her assistant's face. There was discomfiture and something else lurking in his brown eyes. Oh God. Surely he wasn't interested in her. She'd never given him any reason to think she might be remotely attracted to him.

At least, she hoped she hadn't. And yet Ben had automatically assumed Pedro might have his eye on her. Why would he even care?

She touched Pedro's arm. "Ben and I...well, it's complicated."

Complicated. It was. At least for her. And Ben had probably never forgiven her for walking away from their marriage without a word. But what could she have said, really?

Not only do I not want to get pregnant again, I might choose to have my non-cancerous breasts removed.

She could still explain, if she wanted to. But after the way he'd run roughshod over her four years ago, going behind her back and manipulating her into coming home, he'd pretty much snuffed out any feelings of guilt on her part.

Ben had been part of the reason she'd struggled with making a final decision about what to do about her test results. But now that he and the baby were no longer part of the equation, she'd put things on hold, choosing to make a difference in the lives of others instead.

Dragging her attention back to Pedro, she tried her best to finish her earlier statement. Putting more emphasis on the words than was strictly necessary, she wanted to make sure she got her point across to both of them.

"Ben and I are separated. We have been for quite some time. So anything that happens between us will be strictly business."

Now, if she could just convince herself of that, she should be good to go.

CHAPTER FIVE

THERE WAS A reason it was called the Black Death.

There was nothing pretty or romantic about the plague. And the pneumonic form of the disease was the most dangerous, rapidly killing those it touched.

Ben stepped into the tiny house where the patients were being housed, and he fought a wave of pure desolation as he looked over the place. Tracy seemed just as shocked, standing motionless in the doorway beside her assistant.

Simple green cots were packed into what used to be a living room, laid out in two rows with barely enough space between beds for doctors to work.

Ben counted silently. Fourteen patients. And not all of them had IVs started. In fact, when he looked closer, he saw that the wall over some of the cots had a crude "X" penned in black ink.

A chill went over him. Deathbeds.

His gaze moved further and he spotted two men he assumed were doctors, still wearing that hazard gear he'd spotted earlier. The pair stood on either side of a bed, assessing a woman who was wailing, the sound coming in fits and starts that were interrupted by coughing spasms. One of the men leaned past the patient and slashed a mark over the bed.

Just like that. Bile pumped into his stomach in a flood.

Tracy's gaze met his, her eyes reflecting pure horror. She reached out and gripped Pedro's sleeve. "So many."

The man nodded. "I know."

None of the trio had on the protective clothing worn by the other doctors, other than masks and latex gloves, but as Tracy was on antibiotics and Pedro had just been given his first dose, there was no need. He assumed the heavy gear worn by the other men would be done away with pretty soon.

Besides, it was stifling in the room, the number of bodies cranking up the temperatures to unbearable levels. There wasn't even a fan to move the air around, probably out of fear of microbes being carried outside the room. But none of these patients—even the ones without the fatal mark on the wall—would last long if they couldn't cool it down.

Ben decided that one of his first orders of business would be to set up some kind of misting system.

Tracy moved towards him and touched his arm, pointing to the left at a nearby patient. It was a boy who Ben assumed was the one she'd been so worried about. There was a black squiggle over his bed but it was incomplete, as if someone had started to cross him off the list of the living and had then changed his mind.

"I'm going to check on Daniel and Cleo."

Pedro made a move to follow then noticed Ben's frown and evidently thought better of it, shifting his attention to a patient on the other side of the room instead.

Why did he care if the man had a thing for Tracy? Unlike him, the assistant seemed to have no problem with her job. He probably traveled with her every chance he got.

A steady pain thumped on either side of his head, and he squeezed the bridge of his nose in an effort to interrupt the nerve impulses.

While Tracy checked on the boy, he made his way to

the suited pair across the room. He identified himself and flashed his ID card, causing one of the men's brows to lift. "You're the *epidemiologista* General Gutierrez sent for?"

Ben nodded. "Are you marking these beds on his orders?"

"Well, no. He won't be here until tomorrow." They glanced quickly at each other. "But we can't take care of fourteen patients on our own, so we've been…" The words trailed away, but Ben understood. They were deciding who was worth their care and who was beyond saving.

"Well, Dr. Hinton and myself will be joining you, so let's set up a rotating schedule. Between all of us I'm sure we can make an effort to see *all* the patients." He let his emphasis hang in the air.

"But some of them won't last a day."

"And some of them might," he countered. "Why don't you explain to me who you've assessed, and we'll divide the room into critical care and non-critical, just like you would for field triage. It'll help us divide our efforts."

Neither man looked happy to be challenged, but they didn't contradict him either. If he knew General Gutierrez, the man had told them to follow his recommendations. The doctors gave him a quick rundown and Ben made a list, marking "TI"—for *tratamento intensivo*—next to those patients who were in critical condition and needed extra care. Not one "X" went next to anyone's name.

Ben moved over to the older woman who'd cried out as the men had marked her bed and found she was indeed critical, with red staining around her mouth that signaled she was producing bloody sputum. He laid a gloved hand on her forehead and spoke softly to her, her glassy eyes coming up to meet his, even as her breath rasped in and out, breathing labored. "We're going to take good care of you, okay?"

She blinked at him, not even making an effort to speak.

Ben called out to Tracy. "I want IVs started on all the patients who don't currently have one. We're going to push antibiotics into them. All of them." Then he turned to one of the men and nodded towards the radio on his hip. "Can you get me General Gutierrez? He and I need to have a little chat."

She didn't know what he'd done, but Ben had obviously spoken to someone in authority and asked for some changes. The cots—with the help of other soldiers—had been rearranged according to how ill each patient was. Daniel and Cleo had ended up on opposite sides of the room.

Heart aching, she moved from the boy to another patient, trying not to think about his prospects as she quickly filled a syringe from a vial of antibiotics and inserted it into the injection port of the IV line, marking the time and amounts in a small spiral-bound notebook they'd made up for each patient.

She caught Pedro's eye from across the room and smiled. "You doing okay?" she mouthed, receiving a thumbs-up in return. Although not a doctor, Pedro had accompanied her on many of her forays into villages and had helped enough that she knew he could hold his own in an emergency. She also trusted him enough to know he'd ask for help if something was beyond his capabilities.

Her shirt was soaked with sweat and she'd gone through masks at an alarming rate. She hoped Ben had brought a big supply. He'd mentioned setting up a rudimentary misting system to help cool off the room.

Right now, though, he was seeing to the unloading of his car, and she refused to think about where they were going to sleep tonight. Ben had said the same "house"…not the same "room" when he'd made his request. But he'd also made it plain that they were married, so she had no doubt they'd be placed together. What was he thinking? Surely he had no more desire to be with her than she had to be with him?

Okay, maybe "desire" was the wrong word to use. Because put them in a room alone together and they tended to combust at frightening speed. She remembered her fury as she'd walked into that village to confront him on their first meeting. She'd heard there was an epidemiologist heading her way down the river but that he was taking his sweet time.

Unwilling to wait for him to stop at every village and sample the local cuisine, she'd powered back upriver and stomped her way to the heart of the village. He'd been standing in the middle of a group of men, a big smile on his face. She'd opened her mouth to throw a vile accusation his way, only to have the words stop in her throat the second their eyes had met.

He'd stared at her for several long seconds then one eyebrow had quirked upwards. "Are you here for me?"

"I…I…" Realizing she'd looked like a fool, she'd drawn herself up to her full height and let him have it.

She'd let him have it again two days later. In an entirely different way.

Oh, God. She could *not* be in a room alone with the man if she could help it. So what was she going to do?

Stay with her patients as much as possible, that's what. She'd already been here for almost eight hours. And it was now a few minutes past the end of her shift. If she knew Ben, he would make them all stick to the schedule he'd drawn up—whether they wanted to or not.

Even as she thought it, she reached Cleo's bed and leaned over her. The girl gave her a tremulous smile, which she returned.

"Hey, how are you doing?"

"Sleepy, and my head hurts." Cleo's voice was a thread of sound.

"I know." Headaches were one of the symptoms of the plague, but Cleo's episode didn't seem to be progressing as rapidly as Daniel's had. "You need to rest. I'm sure—"

Something cool and moist hit her left ankle and swept up the back of her leg until it reached the bottom of her shorts. Stifling a scream, she straightened and spun around to find empty air. She lowered her gaze and spied Ben, on his haunches, about a foot away, a spray bottle in his hand. Half-thought words bubbled on her tongue but didn't find an exit.

He got two more squirts in before she found her voice. "What do you think you're doing?"

Holding the pump bottle up, he said. "We have a room full of sick people. All we need is to have a dengue outbreak on top of everything."

Repellant. Ah. She got it.

But why was he the one spraying it on her? He could have just handed her the bottle and ordered her to put it on.

"You were busy," he said, as if reading her thoughts. "And sometimes with you it's easier to act than to argue."

Like their first kiss? When he'd dragged her to him and planted his lips on hers without so much as a "May I?"

She swallowed, hoping he couldn't read the direction of her thoughts. Or the fact that seeing him kneeling in front of her reminded her of other times when he'd done just that.

Before she could grab the bottle out of his hand he went back to work and sprayed the front of her legs. "Turn around."

"Are you going to personally spray Pedro and the other workers, too? Or just me?"

"They're not wearing shorts." His brows went up. "Didn't think it was as urgent."

She couldn't stop the smile or the roll of her eyes, but she obediently turned around. In reality the chill of the spray against her super-heated skin was heavenly as he slowly misted the back of her right leg. Looking down, she found Cleo looking up at her.

"He's bossy," the little girl said. Her voice was weak but there was a ghost of a smile on her face.

Tracy couldn't stop the laugh that bubbled out, her heart lightening at Cleo's ability to joke. "Oh, honey, you have no idea."

Ben's bossiness had a tendency to come out in all kinds of ways. Some of those she was better off not thinking about right now.

The spraying stopped and Tracy glanced behind her to find Ben staring up at her. Standing abruptly, he shoved the repellant bottle into her hands. "I'll let you finish up the rest. Give it to the other workers after you're done. And make sure you stay protected while you're here."

With that he walked away without a backward glance.

Stay protected? With him in the immediate vicinity?

She gave a huge sigh.

It would take a whole lot more than a bottle of repellent to do that.

CHAPTER SIX

HE WAS A masochist.

Ben stared at the figure sleeping in the hammock—
her back to him—and wondered what on earth he'd been
thinking by demanding they sleep in the same room. He
obviously hadn't been thinking at all, but the sight of Tracy
standing next to Pedro had sent a shaft of what could only
be described as jealousy through him.

Why?

She could have been sleeping with twenty men a day
after she'd left, and he'd have been none the wiser.

Yeah, but he hadn't had to stand there and witness it.

Even as he tried to convince himself that was the reason, he knew it went deeper than that. Deeper than the desire that churned to life as he stared at the sexy curve of
hip flowing into a narrow waist. A waist that hadn't even
had time to expand much before their baby had been lost.

She'd gotten off work two hours ahead of him, just as
his schedule had dictated, which was a relief because she'd
obviously come right back to the room and gone straight
to sleep.

Which was exactly what he should be doing.

Tomorrow was going to be just as difficult as today.

Having Tracy here brought up all the tangled emotions
he thought he'd already unraveled and put to bed. Sighing,

he toed off his shoes, glad he'd donned a pair of athletic shorts to sleep in, because there was no way he was sleeping in just his boxers.

He slid into his hammock, trying to keep the creaking of the ropes to a minimum as he settled into place.

Someone like Pedro would have been ideal husband material for Tracy. He obviously didn't mind her vagabond spirit. In fact, he traveled with her on a regular basis, if appearances were anything to go by.

But then again, Pedro wasn't married to her. He hadn't had to sit at home wondering why she wanted to be anywhere else but with him. Wondering if, once their child was born, the baby would be dumped in the care of his housekeeper, just as he'd been when he'd been little.

Anger churned in his chest at the thought.

So why had seeing her bending over that little girl's bed, shapely bottom facing him, made the saliva pool in his mouth? And when she'd leaned further over, the long, lean muscles in her calves bunching as she'd gone on tiptoe to adjust the sheet on the far side of the cot, his body had roared to life. There hadn't been a drop of anger in sight.

He'd wanted her. Just as much as he always had.

He'd meant to hand her the bottle of repellent with a brusque order to put some on, but he'd been desperate to erase the images cascading through his mind. Squirting a healthy dose of cold liquid on her had seemed like the ideal way to shock her into moving—and shock his own body back to normal. Like a virtual defibrillator, halting a deadly spiral of electrical impulses before they'd overwhelmed his system.

His actions had backfired, though.

She'd turned around, just like he'd hoped, only his senses hadn't righted themselves, they'd gone berserk. And when he'd heard that low, throaty laugh at something her young patient had said, his stomach had turned inside out, drilling him with the reality of how stupid his move had been.

Besides, he'd had other things he needed to attend to.

Like going out and dunking his head in a bucket of water.

Which he'd done. Literally.

When he'd gone back inside, Tracy had already finished spraying herself down, the shine from the repellant glinting off the tip of her upturned nose, making his gut twist all over again.

He'd spent the rest of the day hanging mosquito netting around all of the patients' beds and caring for the ones who were the farthest away from his ex-wife.

Now, if he could just convince himself she really was his ex, he'd be just peachy.

Only two days into the outbreak and she was dog-tired. And hot.

So terribly hot. And now they were up to twenty patients, rather than fourteen.

The tiny house was still stifling, although Ben had figured out a way to combine fans with periodic jets of fine mist that reminded Tracy of the produce sections she'd seen at US supermarkets. It did help, but still…the place could never be deemed "cool."

Then again, it never really cooled off in this part of the world. Tracy had become soft, working in São Paulo for much of the year. The sticky heat that blanketed the equator—a place where seasons didn't exist—was unrelenting, reaching into every nook and cranny.

It had to be just as hard for Ben, who worked in an air-conditioned office nowadays, rather than doing fieldwork like he'd done when they'd met.

They'd administered a therapeutic dose of antibiotics

into all their patients, but they were already seeing the truth of that narrow window of treatment. The patients who'd been diagnosed after help arrived and given antibiotics immediately were doing better than those who had already been ill when they'd arrived.

The statistics held true, with the sickest of their patients continuing their downward spiral. Still, they had to keep trying, so they stayed their course, using either IV antibiotics, intramuscular injections or, for those who could tolerate it, oral doses. Two more had died since their arrival, but at least Ben had ordered those awful marks above the beds to be scrubbed clean.

Amazingly, Daniel—although gravely ill—was still hanging in there.

She glanced over at Ben, who was injecting his next patient, squeezing the woman's hand and offering her an encouraging smile that she couldn't actually see—because of his mask—but the crinkling at the corners of his eyes gave him away. Oh, how Tracy had loved seeing those happy little lines go to work.

He put the syringe into the medical waste container they'd set up, and Tracy reminded herself to check on the supply of disposable needles. He caught her looking at him from her place beside Daniel's bed and made his way over to her. She tensed, just as she'd done every time they'd had to interact.

"Why don't you take a quick nap?"

She shook her head. "I'm okay. Besides, I've had more sleep than you have."

Something she would know, as she'd heard him get up in the middle of the night and leave their room both nights they'd been in there. Maybe he was as restless as she was.

Well, whose fault was that? He'd been the one who'd insisted they stay together, which had made things incredibly awkward with Pedro.

And there were no real beds, so it wasn't a matter of her getting the bed while he slept on a pallet on the floor. No, all the workers had been assigned military hammocks, the residents' original hammocks having been confiscated, along with most of their fabric or upholstered possessions. Once some of the patients recovered, they'd have the added hardship of knowing many of their household clothes and belongings were long gone. Destroyed for the good of the village.

Tracy, for once, had agreed with the decision when Ben told her about it.

In addition to the bed situation, there wasn't much privacy to be had anywhere in the town. Showers had been set up in a clearing and the stinging smell of strong disinfectant soap had become an all-too-familiar fragrance around the compound. But even that couldn't totally vanquish the warm masculine scent that greeted her each night from the neighboring hammock where Ben lay.

Hanging side by side, the two hammocks were slung on three hooks, sharing one at the lower end, while the two upper ends branched apart onto two separate hooks, so that the hammocks formed a V. Knowing their feet were almost touching each and every night had been part of the reason for her sleeplessness.

So she'd lain awake for hours, despite her growing fatigue, until Ben—like he'd done the previous two nights—had slipped from his bed and out of the room. Only then had she finally been able to close her eyes and relax.

Ben looked like he was about to press his point about her taking a nap when the front door to the house banged open and a fierce argument carried through to where they were standing.

What in the name of...?

Both she and Ben moved quickly into the hallway, not wanting someone to be inadvertently exposed to the sickroom. They found one of the military police who'd been assigned to enforcing the quarantine arguing with a young girl who was around six years old. Tear tracks marked the dust on either side of the child's face, and her feet—clad only in flip-flops—were caked with dirt.

"What's going on?" Ben asked in Portuguese.

"She insists on speaking with a doctor, even though I've explained she can't go in there."

Tracy moved forward. "It's okay. I'll go outside with her."

"Tracy." Ben put a hand on her arm, stopping her.

She sent him a look that she hoped conveyed her irritation. "Someone has to talk to her. Better me than them." She aimed a thumb at the poor soldier.

"You need to at least take off your gear before you go out there."

"I will." She spoke softly to the child, telling her it was okay, that she'd be out in a minute. The girl nodded, the wobbling of her chin as she turned to go wrenching at Tracy's heart.

Ben caught the eye of one of the military doctors and told him they'd be back in a few minutes. They both stripped off their protective gear in the clean area and scrubbed with antibiotic soap. Tracy used her forearm to swipe at her damp forehead, frowning when Ben lifted a hand toward her. She took a quick step back.

"You have suds." He pointed to his own forehead.

She reached up and dabbed it away herself, avoiding his eyes, then pushed through the screen door at the back of the house. They made their way round to the front and the little girl rushed toward them. Ben stepped in front of

Tracy, causing her to give a sigh of exasperation. "Ben, please. She's not going to hurt anyone."

Moving around him, she knelt in front of the child. "What's your name?"

"Miriam."

Tracy wanted to gently wipe a smudge on the little girl's forehead, much as Ben had tried to do with her a second ago, but she was too afraid of spreading germs at this point to touch anyone outside the village. "Okay, Miriam. What did you want to tell us?"

"You are doctors?"

"Yes. We both are. It's okay. Is someone sick?"

The girl clasped her hands in front of her and nodded. "My *mami*. She has been ill for two days, but told me not to tell anyone. But now…" Her voice broke on a low sob. "But now she does not wake up, even when I try to feed her broth."

"Where is she?"

"At my house. But it is a long way from here."

The first twinge of alarm filtered up her back. "How far?"

"The next village."

Horrified, Tracy stood in a rush and grabbed Ben's hand, her wide eyes on his. "Could it have spread beyond São João dos Rios?"

No! They'd been so careful, no one had been allowed to leave the village once the military had arrived.

But before that?"

His fingers closed around hers, giving them a quick squeeze, then addressed the child, whose small forehead was now scrunched in distress. "Was your mother coughing?"

"Yes. She said it was just a cold, but I am afraid…" She motioned around the quarantined village. "We have heard

what happened here. They say the military is shooting anyone who is sick. I had to sneak past them to find you."

Tracy's heart clenched. She knew how suspicious some
of these towns were of government officials. But those
fears only helped spread sickness and disease. Because
people who were afraid tended to hide things from those
who could help them.

Like Tracy had when she'd left Ben four years ago?

No, it wasn't the same thing at all. She forced a smile to
her lips, knowing it probably looked anything but reassuring. "No one is shooting anyone."

"Will you come and help my mother, then?"

Tracy glanced at the house, where one of the military
police watched them closely. Would they let her travel to
the village or would they insist on sending someone else?
It was a tough call. She didn't want to risk spreading anything, but the more people involved, the more places the
disease could be carried. "Yes, honey, I will."

When she tried to move towards the guard, Ben clamped
down on her hand. "What do you think you're doing,
Tracy?" he murmured, sending a whisper of air across her
cheek that made her shiver.

"You heard her. Her mother is sick."

"You could end up making things worse for everyone."

The shiver turned to ice in her veins. Those words were
too close to the message he'd sent with the military four
years ago. Her brows went up and she looked pointedly at
the guard behind them. "I'm going, whether you approve
or not. You could always send your little friends after me.
You seem to be quite good at doing that."

"Come on, Tracy. You know why I sent them. You were
carrying our child."

She did know—and maybe she'd been foolish to travel
alone, but she'd been just six weeks along and she'd al-

ready had her yellow fever shot. She also knew her reason for taking off that week had had little to do with the village and everything to do with the results of her test. Even so, the blinding humiliation of seeing those uniformed officials set foot on that beach—and knowing her husband had been behind their presence—still stung.

They glared at each other. The last thing she needed to do right now was antagonize him further. She forced her voice to soften. "Please, try to understand. I *have* to check on her mother. My job is part of what keeps me going."

"Keeps you going?"

That last phrase had slipped out before she realized it. Leave it to Ben to catch it as it flew by.

"I mean, my job is important to me, that's all."

His gaze raked her face, and she held her breath, hoping the raw fear that slithered up her throat wasn't visible. Breaking eye contact, he glanced down at the girl, whose terror was much more on the surface. "Fine. We'll both go. But we need to take precautions. We're on antibiotics, so I'm not worried about us, but I also don't want us carrying anything back that way."

Was that why he'd been worried? Maybe she'd misjudged him.

"What about Miriam?" She kept her voice just as low, switching to English to make it harder for the little girl to understand what she was saying. "They may not let her leave São João dos Rios, now that she's been exposed."

"I know. I'll talk to the guard and get her started on antibiotics."

Poor girl, she had no idea that by trying to get help for her mother she might become a virtual prisoner. And if the worst came to the worst, and her mother had the deadly disease, she might never see her again.

A familiar pang went through Tracy's chest. Her mother

had died while Tracy had been here in Brazil. Six months after she and Ben had married, in fact. Her mother had had no idea she was sick during the wedding rehearsal or as they'd planned what should have been a happy occasion. But then she'd been diagnosed a few weeks after the ceremony. She'd died months later.

Squaring her shoulders, she went through the motions of going with Ben to talk to the guard, who in turn had to make a phone call up his chain of command. An hour later, she, Ben, and four military personnel were on their way to the next village. Ben had his arm around her in the backseat of the four-wheel drive to help steady her as they hit pothole after pothole, the scarred tract rarely seeing much in the way of motor vehicles.

Loaded to the gills with medical equipment, as well as Ben's lab stuff, she leaned against him, allowing him to pull her even closer as she prayed that whatever they found would not be as bad as she feared.

"Bronchitis," Ben declared.

Tracy almost laughed aloud as a giddy sense of relief swept over her. "Are you sure?"

Ben sat behind the house on a low three-legged stool, studying the last of the slides through his microscope.

"I don't see any sign of plague bacteria. And she's awake now. No fever or symptoms other than some thick congestion in her chest." He leaned back and looked at her. "She probably kept going until she was literally worn out, which was why Miriam couldn't wake her up. Regardless, we don't have a case of the plague here."

"Thank God." Her legs threatened to give out, and she had to put a hand on Ben's shoulder to brace herself.

He glanced up at her, concern in his eyes. "Hey, sit down

before you fall down." Before she realized what he was doing, he'd pulled her onto his left knee.

"Sorry," he murmured. "There's nowhere else to sit."

She nodded. "I'm sorry about what I said earlier. About you sending the military after me."

"Don't worry about it. You were upset."

She blinked. He'd just given her absolution. Whether it was for sins of the past or sins of the present was immaterial right now—not when the blood was thickening in her veins, the air around her turning crystal clear with secret knowledge.

The sudden sound of his breath being let out and the way his arm tightened around her back were her undoing. All she could think about was that she owed him a huge "thank you." Before she could stop herself, she looped her arms around his neck and leaned forward to kiss him.

CHAPTER SEVEN

HER LIPS GRAZED his cheek.

Ben wasn't at all sure how it happened. First she was apologizing then her mouth was on his skin. The instant it happened, something from the past surged inside him, and he brushed aside the gesture in favor of something a little more personal. If she was going to kiss him, he was going to make damned sure it counted. Using his free hand to cup her head, he eased her round until she faced him.

He stared at her for a long moment, taking in the parted lips, glittering eyes…an expression he knew all too well. He lowered his head, an inner shout of exultation going off in his skull when she didn't flinch away but met him halfway.

Their lips connected, and it was as if a match had been struck in the presence of gasoline fumes. They both went up in flames.

A low moan slid between them. One that most certainly hadn't come from him. Taking that as a signal to continue, his fingers lifted and tunneled deep into her hair, the damp moisture of her scalp feeling cool against his overheated skin.

Ignoring the microscope and slides, he shifted her legs sideways until they rested between his, without breaking contact with her mouth for even a second.

The change in position pressed her thigh against his

already tightening flesh, which was pure torture—made him want to push back to increase the contact. He forced himself to remain still instead, although it just about killed him. It had been four years since he'd held this woman in his arms, and he wasn't about to blow it by doing anything that would have her leaping from his lap in a panic. Realistically, he knew they weren't going to have sex behind the house of an ill woman, but he could take a minute or two to drink his fill of her.

Only, he'd never really get his fill. Would always want more than she was willing to give.

He licked along the seam of her mouth, asking for permission. She granted it without a word, opening to him. He went deep, his hand tightening in her hair as he tipped her head sideways seeking to find the best angle possible. She wiggled closer, taking him almost to the brink before he got himself back under control.

He gave a hard swallow. *Slow.*

Exploring the heat and warmth he found between her lips, he tried to rememorize everything and realized he didn't need to. Because he'd forgotten nothing. Not the taste of her, not the shivers he could wring from her by using his teeth in addition to his tongue.

And when he could no longer contain his low groan, her fingers came up and tangled in his hair. He could feel the battle going on within her and fought against his own need to control the situation, letting her lead instead.

Unfortunately, she took that as a signal to pull back, her breath coming in husky snatches of sound that he found erotic beyond belief.

She took a couple more quick gulps before attempting to talk.

"Ben," she whispered, her mouth still against his. "What are we doing here?"

In spite of himself, he smiled. "I thought that was fairly obvious."

"Mmm." The hum of sound drove him crazy, just like it always had. "This is a mistake. You know it is."

"I know." He bit her lower lip, sucking on the soft flesh before releasing it with a growl. "Doesn't mean I didn't enjoy it, though. Or that you didn't either."

"I know." No arguments, no denying that she felt the same. Just an acknowledgement of what was obvious to both of them.

It had been an incredibly long week, and all he wanted to do was wrap his arms around her, make slow, satisfying love and then go to sleep still trapped inside her. Just like they used to.

But he knew that was the exhaustion talking. Not to mention that thing wedged against her hip, which was busy shouting out commands he was doing his best to ignore.

Sorry, bud. You're out of luck.

Tracy leaned her forehead against his and gave a drawn-out sigh. "We need to get back to the other village if this one is in the clear."

She heaved one more sigh, before climbing to her feet, looking anywhere but at his lap, which was probably smart. "I'm sure we're both so tired we're not thinking straight. We'll regret this once we've had some sleep."

She might, but he wouldn't. Not even if he slept as long as Rip Van Winkle. He'd still wake up and want to kiss her all over again.

He closed his eyes for a long moment then started undoing his equipment without a word.

She laid a hand on his shoulder. "If it's any consolation, you're right. I enjoyed it too. You always were a great kisser."

Some of the tension in his spine seeped away. Questions from four years ago resurfaced and he couldn't keep himself from asking, "Then why were you always in such a hurry to leave?"

"Please, don't, Ben. Not right now."

And her response was exactly the same as it had been back then. She hadn't wanted to talk about it—had just wanted to head off on her next adventure.

There was nothing left to say, then. "I'll get some medicine out of the car and explain the dosage."

She nodded. "I'm sure they'll even let Miriam come home as there's no evidence of pneumonic plague here. We'll put her on the prophylactic dosage of antibiotics and she should be fine."

Stowing his equipment in a large box and carefully stacking his microscope on top, all he could do was wish for a prophylactic dose of something that would cut through his current jumble of emotions and put him back on the road to normalcy.

Normalcy. Wow. If he ever found a pill that would restore that, he'd end up a very rich man.

Tracy could have kicked herself. She'd let him kiss her. *On the mouth.* Worse, she'd kissed him back. Crazily. As if she couldn't get enough of him.

Her chaste little gesture of thanks had flared to inferno proportions in a nanosecond.

The chemistry between them was just as potent as ever. Something she never should've doubted. Something she should have been braced for and never allowed to happen.

And why on earth had she let herself be drawn into an argument about the past? Because she was trying to keep her distance emotionally? You sure couldn't tell it from where she stood. Because the only message she'd been sending while perched on his lap had been more along the lines of throw-me-on-my-back-and-take-me-hard.

To allow that to happen, though, would only make things more complicated. Especially now. She could admit that she still cared about him, but it didn't mean they could—or should—be together. If she thought there was a chance, she might try to explain what had happened all those years ago. But it wouldn't do any good at this point. And the last thing she needed was Ben's pity. Hanging onto the anger from the past might be best for both of them right now, because in another week or so they'd be heading in opposite directions.

Lying in her hammock, hours from the time they'd finally climbed into Ben's SUV and headed back to town, she still longed to reach across the space and take his hand. Touch his face. Kiss his lips.

Why? None of it made any sense.

There were less than two feet separating them. Less at the foot end of the hammocks. And she'd never been more keenly aware of that fact than she was now. The village was still and quiet. The military doctors had taken up the night shift, leaving Tracy and Ben to get five or six hours of sleep, which was what she should be doing right now, rather than lying here staring at the ceiling. Luckily, Ben was facing away from her and couldn't see her restless movements. He'd fallen asleep almost as soon as his body had hit the hammock, while she'd pretended to do the same. Was still pretending, in fact.

Just like she'd pretended that kiss today was the result of exhaustion and stress.

He turned unexpectedly, and Tracy clamped her eyelids shut, trying to breathe slowly and deeply, even though her heart was pounding out a crazy tattoo. The sound of a throat clearing, some more rustling and then a low, exasperated curse met her ears. She felt a rush of air against her and the movement of his hammock disturbing hers where they intersected at the bottom.

Soft footsteps. Another oath. Then the sound of a door quietly opening and closing. Just like the last three nights.

She waited for several seconds before she got up the courage to open her eyes again and peek.

Yep. He was gone. Where was he disappearing to each night? The restroom? If so, that meant he'd be back in a matter of minutes—which he never was. She pushed her fingers through the open-weave fabric of her hammock in irritation, squeezing the fibers tight. Instead of wondering where he was, she should be using this time to try to go to sleep.

Fat chance of that now.

She continued to lie very still, waiting, staring at the closed door on the other side of the tiny room.

But fifteen minutes later there was still no sign of him, just like on previous nights. Had he decided he couldn't sleep? Yes, it was hot in the room—the fan doing nothing more than fluffing the balmy air—but it would be just as hot no matter where he went.

Did this have something to do with their kiss, earlier? If that were the case, then what was his excuse on the other nights?

Crossing her arms over her chest, she closed her eyes again and tried for the umpteenth time to go to sleep. Morning was going to come, and with it a whole new day of struggles and trials as they tried to care for their remaining patients.

Seven more days. That's how long Ben figured it would take to get the epidemic under control.

And that's how long she had to kick this stupid attraction to the curb and keep herself out of Ben's bed.

Seven, very long days.

CHAPTER EIGHT

"CLEO'S RIGHT HERE, honey."

Gently placing a moist cloth across Daniel's feverish brow, Tracy nodded at the neighboring cot, where Ben was adjusting the IV pole.

The boy had finally regained consciousness, four days after being found in the field. His first words had been to ask about his sister. The plea had remained throughout the day, sometimes interrupted by bouts of coughing, sometimes gasped between harsh breaths, but he never relented. The question was there each time he rallied for a few moments. And it made Tracy's heart squeeze. It was as if, even in his precarious state, he refused to believe Cleo was alive unless he saw it for himself.

Ben had finally relented and offered to shuffle patients around so that the brother and sister could remain close to each other's sides, despite the fact that he'd wanted patients placed according to severity of illness. Daniel was still gravely ill, whereas Cleo's sickness had not ravaged her young body as much as those of some of their other patients. She said her head still ached, but she hadn't worsened.

Daniel's glassy eyes swiveled to the right. "Clee," he whispered, shaky fingers reaching across the space and then dropping before he succeeded in reaching the other bed.

"She's here, Daniel, but she's asleep right now. We have

to let her rest so she can be strong and healthy again." Her gloved fingers brushed back a moist lock of hair, a rush of emotion clogging her throat. "You need to do the same. She'll still be here when you wake up."

If you wake up.

She immediately dismissed the thought. Daniel's vitals had slowly grown weaker over the last couple of days, but he continued to fight harder than anyone she'd ever seen. And so would she. She'd come here to fight for these kids, against the military's wishes…against Ben's wishes. And she was going to damn well keep on fighting.

Maybe there was a message for her in there somewhere. But she was too tired to dig for it right now. Maybe later.

As if he sensed the direction of her thoughts, Ben came to stand beside her. "You need to get some rest as well. You look exhausted."

"We're all tired." She reached up to wipe a trickle of perspiration from her temple only to have Ben beat her to it, using one of the dry compresses to blot her forehead. She gave him a weak grin. "You'd think after almost a week I'd be used to the heat. I travel down the Amazon all the time."

They both froze, and Tracy wondered if he was remembering that last fateful trip.

Ben had accused her of neglecting their marriage, of being careless with their baby's health. Had she? Had her own plight so blinded her that she'd taken unnecessary chances?

She'd never know. And there was nothing she could do to go back and change things anyway.

Guilt gnawed at her, just as strong now as it had been back then.

"You're good with them, you know."

The change in subject made her blink. "With who?"

He nodded toward the kids. "These two."

"I care about all my patients."

"I wasn't accusing you of anything, Tracy. Just making a statement."

She considered that for a moment. The anger had been so strong at the end of their marriage that it was hard to hear anything he said without the filters of the past. Maybe she should start trying to take his words at face value. Maybe he could start doing the same.

She perched on the side of Cleo's bed, her fingers feathering through the girl's hair. A low sigh came from the child's throat, and she snuggled into her hand.

Tears pricked very close to the surface but she ignored them as best she could. "I can't imagine how they're going to feel when they wake up and realize their mother is gone. For ever."

Well, she took that back. She knew how that felt but she'd at least had her mom with her until she was a grown woman. These kids would never know how that felt. She wished there was some way she could take that pain from them.

"Sometimes a parent doesn't have to die to be gone," Ben murmured.

She glanced up at him, but he was staring through the dusty window across from them.

"Are you talking about your mom and dad?" Ben and Marcelo's parents hadn't been around much as they'd been growing up and both men carried some resentment about that. That resentment had carried over to Ben's marriage.

Her traveling had been a constant source of arguments almost from the moment they'd both said, "I do."

But Ben had been just as gung ho about his job when they'd met. She hadn't understood exactly why he'd wanted to give all that up. Well, that wasn't quite true either. When she'd found out she was pregnant, she'd been all set to let her office take over a lot of *Projeto Vida's* off-site calls. Then things had changed.

And Ben had reacted badly to her need for space…for time to think. In reality, she probably should have told him sooner, but she'd still been reeling from the news and grieving over her mother's and sisters' deaths.

Ben's eyes refocused on her. "No. Just talking in generalities."

He was lying. But it was easier to let this particular subject go. "I forgot to ask. How's Rosa?"

"Fine. Still at the house."

She wasn't surprised. The old housekeeper—who'd been widowed at a young age and had never remarried—had practically raised Ben and Marcelo. Of course Ben would keep her on. It was another thing they'd argued about.

Oh, not about Rosa still living there—Tracy loved her almost as much as Ben—but that he wouldn't hear of the housekeeper having any part in raising their child. The early elation of finding out she was pregnant hadn't lasted long.

When he'd asked about her plans for her job once the baby was born, she'd flippantly responded that Rosa would be thrilled to help during her absences—that she'd already asked her, in fact. Her words had been met with stony silence. Seconds later Ben had stalked from the room and slammed through the front door of the house.

Only afterwards had she realized how her comment might have sounded. She'd apologized and tried to explain once he'd come home, but she'd got the feeling Ben had heard little or nothing of what she'd said.

She sighed. "I miss Rosa."

"I'm sure she misses you as well."

Her heart aching, a silent question echoing inside her head: *And what about you, Ben? Do you ever miss me?*

* * *

"Don't move too quickly. You're still weak."

Tracy put her shoulder beneath Daniel's arm and, with Pedro on his other side, they helped him walk slowly around the clearing in front of the house in an effort to ward off the possibility of deep vein thromboses from all his time in bed. Day five, and the patient who'd set off the frantic race to save a village seemed to have turned a corner—against all odds. Just yesterday they'd wondered if he would even make it. Somehow the twelve-year-old's body was fighting off the disease when by most medical journals' estimations he should be dead.

"M-my sister?" His voice was thin and raspy.

"Cleo is at the cafeteria. You have some catching up to do, you know," she teased. "Do you think you can handle the thought of sipping some broth?"

"I'd rather have *beijú*."

The local flatbread made from cassava flour was typical up here in the northeastern part of the country. Tracy had missed the gummy bread in São Paulo, although she could still find it on occasion.

Pedro shook his head. "I think we'd better stick to broth for today, like Tracy said."

Daniel made a face. "Not even beans and rice?"

"Soon," Tracy said with a smile. "Maybe in another day or two, okay?"

His already thin shoulders slumped, but he didn't argue as they led him over to the temporary mess hall the military had set up. The tent was divided into sides. Medical personnel and healthy villagers on one side and those with active infections on the other. Donning her mask, she ducked beneath the canvas door flap to deliver her patient.

Four long tables with wooden benches were mostly empty. There weren't very many patients at the moment who were well enough to actually walk the short distance from their beds. Huge fans sucked heat from the inside and blew it out, keeping the place from turning into an inferno as the sun baked the canvas roof. In fact, more of the flaps were open today, a sign the military knew things were looking up for the stricken town.

A wave from across the space caught her eye.

Cleo, seated at a front table, smiled, her dark eyes lighting up as she saw them come in. "Daniel, you're awake!" She motioned him over.

Tracy delivered their charge to the table and brother and sister were reunited—outside the sickroom—for the first time in over a week. Cleo's smile wavered and then she wrapped her arms around Daniel's neck and sobbed quietly. Tracy was forced to separate them gently when she grew concerned about the boy's system being overloaded. Before she could ask the person in charge of meals for a cup of broth, one magically appeared on the table in front of them.

Cleo, who'd begun to recover more quickly than Daniel, had black beans and rice on her plate—and Tracy could swear that was a piece of fried banana as well. Her own mouth watered, so she could only imagine how Daniel felt. But he dutifully picked up his spoon and gave a tentative taste of the contents of his cup. Despite the liquid diet, he closed his eyes as if it were the finest caviar.

"Good?" she asked.

He nodded, taking another sip.

Pedro glanced at the serving area. "I'm going to head over and get in line before it closes. What do you want?"

"I already have Tracy's food."

The voice came from behind them just as a tray was plonked down in front of her. A creamy-white *beijú*, slathered in butter, was folded in half and propped up on a neat mound of rice and beans. And, oh! A *whole* fried banana.

"Not fair," muttered Daniel, who looked longingly at the plate and sucked down another spoonful of his broth.

She glanced to the side and saw Ben, his eyes on Pedro as he set down a second tray beside hers. She gave her assistant an apologetic shrug. "Get something before they run out. I'll see you later, okay?"

Ben waited for her to sit before joining her. Irritated, she realized she'd been looking for him all day.

"You're supposed to be on the doctors' side of the tent, you know," she said, cringing as the words left her mouth. Great. No "Thank you" for the food. No "How are you?" Just a veiled accusation.

"Hmm. Well, so should you. I saw you come in and thought you might like an update on our situation."

Our situation?

Oh, he meant here in town. He wasn't referring to that disastrous kiss.

"Is that where you've been? With the military?"

"The guys in charge wanted me to fill them in. General Gutierrez is here and heard most of the news from his own doctors, but he wanted to make sure it matched the civilian report. The military's reputation tends to be a touchy subject."

"Since when?" As soon as the words were out of her mouth she wished she could call them back. "Sorry. That hadn't come out right."

He ignored her and leaned around her back to lay a hand on Daniel's shoulder, smiling at the boy. "I'm surprised to see you out of bed."

Cleo blinked at him with huge brown eyes. "What about me? Are you surprised to see me, too?"

"Definitely. But very glad." He then ruffled Cleo's hair, which caused the seven-year-old to giggle. The happy sound made Tracy's heart contract. The man was a natural with children. He should have lots of them. All swarming around him like a litter of cute puppies.

"I haven't heard a peep about any so-called meetings. Why didn't someone call me?" She wasn't really peeved but needed to get her mind off Ben and his future children. Because it hurt too much to think about it. Not when she'd decided her previous pregnancy would probably be her last.

He glanced away. "I wanted to let you sleep in a little while longer. It's been a difficult week."

Come to think of it, no one *had* come to wake her up for her normal seven a.m. shift. Had that been Ben's doing as well? Her heart tightened further.

He was a good man. He'd deserved so much better than what she'd given him.

She cleared her throat, trying to get rid of the lump that clogged it. "Thank you. You weren't there when I woke up."

Turning to look at her, he lifted a shoulder. "I'm an early riser. Always have been."

Yes, he had been. But he hadn't normally left their bed in the middle of the night and not returned. A thought came to her. Maybe he'd found somewhere else to hole up. A streak of something white hot went through her. She had noticed a couple of female soldiers eyeing him. But surely...

Daniel lifted the last spoonful of broth and leaned back with a tired sigh.

She wanted to know what had been said during the meeting but she also needed to take care of her patients' needs. "Are you guys ready to go back to your room?"

Ben frowned down at her untouched tray, while Daniel shook his head. "Can I please stay here for a little while longer? I'm tired of lying in bed, and I want to talk to Cleo."

There was a sad note in the words, and Tracy had a feeling she knew what he wanted to talk to her about. What were these kids going to do when this was all over? A thought that had plagued her repeatedly over the past couple of days.

She nodded. "We'll move to another table and give you some time alone, okay? If you need me, just wave, and I'll see you."

She and Ben picked up their trays. She noticed he headed for a different table than Pedro's. Thankfully her assistant was busy talking to one of the military doctors. Maybe he wouldn't notice.

She realized she wasn't the only one who hadn't touched her plate. "Eat. Then I want to hear about what went on at the meeting."

He lifted his brows. "I'll eat if you will."

Her lips curled into a reluctant smile, and she realized how little of that she'd done over the last week. "Deal."

The next fifteen minutes were spent in relative silence as she enjoyed her first quiet meal since they'd arrived. When she bit into her *beijú* she couldn't stop a low groan of pleasure. Ben remembered exactly how much butter she liked on it. And even though the bread was no longer warm, it was still as good as she remembered. "I have to take some cassava flour back with me so I can make this at home."

Ben didn't respond, and she only realized how that sounded when she noticed a muscle working in his jaw. Surely he knew she'd have to go back to São Paulo soon. Their life together was over, no matter how much she might wish otherwise.

Shaking off her regrets, she forced her back to straighten. "So, how did things go this morning?"

Cutting a chunk of fried banana and popping it into her mouth, she waited for him to fill her in.

"Tell me something," he said instead.

Her whole body went on alert. Because it was he who was supposed to be telling *her* something, not the other way around. And if he asked her about her reasons for leaving, she had no idea what she was going to say. Because for all her raging about Ben's ridiculous actions in sending in the cavalry when she hadn't been in any real danger, she knew it was only a symptom of an underlying problem.

Yes, he'd betrayed her. Yes, he should have come himself, instead of pretending the military had other reasons for her not being in that village. But her reasons for leaving were way more complex than that. Because in the same way the townsfolk's coughs were only a symptom of a raging wildfire burning below the surface, so were her issues.

"I thought we were going to talk about your meeting."

If she thought she could change the subject that easily, she was wrong.

"Why haven't you filed for divorce? Surely you could meet someone who loves your job just as much as you do." His glance went to the table where Pedro sat.

"I—I told you. It's hard to get a divorce from inside Brazil."

"And you mean to tell me that after four years there's been no one you've wanted to spend your life with?"

"If you're talking about Pedro, we're just coworkers." After Ben, she'd wanted no one. "I just haven't had the time to file the paperwork. It would mean a trip to New York."

She tried to turn the conversation back to him. And realized she really did want to know. "What about you?"

"I have no desire to go down that road again."

A spike of guilt went through her heart. Had she done that to him? Been such an awful wife that he'd never consider marrying again? She'd just assumed he'd be happier once she was out of his life, that he'd find someone who could give him what she didn't seem able to. "I see. But surely someday…"

"I don't think so." He dropped his utensils onto his plate with a clatter.

Surely he couldn't kiss her like he'd done a few days ago and not want that with someone else.

"You'd have eventually hated me, Ben. We both know that. It was better that I left." Defective gene or no defective gene, she and Ben had never seen eye to eye on her job.

But would she have traveled as much without that fear prodding her from behind?

He turned to face her. "I never hated you, Tracy. But I deserved better than a letter left on my desk."

He was right. She'd left him an ugly, anger-filled missive detailing everything about their marriage she found unbearable, ending with the military invasion of the village that had ended in her expulsion. Part of that rage had been due to feelings of helplessness over her test results. Part of it had been caused by grief over the loss of her child. But the biggest part of it had been guilt at having failed him so terribly. She'd been too much of a coward to stick around and tell him to his face that it was over.

"You're right, Ben. It won't help, but I was dealing with something more than my pregnancy at that time."

"Something about your job?"

"No." It was on the tip of her tongue to tell him when Daniel waved from across the room. She realized this was neither the time nor the place to dredge up issues from the past. Not when there were lives in the balance and patients who needed her. "I have to go. I can't change the way things played out, Ben. All I can say is I'm sorry."

"Yeah, well, so am I." Before she could even get up from her place, Ben was already on his feet—had already picked up both their trays and was striding towards the front of the tent where the trashcans were located.

As she went over to Daniel's table, she realized Ben

had never told her what the meeting this morning had been about.

And right now she didn't care.

CHAPTER NINE

THEY'D LOST ANOTHER patient during the night, and now this.

A flash of anger went through Tracy's eyes. "We have to stay for a week *after* the last patient recovers? You've got to be kidding. I can't be gone from my job for that long."

Her job. That's what it always came down to.

Unless it was more than that. She'd talked about dealing with other issues during their marriage that had nothing to do with her job. Or her pregnancy. He'd racked his brains, thinking back over every last detail he could remember.

And had come up blank.

Except for a vivid image of that kiss in the neighboring town a few days ago. He couldn't seem to get it out of his head.

In fact, the memory haunted him night after night and infected his dreams. The dreams that drove him from his bed and into the narrow hallway just outside the door. His back was killing him, but it was better than the other part of his body that was also killing him.

"The army is worried about keeping the disease contained, so they're upping the quarantine time." He frowned. "And because we traveled to that neighboring village, they want to keep tabs on it as well and make sure no one starts exhibiting symptoms."

She glanced around the sickroom at the dwindling number of patients. "We'll be sitting here alone, twiddling our thumbs, by that time, and you know it."

More than half of the surviving patients had gone on to recover, and the ones who'd shown no symptoms at all were still on doses of antibiotics and would be for several more days. She was right, though. Once the remaining cases were under control, there'd be no more risk of person-to-person contamination. And they'd be stuck here for a week with nothing to do.

Tracy walked over to one of the patients and checked the IV bag, making sure it didn't need changing. "We wore masks while we were at the other village, Ben."

"Not the whole time."

He saw from the change in her expression that she knew exactly when they'd gone without wearing their protective masks. Right before—and during—that deadly kiss.

She lowered her voice, even though she was speaking in English and no one would understand her. "No one saw us."

"Someone did." He nodded when her eyes widened. "And they reported it to the general."

"I thought you guys were big buddies."

"We're friends. But he's also a stickler for the rules."

"I found that out the hard way." Her eyes narrowed. "Listen, I can't stay here for ever. I have no cellphone reception, and there's no way I can get word back to *Projeto Vida* that I'll be delayed even longer. They need to at least let Pedro head back to the office."

He sighed. They hadn't seen much of Tracy's assistant since lunch the other day, and he wondered if the other man was actively avoiding them. Then again, why would he? Ben's lack of sleep was obviously catching up with him.

"They're not letting anyone out, and I wouldn't try to press the issue, if I were you."

"Did you set this up?"

"Get over yourself, Trace. This has nothing to do with you. Or me, for that matter."

She closed her eyes for a second. "You're right. Sorry."

He thought she actually might be. "Maybe I can ask him to get in touch with your office. I'm sure they must have a satellite phone or something they're using for communication."

Moving over to stand beside her, he touched her hand. "Listen, I know this hasn't been easy. Maybe I shouldn't have let you come in the first place, I don't know. But I'm really not trying to manipulate the situation or make things more difficult than they have to be. It's just as inconvenient for me to be stuck here as it is for you. I have my lab—my own responsibilities. Mandy can't hold down the fort for ever."

Her gaze softened. "Don't think I don't appreciate being able to come, Ben. I do." She hesitated then wrapped her fingers around his. "It just feels…awkward. And I know this is just as hard for you as it is for me. I really am sorry."

When she started to withdraw, he tightened his fingers, holding her in place. "Whatever else happens, it's been good seeing you again." The words had come out before he could stop them, and he could tell by her sharp intake of breath they'd taken her by surprise.

"You too."

Then what were those other issues you mentioned?

He somehow succeeded in keeping the question confined inside his skull. Because he already knew he wouldn't get an answer. Not until she was good and ready to tell him—if she ever was.

The woman was hiding something. But he had no idea what it was.

The last thing he wanted to do, though, was to fall for her all over again, and then stand around cooling his heels, hoping each time she left that when she returned, she'd be back to stay. He might be a glutton for punishment, but he was no fool.

So what did he do?

For a start, he could act like the scientist he was—examine the evidence without her realizing what he was doing. Just like he found various ways to look at the same specimens in his lab—using dyes, centrifuges, and cultures, until they revealed all their secrets.

He was trained to study things from different angles. His fingers continued to grip hers as he glanced down into those deep green eyes. That's what he had to do. Probe, study, examine—kiss.

Whatever it took.

Until she gave up every last secret. And then he could put his crazy emotions to rest once and for all.

Pure heaven.

Tracy sank into the fragrant bubbles, finding the water cool and inviting. Anything warmer would have been unbearable with the sizzling temperatures outside today. She remembered they hadn't even needed a hot-water heater for their showers in Teresina—the water coming from the taps had been plenty warm enough for almost everything.

She sighed and leaned her head back against the rim of the tub. She had no idea how Ben had arranged to have one of the large blue water tanks brought in and set up behind the house, but he had. He'd also had folding screens erected all around it for privacy.

The tanks were normally installed on residential rooftops as a way to increase water pressure. She'd never heard of bathing in one, but as it was the size of a normal hot tub, it was the perfect depth, really. He'd even managed to rustle up some scented shampoo that had probably come from the local market—although the store hadn't been open since the outbreak had begun.

She hadn't dared strip completely naked, but even clad in her black bra and panties the experience still felt unbelievably decadent. Better yet, Ben had stationed himself outside the screened-off area, making sure no one came upon her unexpectedly—not that they could see much through the thick layer of bubbles.

Why had he done it? Yes, they'd both been exhausted and, yes, despite her tepid showers, her muscles ached with fatigue from turning patients and making sure she moved their arms and legs in an effort to keep blood clots from forming.

Where had he even gotten the tank? It looked new, not like it had been drained and taken off someone's house. Well, once she was done, she'd let him have a turn. Only the bubbles would be gone by then and he'd be getting used water—unless they took the time to refill the thing. And she knew Ben was concerned enough about the environment that he wouldn't want to double their water usage.

Or… She pushed up out of the water and stared down at her chest. Her bra was solid black, so nothing showed through. In fact, her underwear was less revealing than what you'd find on most Brazilian beaches. So maybe he could just join her.

A faint danger signal went off in her head, its low buzz making her blink as she sank back into the water.

What? She wasn't naked. Far from it.

Ben had already seen her with a lot fewer clothes. And it wasn't like anyone was going to venture behind the house. The property itself was walled off with an eight-foot-high concrete fence—which was typical in Brazil. The screens were merely an added layer of protection.

If *she'd* been hot and sweaty when he'd unveiled his

surprise, then he had to be positively baking. Especially as he was now standing guard in the sun just beyond the screens. And the water really did feel amazing.

"Ben?" His name came out a little softer than necessary. She figured if he didn't hear her, she could just pretend she hadn't said anything.

"Yep?"

Okay, so she was either going to have to suck it up and ask him if he wanted to join her or just make up some random question.

"Um...I was wondering if you wanted to— I mean the water isn't going to be as fresh once I get out, so do you want to...?" Her throat squeezed off the last of the words.

Ben's face appeared around the side of one of the screens. "Excuse me?"

"As long as we both have some clothes on, we can share the water." She couldn't stop a sigh as she curled a hand around the rim of the tank and peered over the top. "I know you won't pour a new bath for yourself."

"I'm okay." There was definite tension in his jaw, which should serve as an additional warning, but now he was making her feel guilty on top of everything else. Especially when she spied a rivulet of sweat running down the side of his neck, and he lifted a hand to dash it away.

"Come on. Stop being a martyr. You've earned a break. Besides, it'll help cool you off."

"That, I doubt." The words were so low she wasn't sure she'd heard them correctly but, still, he moved into the space, hands low on his hips.

He was soaked, his face red from the heat.

"Look at your shirt, Ben. You're practically steaming." She wouldn't mention the fact that seeing her husband layered in sweat had always been a huge turn-on. Maybe this *was* a mistake. But there was no way she was going to call back her words now. He'd think she was chicken.

So...should you stand up and cluck now...or wait until later?

He mumbled something under his breath that sounded weirdly like, "You're a scientist. Examine, probe..."

The rest of the sentence faded away to nothing.

"Come on, Ben. You're making me feel guilty."

His lips turned up at the edges. "And are you going to make *me* feel guilty if I refuse?"

"Yes." She realized once she'd answered him that his last phrase could have been taken more than one way. But then again she was hearing all kinds of strange stuff today.

When his hands went to the bottom of his shirt and hauled the thing up and over his head, her breath caught in her throat as glistening pecs and tight abs came into view—accompanied by a familiar narrow trail of hair that was every bit as bewitching as she remembered.

Okay, she had definitely not thought this through. For some reason, in her mind she'd pictured him clothed one second and in the tub the next. But then again, stripping outside the fenced area wouldn't help any, because he would still return *sans* most of his clothes.

His hands went to the button of his khaki cargo pants. "You sure about this?"

She gulped. "As long as you have something underneath that."

His smile widened. "It depends whether you're talking about clothing or something else."

Oh, man. She did remember he'd gone commando from time to time, just to drive her crazy. She'd never known when he'd peeled his jeans off at night what she'd find.

When his zip went down this time, however, she breathed

a sigh of relief, followed by a glimmer of disappointment, when dark boxers came into view.

As if reading her thoughts, he said, "No reason to any more."

That little ache in her chest grew larger. He no longer had anyone to play those games with.

As he shoved his slacks the rest of the way down his hips and stepped out of them, she tried to avoid looking at him as she thought about how unfair life was. This was a man who should be in a monogamous, loving relationship. He'd been a great husband. A fantastic lover. And he would have made a terrific father.

"You do have clothes on under those bubbles, right?"

"A little late to be asking that now, don't you think?" She wrinkled her nose and snapped the black strap on her shoulder as evidence. "Of course I do. That invitation wouldn't have gone out otherwise."

His smile this time was a bit tight, but he stepped into the huge tub and slid beneath the water in a single quick motion. Too quick to see if the thought of them in this tank together was affecting him as much as it was her.

Oh, lord, she was an idiot. But as the water licked the curve of his biceps with the slightest movement of their bodies, she couldn't bring herself to be sorry she'd given the invitation.

"Nice?" she asked, making sure her bra-covered breasts were well below the waterline. Since it was almost up to her neck, they were nowhere to be seen.

He responded by sinking down further until his head ducked beneath the surface then rose again. A stream of bubble-laden water sluiced down his face, his neck...that strong chest of his... She only realized her eyes were tracking its progress when his voice drew her attention back up.

"Wish I'd thought of doing this days ago."

"Huh?"

He shook his head with a smile. "Nothing. Yeah. It's nice." He stretched his arms out along either side of the tub and watched her. "So, how was your day?"

Maybe this wasn't going to be so weird after all. "Tiring. Yours?"

"Interesting."

"Did General Gutierrez call another meeting?" If Ben had left her out of the loop again, she was going to be seriously miffed. Those were her patients as well. And she'd been first on the scene when the distress call had gone out.

"No, still the same game plan in place, from what I understand." He lowered his hands into the tub and cupped them, carrying the water to his face and splashing it. If he'd been trying to rinse away the remaining bubbles he'd failed because now they'd gathered like a thin goatee on his chin.

"Um…" She motioned to her own chin to let him know.

He scrubbed the offending body part with his shoulder, transferring the bubbles, then took up his position again, arms spread along the curved blue rim. She tried to make herself as small as possible.

"So, you said your day has been interesting. How so?" She kept her hands braced on the bottom of the tub to keep from slipping even further down into the water. Besides, the less of herself she exposed, the less…well, *exposed* she felt.

He shrugged. "Just doing some research."

"On our cases?"

"Our cases. That's exactly it."

She narrowed her eyes. Why did she get the feeling that the word "cases" was being thrown around rather loosely—at least on his side.

"Did you come to any conclusions?"

"Not yet. But I'm hoping to soon."

The look in his eyes was intense, as if he was expecting to see something reflected back at him.

She cleared her throat. "Daniel is almost better. A few more days and he should be able to be released. Cleo is still complaining of a slight headache, though, and she isn't progressing as quickly as she was earlier."

"Hmm…I'll check her when I get back." His lips pursed. "I've been thinking about those two—Daniel and his sister, I mean. You're good with them."

Something in her stomach tightened. "Like I said earlier, I try to care for all my patients."

"I know you do."

"I feel terrible that their mother didn't…" The tightening spread to her throat, choking off the rest of her words.

"I know, Trace. I'm sorry." He shifted and one of his legs touched hers, his foot lying alongside her knee. She got the feeling the gesture was meant to comfort her because she was too far away for him to reach any other way. The tub was narrower at the bottom than it was at the top, and even though she knew why he'd done it, it still jolted her system to feel the heat of his skin against hers. She returned the pressure, though, to acknowledge what he'd done.

"Thanks," she said. "That means a lot to me."

She licked her lips, expecting him to move his leg away as soon as she said the words, but he didn't. Instead his gaze held hers. What he was expecting her to do, she wasn't quite sure. A shiver went over her when his foot slid along the side of her calf, as if he'd bent his knee beneath the water. Had he done that on purpose?

There was nothing in his expression to indicate he had.

Not only did he not move away, a second later she felt something slide against her other leg. She gulped. Now, that hadn't been an accident. Had it?

And the bubbles were starting to dissipate, popping at

an alarming rate. Soon she'd be able to see beneath the water's surface. And so would Ben. So she either needed to
wash her hair and get out fast or she needed to stay in and…

That was the question. Just how brave was she?

And exactly how far was she willing to let him go?

CHAPTER TEN

SHE DIDN'T KNOW what to do.

Ben watched the quicksilver shift of expressions cross her face the second his other leg touched hers—puzzlement, realization, concern and finally uncertainty.

"Tracy." He leaned forward and held out his hand to her, keeping his voice low and coaxing. "I know it hasn't been easy coming here—working with me. And I wasn't even sure I wanted you here. But it was the right thing to do."

The right thing to do.

And what about what he was doing now?

He had no idea if it was the right thing or not. But the second she'd invited him into the tub he'd wondered if this was where she'd been heading the whole time. Especially when he'd started shucking his clothes and he'd seen the slightest glimmer of hunger flash through her eyes. She'd quickly doused it, but not before it had registered for what it was. He'd seen that look many a time back when they'd been a couple.

The question was, should he push the boundaries? She was vulnerable. Tired—she'd admitted it herself. Wasn't he taking advantage of that?

He started to pull his hand back when she startled him by reaching out and placing hers within it, saying, "I know it was. So is this."

Without a word she held on tight and tugged, a movement that sent her sliding across the tub towards him. Her feet went up and over his thighs, hitting the curved plastic on either side of his hips. Her forward momentum came to a halt, and his libido took up where momentum left off.

Raw need raced through his system, replacing any ethical questions he'd had a few seconds ago. With a single gesture she'd admitted she wanted him. At least, he hoped that's what it meant.

"When do you need to be back to work?" he asked.

"I'm off until tomorrow." Still two feet away from each other, her gaze swept down his face, lingering on his mouth.

Until tomorrow. That meant he had all night. He forced himself to take a long, slow breath.

He smiled. "You know, we should have thought of putting a tub like this in our back yard. It's almost as big as a pool. The only problem with it is you're still much too far away."

"Am I?" Her thumb swept across the back of his hand beneath the water. "I've come halfway. Maybe it's your turn now."

"Maybe it is." He pushed himself across the space until, instead of being separated by feet, they were now inches apart. "Better?"

She smiled. "Yes, definitely." She released his hand and propped her fingers on his shoulders, smoothing across them and sending fire licking through his gut in the process.

He curled his legs around her backside and reeled her in the rest of the way, until they were breast to chest and she had to tip her head back to look at him.

"So, here we are," he murmured. "What do we do now?"

"Do you have to ask?"

His lips curved in a slow smile. "No, but I thought I should check to make sure we were on the same page."

"Same page of the very same book."

That was all the confirmation he needed. He cupped the back of her head and stared into her eyes before doing as she'd asked: meeting her halfway. More than halfway.

He swore, even as he kissed her, that he was still working on his plan. Still analyzing every piece of information. But that lasted all of two seconds before his baser instincts kicked in and robbed him of any type of higher brain function. He'd hoped to get an inkling of whether or not the old attractions were still there.

They were.

And at the moment that attraction was groveling and begging him not to screw this up by thinking too hard.

So he didn't. The fingers in her hair tightened, the silky strands growing taut between them. A tiny sound exited her throat that Ben definitely recognized. Tracy had always been turned on by control.

His over her. Or at least that's what she let herself believe.

In reality, though, she'd always wanted to control every aspect of her life, whereas he was happy to take things as they came. But in the bedroom it was a different story. Handing him the reins got her motor running, and right now Ben was more than happy to oblige.

Using his grip on her hair to hold her in place, he kissed along one of her gorgeous cheekbones, taking his time as he headed towards her ear.

"Ben."

His eyes closed at the sound of his name on her lips. Oh, yeah. It had been four long years since he'd heard that husky whisper—half plea, half groan. And it drove him just as crazy today as it had back then.

His teeth closed over her earlobe, while his free hand trailed slowly down the curve of her neck, continuing down her spine in long feathery strokes, until the line of her bra interrupted him. He circled the clasp a time or two, his finger gliding over the lacy strap that transected her back. One snap and he had it undone.

A whimper escaped her throat, but she couldn't move, still held fast by his hand in her hair. He tugged her head back a bit further, exposing the line of her throat, and the vein beating madly beneath her ear. He licked it, pressed his tongue tight against that throbbing pulse point, glorying in the way those rhythmic waves traveled straight to his groin, making him harder than he ever remembered being. Unable to contain his need, he whispered, "I want you. Right here. Right now. Say yes."

She moistened her lips, but didn't keep him waiting long before responding. "Yes."

"Yes." He breathed in the word and released her hair, his hands going to the straps on her shoulders, peeling them down her arms and letting the piece of clothing sink to the bottom of the tank. He parted the bubbles on the surface of the water until her breasts came into full view.

"Beautiful." He cupped them. "Get up on your knees, honey."

She did as he asked, a water droplet clinging to the hard tip of her left nipple. Who could blame it? Certainly not him, because that was right where he wanted to be.

Lowering his head, he licked the drop off, her quick intake of breath telling him she liked the way he lingered, her fingers on the back of his head emphasizing her point.

He pulled away slightly, and looked up at her with hooded eyes. "Ask for it, Tracy."

Her lips parted, but she didn't utter a word, already knowing that wasn't what he was looking for. Instead, she kept her hands braced against his nape, and arched her back until the breast he'd been courting was back against his mouth. She slowly drew the erect nipple along his lower lip.

"That's it," he whispered against her skin. "I love it when you do that."

He opened his mouth, and she shifted closer. When his lips closed around her and sucked, her body went rigid, and she cried out softly. He gave her what she wanted, using his teeth, his tongue to give her the same pleasure she'd just given him. God, he loved knowing what she wanted and making her reach for it. His arms went around her back, his hands sliding beneath the band of her panties and cupping her butt. He slipped his fingers lower and encountered a slick moisture that had nothing to do with the water all around them. Raw need roared through him.

Knowing he was coming close to the edge of his own limits, he found her center and slid a finger deep inside her, then another, reveling in the way she lowered herself until they were fully embedded. He held her steady with one hand while his mouth and fingers swept her along re-membered paths, her breathing picking up in time with his movements.

Not long now.

And he was ready for her. More than ready. He ached to be where his fingers were.

He clamped down with his teeth and at the same time applied steady pressure in the depths of her body, and just like in days past, she moaned loudly, her body stiffening as she trembled on the precipice before exploding around his fingers in a series of spasms that rocked his world. Within seconds he'd freed himself and lifted her onto his erec-tion, sweeping aside the crotch of her panties as he thrust hard and deep.

Hell. His breath left his lungs as memories flooded back.

Except everything was even better than he remembered, her still pulsing body exquisitely tight, her head thrown back, dark, glossy hair tumbling free around her bare shoulders as she rode him. Over and over, squeezing and releasing, until he could hold back no longer and with a sharp groan he joined her, falling right over the edge into paradise.

CHAPTER ELEVEN

A DISASTER. THAT'S what yesterday's session in the water tank had been.

Tracy stood in front of the tiny mirror in the bathroom and examined her bare breasts. Really looked at them for the first time in a long time. She'd spent the last several years avoiding everything they represented.

And yet they'd brought her such pleasure yesterday.

It was a paradox. One she'd tried to blank out by pretending they didn't exist. Only Ben had forced an awareness that was as uncomfortable as it was real. How much longer was she going to keep running away?

I'm not!

Tracy continued to stare at her reflection, her lips giving a wry twist. She'd believed those two words once, even as she'd scurried from one place to another. Now…? Well, now she wasn't so sure.

She should tell him. Now that the anger was gone, he should know the truth of what she'd been facing back then.

Why? What good could possibly come of it now that they were no longer together? Did she want him to feel guilty for what he'd done? For touching her there?

No. She wanted him to remember it the same way she did—as a pleasurable interlude that shouldn't be repeated.

She raised her hands and cupped herself, remembering

the way Ben's fingers had done the same—the way he'd brought his mouth slowly down…

Shaking her head, she let her arms fall back to her sides.

As great as their time together had been, retracing her steps and venturing back into an unhappy past was not a wise move. Ben had been miserable with her by the end of their marriage.

But how much of that had been her doing? Had been because of what she'd become? A phantom, too scared to sit in any one spot for too long—who had felt the walls of their house closing in around her any time she'd spent more than a couple of weeks there.

So how could she have let yesterday happen?

She had no idea.

Even though she could freely admit it had been a mistake, could even recite each and every reason it had been the wrong thing to do, she couldn't force herself to be sorry for those stolen moments. She'd always known what she'd felt for Ben was powerful—that she'd never feel the same way about another man—and being with him again had just driven that point home.

Which meant she couldn't let it happen again.

Reaching for her clothes, she hurriedly pulled them on, turning her back to the mirror like she always did and feeling like a fraud. It was one thing to admit her reasons for doing something. It was another thing entirely to change her behavior. Especially when that behavior had served her perfectly well for the past four years.

At least…until now.

By the time she made it to the makeshift hospital, Daniel was sitting in a chair next to his bed, his chin on his chest. His eyes were dry, but his arms were wrapped around his waist as if he was in pain.

She squatted next to him. "Daniel, what's wrong? Does something hurt?"

He shook his head, but didn't move from his slumped position.

"Then what is it?"

Several seconds went by before he answered her. "Where will we go?"

The question was so soft she had to lean forward to hear it, and even then she wasn't sure she'd caught his words.

"I'm sorry?"

Lifting his head, he glanced around the space. She twisted to do the same and noted several of the beds were newly empty—fresh sheets neatly pulled up and tucked in as if ready for new patients. Only there probably wouldn't be any.

There'd been no deaths in the last day or so, and the people who'd become ill after the teams had arrived had ended up with much less severe versions of the illness. It definitely made a case for early intervention.

"This is…was our living room…before my mom—before she…" He stopped and took a deep breath. "Once Cleo and I are well enough to leave here, where will we stay?"

Tracy's heart broke all over again. She'd been worrying over her little tryst with Ben when Daniel and Cleo were now facing life without the only parent they'd ever known. And because the two had no relatives that anyone knew of, and as their home was now being used as a temporary hospital, there was literally nowhere for the siblings to go once they were cleared of infection. Oh, the military would probably take them to a state-run orphanage once the quarantine period was lifted. But until then? No one was allowed in or out of the village.

Surely they could stay here in what had once been their home. But where? Every room was being used, whether to house soldiers or medical personnel. It was full. More than full. Even Pedro—whom she'd barely had a chance to speak to in recent days—had moved from where he'd been staying and was now bunking with members of the military unit assigned to São João dos Rios.

She thought for a minute. Ben kept talking about how much he cared about these kids. Maybe it was time to put that to the test. "We can ask to have two more hammocks put up in the room where Dr. Almeida and I sleep. At least until we figure something else out."

Once she'd said it she wondered if that wouldn't make the whole thing feel a little too much like a family for comfort. And she didn't want to give Daniel and Cleo the idea that they could stay together permanently. Because that wasn't on the cards.

Besides, she wasn't sure Ben would be thrilled about sharing his room with a preteen and a child, especially after the slow smile he'd given her that morning. The one that had her face heating despite her best efforts. He'd even stayed and slept in his own hammock last night—a first since they'd arrived. Was it because of what they'd done?

She must have thought so because it was what had set off the self-examination in the bathroom. She hadn't touched herself like that in a long time.

"Will the soldiers let us go with you?" Daniel gave her a hopeful smile.

No backing out now.

"I don't see why they wouldn't, but you'll have to get well first, which means you'll need to get some rest." What else could she say? They couldn't just let Daniel and Cleo wander the streets or sleep in one of the unoccupied houses. The pair had had a home and a family not three weeks ago. And now it was all gone.

She'd been there, done that. She could at least try to

help these children as much as she could before she had to leave—be their temporary family, kind of like a foster-care situation. At least until they figured out something a little more permanent.

How was she supposed to do that before she headed back to São Paulo?

Something she didn't want to think about right now.

Just then, Ben walked into the room, his brow raised in question when he saw the two of them sitting together. She stood, glancing down at Daniel, and noted with horror he had a huge smile on his face.

Don't, Daniel. Not yet. Let me talk to him first.

But even as she thought it, the boy spoke up. "Tracy says Cleo and I can stay with you once we are well."

Ben's glance shot to her. "She did? When?"

"Just now. I explained we did not have any place to go, and she offered to let us stay with you. Cleo was scared." He blinked a couple of times as if that last statement had been hard for him to admit. "We both were…about what might happen. If they tried to take Cleo away from me…" He didn't finish the rest of his statement.

Ben's face grew stormy. "Tracy? Would you like to explain?"

"I, um… Well, I simply said we would figure something out…"

"Figure something out," he parroted.

Daniel's smile never wavered. He had no idea Ben's now icy glare was sucking the heat right out of the atmosphere.

Nodding, Daniel continued, "Yes, so Cleo and I wouldn't be alone—so we could stay together."

Oh, no! He'd obviously misunderstood her intentions— had thought she'd meant the living arrangements would continue even after they left the town. Ben was going to blow his top.

"Well, Daniel, I'm glad to hear she's making those kinds of plans." He moved toward her. "Can I borrow her for a minute?"

"Yes, I have to tell Cleo the good news, anyway. One of the doctors is helping her walk around the yard outside. She should be back in a minute."

Right on cue, Cleo and her companion came through the door and made their way slowly towards them.

"Tracy, do you mind?" Giving a sharp nod toward the door to indicate she should follow him, Ben stalked toward it.

Gulping back her own dismay, she forced a smile to her face. "I won't be long. Could you tell Cleo I'll be back to check on you both in a few minutes?"

As upset as Ben was, she couldn't help but feel a fierce sense of gratitude over the kids' steady improvement. From all indications, they were going to recover fully.

Two miracles in a sea of sorrows.

They'd lost fourteen patients in all. In such a tiny village it was a good percentage of the population. They'd have a hard time coming back from this without some type of government aid. Whether that meant sending them to another town and bulldozing these homes, or finding a way to get things up and running again, nothing would truly be the same again. They would not soon forget what had happened here.

Neither would she.

Pushing through the door, she saw that Ben was already striding down the hallway on his way out of the house. She hurried after him, knowing he must be furious. But once he heard her explanation, he'd understand that…

The second the bright noonday sun hit her retinas, a hand reached out and tugged her to the side, into the shadow of the house.

"Would you like to tell me what the hell that was all about? You expect those kids to stay with us once we leave here? Kind of hard, as we no longer live in the same house. Or even the same state."

"No. Of course not. He took my words the wrong way. I was only talking about here in the village. That they could stay in our room once they left the hospital." She reached out to squeeze his fingers then let go. "They have nowhere else to go. I didn't know what to say."

"So you said they could stay with us?" He swore softly. "Are you that worried about being alone with me, Tracy?"

She looked at him blankly for a second or two. "What are you talking about?"

"I'm talking about what happened between us yesterday." He propped his hands on his hips. "I think it's a little late to start worrying about your virtue—or reputation—or whatever you want to call it."

What a ridiculous thing for him to say. "You're wrong. This has nothing to do with what happened. Nothing."

"Then why?"

Was it her imagination, or was there a shadow of hurt behind his pale eyes?

"They have nowhere to go until the outbreak is over. This was their house, remember? Once they're released from care, they'll be expected to leave, just like our other patients have. They have no relatives here—or anywhere else, if what Daniel said was true."

Ben pivoted and leaned against the wall, dragging a hand through his hair, which was already damp from the heat of the day. "You're right. I thought…"

Since he didn't finish his sentence, she had no idea *what* he thought.

Maybe he was worried she was making a play for him. That she wanted to move back to their old house. No, that didn't make any sense. He'd given no hint he wanted to start things back up between them. For all she knew, he'd just needed to get laid, and she'd practically put up a neon sign saying she was ready, willing and able to take care of that need.

What had she been thinking, inviting him to get in the tub?

Well, it was over and done with. They were both adults. They *both* had needs—heaven knew, hers hadn't been met in quite some time. Four years, to be exact. She hadn't been with anyone since she'd left him.

To say that the experience yesterday had been cataclysmic was an understatement. A huge one.

"Maybe we can put up a curtain or something." She pressed her shoulder to the wall and looked up at him. "Can they stay with us? At least for a little while?"

"Of course they can." The words were soft, but he seemed distracted, almost as if his mind was already on something else entirely. "I'll check with General Gutierrez, and see what he can do about finding them a place to stay after the quarantine is lifted."

"Thank you." She leaned closer and stretched up to kiss his cheek, her hand going to his arm and lingering there. "And I'm sorry Daniel dropped it on you like that. He asked, and it was the only thing I could think of. I was hoping to talk to you alone before we made any decisions."

"What are you going to do about the other part? If he misunderstood, someone is going to have to talk to him."

"I know." She blew out a breath. "Let's give it a few days, though, okay? Until they're stronger and we see how things are going to play out here. Maybe someone in the town can take them in."

"That might pose a bit of a problem." He paused before

covering her hand with his own. "I came by to tell you something is getting ready to happen."

Her internal radar went on high alert. "With the military?"

"Yes. I sat in on another meeting today." His jaw tightened. "The news wasn't good. And despite what you think, my opinion doesn't always hold that much sway."

Her skin grew clammy at the way he said it. "What are they going to do?"

Tracy had heard tell of things going on behind the scenes where the military police were concerned. Although many were honest, hard-working, family men, there were others who wouldn't think twice about asking for a bribe.

She'd also heard stories about other branches of the police colluding with the drug cartels that worked out of the *favelas*. The shanty towns were notorious for narcotics and illegal dealings. Many of the slums actually had armed thugs guarding the roads leading to the rickety housing developments. It was not only dangerous for the police to enter such places, it was often deadly. Only the corrupt cops could enter and leave with impunity.

"Nothing's been decided for sure. They're still discussing options with the central government."

The hair on the back of her neck rose at the quiet way he said it. She thought again about Daniel's words and the way she'd found him sitting in that chair. He'd seemed almost hopeless. An unsettling thought occurred to her.

"When Daniel mentioned having nowhere to go, I assumed he was talking about for the next several days. But you and he both jumped to the same conclusion about my offer. You both thought the offer was something more permanent."

"Yes."

"Why is that?" Her voice dropped to a whisper. "What's going to happen here, Ben?"

When she tried to drop her hand from his arm, he held on, fingers tightening around hers. "Remember I told you they were going to lift the quarantine in another week? That we—along with the rest of the medical and military personnel—would be allowed to leave once there were no new cases of the plague?"

"I remember."

"Have you looked around you lately? At the survivors?"

She tried to think. One young mother said her husband was trying to pack all their belongings. She'd assumed it was because they wanted to leave for a while to try to forget the horrors of what had happened here. But what if that was not the reason at all? "I know one couple is preparing to leave. So the military must be planning on lifting the quarantine for everyone at the same time."

"Oh they're lifting it all right. The people you mentioned aren't the only ones getting ready for a big move. There are signs of packing going on all over town. Windows being boarded up. *Acerolas* being bulk-harvested from trees."

She had noticed the berries being picked and put into baskets.

"So everyone is going to leave when this is over? They're going to board up the entire town?" If so, what did that mean for Daniel and Cleo?

"No, they're not going to board it up."

"What, then?"

He drew a deep breath then released it on a sigh. "They're planning to destroy the town once this is all over."

Her eyes widened. "Destroy it? How?"

"The same way they're destroying the bodies. They're going to torch everything, until nothing is left of this place but ashes."

CHAPTER TWELVE

A FAMILY. HE'D always wanted one, but not this way. Not at someone else's expense. And certainly not at the expense of an entire village.

He could still hear the pained cry Tracy had given when he'd told her the news.

Ben leaned against the wall as she helped Daniel attach one end of the hammock to the protective iron grating that covered the window. She gave the rope a tug to make sure it would hold. He'd offered to help, only to have her wave him off, saying Daniel needed something to do.

Maybe she did as well.

He tried to read her body language and the furtive glances she periodically threw his way. They hadn't had much of a chance to talk since she'd had to go back to work at the hospital, but her horror when he'd shared the military's plans had been obvious. They both knew it happened in various countries. Not just in Brazil. It could even happen in the United States, if there were ever a deadly enough epidemic. The same heartbreaking choice might have to be made: contain it, for the good of the general population.

In this case, he wasn't sure it *was* the only option. But in a poor state like *Piauí*, it was the easiest one. São João dos Rios was pretty far off the beaten path. It would be expensive for the military to come in and check the village periodically to make sure the outbreak didn't erupt again, as they still hadn't isolated the initial source of the infection. And if it did recur and spread to a place like *Teresina*— the state capital—it could affect hundreds of thousands of people. If he thought fourteen deaths were far too many, how would he feel if that number was multiplied tenfold?

Hopefully Tracy realized he'd been upset for another reason entirely when she'd explained about Daniel and Cleo sharing their room. And the spark that had lit in his gut when Daniel had talked about them all living together had been hard to contain once it had started burning, although he'd better find a way to extinguish it quickly, because Tracy had no intention of letting this arrangement become permanent.

Well, neither did he.

But he *had* been hoping to have Tracy to himself a little while longer before they went their separate ways. Why he wanted that, he wasn't sure. Maybe just to understand her reasons for inviting him into that tub. To say it had been unexpected would be an understatement.

That was the least of his worries right now, however. The folks in charge were concerned about this getting out to the press. Yeah, hearing that your own military had sluiced cans of gasoline over an entire village and set it ablaze would not be the most popular story. Which was why they were trying to go about it quietly and peacefully. They'd spread the word that stipends would be awarded to anyone who agreed to leave town after the quarantine was lifted.

If they could relocate all the townsfolk before the match was struck, no one would be the wiser—except Ben and a few other key people—until long after the fact. Telling Tracy had probably been a mistake, in fact. But given their history—and her distrust of the military—what else could he have done? Keeping this to himself would have given her one more reason to hate him.

As far as Ben was concerned, as long as no one was hurt, these were just buildings. But he knew Tracy would feel differently. It was one point they'd argued about in the past. He tended to see things with a scientific bent, rather than an emotional one. But it was also one of the things he'd loved about her. She was the balance to his cold, analytical stance, forcing him to see another side to issues. Which made his actions in the past seem childish and petty. If he'd waited until she'd gotten home to talk to her calmly and explained his concerns, would things have turned out differently?

Possibly. There was no way to know.

But it was another of the reasons he'd talked about the military's plans this time. Nothing good could come from discovering the truth from someone else. If she realized he'd kept the information to himself, she'd be furious. And that's the last thing he wanted. Especially after their time in that home-made hot tub—or cooling tub, in this case.

Daniel secured the last of the knots and tried to hop onto the hammock to check it out, but ended up being flipped back onto the floor instead. He lay there panting as if he was exhausted, which he probably was. He was still weak from his illness. Ben pushed away from the wall and reached the boy before Tracy did, holding out a hand. "Easy. You need to regain some strength before trying stuff like that. Besides, you've been on a cot for the last week and a half. You'll have to get used to sleeping in a hammock again."

Daniel let Ben help him up and then rubbed his backside with a rueful grin. "I feel so much better than before, so I forget." He glanced around the space, already cramped from three hammocks. "Where will Cleo sleep?"

"We'll string another hammock above yours. Kind of like bunk beds. Only you're taller, so you'll sleep in the top one." Ben nodded at the bars on the windows. "They're strong enough to support both hammocks."

Tracy stood next to him. "Good idea. I was beginning to wonder how we were all going to fit."

He gave her a pained smile. "I could always put you up on top, but…" He let the words trail off, knowing she'd catch his implication.

True to form, pink stained both her cheeks, and she turned away to adjust the fan they'd brought in from one of the other rooms. "This will help keep the mosquitoes away, as most of nets are being used by the hospital."

"We never used them at home anyway," Daniel said.

Tracy's sister had died of dengue fever, so she was a little more paranoid about using the netting than many Brazilians. He couldn't blame her. He still remembered the day he'd come home to find the milky netting draped across their huge canopy bed. Despite the fact that her reasons for putting it up had had nothing to do with romance and everything to do with safety, he still found it incredibly intimate once they were both inside. And when he'd made love to her within the confines of the bed, there'd been a raw, primitive quality to Tracy that had shaken him to the core. She'd fallen pregnant that night.

A shaft of pain went through him.

Her eyes met his and she gave a rueful smile, her face growing even pinker. She was remembering those nights as well. He could at least be glad some of those memories made her smile, rather than filling her with bitterness.

And then there were these two kids. What was going to happen to them if the village really was burned down?

Something else he was better off not thinking about, because there wasn't a thing he could do about it.

Tracy says Cleo and I can stay with you once we are well.

If only it were that easy.

Wasn't it?

He swallowed, the words replaying in his head again and again. Evidently that "bath" had permanently messed something up in his skull. Was he actually thinking about taking on somebody else's kids?

He forced his mind back to the mosquito-net conversation between Tracy and Daniel, which was still going strong.

Interrupting her, he said, "We haven't been using nets either, Trace. It's not dengue season anyway."

"I know."

He sensed she wanted to say something further, maybe even about their current situation, but Daniel's presence made sharing any kind of confidences more complicated, if not impossible. And that went for any other kind of intimacies they might have shared in this room. Because with Daniel officially sprung from the infirmary, there was no possibility of that. But he would have liked to have talked to Tracy about…stuff.

Maybe even apologize for his actions four years ago.

"Will they still let me see Cleo?"

Surprisingly, Daniel had recovered faster than his sister, who would be in the infirmary for another day or so. And if he knew Tracy, she'd be sleeping in a chair next to the girl's bed, in case Daniel's absence made her jittery.

Tracy glanced at her watch. "I don't see why not. It's only seven o'clock. Curfew isn't for another three hours."

That was another thing. Yesterday, the military had suddenly instituted a curfew without warning. They'd said it was to prevent looting now that more people were recovering, but Ben had a feeling it had more to do with news being passed from person to person than anything else. Why prevent looting in a place they were planning to burn down?

No, it made no sense, other than the fact it was easier to keep an eye on folks during the daytime. If they imposed a curfew, they had more control over what went on after dark.

"Okay," Daniel said, then hesitated. "Do you need me to help with anything else?"

Tracy shook her head and smiled at him. "No, just be back by ten—tell Cleo I'll be there in a little while. And we'll try to rustle up a snack before bedtime, okay? We need to build up your strength."

The concern in her voice made Ben's heart ache. Tracy would have been a good mother had her job not consumed her every waking moment.

Job or no job, though, his own behavior back then wasn't something he was proud of.

It made him even more determined to set the record straight and see if they could make peace about the past. With Daniel sharing their room, he wasn't sure when he'd get the chance. But he intended to try. The sooner the better.

Tracy glanced at the door as it closed behind Daniel. She was still having trouble processing what Ben had told her. They were going to burn the town down? Without letting anyone have a say?

What would happen to Daniel and Cleo if that happened? She'd hoped maybe someone here would be willing to take on the kids since places like São João dos Rios tended to be close-knit communities. But if they all were forced to scatter in different directions, the kids might end up in a slum or an orphanage...or worse.

"What are those kids going to do now, Ben?" She pulled

her hair up into a loose ponytail and used the elastic she wore around her wrist to secure it in place. Her neck felt moist and sticky, despite the gusts of warm air the fan pushed their way from time to time.

"I don't know." He leaned down to the tiny refrigerator he'd brought from his lab and opened the door. Tossing her a cold bottle of water, he took one out for himself, twisting the top and taking a long pull.

Tracy paused to press her bottle against her overheated face, welcoming the shock of cold as it hit her skin. Closing her eyes, she rolled the plastic container along her cheek until she reached her hairline, before repeating the action on the other side. Then she uncapped the bottle and sipped at it. "There's something to be said about cold water. Thanks."

"No problem. How long do you think he'll be?"

"Daniel?" She turned to look at him, suspicion flaring within her. "He'll probably be a while. He and Cleo are close."

"They certainly seem to be."

Surely he wasn't thinking about trying something in the boy's absence. "Why did you ask?"

"What Daniel said made me think about their future, and I thought we could try to figure something out, especially if the military's plans become a reality."

"What can we do?"

"I'm not sure." He scrubbed a hand across the back of his neck. "Maybe one of the villagers could take the kids with them when they leave."

"I thought about that as well, but I don't see how. The whole town will be uprooted and scattered. Most of them will have to live with other people for a while, until they get back on their feet. Adding two more mouths to the equation…?" She took a quick drink.

"You know how these things work, Ben. The people here

are barely scraping by. To lose their homes, their livelihood? The last thing they'll be thinking about is two orphaned kids—no matter how well liked they are."

And how was she going to walk away from them when the time came? How could she bear to look those children in the eye with an apologetic shrug and then climb into Ben's car?

There was a long pause. Then Ben said in a low voice, "Ever since Daniel misunderstood what you meant, something's been rattling around in my head."

"Really? What?"

Before he could say anything, Daniel came skidding down the hallway, his face as white as the wall behind him. "Please, come. Cleo is sick. Really sick."

CHAPTER THIRTEEN

Tracy stroked Cleo's head, while Ben glanced at the read-out. "Almost three hundred. No wonder she's not feeling well."

Her blood-sugar levels were sky-high.

"She's mentioned having a headache on and off, but I thought it was because of the plague. I had no idea. Is she diabetic?"

"I don't know." He glanced at Pedro, who was standing near the head of the bed and had been the one to send Daniel to find them. "Did anyone notice her breath smelling off?"

A fruity smell was one sign of diabetes, and something one of them should have noticed.

Tracy bristled at his tone, however. "We've been fighting the plague for the last week and a half, Ben. We weren't looking for anything else."

"It wasn't a criticism. Just a question. Would you mind calling Daniel back into the room?"

Poor Daniel. He'd been banished as they'd tried to assess a thrashing Cleo, who not only had a headache but stomach cramps as well. It had seemed to take ages for Ben to get the finger-prick. They'd need to get a urine sample as well to make sure the child's body wasn't flooded with ketones. Without enough insulin to break down sugar, the body would begin converting fat into energy. That process resulted in ketones, which could quickly grow to toxic levels.

Cleo had quieted somewhat, but she was still restless on her cot, her head twisting back and forth on the pillow.

The second the boy came into the room, Ben asked him, "Does your sister have diabetes?"

"Diabetes?" A blank stare was all he received. "Is it from this sickness we had?"

Of course he wouldn't know anything about glucose levels or what too much sugar circulating in the bloodstream could lead to. Many of these people didn't get regular medical care. And what they did get was confined to emergencies or critical illnesses. Surely if the girl had type-one diabetes, though, someone would have figured it out. "Could her glucose levels have been affected by the plague?" Tracy asked.

"Possibly. Serious illnesses can wreak havoc on some of those balances. Or maybe her pancreas was affected. The plague isn't always confined the lungs. We'll pray the change is temporary, but in the meantime we need to get some insulin into her and monitor her blood-sugar levels."

"And if it's not temporary?"

"Let's take one thing at a time." Ben stripped off his gloves and tossed them, along with the test strip, into the wastebasket. "If the glucose doesn't stabilize on its own, we'll have to transport her somewhere so she can be diagnosed and treated."

"The hospital in *Teresina* is good."

Jotting something in a spiralbound notebook, he didn't even look up. "But she doesn't live in *Teresina*."

"She doesn't live anywhere. Not any more."

Unfortunately, she'd forgotten that Daniel was in the room. He immediately jumped on her statement. "But I thought we were going to live with you."

She threw Ben a panicked glance and was grateful when he stopped writing and came to the rescue.

"We're still hammering out the details."

Oh, Lord, how were they going to fix this? Hoping that one of the villagers would take the kids had already been a long shot. But if Cleo did have diabetes, it was doubtful if anyone from São João dos Rios would have the resources to take on her medical expenses.

She could offer to take the kids herself, but things in her life could change at any moment. Just that morning she'd faced that fact while staring in the mirror. She was going to have to do something about those test results—like sit down with a doctor and discuss her options. The more she thought about it, though, the more she was leaning toward a radical solution, a permanent one that would give her peace of mind once and for all. For the most part, anyway.

Maybe she could talk to Ben. Tell him what she was facing. And ask him if he would take the kids instead, at least on a temporary basis. Just until they figured out what was going on with Cleo.

And if he said no?

Then she had no idea what she was going to do. But one thing was for sure. She was not going to abandon Cleo. Not without doing everything in her power to make sure the girl was in good hands.

After they got a dose of insulin into her, they monitored her for the next two hours, until her blood-sugar levels began to decrease. An hour before curfew and knowing there would be little sleep to be had, Tracy asked Ben to walk with her to get a cup of coffee from the cafeteria, leaving Pedro and Daniel to stand watch. Several carafes were still on the buffet table, left over from the evening meal. Two of the pitchers even had some warm dregs left in them. Ben handed her a cup of the thick, black liquid and she spooned some sugar into hers to cut the bitter edge, while Ben drank his plain.

He made a face. "Not quite like I make at home."

Tracy smiled. "You always did make great coffee."

They wandered over to one of the tables at the back of the room. Ben waited for her to sit then joined her.

She nursed her cup for a moment before saying anything. "Do you think Cleo's blood sugar is going to drop back to normal once she's better?"

"I hope so."

"Ben…about what Daniel said…" She drew a deep breath and then blurted it out. "Maybe you could take them."

"Take them where? They don't have family that we know of."

Oh, boy. Something was about to hit that wheezy fan in the window behind her. But she had to ask. Had to try. "No, I mean maybe you could take them in for a while. Make sure Cleo gets the treatment she needs. It wouldn't have to be permanent."

Ben's brows drew together, and he stared at her for several long seconds. "What?"

Once the words were out, there was no retracting them, and they just seemed to keep tumbling from her mouth. "You always said you wanted kids. Well, this is the perfect solution—you won't even need a wife to birth them for you."

"I won't need a wife to…birth them?" His frown grew even stormier. "Is that how you felt about your pregnancy? That I was dooming you to be some type of brood mare? And our baby was just an inconvenience to be endured?"

"Oh, Ben, of course not. I wanted that baby as much as you did." She set her coffee down and wrapped her hands around the cup. "There were just circumstances that… Well, it doesn't matter now."

"What circumstances?"

"I don't want to talk about that. I want to figure out how to help these kids."

"And your way of doing that is by asking someone else to take them on?" He blew out an exasperated breath. "What are they supposed to do while I'm at work? Cleo can't monitor her own blood sugar."

"Daniel is practically a teen. And he's already displayed an enormous amount of responsibility. If she is diabetic, he could help." She plowed ahead. "You've seen how well behaved they are. They could—"

"I can't believe you're putting this all on me, Tracy." His fingers made angry tracks through his hair. "If you feel so strongly about it, why don't *you* take them?"

She knew it was an illogical thought, but if she ended up having surgery, who would watch the kids while she was recovering? It wasn't simply a matter of removing her breasts and being done with it. She wanted reconstruction afterwards. Each step of the process took time. Hospital time. Recovery time.

Both physical and emotional.

She decided to be honest as much as she could. "I can't take them, Ben. If I thought there was any way, believe me, I'd be the first to step up to the plate. They beat the odds and survived the outbreak—when none of us thought they could—so it just doesn't seem fair to abandon them to the system."

"Said as if it's a jail sentence."

"*Teresina* is poor. I've seen the orphanages, remember? I was one of the physicians who helped care for those children when I lived there."

"Let's go for a walk." He stood, collecting both of their

half-empty cups. "I don't want Daniel to come in and find us arguing over his fate."

Fate. What a funny word to use. But it was true. What Ben decided right here, right now, would determine those kids' futures. He could make sure Cleo got the treatment she needed. Even if this was a temporary setback, getting her glucose levels under control could take time.

Ben tossed the cups in the wastebasket and headed out the door, leaving Tracy to hurry to catch up with him.

"Won't you at least consider it?" she asked, turning sideways as she walked next to one of several abandoned houses.

He blew out a rough breath. "I don't know what you want me to say here, Tracy. I'll have to think about it. It would help to know why you're so dead set against taking them yourself."

"I travel a lot. My career—"

"Don't." The angry throbbing of a vein in his temple showed how touchy a subject this was. "Don't even play the travel card—you already know how I feel about that. Besides, I have a career too. So do millions of parents everywhere. But most of them at least want to spend a little time with their husbands and kids."

Shock roiled through her. Was that how he'd seen her? She'd known he hadn't like her traveling. Known it was because of how his parents had treated him and his brother, but hearing him say it outright hurt on a level it never had before.

"I did want to spend time with you." Her voice was quiet when it came out.

She should have told him the truth, long ago. But when he'd sent the military after her as she'd been trying to figure out how to tell him about the test results, she'd felt hurt and betrayed. And terribly, terribly angry. Angry at him, angry about her mother's death and angry that her future might not be the one she'd envisioned.

Maybe she'd turned a large part of that anger on Ben, somehow rationalizing that he didn't deserve to know the truth after what he'd done to her. Convinced herself that she didn't care what he thought—or that he might view her behavior through the lens of his childhood.

Abandoned by his parents. Abandoned by his wife.

What did that make her?

She closed her eyes, trying to block out the thought of Ben sitting alone at home night after night, while she'd tried to outrun her demons. "It's okay. If you can't take them, I'll find someone else."

"Who?"

"Pedro, maybe."

The frown was back. "You'd really ask your assistant to take two kids that you're not willing to take yourself?"

Her eyes filled with tears. "It's not that I'm not willing to. There are times I think about what our child might have looked like and I... Maybe I can take them for a while and then figure something else out." She bit her lip, unable to control the wobble of her chin.

Ben took a step forward so she was forced to look up at him then brushed wisps of hair from her temples. His hands slid around to cradle the back of her head. "I didn't say I wouldn't take them. I just said I needed to think about it. So give me a day or two, okay?"

She nodded, her heart thumping in her chest as his touch chased away the regret and did strange things to her equilibrium. "Okay."

"How do you do it?" He leaned down and slid his cheek

across hers, the familiar coarseness of his stubble wrenching at her heart.

"Do what?"

"Talk me into doing crazy stuff."

"I—I don't."

"No?" His breath swept across her ear, sending a shiver over her. "How about talking me into getting in that tub?"

Oh. He was right. She had been the one who'd invited him in. "Maybe it's not me. Maybe it's this climate. The heat messes with your brain."

"Oh, no. This is all you. *You* mess with my brain."

She didn't know if he thought she messed with it in a bad way or a good way. She suddenly hoped it was good. That he remembered their life together with some fondness, despite the heartache she'd caused him.

His lips touched her cheek then grazed along it as he continued to murmur softly to her. "Tell you what. The kids can come live at the house—temporarily, until Cleo is better and we can find something else."

She wasn't sure she'd heard him correctly. She pulled away to look at him, although the last thing she wanted was for his mouth to stop what it was doing. "You'll take them?"

"I think you missed the pronoun. I said 'we.'"

"What do you mean?"

"I'm not going to do this by myself. If Cleo's condition doesn't stabilize and this turns into full-blown diabetes, she'll need to be transported back and forth to a specialist. Her insulin levels will need to be monitored closely at first."

"Daniel—"

"Daniel is responsible, yes, but he's still just a kid. He's grieving the loss of his mother. I don't think it's fair to expect him to take on the bulk of Cleo's care."

"I agree."

"So the 'we' part of the equation means we share the

load. You and me." His sly smile warned her of what was coming before his words had a chance to register. "Until *we* can arrange something else, you'll need to come back to Teresina. With me."

CHAPTER FOURTEEN

"WHAT?"

Ben had expected an angry outburst the second she realized what he was asking. What he didn't anticipate was the stricken pain that flooded her eyes instead.

Warning bells went off inside him.

"It won't be that hard. You can relocate for six months to a year—help the kids get through one school year. You'll be closer to the Amazon, anyway, if you're in *Teresina*, because *Projeto Vida's* medical boat operates out of *Manaus*."

She stopped walking and turned to face him. "Ben, I—I can't."

Something in her face took him aback. What was going on here?

"Why can't you? And if you mention the word 'travel,' the deal is off." He held his ground. "I want Cleo to get the best treatment available. In fact, I want that just as much as you do, but you've got to tell me why you can't sacrifice one year of your life to help make sure she does."

She turned away from him and crossed over to the trunk of a huge mango tree, fingering the bark.

Not about to let her off the hook, he followed her, putting his hands on her shoulders. She whirled round to face him.

"You want to know why I'm reluctant to commit to a

year in Teresina? Why I traveled so much while I was carrying our child?"

"Yes." He kept his eyes on hers, even as the first tears spilled over her lashes.

"Because I have the BRCA1 mutation. And I don't know when—or even if—that switch might suddenly flip on."

"BRCA…" His mind went blank for a second before his training kicked in. "One of the breast-cancer markers?"

A lot of information hit his system at once: Tracy's mother's early death from the disease, her grandmother's death. Next came shock. She'd been tested for the gene variation? There's no way she'd draw that kind of conclusion without some kind of definitive proof. "When did you find out?"

"A while ago." Her green eyes skipped away from his. "After my mother passed away."

An ugly suspicion went through his mind. Her mom had died not long after they'd married. A lot of things suddenly became clear. The frantic pace she'd kept. Her withdrawal a month or so before she'd finally walked out on him. "It was while you were pregnant, wasn't it?"

She nodded.

"You went through genetic testing and never said a word to me?"

"I didn't want to worry you. And then when the test came back positive…" She shook her head. "I was trying to think of a way to tell you. Before I could, you sent the military into that village. I was angry. Hurt. And then I lost the baby."

And then she'd lost the baby.

A streak of raw fury burst through his system closing off his throat and trapping all kinds of angry words inside as he remembered that time. She'd stood in his office a week and a half ago and accused him of going behind her back, and yet she'd traipsed around the country, carrying this huge secret.

Oh, no. That was where he drew the line.

"Yes, I did go behind your back, and I was wrong for doing that. But how is that any different than what you did? You went behind *my* back and had yourself tested for a gene that could impact your life…our future as a couple. How could you have kept that a secret?"

"You're right, Ben. I'm sorry." Her hands went to his, which had drawn up into tight fists as he'd talked. Her fingers curved around them. "At first I was just scared, wondering what it meant for our baby—and if it was a girl, if I would pass the gene to her. Then I worried about how this would affect us as a couple. I—I didn't want your pity."

"Believe me, pity is the last thing I'm feeling right now." At the top of the list was anger. Anger that she'd suffered in silence. Anger that she hadn't trusted him enough to say anything.

"I probably should have told you. I know that now."

"Probably? *Probably?* I cannot believe you just used that word."

She swallowed. "Okay, I *should* have told you."

"We were supposed to be a couple, Tracy. A team. I shared every part of my life with you. Didn't keep one thing from you."

"I know it doesn't seem right. But when you've had some time to think about it—"

"I don't need time to think."

When he started to pull away from her completely, she gripped his wrists, holding him in place. "Try to understand, Ben. My mom had died of cancer six months after we were married. We got pregnant sooner than we expected to, and I started to worry. Being tested was something I did on impulse, just to put my mind at ease. I didn't expect the results to come back the way they did."

"And yet you kept them to yourself. Even when they did."

"Yes."

The anger drained out of him, leaving him exhausted. "It explains everything."

And yet it explained nothing.

Not really. Millions of women faced these same kinds of decisions. And most of them didn't shut their loved ones out completely. Only Tracy had also been facing the loss of their child in addition to the test results. Not to mention what she'd viewed as a betrayal on his part.

He wrapped his arms around her and pulled her close, tucking her head against his shoulder.

"I'm sorry, Ben," she repeated. The low words were muffled by his shirt, but he heard them, sensed they were coming from her heart.

He didn't respond, just let the charged emotions crash over him until they were all spent.

Nothing could change what had happened back then. It was what it was. She'd made her decision, and now he had to make his. How he was going to handle this newfound knowledge?

"This is why you don't want to take Daniel and Cleo yourself."

"Yes."

Wow. He tried to find the right words but found himself at a loss. Maybe like she'd been when she'd found out?

He gripped her upper arms and edged her back a little so he could look at her face. Fresh tear tracks had appeared, although she hadn't let out any kind of sound.

"This isn't a death sentence, Tracy." He wiped the moisture from her cheeks and eyes with the pad of his thumb.

"Carrying the gene mutation doesn't mean you'll develop the disease."

"My mom and grandmother did."

"I know. But knowledge is power. You know to be vigilant."

"I know that I might have to take preventative measures."

Something she'd hinted at earlier. "Tamoxifen?" He'd heard that some of the chemo drugs were being used as a preventative measure nowadays, much like the antibiotics they'd used on those exposed to the plague in São João dos Rios. All in the hope of killing any cancer cells before they had a chance to develop and multiply.

"Some women choose to go that route, yes."

"But not you." It was a statement, because from her phrasing it was clear that she wasn't looking at that option. Or had looked at it and rejected it.

"No. Not me." She licked her lips. "I've been weighing the benefits of prophylactic surgery."

"Surgery…" He blinked as he realized exactly what she was saying. "You're thinking of having an elective mastectomy?" Against his will, his glance went to her chest and then back to her face.

"Yes. That's what I'm saying. I don't know the timing yet, but I realized not long ago that if I can head it off, that's what I'm going to do."

Shit.

He remembered their time in the tub and how he'd gently caressed her breasts. Kissed them. What had she been thinking as he'd brought her nipples to hard peaks? Even then, she hadn't said a word. Maybe she had been committing the sensations to memory.

Okay, now *his* vision was starting to go a little funny. He tightened his jaw. Tracy had said the last thing she wanted from him was pity. He needed to suck it up. Then again, she'd had a whole lot longer to process the information than he had. And ultimately she was right. It was her decision to make. He might disagree or object or even urge her to go ahead and do it, but he wasn't the one who'd have to live with the aftermath. Tracy was.

And he'd had no idea what she'd been facing all this time. He was surprised she hadn't chosen to have the surgery right after their break-up.

He decided not to say anything. Instead, he opted to go a completely different route.

But before he could, she spoke again. "So you see why I'm reluctant to say yes. I was planning to meet with a doctor when I got back to São Paulo."

"Give it some time, Tracy. Neither one of us should make any hard and fast decisions right on the heels of fighting this outbreak." He tucked a lock of hair behind one of her ears. "I'll be honest, though. I don't think I can commit to taking on Cleo's treatment on my own. And I'm not sure it would be fair to her or Daniel. I'm away a lot. Sometimes for days at a time."

"Kind of like I used to be." The words had a ring of challenge to them.

"The difference is I don't have a partner or children at home. Not any more."

She sighed. "And I did."

His thumb stroked her earlobe, watching as her pupils dilated at his touch. "Give me six months to a year of your time, Trace, and I'll take the kids on. I'm not asking you to renew our wedding vows or even get back together. We just have to…work as partners. For the sake of the kids, until Cleo is fully recovered and we can find a better place for them."

"I don't know. Give me a couple of days to make a decision, okay?"

"You've got it. But as for timeframes, we don't have that long, remember? São João dos Rios has less than a week. And then Cleo—and everyone else—will be escorted out."

CHAPTER FIFTEEN

INSULIN WAS A blessing and a curse.

A blessing because the change in Cleo had been almost immediate when they'd pushed the first dose into her. A curse, because this might be something she'd have to do for the rest of her life.

It explained why her body had taken so much longer to recuperate from the plague than that of her brother. She'd improve a little bit and then go back three steps for seemingly no reason. They'd assumed it was because she was one of the first victims. In reality it had been because the sugar had built up in her system like a toxin, infecting her tissue as surely as the plague had.

The insulin had worked. Today the little girl was well enough to walk the short distance from the village to a clearing to accompany Daniel, Ben and herself as they took care of some important business.

Just like a little family.

And that made her heart ache even more as they caught sight of the first of the cement markers on the other side of a small wooden fence.

"Will I see Mommy again?" Cleo's voice wobbled the tiniest bit.

"I think you will, honey. But only after you've had a long and healthy life."

Tracy wanted to do everything in her power to make sure that happened.

Even move back to *Teresina* for a while?

Ben stopped at an empty site beneath a tree, carrying a flat sandstone rock in one hand and a hammer and chisel he'd found in a neighbor's shed in the other. "How does this spot look?"

"Beautiful," Tracy said. "How about to you guys?"

Cleo nodded, but Daniel remained silent, his mouth set in a mutinous line, looking off to the left. He'd been silent since Cleo had asked if their mother would have a grave and a stone like their grandparents did. But when they'd given the boy a chance to remain behind, he'd trailed along at a distance, before steadily gaining ground until he'd been walking beside Ben.

"*O que foi?*" Cleo went over to Daniel and took his hand in hers, her concern obvious. "*Estás triste?*"

He shook his head. "*Vovô está por aí.*"

Ah, so that's why he was looking in that direction. His grandparents' graves were to the left. Cleo had assumed, like Tracy had, that Daniel was struggling with his grief. And maybe that was partially true. But he also wanted his mom's grave to be next to that of his grandparents.

"Can you show us where they are?" she asked.

Without a word, Daniel trudged to a spot about twenty yards to his left, where a weathered tombstone canted backwards.

Ben laid his tools on the ground and set to righting the stone as best he could, packing dirt into the furrow behind it. The names Louisa and Jorge were inscribed on the top, along with the surname Silva. Louisa had outlived Jorge by fifteen years.

Other than the leaning headstone, the graves were neat, with no weeds anywhere to be seen. They'd been well tended—probably by the mother of Cleo and Daniel. It made it all the more fitting that her grave be next to theirs.

"This is perfect," Tracy said.

Daniel gave a short nod, to which Cleo added her approval.

Kneeling on the packed ground next to her, Ben pulled out the sheet of paper that had the children's mother's full name on it and picked up his chisel and hammer. The first strike rang through the air like a shot, and Cleo flinched. Tracy put her arm around the girl and they stood quietly as the sound was repeated time and time again. A cadence of death…and hope.

Sweat poured down Ben's face and spots of moisture began to appear on his dark T-shirt, but still he continued, letter by letter, until the name of Maria Eugênia da Silva Costa appeared on the stone, along with the dates of her birth and death.

Cleo had stood quietly through the entire process, but when Ben glanced up at her with his brows raised, she knelt beside him. With tender fingers she traced the letters one by one while Daniel stayed where he was. He'd brushed his palm across his face as if chasing away sweat—but Tracy had a feeling a rogue tear or two might have been part of the mix.

Handing a bunch of wildflowers to the little girl, she watched as Cleo and Ben carefully placed the stone and cross, setting the tiny bouquet in front of the objects. Glancing at Ben, who'd slicked his hair back, she cleared her throat. "Would you mind saying a few words?"

Blotting a drizzle of perspiration with his shirt sleeve, he stood, lifting a brow. "It's been a while since I've gone to church."

"I'm sure you can think of something." Tracy knew she'd lose it if she tried to say anything.

Cleo rose as well and gripped her hand fiercely.

"Right." He put his hand on one of Cleo's shoulders and motioned Daniel over. The boy moved forward, his steps unsure as if he didn't want to face the reality of what was about to happen. Tracy knew just how he felt. Somehow seeing your mother's name carved into cold, hard stone made things seem unbearably permanent. Even more permanent than the granite itself.

As if aware of her thoughts, Ben started talking, his voice low and somber. "We want to remember Maria Eugênia and give thanks for her life. For the brave children she brought into this world and nurtured to be such fine, caring individuals." Ben's eyes met hers. "We leave this marker as a reminder of her time on this earth. A symbol that she was important. That she was loved. That she won't be forgotten. By any of us."

Cleo's hands went up to cover her face, her small shoulders shaking in silence, while Daniel stood unmoving. Ben knelt between them. One broad-shouldered man flanked by two grieving children.

Oh, God.

One of the tears she'd been blinking away for the last several minutes threatened to break free. But this was not the time. This wasn't about her. It was about these kids. About helping them through a terrible time in their lives. About helping Cleo get to the root of her medical problems.

She went over and gave Daniel a long hug. And then she knelt in front of Cleo, her eyes meeting Ben's as she brushed a strand of hair from the child's damp head and then dropped a kiss on top of it.

Suddenly she knew she wouldn't need a few days to decide. In the scheme of things, what was six months or a year when she could make a difference in these kids' lives for ever? Wasn't that what she'd come here to do? What she'd done even as she'd faced her test results? As impossibly hard as it might be to see Ben each and every day, she was going to *Teresina*. She was going to help make sure Daniel and Cleo were put in a situation where they could flourish and grow. And where Cleo—as Tracy had promised her—would have that chance at a long and healthy life.

Ben stood in the door of the sickroom and peered around one last time. Every bed was empty of patients, the IV poles disassembled and the military vehicles had headed out one by one, leaving only a small contingent to carry out General Gutierrez's final order. Ben had insisted on staying behind to make sure the last survivors had packed up and moved out of town, which they had.

Maybe it was the life-and-death struggle that had gone on here, maybe it was the unrelenting horror of what they'd seen, but most of the inhabitants had seemed only too happy to clear out. Most of them—except Cleo and Daniel—had relatives to turn to and those who didn't would have help from the government to start over, including jobs and subsidized housing, until they got back on their feet.

Several of the villagers, when they'd discovered what Ben had done for Daniel and Cleo's mother, had made similar monuments for their own loved ones and set them in various locations around the cemetery. Ben had wrung a promise from the general that the graveyard would remain untouched.

São João dos Rios was now a ghost town—already dead to all intents and purposes.

And soon his wife would be moving back into his house with a ready-made family in tow. He wasn't sure what had suddenly caused her to say yes. He only knew as the four of them had knelt in front of Maria Eugênia's grave, she'd met his eyes and given a single nod of her head.

He'd mouthed the words, "You'll go?"

Another slow nod.

There'd been no emotion on her face other than a mixture of grief and determination, and he'd wondered if he'd done the right thing in asking her to come. But he couldn't take on two kids by himself and do them justice. Daniel was a strong young man, a few years from adulthood, and Cleo a young girl whose body was still battling to adapt to diabetes, while her mind buckled under a load of grief and loss.

Right now, Tracy and the kids were going through Daniel and Cleo's house and collecting an assortment of sentimental items, and if he knew Tracy, she was making the case for each and every object with the soldier General Gutierrez had left in charge. His friend wasn't an unreasonable man, but he took his job seriously. He was not going to let this pathogen out of the city, if he could help it.

All clothing and linens had to be boiled before they were packed into crates and given a stamp of approval. The hours had run into days as people waited in line for their turn to sanitize their belongings.

A movement caught his eye and he frowned as he spotted Tracy's assistant heading over to the house. He hadn't realized the man was still here, although in the confusion of the last few hours he couldn't remember seeing him leave. Obviously, he wouldn't have without saying goodbye to his boss.

He turned, ready to follow, when Tracy came out of the house and met him. Pedro said something to her and she shrugged. But when the man laid his hands on her shoulders, a slow tide began to rise in Ben's head and he pushed off to see what was going on.

The first voice to reach his ears was Pedro's. "You can't be serious. *Projeto Vida* is your life. You can't just abandon it. What about the medical ship?"

Tracy shook her head and said something, but he couldn't quite make out her words. Ben moved a little faster.

"Why can't someone else deal with them?"

"Because there is no one else, Pedro. It's something I have to do. You and the rest of the crew can hold the fort until I get back."

Until she got back. Why did those four words make his gut churn?

Pedro evidently saw him coming and took his hands from her shoulders. It didn't stop him from continuing his tirade, though. "How long do you think that will that be?"

"Six months. Maybe a year." She glanced back at the door to the house. "Please, keep your voice down. We haven't talked to the kids about time frames."

"Why don't you just bring the kids down to São Paulo?"

"You know I can't do that. It wouldn't be fair to them or to you all. Our hours are all over the place and we're rarely in the office a week before we're off again."

The turning and shifting in Ben's gut increased in intensity. He hoped that didn't mean she was planning on keeping the same schedule once she got to Teresina. He expected her to be an active partner in Cleo's care, not an absentee parent.

He forced a smile as he addressed Tracy. "Is there a problem?"

She shook her head. "No, we're just working out some details about the office."

That's not what it sounded like to him.

Moistening her lips, she leaned forward to give Pedro a quick hug. "It's going to be all right. Give me a call when you get in. I should have cellphone service once I get on the road."

"Speaking of roads," Ben said, his eyes locked on Pedro,

"we should all be heading in that direction. Do you need a ride anywhere?"

"Nope. I offered to help with the clean-up then I'll catch a ride to the airport."

Tracy smiled. "I thought you said the soldiers were 'scary dudes.'"

"They're not so bad once you get to know them. Other people...not so much."

Yeah, Ben could guess who that little jab was meant for. Luckily, his skin had grown pretty thick over the last several years. Not much got through.

Except maybe one hot-tub episode.

And a few hot tears that had splashed on his shoulder as Tracy had confessed her deepest, darkest secret. Oh, yeah, that had gotten through more than he cared to admit.

"I have a crate of embroidered linens that need to be boiled and then we can go."

Pedro, as if finally realizing she was serious about going to *Teresina*, spun on his heel and walked away.

Maybe he should give Tracy one more chance to walk away as well. But as much as he tried to summon up the strength, he couldn't. Not just yet.

He had two kids to worry about.

And maybe someday he could convince himself that was the real reason.

"Where are the beds?"

Ben found Daniel standing in the middle of his new room, the backpack with all his clothes still slung over one of his thin shoulders. At least the boy's cheeks had some color back in them. "It's right there against the wall."

And then he realized why the kid had asked that question. He'd probably never slept on a spring mattress in his life. The military had used canvas cots for sickbeds, while

most of the houses in São João dos Rios contained *redes*...
hammocks. Ben had nothing against sleeping in them. The
things were pretty comfortable, in fact. And making love
in one...

Yeah, better not to think about the times he and Tracy
had shared one on various trips in their past.

Ben moved past Daniel and sat on the double-sized bed.
"This is what we normally sleep on."

"But it's not hanging up. Doesn't it get hot?"

The kid had a point.

"That's why we have fans." He nodded at the ceiling
fan that was slowly spinning above them. "It goes at different speeds."

"I don't know..." Daniel looked dubious.

Ben smiled. "Tell you what. Try it for a week or so and
if you absolutely hate it, we'll go buy you a *rede*."

"My mom made mine herself. And Cleo's."

His throat tightening, Ben nodded. By now the military would have burned everything. Houses, most material possessions that could carry bacteria out of the city.
That included Daniel and Cleo's hammocks. "I know. I
wish we could have brought them, but there was no way
to boil them."

They'd been able to sterilize a few of Maria Eugênia's
aprons and embroidered towels, but hammocks had been
too unwieldy. They'd been forced to leave so much behind.

"I understand." He looked around again. "Why is there
only one bed, then?"

That was another thing. The siblings had shared a bedroom in their old house, but there were enough rooms here
that they wouldn't need to any more. But how to explain
that to a boy who'd never had a room of his own. "Cleo
will have her own bed, in the room next door to this one."

Tracy was currently in there with the girl, making up the

couch with sheets and pillows. He tried to look at his home through their eyes. He wasn't a wealthy man by American standards, but it would certainly seem that way to Cleo and Daniel. There was even an air-conditioner in each of the rooms for when things got unbearably hot. But he didn't mention that right now. He wanted to give them some time to adjust to their new surroundings before springing too much on them.

The local government had been overwhelmed, dealing with the aftermath of the outbreak, so when Ben had asked permission to take the kids with them, they'd made copies of Ben's and Tracy's identity papers, called in a quick background check, then promised a formal interview in the coming weeks. He knew it would only be a formality. And maybe some long-lost relative would come forward in the meantime and claim the children.

He wasn't sure how he felt about that. In just two weeks Ben had grown fond of the kids. Too fond, in fact.

What had he been thinking, agreeing to this? And what had Tracy been thinking, saying yes?

A question that made something in his chest shimmy to life.

As if she knew he'd been thinking about her, Tracy showed up at the doorway with Cleo in tow. "We're all set up. How are you doing in here?"

Daniel looked up at the sign Rosa had hung on the bedroom wall when Ben had called to tell her the news.

Bem Vindo, Daniel!

There was a matching "welcome home" sign in Cleo's room, with her name on it.

Giving the first tentative smile Ben had witnessed since he'd known the boy, Daniel nodded. "I think we will do very well here."

"So do I."

The soft words came from Tracy, who also had a ghost of a smile on her face. She walked over and took one of his hands, giving it a quick squeeze before releasing it. Then she whispered the two most beautiful words he'd ever heard. "Thank you."

CHAPTER SIXTEEN

"I HAVE A surprise for you outside."

Ben had rounded them all up in the living room.

A surprise—anything, in fact—was better than Tracy trying to avoid looking into the bedroom she'd once shared with Ben. The one that seemed to call to her, no matter where she was in the house.

Tracy glanced at Rosa to see if she knew anything, but she just shrugged.

If the housekeeper was surprised to see Tracy back in *Teresina*, she didn't show it. She'd just engulfed her in a hug so tight it had squeezed the air from her lungs. She'd then dabbed the corners of her eyes with her apron before embracing each of the children.

"A surprise?" asked Cleo. "What is it?"

Giving Ben a puzzled look, Tracy wondered what kind of surprise he could possibly have. They'd only arrived a few hours ago. The kids hadn't even had a chance to explore properly yet.

"I bought a water tank," he said in English. "I thought we could convert it into a makeshift pool for the kids. Maybe even sink it partway into the ground to make it easier to climb into. I had it delivered when you agreed to come to *Teresina*."

Heat suffused her face as she processed this, ignoring

the kids who were asking to know what he'd said. "Is it the one from São João dos Rios?" Lord, she hoped not. Those memories were even fresher than the ones from the bedroom down the hall.

"No. Bigger."

"We could have bought an inflatable pool."

"I figured this would be more permanent and less likely to rupture. I can't afford to have a built-in pool put in, but I figured the kids could help with the upkeep. It'll also give them a place to entertain any new friends they might make."

"That was nice, Ben." She refused to wonder what would happen to it once everyone went their separate ways. "I think they'll love it."

Tracy switched back to Portuguese and twitched her index finger back and forth at the kids' expectant glances. "I can't tell you what we said without spoiling the surprise."

Standing aside as Ben pushed the door open, she watched the kids lope into the back yard. A large oval water tank sat in a sandy area. Daniel's eyes touched it then skipped past, still looking for whatever the surprise was.

Ben was right, it was huge. The thing must hold a couple of thousand gallons. Why had they never thought of using one as a pool before? Perched on rooftops everywhere in Brazil, the blue fiberglass tanks came in various shapes and sizes. This one must have been meant for a commercial building.

Cleo seemed just as lost as Daniel was. "Where's the surprise?"

To them, evidently, a *caixa de água* was just that: a holding tank for water. They couldn't see the possibilities.

Ben walked over to it and put his hand on the curved rim. "This is it."

The way both kids' faces fell brought a laugh up from Tracy's chest. "What? You don't think this is a good surprise?"

Cleo shook her head, and Daniel said, "It's fine. I'm sure you needed a new one."

"Oh, it's not for our roof." Ben motioned them round to the other side of the tank. They followed him, Tracy wondering what he'd hidden over there.

Taped to the outside edge was a glossy magazine ad showing a family playing in an above-ground pool, an inflatable raft bouncing on happy waves.

"This…" Ben patted the side of the tank "…is going to be a pool once we're done with it."

"A *piscina*?" Cleo's voice held a note of awe. "We're going to have a pool?"

"We're going to use the tank as a pool." He ran a hand over the top edge. "You're going to have to help me get it ready. And you'll have to help take care of it once it's set up. But, yes, we're going to have a pool."

"Beleza!" The happy shout came from Daniel, who now walked around the tank with a completely different mindset. "The water will be almost up to my neck."

"Yes, and you'll have to be careful with your sister," Ben said, "because it'll be over her head. I don't want you guys using this without supervision. In fact, I'm going to have a cover installed when it's not in use."

Cleo's fingers trailed over the image of the raft on top of the water.

Catching Ben's grin, Tracy could guess what was coming. "There's a bag on the far side of the tank, Cleo. Why don't you go and look inside?"

The little girl raced around to the other side. They soon heard a squeal. "A float. Just like in the picture. And there are two!"

"One for each of them," Tracy murmured to Ben. "You thought of everything, didn't you?"

"No. Not everything." Something in the words had her gaze swiveling back to him.

"I don't understand."

"I don't imagine you do, but it doesn't matter." He moved away from her before she could really look at him. She heard him talking to the kids then they all came around and walked across the yard behind the house, trying to decide on the best place for the pool. They finally came up with a spot near the *acerola* tree, where they'd at least get some shade during the heat of the day.

As soon as the kids had uncovered all the secrets of the soon-to-be pool, they went off to explore the rest of the backyard, leaving Ben and Tracy alone together.

When her eyes met his, the look was soft and fluid, reminding him of days gone by when he'd brought her flowers unexpectedly or had taken her on a long walk in the park.

Hell, he'd missed that look. Placing his hand out, palm up, he held his breath and waited to see if she'd take it. She did, her cool skin sliding across his. He closed his fingers, his gaze holding hers. "Are you okay with all this?"

"I am."

He'd felt the stab of guilt more than once since she'd agreed to come back with him. Especially after the way they'd parted four years ago.

With a sigh he opened his hand and released her. He'd never really known what she'd been thinking during those last dark days of their marriage. And he wasn't sure he wanted to. Maybe it would just make the rift between them that much deeper.

"I guess I'd better go help Rosa with dinner." She

stepped up on tiptoe and gave him a soft kiss. "The kids love their surprise, I can tell. Thank you."

Tracy stood back with a smile, the corners of her eyes crinkling. Oh, how he loved seeing that. The urge to kiss her came and went without incident. After screwing up so badly in the past, he didn't want to do anything that would send them spinning back to uglier times just when he was beginning to feel he'd made up some ground with her. Maybe with time they'd be able to move past those days and become friends again.

At least that was his hope.

Dr. Crista Morena gently palpated Cleo's abdomen, her brow furrowed in concern. "You know that type-one diabetes can occur at any age." She glanced up at them, and Ben could see the curiosity in her eyes. "You know nothing of her background, her medical history?"

"Just what we observed during the plague outbreak," he said. "Could her pancreas have been affected by the illness?"

She stood and straightened the stethoscope around her neck. "Some cases may be triggered by a viral infection— something in the enterovirus family—that causes an auto-immune response." She helped Cleo sit up. "I want to get some bloodwork done on her, but the finger prick we did when you first came in is right around two-twenty. We'll need to do another with her fasting. I'll send some testers home with you."

Tracy nodded. "Her glucose levels seem to fluctuate for no apparent reason, just like they did while she was sick, so her pancreas must be producing some insulin."

"If it's type one, she could be in the honeymoon phase. You administered insulin to bring her levels back down, right?"

"Yes."

"Doing that can sometimes give the organ a rest, stimulating those last remaining beta cells, which then pump out small quantities of the hormone." She looked at each of them. "If it's type one, the honeymoon phase is only a temporary reprieve. Those cells will eventually stop producing all together."

Ben swallowed. If that was true, Cleo would need constant monitoring for the rest of her life. Temporary would become permanent. He glanced at Tracy to see if she'd come to the same conclusion he had.

Yep. Her hands were clasped tightly in her lap, fingers twisting around each other. Well, taking the kids had been her idea in the first place.

But you agreed.

Besides, it had done him a world of good to hear Cleo's happy laugh when she'd realized what the water tank in the backyard meant. How her eyes had widened when she'd discovered she was getting a room of her own with a new pink bedspread—once the bed they'd ordered for her arrived. He wouldn't trade those moments for anything.

Ben helped Cleo hop off the exam table and motioned to the chair he'd occupied moments earlier. She chose to go to Tracy instead, who opened her arms and hauled the child onto her lap, hugging her close.

His throat tightened further. Tracy looked so right holding a child. Would she have cut back on her traveling if their baby had been born?

If the evidence he'd seen was any indication, the answer to that was no. She'd rushed to São João dos Rios during the outbreak, and Pedro had indicated they'd made quite a few trips during the year.

She saved lives by being in that city.

But at what cost to herself?

None, evidently.

Dr. Morena looked up from Cleo's chart and focused on Tracy. "I understand you practiced pediatric medicine in the past. We could use another doctor here at the clinic. Would you be interested?"

"How did you know that?" She shot him a glance that he couldn't read.

"Ben mentioned you were a doctor when he called to make the appointment."

His heart sped up as he waited to see her reaction. Although his slip had been unintentional, when Dr. Morena had mentioned an opening, he'd wondered if she'd say anything to Tracy.

"I haven't practiced pediatric medicine in quite a few years. I've been dealing more with indigenous tribes so—"

"You treat children in those tribes, don't you?"

"Of course."

Dr. Morena closed the cover of the chart with a soft snap. "It's like riding a bicycle. You never really forget how to deal with those little ones. And you obviously have a knack with them." She nodded at Cleo, who was now snuggled into Tracy's lap. "Give me a call if you're interested."

CHAPTER SEVENTEEN

IT WAS LIKE riding a bicycle.

Dr. Morena's words rang through her head a few days later as she stood in the doorway of her old bedroom.

Being with Ben in that water tank had been like that. Remembered responses and emotions bubbling up to the surface. She ventured a little further into the room, sliding her hand across the bedspread. The same silky beige-striped one they'd had years ago. She was surprised he hadn't bought a new set.

She glanced at the door and then, on impulse, lay across the old mattress and stared up at the ceiling. No one would know. Ben was safely at work right now, and Daniel had taken Cleo to explore the neighborhood. Even Rosa was off shopping for groceries, which meant she had a couple of hours to herself.

She wouldn't stay long, just enough to satisfy her curiosity. She'd passed this room for the last couple of days and had wanted to step inside, but she'd resisted the temptation.

Until now.

So, what does it feel like to lie here?

Just like riding a bicycle.

That thought was both terrifying and exhilarating.

The only thing lacking was Ben. And if he could see her now, he'd probably hit the roof. They'd patched together an uneasy truce since arriving in the city, and she was loath to do anything to rock that particular boat. But the open bedroom door had winked at her, inviting her to step through and relive the past.

Rolling onto her stomach, she grabbed the pillow and buried her face into it, sucking down a deep breath of air.

Yep, Ben still slept on the right side of the bed. His warm masculine scent was imprinted on the soft cotton cover, despite Rosa fluffing the pillows to within an inch of their lives. She'd have to make sure she left things exactly like she'd found them.

Being here felt dangerous…voyeuristic. And incredibly erotic. They'd made love in this bed many, many times. All kinds of positions. Her on top. Him. Her hands trapped above her head. His hands molding her body…making her cry out when the time came.

Just that memory made her tingle, her skin responding to the sudden flurry of images that flashed through her head. Oh, Lord. This was bad.

So bad.

Just like riding a bike.

Sitting on a bicycle was one thing. Putting your feet on the pedals and making them go round and round was another thing entirely.

She knew she should get up. Now. But the temptation to linger and let her imagination run wild—to remember one of their lovemaking sessions—was too great. The one that came to mind was when Tracy had been lying on the bed much like she was now. Only she'd been naked.

Waiting.

The covers pulled down so that Ben would find her just like this when he came home from work.

And he had.

Her nipples drew up tight as she recalled the quiet click

of the front door closing. The sound of his indrawn breath as he'd stood in the doorway of this very room and spotted her. Without a word, warm lips had pressed against her neck. Just when she'd started to turn her head, eyelids fluttering open, she'd heard the low command, "Don't look.

She'd obeyed, letting him explore her body and whisper the things he wanted to do to her. His hands had slipped beneath her to cup her breasts, drawing a whimper from her when he'd found the sensitive peaks and gently squeezed.

Even now, Tracy couldn't stop her own hands from replaying the scene, burrowing between her body and the mattress.

"Mmm. Yes."

He'd touched her just like this. Her teeth had dug into her lower lip as she'd let the sensations spiral through her system. Just a hint of friction then more as he'd seemed to sense exactly what she was feeling.

"Ben." The whispered name was low, but in the silence of the house it carried. She let out another puff of breath between pursed lips, even as one hand trailed down her side, her legs opening just a bit.

It wouldn't take long. She was so turned on. Just a minute or two. And she'd relieve the ache that had been growing inside her since their time in the tub. She undid the button on her jeans and her fingers found the juncture at the top of her thighs, sweet, familiar heat rippling through her.

Maybe she should close the door. Just in case. Her head tilted in that direction.

Instead of empty space, her gaze met familiar broad shoulders, which now filled the doorway.

She yanked her hands from beneath her in the space of a nanosecond, molten lava rushing up her neck and scorching her face.

Oh, God! Had he heard her say his name?

"Wh-what are you doing here?"

"I would ask you the same thing, but I think it's fairly obvious from where I'm standing." He took a step closer, his eyes never leaving hers. And the heat contained in them nearly burned her alive.

The door closed. The lock snicked.

"I was just taking a…" She rolled onto her back and propped herself up on her elbows, realizing her mistake when his gaze trailed to her chest and saw the truth for himself. Even she could feel the desperate press of her nipples against her thin shirt.

He stood at the foot of the bed. "Nap?" He gave her a slow smile. "Must have been having quite some dream, then."

Oh, it was no dream. More like a wish. And Ben had been at the heart of it.

"Wh-why did you just lock the door?" Sick anticipation began strumming through her, even though she already knew the answer.

His hands wrapped around her ankles and hauled her down to the foot of the bed, giving her all the confirmation she needed. "Isn't it obvious, Trace? *I* intend to be the one to finish what you started."

Ben wasn't sure what he'd expected when he'd come home early to spend the weekend with Tracy and the kids, but he certainly hadn't expected to find her in his bed…face buried in his pillow, her hands sliding down her own body.

Then, when she'd said his name, he'd known. She'd been fantasizing about him. About them. About the way they used to be.

He'd gone instantly erect, instantly ready for business. And then she'd turned and looked into his eyes, and he'd seen the fire that had once burned just for him. She still felt it. Just like he did.

It inflamed him. Enticed him.

And he wasn't above taking full advantage of it.

Leaning over the bed and planting his hands on either side of her shoulders, he stared down at her, hungry for the sight of her, hair in gorgeous disarray from being dragged down the bed, her slender body encased in snug jeans and a thin cami top. "Tell me you want me."

She licked her lips. "We shouldn't…"

"Maybe not. But I want to know. Was it me you were imagining?"

"Yes." The airy sigh was all he needed.

He bent down and closed his lips over the nipple he could see so clearly through her shirt, his teeth gripping, loving the tight heat of her against his tongue. She whimpered when he raised his head. "Did you imagine me here?" His knee parted her legs and moved to press tightly against her. "Here?"

Tracy's throat moved as she swallowed. "Yes."

His breath huffed out, and he moved up to whisper in her ear, "Let me, then. We'll sort all the other stuff out later."

She didn't say anything, and he wondered if she might refuse. Then her hands went to the back of his head and pulled him down to her lips, which instantly parted the second their mouths met. He groaned low and long as he accepted the invitation, pushing his tongue inside, tasting, remembering, pressing deep and then withdrawing…only to repeat the act all over again—a mounting heat growing in another part of his body.

Desperation spread through his veins, and he tried to rein in his need, knowing that soon kissing her would no longer be enough. The tiny sound she made in the back of her throat said she felt the exact same way.

This was how it had always been with them. The flames burned higher and faster than either of them wanted, until they were writhing against each other, fighting off the inevitable—knowing it would be over far too soon.

He pulled away, his breath rasping in his lungs. "Take off your shirt," he whispered. "I want to see you."

Tracy's hands went to the bottom of her cami without hesitation and lifted it over her head in a graceful movement that made him want to tear off the rest of her clothing and bury himself deep inside her. But he knew it was better if he didn't touch her for the next couple of minutes.

He nodded at her undergarment. "Bra next."

"Say please."

He swallowed, knowing she was teasing, but at this point he'd say anything she wanted. "Please."

She unclipped the front of the thing and shimmied it off her shoulders, the jiggle of her breasts making his mouth water. God, he wanted her.

He drank in the sight and, just like she always had, she took his breath away. "Touch them. Like you were when I came in." He gave her a wolfish grin as he added, "Please."

Her face turned pink, and this time he wondered if she might leap off the bed and stomp out of the room, but her hands went to her breasts and covered them, her head falling back as she gently massaged them.

This woman got to him like no other ever had. He slid his hand into the tangle of her hair and kissed her long and deep, drinking in everything he could.

He stood again, watching her eyes open and meet his. "Slide your thumbs over your nipples. Slowly. Just like I'm aching to do."

Again she hesitated, but then her hands shifted, the pads of her thumbs skimming over the tight buds in perfect synchrony. She repeated the motion, her gaze never leaving his. "Like this?"

"Oh, exactly like that." His voice had gone slightly hoarse, and he knew no amount of clearing his throat would chase it away. "Don't stop."

Her low moan sent heat skimming down his stomach and beyond.

"Where are the kids?"

"Outside. Rosa's shopping."

"Ah, so that's why you were in here." He stepped between her legs, which were still dangling over the side of the bed. He slowly spread them wider with his stance. "You thought you wouldn't get caught."

"I—I didn't plan it."

"But the second you got on that bed you felt it, didn't you? The things we used to do. Imagined me right here—just like this."

"Ben—"

"Shh. Don't talk. We're alone. We both want this." His fingers moved down to the waistband of her jeans. Her teeth sank into her bottom lip, her hands going completely still. "Uh-uh. I didn't tell you you could stop." He placed his hands over hers and showed her how he wanted her to stroke her breasts.

She moaned again, her hips shifting restlessly on the bed. "I want *you* to do it. Please?"

"Soon." His fingers returned to her jeans and dragged them down her thighs, stepping back so he could tug them the rest of the way off. "I don't want to waste a second of this time."

"The kids—"

"Will find the door locked." He smiled at her. "And you're sleeping. You need your rest."

Her panties were black, just like her lacy bra had been.

His hand glided down her sternum, past her bellybutton and stopped, fingers trailing along the line formed by her underwear. He wanted to watch her do that too.

"Tracy." His eyes met hers, and he took her hands in his, running both sets down her stomach until he reached the satin band. "Take them off."

She hooked her thumbs around the elastic and eased them down her hips, over the curve of her butt. When she'd pushed them as far as she could go without sitting up, Ben slid them off the rest of the way.

She was naked. His hands curled around her thighs and pushed them apart, his thumbs caressing the soft inner surfaces, then shifted higher, watching her eyes darken with each excruciating inch he gained. When he reached her center, he found her wet...open. He delved inside, still holding her thighs apart. A low whimper erupted from her throat when he applied pressure to the inner surface, right at the spot she liked best.

Her flesh tightened around his thumb, and she raised her hips stroking herself on him.

"Please, Ben. Now."

He didn't want to. Not yet. But he couldn't hold off much longer. He was already shaking with need.

With one hand he reached for his zipper and yanked it down, freeing himself. They could take it slowly later. Gripping her thighs again, he pulled her closer before filling his hands with her luscious butt and lifting it off the bed. He sank into her, watching as she took him in inch by inch.

Buried inside her, he savored the tight heat, trying his best not to move for several seconds. Tracy had other ideas. She wrapped her legs around him, planting her heels against his lower back and pulled him closer, using the leverage to lift her hips up then let them slide back down, setting up a sensual circular rhythm that wouldn't let up. The result was that, although he held perfectly still, his flesh was gripped by her body, massaged and squeezed and rubbed and…

He gritted his teeth and tried desperately to hold on, but it was no use. Nothing could stop the avalanche once it began.

With a hoarse groan he grabbed her hips and thrust hard into her, riding her wildly, feeling her explode around him with an answering cry even as he emptied himself inside her.

Heart pounding in his chest, he continued to move until there was nothing left and his legs turned to jelly. Slowly lowering her to the bed, he followed her down, pulling her onto her side and gathering her close.

Her breath rasped past his cheek, slowing gradually.

The moment of truth. Was she going to bolt? Or accept what had happened between them?

He took a minute or two to get his bearings then kissed her forehead. "Was it as good as you imagined?"

"Better." Her soft laugh warmed his heart. "Only you had your clothes off in my imagination."

"We'll have to work on that."

"Mmm." She sighed against his throat then licked the moisture that had collected there. "Someone will be coming pretty soon."

"Exactly."

"I meant coming *home*."

Something in Ben's throat tightened at the sound of that word on her tongue. *Home.*

Was that what she considered this place? Or would she take off again the second she had the opportunity?

He'd better tread carefully. Not let himself get too comfortable. Because she considered this a temporary arrangement. And if not for the kids, Tracy wouldn't even be here right now. The fact that she hadn't automatically expected to share his bed spoke volumes. She hadn't planned on returning to their old relationship, no matter how good their little interlude in the water tank had been. Or how much she'd seemed to enjoy their time in this bed.

And she had enjoyed it.

Seeing her pleasuring herself on his bed...*their* bed... had done a number on his heart. As had her admission of fantasizing about him...not about Pedro or some other faceless man as she'd touched her body.

Yeah. He'd liked that a little too much.

Well, somehow he'd better drag himself back from the edge of insanity and grab hold of reality. Because it wasn't likely Tracy was going to change her mind about staying with him for ever. And, unfortunately, with each day that passed he found that's exactly what he wanted.

CHAPTER EIGHTEEN

TRACY DREW THE insulin into the syringe and gave Cleo a reassuring smile. "You're becoming a pro at these."

This was Cleo's tenth shot, but her glucose levels were still fluctuating all over the place. Whether it was the honeymoon phase that Dr. Morena had mentioned or whether her pancreas would again start pumping out its own supply of insulin was the big question. One no one could seem to answer.

"It still hurts."

"I know. It always will. But sometimes we have to be brave and do what we know is best—even if it hurts."

Like leaving had been four years ago? Because that had hurt more than anything else ever had—that and her miscarriage. Looking back, she knew all kinds of things had led to her flight from *Teresina*. Anger, grief, shock. If Ben hadn't done what he had, she might have stuck it out and tried to make things work. But his actions had been the proverbial last straw...her whole world had collapsed around her, unable to keep functioning under the load she'd placed on it.

And now?

She and Ben hadn't talked about what had happened between them two days ago. There was still a part of her that was mortified that he'd caught her on his bed, but the result had been something beyond her wildest dreams. He'd been arrogant—and sexy as hell—standing there at the foot of the bed, ordering her to touch herself.

If the front door hadn't clicked open and then shut again, they might have started all over again. But the second the sound had registered, there had been a mad dash of yanking on clothing interspersed with panicked giggles as they'd snuck out of his room to face Rosa and her armloads of groceries.

Ben had been a whole lot better at feigning nonchalance than she had as he'd taken the canvas sacks from the housekeeper and helped her put things away. But the burning glances he'd thrown her from time to time had told her he'd rather be right back in that bed with her.

Heat washed over her as she tried to corral her thoughts and keep them from straying any further down that dangerous path.

Tracy rolled up Cleo's shorts. "Ready?"

"I—I think so."

With a quick jab that was designed to cause as little pain as possible, she pushed the needle home and injected the medicine. Other than the quick intake of breath, the little girl didn't make a sound. As soon as Tracy withdrew and capped the syringe, she tossed the instrument into the mini medical waste container they'd set up.

Cleo's voice came from the stool where she was still seated. "Are you going to work for Dr. Morena?"

Ah, so she had heard the doctor as she'd talked to them in the exam room. Tracy didn't have an answer today any more than she'd had one for Ben when he'd asked her much the same question after making love.

They hadn't been together again since that night but he'd gotten into the habit of dropping a kiss on her cheek before he left for work each day. She probably should have moved away the first time he'd done it, but this morning she'd found herself lifting her cheek to him in anticipation. At this rate, she'd be puckering up and laying one right on his lips very soon.

Probably not a smart idea.

She'd never fooled herself into thinking she didn't love Ben. Of course she did. She'd never stopped. She had been furious with him after the yellow fever incident and had needed time to think about how to deal with everything that had been going on in her life. Only she'd taken too much time, and hiding her condition had become second nature—and had seemed easier than returning to *Teresina* to tell him the truth.

During all those years she'd been gone he'd never called her, never begged her to change her mind. Although she couldn't imagine Ben ever doing that. He was strong, stoic. He'd had to be self-sufficient as a child in order to cope, since his parents had rarely been there for him.

She hadn't been there for him either.

But now he knew why. Didn't that change everything? Wasn't that what those little pecks on the cheek had meant?

She could say she hoped so, but in reality she had no idea. He'd barely had any time to process the information, but how would he feel once he had? She knew she was more than just the sum of her parts, but Ben loved her breasts. That much had been obvious from the heat in his eyes as her hands had cupped them. Stroked over the tips.

And, yep…her mind was right back in the gutter, despite her best efforts.

With a start she realized she was still standing in front of the cabinet, and that Cleo was now frowning up at her with a look of concern. Oh, she'd asked about Dr. Morena and whether she was going to work for her.

"How do you feel about what the doctor said? About working at the clinic?"

Cleo hopped down from the stool and unrolled the leg of the shorts. "Does that mean we'll keep on staying with you?"

Afraid to get the girl's hopes up too high, she said, "Why don't you leave the worrying about that to us, okay?" She dropped a quick kiss on her head. "Just know that you are loved."

Ben pushed through the front door, stopping short when the sounds of screaming came from the backyard. Dropping his briefcase on the floor, he yelled for Tracy, but other than those distant shouts his call was met by silence. A sense of weird *déjà vu* settled over him. This was much like the day he'd come home to find Tracy gone.

Except there'd been no shouting that day. Speaking of which…

Moving to the back of the house, he threw open the door that led to the patio. There, in the pool, were three bodies. Only they were very much alive.

In fact, it looked like he'd arrived in the middle of some kind of battle from the looks of the water guns in each person's hands. He walked up the steps to the top of the deck, which was still under construction, and all three pairs of eyes turned to him in a synchronized fashion. Too late, he realized his mistake when Daniel shouted, *"Atire-nele!"*

They all took aim and squeezed their triggers. Water came at him from three different angles, soaking his blue dress shirt and plastering it to his chest. "Hey! Enough already!"

No one listened, but then Tracy, clad in a cherry-red bikini that held his eyes prisoner for several long seconds, ran out of water first. As she was dunking her gun to reload, he pounced, going over the side of the water tank in one smooth move and capturing her gun hand as he hit the water—before she had time to bring it back up. She gave a startled scream when he wrapped his arms around her and took her with him beneath the water. Out of sight of the kids, who were bobbing around him, he planted his lips on Tracy's, a stream of bubbles rising as she laughed against her will. He let her up, where she coughed and spluttered. "Not fair!"

He slicked his hair out of his face, brows lifted. "And shooting me without any warning was?"

"You saw the water guns. We figured that was all the warning you deserved."

Ben stood there, dress shoes lying at the bottom of the pool, obviously ruined by now.

But he wouldn't change this scene for anything in the world. This was what he'd always dreamed of. Except in his daydreams Tracy had stayed by his side for ever. For a minute or two he allowed himself to mourn what might never be. But Tracy was here, right now. And all he wanted to do was pull the loose end on that bikini and see what happened. Only they weren't alone.

But at least she was playing. Laughing at his attempt to kiss her beneath the water. Maybe it was enough for now. He could wait and see how things went. If he didn't get his hopes up too high, they couldn't be dashed. Right?

"So. You planned to ambush me the minute I arrived, did you?"

Daniel gave him another squirt—which hit him squarely in the eye. "Ow!"

Another laugh from Tracy. When was the last time he'd heard her laugh with abandon? Far too long ago.

Her gun was still on the bottom of the pool. Diving beneath the water, he retrieved it and came back up, his head just barely above the surface as he let water fill the reservoir. Then he went on the attack, giving back as good as he got. Tracy stayed well out of the line of fire this time, double checking her bikini to make sure she was still in it. The act distracted him for a second and both the kids got him again.

He glared at his wife, mimicking her earlier words. "Not fair."

"Oh, but you know what they say. All's fair in…" Her voice trailed away, her smile dying with it.

He cursed himself, even though he knew it wasn't his fault. Instead, he waved the kids off for a minute and jogged over to her. Draping an arm around her waist, he whispered in her ear. "Let's just take it a day at a time, okay? No expectations."

The smile she gave him was tremulous. "I feel awful, Ben."

"Don't." He kissed her cheek. "Although I think you owe me a new pair of shoes."

"Done." She slid back beneath the water and leaned against the side. "This was a great idea. The kids love it. I'm thinking of enrolling Cleo in swimming lessons. Did you know she doesn't swim?"

Tracy had switched to English so the kids wouldn't understand her. He glanced at Cleo, who was hanging onto the side of the tank with one hand while maneuvering the water gun with the other. He answered her back in the same language. "She definitely needs to learn if the pool is going to stay up year round. How about Daniel?"

"He had lessons in school, but he's never had a place to practice. So it might not be a bad idea for him to brush up on his skills as well."

"Right." He leaned back beside her, stretching his legs out beneath the water. Tracy's limbs looked pale next to the black fabric of his slacks. "Did you put sunscreen on?"

"SPF sixty. The kids have some on as well."

He touched her nose, which, despite her sun protection, was slightly pink. "How long have you guys been in the water?"

"About an hour. We were making a list of recipes that the kids' mother used to fix, and I felt like we needed to do something fun afterwards. I don't want every memory of their mom to end on a sad note."

"Smart." Ben paused, wondering how to ask the question that had been bothering him for the last couple of days. His timing tended to suck, so why worry about that now? "Listen, I've been meaning to ask. About the other night…"

She tensed beside him. "I don't think now is the best time to talk about this."

"I haven't exactly been able to get you alone." Whether that had been on purpose or not, only Tracy could say. "I'll say it in English, so no one else will understand. Are you okay?"

"Okay?"

"Are you upset with me for the way I…?"

He didn't know how else to ask it. And he wasn't sure if he was asking if Tracy was okay, or if "they" were okay.

She shook her head, eyes softening. "No. Of course I'm not upset."

"You've been acting a little funny."

"This whole situation is a little funny." She sighed. "I never expected to be back in *Teresina*."

"Are you sorry you came?"

Ben wasn't sure why he was pushing so hard for reassurance, but he felt like he was slipping and sliding around, searching for something that might or might not be there.

"No. But I was going to tell you something later today. I made a phone call and talked to my old doctor here. She got me an appointment with a surgeon on Monday."

He froze, then a million and one questions immediately came to mind. She gave a quick nod at the kids, who, Ben realized, were both looking at them, trying to figure out what was being said. "Okay. Let's discuss it after dinner, okay?"

"Thank you." She switched back to Portuguese. "Is the military still monitoring your movements?"

He'd mentioned an unmarked vehicle parked in the lot at the hospital since they'd gotten back to *Teresina*. He hadn't recognized it and the driver was always the same person. It was either the military or a terrorist, Ben had told her with a rueful smile. The latter wasn't very likely in Brazil, since it was a pacifist country.

"The car hasn't been in the lot for the last two days so hopefully, if it was the General's doing, they've decided I'm too boring to keep tabs on." He pulled a face at the kids.

Tracy laughed. "Those guys don't know you very well, then, do they, Dr. Almeida? You're quite unpredictable."

The way she said it warmed his heart, despite the chill he'd felt when she'd mentioned the word "surgeon."

He planted a hand on his chest as if wounded and winked at Cleo. "You think I'm a pretty boring guy, don't you?"

The little girl giggled then shook her head.

"What about you?" he asked Daniel.

The boy scratched his head with the tip of his water gun. "I guess you're okay. Not too boring."

Tracy grinned then shot Ben a smug look. "See? Told you."

They were throwing playful barbs at each other again. His spine relaxed. How good it felt to be back on solid footing, instead of crashing around in a scary place where you couldn't see the bottom for the muck.

At least for today. Monday might bring something altogether different.

Ben had knocked on her door that night around midnight. She'd been half expecting him to come and see her out of earshot of the kids. What she hadn't expected was for him to push the door shut with his foot and stand there, staring at her.

Then he'd swept her in his arms and kissed her as if there was no tomorrow. They'd made love on her bed, and it had been as fresh and new as the other two times they'd been together. Afterwards, he'd held her in his arms.

"Whatever happens on Monday, we'll face it together, okay?"

A little sliver of doubt went through her chest. "Are you saying you want to go with me?"

"Would that be okay?"

Tracy had to decide to let him in completely or shut him out. "What about your work?"

"I can take off for a couple of hours." Ben caught a strand of her hair, rubbing it between his fingertips.

"Okay." Whew. Why did that feel so huge? "I won't make any firm decisions until Cleo's diabetes is under control, but I just need to see where I am. I've been neglecting my tests and want to get caught up with them."

"Why now?"

"I don't know. Maybe I've been running away from making a decision one way or the other."

He nodded and wrapped the lock of hair around his finger. "If I asked you to start sleeping in our old bed again, would you say yes?"

"Tonight? Or…?"

"Not just tonight. From now on."

Wow. This had gone from talking about her appointment to Ben asking her to make their marriage a real one. At least that's what she thought he was asking. "I assume by sleeping, you don't actually mean closing our eyes."

The right side of his mouth quirked up. "I definitely think there might be some eye closing going on, but it would take place well before any actual sleeping."

Tracy's body quickened despite having just made love with this man fifteen minutes ago. She tilted her head as if in deep thought. "Hmm. I don't know. Do you snore?"

"Interesting question. I do make sounds from time to time, but I don't know if I'd call them snoring." His fingers tunneled into her hair, massaging her head in tiny circles that made her shiver.

"I think I remember those sounds. I kind of liked them."

"Did you, now?" His thumb trailed down the side of her throat, stroking the spot where her pulse was beginning to pick up speed in response to his words and his touch.

"Mmm."

He leaned over and kissed the side of her jaw. "And I kind of like the little sound you just made."

"I'm glad, because if you keep that up, I'm going to be making a lot more of— Oh!" Her breath caught as his teeth nipped the crook of her neck, sucking the blood to the surface and then licking over it with his warm tongue.

"Say yes," he whispered.

"Yes." She wasn't sure what she was agreeing to, but it didn't really matter at this point. She wasn't about to hold anything back, and she trusted him enough to know he wouldn't ask her for more than she could give.

He moved to her lips. "Yes to sleeping in my bed?"

"I thought we'd already decided that."

"No, you were still questioning whether or not I snored." His tongue slowly licked across her mouth.

"No snoring. Just sounds." As she said each word, his tongue delved into her mouth before finally cutting off her speech altogether.

I didn't matter, though, because Tracy was already beyond rational thought, her arms winding around his neck.

She was ready to lose herself to him all over again—for as long as he wanted her.

CHAPTER NINETEEN

BEN WAS STILL groggy with sleep when he reached across the bed and realized Tracy was no longer there. He could hear her talking softly from somewhere nearby, and he woke up the rest of the way in a flash.

"But I have a doctor's appointment on Monday." There was a pause. "I suppose I could. It's not urgent."

Ben sat up in bed, looking for her. She must be in the bathroom.

He wasn't purposely trying to eavesdrop, but something about the way she kept her voice hushed said she wasn't anxious for anyone to hear the conversation.

"I don't want to be gone long. Cleo's still getting her shots regulated."

Climbing out of bed and reaching for his boxers, he padded to the door. "Pedro, I can't leave right this second. No, I know. I'm sure Rosa won't mind watching them while Ben is at work. She used to watch him when his parents were gone. I'd have to teach her how to give Cleo her insulin shots, though."

Rosa won't mind watching them.

The soft warmth he'd felt during the night evaporated. Why would Rosa need to watch the kids? Or give Cleo her shots?

Unless Tracy was planning to be gone for a while.

And why was she talking to Pedro in the bathroom, unless she was keeping something from him?

It wouldn't be the first time.

They'd been home less than a week, and she was already off somewhere?

A jumble of emotions spun up inside him like a tornado, anger being the first to reach the top.

No. He was not heading down this path again. He turned the knob and pushed the door open.

Tracy's mouth rounded in a perfect "O" that had looked incredibly sexy last night. But all he saw this morning was betrayal.

"Pedro, hold on just a second."

She put her hand over the phone, but Ben beat her to the punch. "You're leaving."

Licking her lips, she nodded. "Just for a few days. The medical boat docked at a flooded village. There are five cases of cholera and there's certain to be dozens more, as they've all been drinking from the same water source."

"Send someone else." His voice was cold and hard, but that's how he felt inside. "Let Pedro deal with it."

"He's not a doctor, Ben. I am. Matt called him, they're expecting to be overwhelmed by—"

"You're *a* doctor. Not the only doctor in the whole country. You have responsibilities here."

"Rosa can—"

Fury washed over him. "Rosa practically raised my brother and me. These kids need a steady presence in their lives, not be pushed off on someone else every time your assistant has a runny nose. You promised me at least six months."

"It's only this one time."

He closed his eyes for a second, his hand squeezing the doorknob for all he was worth. Then he took a deep breath.

"I'm going to lay it out for you, Tracy. Either you let someone else handle this, and we start looking toward a future. Together. Or I'm filing for divorce. Even if I have to go all the way to New York to do it."

Every ounce of color drained from her face. "Wh-what about Daniel and Cleo? You said you couldn't do this alone."

"It doesn't look like I have much of a choice." He shot her a glance. "*I* made a promise that I intend to keep. Besides, I've been through the same rinse-and-spin cycle a couple of times already. I'm sure I can figure things out."

Just before he pulled the door shut he added, "Finish your conversation, then let me know what you decide."

Tracy draped a moist cloth over the forehead of the woman she was treating then used a gloved hand to check her vitals. They were through the worst of the cholera outbreak. There were several army doctors among their group, but this time they hadn't been sent at the request of her husband but were instead digging drain fields and latrines in an effort to prevent a recurrence.

Ben wouldn't send anyone for her this time, because he was through with her. He'd said as much.

She wasn't sure why Pedro's call had spurred her to action. Maybe her instincts were programmed to bolt at the first sign of trouble.

Like having an actual appointment with a doctor? Was she still running...still having to move and work to feel alive?

No, she'd felt alive with Ben as well. And this trip felt hollow. It didn't fulfill her the way it might have a few years ago. She missed the kids. Missed Ben.

Matt's wife sat down beside her on an intricately woven mat. "How are you holding up?"

Stevie had been with *Projeto Vida* for two years, working alongside her husband. They had a daughter as well, but she was confined to the boat this trip. Neither Matt nor Stevie wanted to run the risk of her becoming ill.

"As well as anyone."

Stevie gave her a keen look. "Are you sure about that?"

"We're all tired. I came here to help."

"And you have." Stevie touched her gloved hand to Tracy's. "How's Ben?"

She flashed the other woman a startled look. Word evidently traveled fast. "I wouldn't know. I won't be heading back there."

"I'm sorry."

"Me too." She gave her patient's shoulder a gentle squeeze and murmured that someone would check on her in just a little while then she stood with a sigh. "How do you do it?"

Stevie got to her feet as well. "What do you mean?"

"How do you keep your marriage together and travel on the boat?"

"We both believe in what we do." She stripped her gloves off and motioned for Tracy to follow her. Once outside the tent she leaned against a tree. "Sometimes I just need a breath of fresh air, you know?"

Tracy did know. The smells of illness got to you after a while.

Letting her head bump the bark of the tree trunk, Stevie swiveled her head toward her. "Matt wasn't sure he wanted to come back to Brazil after losing so much here. If he'd chosen to stay in the States, I would have stayed with him. Because that's the only important thing—that we're together."

"So you're saying I shouldn't have come."

"No." Stevie gave her a soft smile. "Only you know what's right...what's in your heart."

"I don't know any more. Ben never liked me traveling."

"I'm sure he missed you very much when you were gone."

"Yes, I suppose he did. But other wives travel."

"As much as you do?" Stevie paused for a moment or two. "I think you have to examine your heart and decide what it is you want out of life. Why you're so driven to do what you do."

Because she didn't have to think about anything else when she was helping people?

In the past she'd worked herself to exhaustion day after day—had fallen into bed at night, her eyes closing as soon as her head had hit the pillow.

Movement equaled life.

But was this really living? Was she doing this because she believed in her work or because she was afraid to stay in one place, where she might start feeling trapped—claustrophobic?

She'd missed her doctor's appointment to be here. Could she not have delayed her flight for a few hours? In reality, despite Pedro's dire predictions, there'd been enough hands to fight the cholera outbreak, even if she hadn't been here. She'd been living her whole life as if she were single with no commitments. Yes, she'd had this job before she'd met Ben. But in choosing it over him time and time again she'd been sending the message that he meant no more to her than he'd meant to his parents.

Lord, she'd made such a mess of things. Such a mess of her life.

And in staying so incredibly busy, she'd not only risked her long-term health but she'd also lost sight of the person she loved most: Ben.

Maybe it was time to start pulling away. Let someone else take the helm of her organization—Pedro maybe—and go back to practicing medicine in a clinic. She might not be able to help whole swaths of people but she could help them one at a time.

Which path was more valuable in the long run? Maybe it wasn't a question of either/or. Maybe each had its own place in the grand scheme of things. And there were two children who'd trusted her to be there for them.

She turned and hugged her friend. "Thank you. I think I've just realized where I should be."

"In *Teresina*?"

She nodded. "I don't know why I didn't see it before now."

"Maybe because 'now' was when you needed to see it." With a secretive smile Stevie waved to her husband, who was working off in the distance. He winked back.

And Tracy did what she should have done four years ago: she walked to the nearest soldier and asked if she could hitch a ride on the next boat out of the Amazon.

Ben sucked down a mouthful of tepid coffee and grimaced before going back to his microscope and glaring down at the slide beneath the lens. He had no business being here today. He'd had no business here all week.

Why had he drawn that ridiculous line in the sand and dared her to cross it? Maybe because he'd never forgiven his parents for withholding their affection when he'd been a child?

Yeah, well, he was an adult now. Well past the age of holding grudges.

He hadn't heard from Tracy since she'd left, and he'd cursed himself repeatedly for not being more sensitive the last time they'd talked…for not trying to really listen to what she'd been saying.

He wasn't the only one who was upset.

Rosa had chewed his butt up one side and down the other when she'd found out Tracy wasn't coming home.

"I used to think I raised you to be a smart boy, Benjamin Almeida. Now I'm not so sure."

"You shouldn't have had to raise me at all."

"Was it so bad? Your childhood?"

He thought back. No, his parents had been gone for months at a time, but when they had been there there'd been laughter…and then, when they'd left again there'd been tears. But through it all Rosa had been there. How many children grew up not even having a Rosa in their lives?

If he thought about it, he was damned lucky.

And if he'd given Tracy a little more time to settle in before jumping to conclusions at the first phone call she'd got from the office, maybe he could have done a better job at being a husband this time.

He rummaged around in his desk until he came up with an old tattered business card that he'd saved for years. Staring at the familiar name on the front, he turned it over and over between his fingers, battling with indecision. He knew from their time in São João dos Rios that the phone number was still the same. Finally, before he could change his mind, he dialed and swiveled around in his chair to face out the window.

Did she even have cellphone reception wherever she was?

He heard the phone ring through the handset, but there was something weird about it. Almost as if it was ringing in two places at once—inside his ear and somewhere off in the distance. On the second ring the sound outside his ear grew louder in steady increments, and he frowned, trying to figure out if he was just imagining it. On the third ring her voice came through. "Hello?"

Ben's breath seized in his lungs as he realized the greeting came not only from the handset pressed to his ear but from right behind him. He slowly swiveled and met sea-green eyes. They crinkled at the corners as they looked back at him.

Keeping the phone pressed to his ear, he gazed at her in disbelief, while she kept her phone against her own ear as well.

"Tracy?"

"Yes."

God, he could just jump up and crush her to him. But he didn't. He said the words he'd been rehearsing for the last half-hour. "I've missed you. Please come home."

Tears shimmered in her eyes, her throat moving in a quick jerking motion. "I've missed you too. I'll be there soon."

With that she clicked her phone shut and moved towards him. When she stood before his chair, he reached up and pulled her down onto his lap. "You're home."

"I am. I'm home." She wrapped her arms around his neck and pulled him against her. "And this time I'm here to stay."

One year later

Ben strode down the hallway of Einstein Hospital in São Paulo, Brazil, until he reached the surgical wing. Tracy's dad was already in the waiting room. He stood as he saw Ben heading his way. The two men shook hands, Sam taking it one step further and embracing his son-in-law.

Ben said, "I'm glad you were able to come, sir."

"How is she?"

"Still in surgery."

The months since Tracy had stood in his office and they'd shared declarations of love had passed in a flurry of medical tests for both Cleo and Tracy. Cleo's initial diagnosis of diabetes had been confirmed, but it was now under control. They'd even been granted custody of both children.

Tracy's mammogram had come back with an area of concern and whether it was cancer or not, they both knew it was time. They'd made this decision together soon after she'd come home. She'd shed tears while Ben had reassured her that he'd love her with breasts or without.

Nodding to the chair Sam had vacated, they both sat down.

"She did it, then," his father-in-law said.

"Yes." Ben leaned forward, elbows on his knees, clasped hands dangling between them. "She wanted to be proactive."

Tracy's dad nodded. "If her mother had known she carried this gene, I know in my heart she would have done the same thing. And I would have stood beside her." He dragged a forearm across his eyes, which Ben pretended he didn't see. "How long will she be back there?"

"Two to four hours." He glanced at his watch. "It's going on three hours now. We should be hearing something fairly soon."

Two to four hours. Such a short time. And yet it seemed like for ever.

Unable to sit still, he settled for pacing while Sam remained in his seat. Ben had already made all kinds of deals with God, so many he wasn't sure he'd be able to keep track. But Tracy had been so sure of this, so at peace with her decision in the past week.

A green-suited man came around the corner, a surgical mask dangling around his neck. "Mr. Almeida?"

Ben moved towards him, Sam following close behind. The surgeon frowned, but Ben nodded. "This is Tracy's dad. He's just arrived in town."

The man nodded. "The surgery went fine. I didn't see any definite areas of malignancy, but I'm sending everything off to pathology for testing just in case."

"Tracy's okay, then?" Ben didn't want to hear about malignancies or what they had or hadn't found.

"She's fine." The man hesitated. "Reconstruction shouldn't be a problem. We'd like to keep her here for a day or two to observe her, however. Will she have someone to help her at home afterwards?"

"Yes." Ben's and Sam's answers came on top of the other, causing all of them to smile.

Ben finished. "We'll make sure she gets everything she needs." He knew the kids would both be beside themselves, desperate for a chance to talk to Tracy. But he'd left them in *Teresina*, in Rosa's care—though he'd realized the irony of it. Kids survived. And these two kids had survived more than most…more than he'd ever had to, even on his worst days.

"Good," the surgeon said. "Give us a few minutes to get her settled then someone will come and get you. Please, don't stay long, though. She needs to rest."

Ben held out a hand. "Thank you. For everything."

The surgeon nodded then shook each of their hands and headed back in the direction from which he'd come. Before he rounded the corner, though, he turned and came back. "I wanted to tell you what a brave young woman Tracy is. I don't know how much you've talked about everything, but whether you agree with her decision or not it was ultimately up to her. Support her in it."

"Absolutely." Ben wasn't planning on doing anything else. He'd spend the rest of his days supporting whatever decisions she made. He was just grateful to have her back.

"Thanks again."

"You're welcome. Take care." This time the surgeon didn't look back but disappeared around the corner.

"Why don't you go back and see her first?" Ben told Sam.

"My face is not the one she'll want to see when she wakes up. There's plenty of time."

Yes, there was. Ben swallowed. "Thank you. I'll tell her you're here."

Sleep.

That's all Tracy wanted to do, but something warm curled around her hand and gave a soft squeeze. Someone said her name in a low, gravelly voice she should recognize.

Did recognize.

"Trace."

There it was again. Her heart warmed despite the long shivers taking hold of her body. She was cold. Freezing. Her body fought back, shuddering against the sensation.

Something settled over her. A blanket?

She focused on her eyelids, trying to convince them to part—wanted to put a hand to her chest to see if they were still there.

Oh, God. Moisture flared behind still closed lids and leaked out the sides.

"Tracy." Warm fingers threaded through her own. "You're okay. Safe. I'm here."

She wanted to believe. But she was afraid the last year had all been a dream. At least the blanket was starting to warm her just a bit.

Her throat ached. From the tube she'd had down her throat.

Wait. Tube?

Yes, from the surgery. Ben was here. Somewhere. He promised to be here when she woke up.

So why was she even doubting she'd heard his voice?

Okay. Moment of truth.

Eyelids...open.

As if by magic, they parted and the first thing she saw was the face. The gorgeous face that matched that low, sexy voice. Broad shoulders stretched wide against the fabric of his shirt. Ruffled brown hair that looked like he'd shoved fingers through it repeatedly, a piece in the back sticking straight up.

Long, dark lashes. Strong throat. Gentle hands.

Her husband.

"Ben?" The sound rasped out of her throat as if coated by rough sandpaper—and feeling like it as well.

"I'm here."

Yes, it was Ben. He was here. Crying?

Oh, God. He was crying because she no longer had breasts. No, that wasn't it. They'd made this decision together. Had they found something during the surgery?

She tried to glance down at herself, but everything was buried under a thick layer of blankets. But there was no pain. Could the surgeon not have taken them?

"Are they...?"

"Shh. You're fine."

Closing her eyes, she tried to clear her fuzzy head. "The kids?"

"I spoke to Rosa a few minutes ago. They're fine. They miss you."

I miss you.

Her lips curved as she remembered Ben saying those very words as she'd stood in the doorway of his office a year ago. That he'd actually called her—wanted her to come home—was a memory she'd treasure for ever.

Where was the pain? Shouldn't it hurt to have something sliced off your body?

"I miss the kids, too."

He smiled and smoothed strands of hair back from her face. "Your dad's here. They'll only let one of us in at a time, and he insisted you'd want to see me first."

"He was right."

Lifting her hand to his lips, he kissed the top of it. His touch was as warm as his voice. "I love you, Tracy. And I'm going to spend the rest of my life showing you how much."

She closed her eyes, only to have to force them open again. "I like the sound of that."

One of the nurses appeared in the doorway, leaning against the frame. "We probably need to let Mrs. Almeida get some sleep."

"Mrs. Almeida." Tracy murmured the words as her eyelids once again began to flicker shut. She loved having his name.

Almost as much as she loved the man who'd given it to her.

EPILOGUE

THE SUNRISE WAS gorgeous, a blazing red ball of fire tossed just above the horizon by the hand of God.

Today promised to be a scorcher—just like most days in *Teresina*. And she relished each and every one of them. Curling her hands around the railing of the deck off their bedroom, Tracy let the warmth of the wood sink into her palms and gave a quiet sigh of contentment. She loved these kinds of mornings.

Five years since her surgery and no sign of cancer.

Tracy was thrilled to be a part of Crista Morena's thriving pediatric practice. And twice a year she and Ben took a trip along the Amazon to do relief work. Together. Something that might have been impossible in the past.

A pair of arms wrapped around her from behind, sliding beneath the hem of her white camisole and tickling the skin of her tummy. She made a quiet sound, putting her hands over his and holding him close. Leaning her head against her husband's chest, she thought about how truly blessed she was.

Except for one thing.

"I miss Daniel." The wistfulness in her heart came through in her voice.

Their adopted son had left for college in the States last month and was busy studying to be a doctor—hoping to return to Brazil and help people in communities like São João dos Rios. His mother would be so very proud of the man her son had become. The four of them had made several trips back to the kids' home town, and although the razed village was sad testament to what had happened there, it was also a place of joy. A place of new beginnings.

They'd had a permanent stone marker made and had placed it on Maria Eugênia's grave—although both Daniel and Cleo had decided the crude rock Ben had carved should remain there as well.

They'd also made a pact to go back once a year to put flowers on her grave.

Cleo, now thirteen, was growing into a beautiful young woman who was sensitive and wise beyond her years. All too soon she'd be grown as well, leaving them to start a life of her own.

"We can always phone Daniel later this afternoon." Ben planted cool lips on her neck.

"We'll wait for Cleo to get home from school. I can't believe how fast time has gone by."

"I'm grateful for every moment." His lips continued to glide up her neck until he reached her earlobe, biting gently.

She shivered, her body reacting instantly, the way it always did for this man. "So am I."

A thin cry came from the back of the house. Tracy squinched her nose and sighed. "So is someone else."

Their baby girl, just three months old, was letting them know she was hungry. Although she would never replace the baby they'd lost all those years ago, trying to have another child had seemed the right thing to do. Tracy was grateful for second chances, no matter how they came.

Ben had taken a little more coaxing—a year to be exact. He'd been worried about the ramifications to her health, but in the end he'd agreed. And Grace Elizabeth Almeida had come into the world kicking and screaming.

Someone ready to take on the universe and everything it held.

"I guess we'd better go feed her before she gets really wound up." Ben turned her in his arms and nipped her lower lip. "Although I was hoping we might get a little alone time. Just this once."

"Don't worry, Ben. We have plenty of time. Our whole lives, in fact."

Tracy sighed, her happiness complete. She had everything she could possibly want out of life. She and Ben had found their middle ground, despite seemingly impossible odds. And she'd discovered there was more than one path to happiness, as long as the man she loved was by her side. And as her three children had taught her, there was definitely more than one way to make a family.

* * * * *

THE REBEL DOC WHO STOLE HER HEART

BY
SUSAN CARLISLE

Published in Great Britain 2014
by Mills & Boon, an imprint of Harlequin (UK) Limited,
Eton House, 18-24 Paradise Road, Richmond, Surrey, TW9 1SR

© Susan Carlisle 2014

ISBN: 978 0 263 90739 1

Harlequin (UK) Limited's policy is to use papers that are natural,
renewable and recyclable products and made from wood grown in
sustainable forests. The logging and manufacturing processes conform
to the legal environmental regulations of the country of origin.

Printed and bound in Spain
by Blackprint CPI, Barcelona

Dear Reader

I've always been fascinated by the attraction between two people. So many times men and woman are complete opposites and still find that special spark. A good-looking man and an unattractive woman, or the reverse. The introvert and the extrovert. The super-popular person and the one in the corner. The person who loves adventure and the one who prefers to watch TV. It amazes me how humans manage to pair off.

These extreme differences are what I explore in Michelle and Ty's story. They couldn't be more dissimilar and yet they fit—complement each other as if they are puzzle pieces finding their spot. What made writing this book especially fun was watching the two characters squirm as they find that they truly do belong together.

I would be remiss if I didn't mention and thank Dr Bruce Miller, who is an anaesthesiologist extraordinaire. Much of Ty's doctoring skills and sensitive interactions with patients were influenced through knowing Dr Miller and witnessing him in action. I also have to say a big thanks to Dr Kirk Kanter, a heart surgeon with a big heart. There is none better in the world. Through him I received amazing technical assistance that helped Michelle's world become real. All doctors should be as good and as dedicated as these two men are to their patients.

I hope you enjoyed reading Michelle and Ty's story as much as I enjoyed writing it. I love to hear from my readers. You can contact me at www.SusanCarlisle.com

Susan

Dedication

To Andy, the Mr Romance in my life.
I love you.

Recent titles by Susan Carlisle:

SNOWBOUND WITH DR DELECTABLE
NYC ANGELS: THE WALLFLOWER'S SECRET*
HOT-SHOT DOC COMES TO TOWN
THE NURSE HE SHOULDN'T NOTICE
HEART SURGEON, HERO...HUSBAND?

NYC Angels

**These books are also available in eBook format
from www.millsandboon.co.uk**

**Praise for
Susan Carlisle:**

'Susan Carlisle pens her romances beautifully…
HOT-SHOT DOC COMES TO TOWN is a book
that I would recommend not only to Medical Romance™
fans but to anyone looking to curl up with an
angst-free romance about taking chances
and following your heart.'
—*HarlequinJunkie.com*

CHAPTER ONE

HEART SURGEON MICHELLE ROSS used her hip to nudge open the swinging door to the number four operating room in Raleigh Medical Center in North Carolina.

Her patient, Mr. Martin, waiting on her to begin repairing his artery, was the type of person that affected her most. There were almost always young children waiting at home for their parent to get better. She had to save this father. Make sure he lived to return to his family.

Dressed in sterile gown and with hands covered in latex gloves, she eyed her team and asked in a crisp voice, "Are we ready to begin?"

The quietly speaking group gathered around the middle-aged patient suddenly became mute. If a scalpel had been mishandled and fallen to the floor it would have echoed in the soundless room.

She looked at each of them and watched as every set of eyes refused to meet her gaze. What was going on? Normally her team was ready to proceed without hesitation. She asked the same question before each operation out of habit.

Glitches weren't allowed in her OR. Efficiency was her motto. Her patients deserved the best and she saw that they got it. She'd hand-picked her team and they knew what was expected, she trusted them, so what was the issue?

Her team's unwillingness to answer didn't alleviate her

anxiety over a case that would require her complete attention. She stepped to her place beside the table before her gaze landed on the *anesthesiologist resident* at the head of the patient. "Where's Schwartzie?" she demanded.

The younger doctor's eyes flickered a couple of times above the top edge of his surgical mask and he said, "Dr. Schwartz's replacement isn't here yet."

Annoyance blistered in her. Her patient deserved better. She opened her mouth to respond but someone entering the door stopped her. A man with wide shoulders had his back to her. He made an agile pivot and faced the group. A bright orange zebra-striped surgical cap screamed for attention in her sterile and ordered world. The basic blue surgical uniform of the hospital covered his body but what caught her attention again were the glowing lime-colored clogs that shone through the surgical paper booties on his feet.

Who was this clown? All that was missing was the red nose. As he approached the group her focus centered on his striking jade-colored eyes above his mask. Those orbs met hers expectantly, held her gaze before the twinkle in them put her off guard.

Surely this wasn't her missing anesthesiologist?

"Hey, I'm Ty Smith. I'm filling in for Schwartz." Despite the mask covering his mouth, she could tell he was smiling as he made eye contact with each person.

"We have a patient waiting," she said, halting any further pleasantries.

"You must be Dr. Ross," he stated in a cheerful tone.

"I am. And I'm ready to begin."

He pulled the stool forward with his foot and sat with one easy movement. He didn't seem to give her a further thought or show any concern that they had all been waiting for him.

Looking at the resident, he said, "Nicely done."

The young man who had been so flustered by her question earlier visibly relaxed.

Dr. Smith checked the anesthesia set-up and looked at her. "Ready when you are, Doc."

Once again his eyes caught her off guard. They reminded her of a spring lawn after a rain they were so green. She couldn't let him divert her attention from the patient. She never forgot her duty. "It's Dr. Ross," she corrected.

"Patient is ready, Dr. Ross." He said her name with a subtle twist that implied he might be making fun of her.

Hours later, as she began making the final sutures, Michelle was pleased the procedure had gone without a glitch. Her patient would live a long time and get to see his children grow up. Of that she was particularly proud.

Her father had died of a heart attack when she'd been twelve. They'd been out shopping for new school clothes, something she and her mother hadn't been able to agree on, when he'd clutched his chest and fallen to the floor of the mall. She could still hear the yells to call 911 and the running of feet, but mostly it was the sound of her own crying that she remembered.

At the funeral, as she'd sat beside her mother in the front pew of the church, she'd vowed that she'd help ensure that as many children as possible never experienced what she had. Her answer had been to study and work hard to become a heart surgeon. Her personal experience had taught her there was no room for humor here. This was serious business.

Michelle was in the process of closing when a soft hum, which began at the head of the table, distracted her. During the operation she hadn't looked at the new guy. Instead, she had given Mr. Martin her complete attention, even when her surgical resident had been making the opening incision. She glanced toward the head of the table to find Dr. Smith busily studying a monitor. The others around the table shifted restlessly. As far as she was concerned, the OR was no place for music. She wanted nothing to distract their concentration. She'd always seen to it that any noise remained at a minimum.

Tension as thick as the polar icecap and just as cold filled the space. She didn't miss the covert glances directed her way or towards the humming man.

The new guy looked up, his gaze meeting hers. The lines around his eyes crinkled. "You can join in if you wish."

The man was too disrupting to her OR. He had to go. She'd see that he wasn't assigned to her cases again. "How's the BP?" she asked in a crisp voice.

"Holding steady," he responded.

"Then let's finish this up and get him to CICU. And no more humming."

"Yes, ma'am."

He sounded like a mischievous fourth-grade boy who'd just gotten into trouble for pulling a girl's hair. Not very sincere and determined to do it again.

Ty rubbed the back of his neck to ease his strained muscles as he stepped out of the OR. Having traveled most of the night to arrive on time, he was tired. The car accident he'd assisted with at the city limits hadn't made the situation any better. He didn't like being late but it couldn't be helped. He'd been the first one on the scene and it had been necessary to stay. He took his oath as a doctor seriously.

Moving from one place to another didn't bother him. Heck, he'd done it all his life. That had been one of the problems. His parents had been follow-the-band, sixties wannabe hippies who'd had no business having children but they had. Joey, his younger brother by six years, had needed to stay in one place and have stable medical care but that hadn't been for his parents. They had sought help from this guru here, a herb there or "If we only lived in the desert climate" Joey could breathe better—get better. They had been wrong. Dead wrong.

His parents had said it was just how it was supposed to be. For him, Joey being alive and pestering him about wanting to follow him somewhere was how it should have been. Sitting on the ground in the middle of the moaning and groaning and incense-smoke rising, Ty had decided that he couldn't live like that any more.

He hadn't been able to accept that his parents had refused to take Joey to a traditional doctor. That he'd not done so himself. He'd let Joey die. That had been when he'd made the decision to leave the community and go and live with his grandparents.

He was intelligent enough and with excellent grades he'd decided to attended med school. Maybe by helping others he could make amends for what had happened to his brother. Just out of med school he'd been offered a job by a friend who had been starting up a company supplying fill-in doctors to hospitals. He'd taken it. As a supply doctor he'd gone wherever he'd been needed, normally only staying a few weeks in each place. He was familiar with that type of lifestyle. But right now all he wanted was to find the apartment he'd been promised and fall into bed.

"Dr.…"

"Ty Smith." He offered his hand to the woman surgeon he'd shared the OR with.

She was a looker. Shiny brown hair, rosebud lips, and creamy skin. Too bad she had such an abrasive personality. She was a stuffed shirt if he'd ever met one. He'd met a number of them over the years, but this one took the prize.

"We haven't been formally introduced. I go by Ty. What may I call you?"

"Dr. Ross."

Brr…a cold wind. Even the color of her eyes fit her attitude. Normally he was a sucker for a woman with clear blue pools for eyes, but not this time. He'd worked with others who hadn't been completely comfortable with his less than "buttoned-up" ways but she was the iciest to date. No warm welcome here.

"May I speak to you a moment? Privately," she said, in one of the primmest tones he'd ever heard.

"Certainly." He stepped towards a quiet corner and she followed.

Finding his best professional voice, he said, "Well…Dr. Ross, it is a pleasure to meet you. I look forward to working with you."

"That isn't going to happen again. I don't think we're right for each other. I expect my anesthesiologist to be punctual."

What had happened to put such a chip on this woman's shoulder?

"I'm sorry you feel that way. I wasn't intentionally late. And the resident was more than capable of putting the patient under. Our patient was in no danger. So, no harm. No foul. See you around, Dr. Ross." He wanted her to understand that just because he was new to the hospital it didn't mean he couldn't stand his ground.

She sputtered in her effort to respond.

Ty didn't wait to hear what she came up with. He turned and headed towards the locker room to change his clothes.

Two hours later, Ty sat behind the nurses' station in the CICU. He'd not managed to get away as soon as he'd hoped. Busy making notes on the latest patient's chart, he looked up to see Dr. Ross enter, along with a woman and a couple of teenagers. Dr. Ross led the way to Mr. Martin's bed.

The nurse sitting to his left muttered to the clerk on her right, "Well, I see the ice queen has arrived."

So he wasn't special. She was cool to everyone.

"Yeah, but the woman sure can dress," the clerk responded. "Too bad she isn't as nice as her clothes."

These women were jealous.

He couldn't blame them. Dr. Ross was a stately woman with regal bearing. Dressed in a form-fitting pale pink suit jacket and skirt that left no curve untouched, she was eye-catching. He sat up taller in the chair. From his vantage point he could see her from head to toe. He perused her trim calves, following their well-defined length until he stopped at heels that perfectly matched her suit. He'd bet his motorcycle that they were designer, hand-made shoes.

His gaze returned to her dark sable-colored hair. It was pulled back and held by a large silver clasp, which added to the woman-in-control look. She had certainly been hiding some fetching bends and turns under that surgical garb. Too bad that if you touched her with a wet finger it might stick because she was so cold.

She spoke with gracefully arcing hands, pointing and gesturing to pumps and machinery encircling the patient's bed. She must be explaining what they were and how they worked. To his surprise, occasionally she gave the small group a reassuring smile. So there was some warmth under that freezing exterior. She just didn't choose to share it with him.

She glanced toward the desk and for a second her gaze met his. Did he see anxiety in those eyes?

No, that would be the last emotion he'd attribute to Dr. Ross. Self-confidence oozed from her.

Sliding back the chair, Ty continued to watch the family

as they hovered around the patient. Dr. Ross no longer stood in the center of the group. She now blended into the background as she answered an occasional question. Standing, Ty came around the desk, planning to leave the unit. When she looked in his direction again he changed his angle and walked towards the group. Stopping beside her, he asked in hushed tones, "Is there a problem?"

She stiffened. "No. Why would you ask that?" she hissed.

Her eyes were on the family members, as if she was making sure they didn't overhear their conversation.

"Good. From my end he looks good. I don't see any reason the tube can't be pulled out tomorrow morning if he continues on this path."

"I appreciate—"

Her remark was interrupted by the woman he assumed was their patient's wife. She looked at him and then back at Dr. Ross.

The sound of Dr. Ross clearing her throat and the almost imperceptible hesitation didn't get past him but only because he was standing so close to her. She'd had no intention of introducing him but now if she didn't she would appear impolite.

Ty smiled at the woman and extended his hand. "Hi, I'm Ty Smith, I'm the anesthesiologist who worked with Dr. Ross on Mr. Martin's case."

"Thank you for taking such good care of my husband. Our family, my son and daughter…" the woman nodded toward the teens "…are grateful for everything you've done."

"I assure you your husband received the best of care. Dr. Ross is an excellent surgeon." He glanced at Dr. Ross. A flicker of skepticism entered her eyes. She must be wondering what he was up to. He'd meant what he'd said about her skills. Her abilities exceeded many he'd shared an OR with but praise appeared to make her uncomfortable.

"I'm sorry that this could only be a short visit," Dr. Ross said to the woman. "After shift change you may stay longer. Why don't you have dinner and then come back to visit?"

"We will. Come on, kids. Thanks, Dr. Ross. Dr. Smith, nice to meet you."

He nodded as the family passed him on their way to the door.

Dr. Ross moved to where the nurse stood and began discussing the patient.

Ty silently stepped away. Based on the conversation he and Dr. Ross had had after the surgery, she probably hadn't appreciated him coming over to meet the family. There had been a couple of seconds there when he'd seen past her cold exterior to some emotion he couldn't give a name to.

Minutes after leaving the CICU Michelle knocked on the chief of surgery's office door.

"Enter," she heard from the other side of the door.

She didn't always agree with Dr. Marshall's decisions or directives but she did think he was fair. He had been a mentor of sorts to her and more than once had gone to bat for her when there had been a problem between her and Administration. For the most part, though, he left her alone to do her job. He was old school but supportive. When he'd gone through medical school it had been almost entirely a man's profession so a female heart surgeon had made him feel a little uneasy.

She opened the door, stepped in and closed it behind her. The balding doctor leaned back in his chair, interest written on his face.

"To what do I owe this visit? I don't think you've been in my office for some time."

"Bob, you know I don't complain much."

He nodded, his eyes intently watching her.

"But I can't allow the new supply anesthesiologist to work in my OR again."

Dr. Marshall propped his arms on his desk, concern on his face. "Is the patient okay?"

"The patient is fine. Doing very well really."

He relaxed. "Then what's the problem? Smith, I think his name is, came highly recommended. Good CV. Excellent, actually."

"I cannot have the man showing up late for procedures."

Bob looked at her incredulously. "Why did he show up late?"

"I don't know. He didn't say."

"Did you ask him?"

"No. I didn't. I just need the people on my team to be on time."

"If that is the only fault you can find I think you should ask him why. I know you run a tight ship but we are all late sometimes."

"I'm not."

Bob released an exaggerated huff. "I know you're not. It might be good if you were occasionally." He said the last few words so quietly that she almost missed them. "Michelle, I think you're overreacting a bit. We're short an anesthesiologist and I can't shift everyone around just to suit you. Smith is more than qualified in cardiothoracic surgery. Unless he has or is doing something to harm a patient, you're just going to have to find a way to work with him."

"But—"

"Michelle, I know you're a driven physician. I can appreciate that but I think you can work this out without involving me. Smith is only here for six weeks. Surely you can handle working with him that long."

His desk phone rang and his hand hovered over the receiver. "Let me know if there's an issue involving a patient." He picked up the phone and said, "Hello?"

She'd been dismissed. Opening the door, Michelle stepped out into the hall and closed it behind her.

With no support, she was left no choice but to get along with the new guy. How was she going to manage that? Everything about him rubbed her the wrong way.

Ty stepped out into the warm, damp May evening, glad to head home or at least to the place he'd call home for the next few weeks. He'd never known a real brick-and-mortar house until he'd been sixteen and had left his mother and father to go and live with his grandparents.

He shoved a hand through his hair and rolled his neck one way and then the other to get the kinks out. It had taken him longer than he'd anticipated but he'd finished introducing himself to the next day's OR patients before he'd left the hospital.

Hooking his black leather bomber jacket on his index finger, he slung it over his shoulder and started in the direction of his motorcycle. A woman dressed in what he could see was a trim-fitting skirt was walking some distance ahead.

In the dim light he couldn't make out the color of her hair or clothes but as a red-blooded man he couldn't help but notice the provocative sway of her hips as she walked in and out of the shadows. She moved as if she was a model strutting on a runway in Paris. It was a sexy stride if he'd ever seen one. He wouldn't mind making the woman's acquaintance while he was here. Maybe she worked in one of the business departments in the hospital. He'd have to make a few inquiries in the morning.

With a feeling of disappointment he watched her step

between two parked cars, leaving only her head visible. A minute later Ty approached the back of what must be her car. She glanced at him. The male anticipation he'd developed and fostered while watching her walk suddenly received an icy shower.

"Dr. Ross!" He couldn't have contained his astonishment if he'd tried. That amazingly hot strut belonged to the ice queen.

Her eyes widened in disbelief. The key fob she held fell to the ground.

"Dr. Smith. Are you looking for me?" Her voice sounded a little high.

He'd certainly been looking *at* her, admiring her even.

She kneeled gracefully to retrieve her keys. "Is something wrong with our patient?"

"As far as I know, the patient is fine."

"Then why are you here?"

"This is a public parking lot. My bike is just over there." He pointed past her.

She glanced over her shoulder in the direction he indicated. "You ride a motorcycle?" Her voice was both shocked and accusatory. "They're so dangerous."

"Ever been on one?"

"No!"

"Try it. You might like it."

He looked down at her trim ankles balanced on spiky high heels. "Of course, that outfit might draw attention if you did. You'd show so much thigh that you might be stopped for being a traffic hazard." He chuckled.

His grin grew when her head dipped in what could only be described as embarrassment. Unless he was mistaken, her cheeks were the same rosy pink he remembered her shoes as being. Something about her reaction made him believe that she wasn't used to receiving compliments from men. That barbed-wire attitude of hers probably kept her from getting many. She was certainly attractive enough to receive them.

"I have no interest in being a traffic hazard." She opened the door of the car, slid in and slammed the door between them.

She might not want to be one but the woman certainly had everything required.

Ty moved on through the lot. It was necessary for her to pass him to leave. As she drove by her gaze found his and held for a second of awareness before she sped up and was gone.

Yes, the next few weeks would unquestionably be interesting.

Michelle pulled into the drive of her mother's simple red-brick suburban home. It was located in a neighborhood where all the houses along the street looked similar. The curtains of the living-room window fluttered and her mother's face appeared. Getting out of the car, Michelle opened the back passenger door and removed two plastic bags of groceries.

She headed for the front door. Seconds before she reached it the door opened. "Mom, you didn't need to get up. I could have let myself in."

Her tall but frail-looking mother, with a dusting of gray in her hair, smiled. "I know, dear, but you have your hands full."

"And the doctor said to take it easy for a while."

"I have been. You worry too much. What do doctors know anyway?" Her smile grew.

Michelle returned her grin. It was a running joke between them. Her mother was very proud of Michelle and told her so often. As the only parent Michelle had left, she worried about her mother, unable to stand the thought of losing her in both body and spirit. Then she would be alone in the world.

"Mom, why don't you come and sit in the kitchen while I put these groceries away and see about getting us some supper?"

"I'd like that. You can tell me about your day. You work too hard, you know. Doing surgery all day and then coming here to see about me."

That was also a continuing argument between them. One that neither one of them seemed to ever win.

Her mother followed Michelle along the familiar hallway to the small but cozy kitchen. This was Michelle's favorite room in the house. It was where she remembered her father best. Even years after his death she and her mother still didn't sit in what was considered "his chair".

As Michelle prepared the simple meal, her mother chatted about the book she was reading and the neighborhood children who had stopped by to sell her cookies. Michelle felt bad that her mother had to spend so much time alone. She'd been such an active woman until the cancer had been discovered. Her recovery was coming along well but Michelle worried that her mother had lost hope. Worse, Michelle feared *she* might have. She fixed hearts. Cancer wasn't her department. She had no control here and she was having a difficult time dealing with that fact.

With all those years of medical school and all her surgical skills, she was no more capable of saving her mother than the guy down at the gas station. Cancer had a way of leveling the playing field. No one was more likely to live than another. The only thing anyone really shared was hope. That knowledge not only made her angry but it made her feel desperate.

Michelle placed a plate in front of her mother and another at her own lifelong place. Filling their glasses with iced tea, she set them on the table and took her chair.

"So, how was your day? Anything special happen?" her mother asked, as she poked at the roast chicken in front of her.

Suddenly the broad-shouldered, unorthodox anesthesiologist with the dark unruly hair flashed into her mind. Of all the people to be the highlight of her day.

"No, nothing special. My surgery cases went well, which always makes it a good day."

"You know you really should go out some."

Michelle let out an exasperated breath. She changed lives through surgery for the better almost daily and some days saved a life that would soon be lost. Despite that, her mother was still only interested in her dating. No matter how old or successful she became, her mother wanted her to find someone special.

Michelle wasn't against the idea. The right person just hadn't come along. She had to admit that it would be nice to have a man in her life. A serious man who could understand her. It would be wonderful to have a marriage like her mom and dad's had been.

"Michelle, you have no fun in your life. You worked too hard. When you're not at the hospital you spend your evenings here, visiting me. You need to live a little."

This had become an almost daily conversation. "Mom, I love spending time with you."

"Aren't there any young men working at that hospital you might like?"

The aggravating anesthesiologist's twinkling eyes popped into her mind. "None that I'd ever be interested in."

Ty opened the door to the nondescript furnished apartment. His surroundings didn't bother him. After years of living in other spaces like it, he was more than used to this type of place. At least there would be a roof over his head, which was more than he could say about his childhood.

Pushing the large brown box with his name on it inside with his foot, he closed the door behind him. A cardboard box had become his suitcase of choice. His guitar should be delivered tomorrow. He'd arranged to have it shipped to the hospital so that someone would be around to sign for it and put it in a safe place. Sometimes he traveled with it on the bike but he didn't like to. It was one of the few things he'd taken with him when he'd left his parents.

He dropped his helmet on the chair closest to the door and headed for the kitchen. He placed the sack holding the package of gourmet coffee on the counter then looked for the coffeemaker. Great. The machine was a good one. It had been his only request.

Doctors to Go, the service he worked for and was a fifty percent owner of, had seen that he had one. Ty had been working for the company a year when his friend had offered Ty part of the business. Owning nothing but a motorcycle and the clothes on his back, he'd saved his paychecks. There had also been the small amount he'd inherited when his grandfather had died, so he'd had the funds to invest.

His partner ran the show and Ty stayed in the background as a very silent partner. No boardrooms or conference calls for him. One of the ideals that his grandfather had drummed into him early after he moved in with his grandparents had been to plan for the future. Something his parents would have never considered. He'd done as his grandfather had suggested, but he loved working with people so he still continued to practice medicine.

He didn't generally frequent grocery stores when he moved to a new city. Instead, he chose to take most of his meals at the hospital. Otherwise he asked around about local mom-and-pop places that served good down-home cooking. Ty had already been given a few names of places from a couple of the surgery team members. He'd try one of the restaurants on his day off.

Ty prepared and set the coffeemaker to start percolating at five a.m., before he headed for the shower. Stripping off and turning the water on, he stepped under the shower head. Not all the places he'd stayed had had great showers but having one available was more than he'd had growing up. Rain barrels and creeks just didn't compare to a hot spray with excellent water pressure.

A muffled ring came from the clothes he'd dropped on the floor. He pushed the shower curtain back, picked up his discarded jeans and dug into the pocket for his phone. His partner had texted earlier that he would be calling about an issue with the business.

"Smith here. Let me call you right back. I'm in the shower."

"Uh, Dr. Smith. It's Dr. Ross," came a soft, stilted voice.

"Who?"

"Dr. Ross." Emphasis and impatience surrounded the enunciation of the name.

"Oh, Michelle. I thought you were someone else."

"Obviously."

He could just see her nose turning up as she said the word. The woman was far too stuffy. "How can I help you, Michelle?" He did like the sound of her name. It suited her.

"Our case has been moved up to first thing in the morning."

He held the phone with two fingers to keep water from running over it. "I thought that the anesthesia department clerk made these calls."

"Normally she does, but I was called and couldn't get her, so I'm calling."

If nothing else, she was thorough. He couldn't fault that. It no doubt made her a good doctor. "How did you get my number?"

"I make it a point to have the numbers of everyone on my team."

"I see." He let the words drag out for emphasis. "You have it for no other reason?"

"No. There is no other. I'll see you at seven sharp."

He chuckled at her haughty tone. It sounded as if she were saying the words through a clenched jaw. He couldn't help taunting her. She seemed like the kind of person who always rose to the bait. If only he could see her face.

"I'll be there. Now, if you don't mind I'll finish my shower."

"Oh. Uh…sure. Bye."

So the frosty woman could be rattled. Stepping back into the shower, he thought he might have to do that more often. But what had him giving the stiff, buttoned-up woman even a second thought? She certainly wasn't his type. Everything about her screamed of stability.

He'd been accused on more than one occasion of being the love-them-and-leave-them type. No woman got promises or commitments from him. That way he didn't hurt them. Others could plant roots but they weren't for him.

There had been a couple of women he'd dated who had made noises about him settling down. When that had happened it hadn't taken him long until he'd been on his way to the next hospital in the next town. He wasn't the type of person someone should depend on. When the going got tough he'd only let them down.

He liked women who enjoyed life, laughed, had fun and that was all they were interested in from the relationship. Michelle seemed far too serious about everything. She didn't strike him as a short but enjoyable affair type of woman, even if he had been interested in having one with her. Which he wasn't.

Enough about her. He needed some rest, especially if he was going to have to face her early in the morning and be on his best behavior. Which he wasn't sure he could do.

He turned off the water and stepped out of the shower. Snatching a towel off the rack, he dried off. Thank goodness he'd requested maid service to start yesterday. Minutes later, naked, he slipped between cool sheets.

Dr. Ross's strut across the parking lot came to mind. His weeks in Raleigh might be far more fascinating than he'd anticipated.

CHAPTER TWO

EARLY THE NEXT morning, Michelle tapped lightly on the door of her first case for the day.

Shawn Russell. Twenty years old. His procedure would be difficult. As a congenital heart patient he'd grown up in the hospital system and would never really leave it. Shawn was quite unhappy with the prospect of having surgery again. This time he needed to have the heart valve he'd outgrown replaced. Not a demanding surgery in most patients but in those with multiple surgeries the development of scar tissue added a degree of difficulty.

At the sound of "Come in", Michelle pushed the door open further. The room was filled with people, undoubtedly family and friends. Dr. Smith stood beside Shawn's bed with his back to her. Having only known him a day, she still recognized his dark hair and broad back.

He glanced around. "Good morning, Dr. Ross. We were just talking about you," he said with a grin.

Michelle raised an uncertain brow. Never a fan of people discussing her, she wasn't sure she was happy with what Dr. Smith might have been saying.

More than once she'd heard the whispers after she'd gone by the nurses' desk. But instead of those negative thoughts his grin brought back memories of their conversation the evening before when he'd announced unabashedly that he was in the shower. He'd been trying to get a reaction out of her. She planned to see he didn't get one.

"I was checking on Shawn to see if he had any questions for me before he goes into the OR," Dr. Smith offered.

She nodded. "Good."

Dr. Smith pushed his dark hair back away from his face. There was nothing conservative about its length or cut. Worn long and being wavy and thick, it curled behind his ears. It was the kind of hair that women envied. He certainly didn't meet what she considered the standard dress code.

"Did you know that Shawn is a master gamer?"

What was he talking about? "No, I didn't. That's great." She looked at Shawn. "Do you have any questions about the surgery?"

The far-too-thin young man shook his head. "I think my mother does."

"I'll go and let Dr. Ross speak to your parents. I'll see you in the OR in a few minutes. The nurse will give you something to make you happy." Dr. Smith grinned. "Don't get too used to it because you don't get to carry any of it home." He put out his fist and Shawn butted his against it. "Later, man. Remember you promised me a game."

"Sure, Dr. Smith."

"Make it Ty, man. See you soon."

Shawn nodded and gave him a small smile. For the first time since she'd met Shawn he didn't look terrified. She and Dr. Smith might have gotten off on the wrong foot but she had to give him kudos for making patients feel comfortable. She would like to be that easy with people but it wasn't her strong suit.

Half an hour later Michelle entered the OR prep area. Dr. Smith stood at the scrub sink along with three of the OR nurses. The group was chattering non-stop. Dr. Smith seemed to be the ringleader, interjecting a random comment which would bring on a burst of laughter from the women around him.

For the first time Michelle felt like an outsider. She couldn't remember ever feeling that way so intensely before, or caring. She had no idea how to join their conversation. Worse, she couldn't understand why all of a sudden she wanted to. What would it be like to belong? To know what was happening in the staff's lives, for them to know what was happening in hers? Could she ever have that type of relationship with her coworkers? With anyone?

She remembered having friends over to spend the night as a kid. After her father had died that had become less frequent. She'd found out pretty quickly that her friends hadn't felt comfortable with her any longer. The sadness she'd felt over the loss of her beloved father had been far too much for them. She'd started spending more and more time at home, reading and studying. It had been easier than trying to pretend to be having a good time with people who didn't understand.

Her father was gone and her friends had slowly left also. Michelle's mother had encouraged her to go out to football games, to the prom, but to Michelle all those things had seemed silly. She'd also hated to leave her mother alone. They'd become a team. As the years had gone by Michelle had lost most of her small-talk skills, choosing to focus on medicine instead of a social life. Her mother, school and then her job had taken all her time, leaving little to devote to building outside relationships. There had been a few men who had shown her attention. Most had only been interested in her for her looks. Few had appreciated her intellect. They hadn't stayed around long.

A second later another nurse joined the group. Dr. Smith did have a way of drawing not only women to him but men as well. People liked him. She had to admit she was as aware of the man as the rest of them. She just refused to let it show, had more command over her reactions.

Unable to wait any longer to scrub in so that she could begin her procedure on time, she stepped towards the sink when a spot became available. Just as she took her place, the group erupted in laughter.

Dr. Smith turned, almost bumping into her. "Hey, Michelle."

Out of the corner of her eye she noticed the other women drifting away. She placed a foot on the pedal to start the water. "Hi," she said, concentrating on washing.

"We were just talking about getting together tonight at a bar downtown. I've been asked to fill in as part of the surgeons' band."

"You play?"

"Don't sound so surprised. I play a mean guitar. I think that's why Schwartz requested me to take his place. More for my guitar skills than my medical ones."

"I didn't know Dr. Schwartz played in the band."

Had he said he wasn't surprised? She refused to let him make her feel like she didn't belong. "No, it doesn't surprise me that you play guitar. I was just making conversation."

"Interesting. You don't strike me as someone who makes small talk." Was he trying to needle her on purpose?

"I don't believe you know me well enough to know what I do."

He pressed his lips together and nodded as if in deep thought. "You're right. Maybe we should try to change that."

Michelle looked at him. Where was this going?

"A group of us are getting together after the band plays on Saturday night. Why don't you join us then? Practice that small talk."

"I'm busy."

"Well, if your plans change we're going to be at Buster's. Wherever that is."

"It's right in the central part of the old city."

"A surgeon and a tour guide. Two for one," he said with a grin.

She smirked at him. "My father used to take me there for burgers when I was a kid." Why was she telling him this?

"Really, your father took you to a bar?" His tone implied he was teasing.

She made an exasperated noise. "My father would never have taken me to a bar."

Dr. Smith chuckled. The man was baiting her again. Wasn't he ever serious?

"It wasn't a bar then. Just a grill. Mr. Roberts owned the place and was a friend of my father's. I don't know what it's like now, but it was once a place with brick walls and had these old wooden tables."

"You haven't been lately?"

"Not since I was a child."

"Why not?"

"I just hadn't thought about going." That wasn't true. It had been her and her father's special place. The memories were just too strong there. They made her miss her father more.

"Maybe it's time to try it again."

She finished scrubbing her nails. "I don't think so."

"Well, I hope you change your mind. It could be fun. If they still have burgers, I'll buy you one," he said, passing her on his way toward the OR.

A few minutes later she entered behind him. The team was talking and softly laughing at something Ty must have said. He seemed to always be saying something outrageous. She couldn't blame her team for reacting. She'd smiled more since she'd met him than she had in a long time, but her nerves had been on edge just as often.

Everyone quieted down and became attentive when she joined them. "Are we ready to begin? By the way, it's nice to see you here ahead of me, Dr. Smith." Her voice carried a teasing tone. She didn't tease. What was happening to her?

"Glad to be here. This time I wasn't stuck helping out at a car accident." His gaze caught and held hers.

He'd made his point. It figured he'd have a good reason that would make her feel bad about her actions the day before. "Understandable. I hope everyone was okay."

"Everyone was fine. I'm ready to begin when you are, Michelle." His eyes twinkled when he said her name.

Her jaw tightened beneath her mask. Demanding that the aggravating man call her by her formal name in the OR was a battle she didn't think she could win. She'd let it go unless it happened at an improper time, like in front of a patient.

She glanced around to find all eyes on her. Their faces were covered but she had a sense that their mouths had dropped open. She imagined they were following the interaction between her and Ty with great interest.

Unwilling to let the team know he'd gotten a reaction out of her, she cleared her throat and said in her most efficient tone, "Let's begin."

Later, Ty sat behind the nurses' station on the heart floor, reviewing patient charts before his pre-op visits. He and Michelle would share three cases the next day. Finished with the chart he'd been reviewing, he closed it as the clip-clip of heels tapping tiles drew his attention. He looked up to see Michelle coming towards him. Her hair was pulled tight behind her head and she was dressed in soft gray pants with a silky pale pink blouse. Over that she wore a finely pressed lab jacket. There wasn't a wrinkle on it and he'd bet a weeks' pay it was starched. Her high heels were the same dove-gray as her pants except for the tips of the toes, which were hot pink.

Disappointment filled him over missing a view of her legs. She had exceptionally fine legs.

For such a strong-willed woman she sure wore feminine colors. This outfit was just as tailored as yesterday's, letting no one mistake her as anything other than a female. She was a paradox. All hard edges in manner and all soft and sensual curves in looks. Which was the truer Michelle? He'd like to know.

She glanced in his direction. When he smiled she quickly looked away and continued towards the room of one of her cases. He returned his attention to the computer screen and the chart of his next patient.

Opening another file, he looked up to see the nurse assigned to Shawn stamping toward the desk. Her lips were clamped into a tight, thin line. She stopped in front of the nurse sitting two chairs down from him. Through clenched teeth she hissed, "Abby, please watch my patient for a few minutes. The ice queen is riding her broom again."

The nurse she spoke to looked none too happy but she said, "Okay. But don't be long. I don't want to be in her line of fire either."

"I just need to blow off some steam for a minute. At least she has moved on to poor Robin's patient."

Ty saw Michelle approaching, but the two nurses had not. He didn't miss the look of glass-shard pain in Michelle's eyes before she blinked and her face became an unemotional mask. He had no doubt she'd heard every word. It had hurt her. By the look in her eyes—deeply.

"Excuse me, if you are not too busy, could you get me a number where I can reach Shawn's family?"

The first nurse wheeled about, shock covering her face. "Uh, yes, yes, ma'am. I have it in the chart."

The nurse must have forgotten about blowing off steam because she hurried to pull up the chart on one of the computers behind the desk.

Ty focused his attention on Michelle but she didn't even glance at him.

The nurse handed a slip of paper to Michelle.

"Thank you," she said stiffly.

She walked off. For once Ty felt sorry for her.

Not long afterwards, Ty started his pre-op rounds, visiting the patients on the next day's surgery schedule. One of them was running a fever. He'd have to speak to Michelle about postponing surgery at least a day.

He could call her but after what had happened earlier he felt compelled to talk to her personally. Just for a second when she'd turned to leave he'd seen a crack in her mask, a deep sadness. He asked a nurse where to find her office. While he walked down the long hall in that direction, he told himself that he would be concerned about anyone who might have had their feelings hurt so publicly. It had nothing to do with Michelle in particular. He made a point not to get involved on a personal level. So why had her reaction gotten to him?

Stopping at the woodgrained door with her name on a plate beside it, he tapped. Seconds later a subdued, "Come in," reached his ears.

Opening the door, he stepped in. The blast of color before him made him jolt to a stop. The walls of Michelle's office were a warm yellow but what really got his attention was the huge bright red poppy painting hanging behind Michelle's head. That, he hadn't expected. The woman just got more interesting all the time. Her desk was the traditional hospital style but on it were modern office supplies, not typical business issue. There were two bright ultra-modern chairs covered in a fabric that coordinated with the painting and the color of the walls in front of her desk. This was obviously her haven.

Michelle's eyes widened when she saw him. They were bloodshot, pink-rimmed. His gut squeezed. She'd been crying. She wouldn't be happy he'd noticed either. He moved toward her desk.

"What can I help you with, Dr. Smith?" Her flat tone said she wanted to get rid of him as quickly as possible.

"Please make it Ty."

With a sound of annoyance she said, "Is there a problem…Ty?"

Michelle said his name as if it was painful. She still resisted any relationship that being on a first-name basis implied.

"Mr. Marcus has spiked a fever." He glanced down at the garbage can sitting beside her desk. Inside were Cellophane wrappers and white paper squares. She'd been eating chocolate cake rolls, no doubt feeding her emotions. So the woman was undeniably human.

When his gaze came back up it was seconds before hers met his. It quickly fluttered away again.

"I'm sorry you overheard them." He didn't take his eyes off her.

She didn't question to what he referred. Instead, she sat straighter and said, "We need to start Mr. Marcus on prophylactic antibiotics and postpone his surgery until the day after tomorrow."

"I agree."

"Is there anything further?" Michelle shifted some papers on her desk that he suspected she really hadn't been working on. She was trying to get him to leave without coming out and saying it. Still, he couldn't bring himself to just forget that she'd been crying before he'd entered the office. Despite her less than warm demeanor toward him, he wanted to help her. He wanted to peel away the layers and find out what made the woman tick.

"I can *see* that you've already had dessert but I was wondering if you might like to grab a meal with me. I heard there is a place not far from here that serves a great roast-beef platter."

She looked up at him as if he had snakes in his hair. "No, thank you. I have work to do."

"Then maybe another time."

"I don't think so."

He leaned his hip against her desk and looked down at where she sat. She glared at him pointedly.

"What sticks in your craw about me? Or is it you can't stand anyone?" He raised a hand to stop her from interrupting. "It's none of my business, and you can pretend differently, but I know your feelings were hurt a while ago. All you have to do is show them that you're human. Smile, ask about their families. Win them over a little."

Michelle stood with a jerk. Placing both hands on the edge of her desk, she leaned towards him. "You think I don't know what the staff thinks about me? It isn't my job to be friends with them. My patients' care comes first and foremost. How dare you come in and try to tell me how to run my life? I don't need some flit-in and flit-out doctor to tell me how I need to interact with the nurses."

A slow grinned came to his lips. He'd expected her righteous indignation. "I'm just saying you can catch more flies with honey than you can with vinegar."

She sputtered her disgust as he turned to leave.

At two in the morning Michelle pushed open the door of the physicians' entrance to the hospital and stepped out into the night. Her team had been called in to handle an emergency. Thankfully she didn't do too much surgery in the early hours of the morning. A hospital took on an other-world feeling late at night. Spooky yet peaceful.

She was so tired she hadn't bothered to change out of her scrubs. Something that rarely happened. Her hair was still pulled back and secured by a rubber band, producing a small ponytail that brushed her neck. Holding her small purse in her hand, she was taking her first step towards her car when the door behind her opened. She jumped. Glancing back, she saw Ty. In one way it was a relief that it wasn't someone with nefarious ideas; in another he wasn't her favorite person.

This was the first time outside the OR she'd seen him since their conversation, turned blow-out on her part, hours earlier. She had cooled off but she still didn't know why he thought he had the right to offer her advice. Especially the unsolicited kind.

She started walking.

"Nice work in there, Michelle," he called.

She stopped and looked back at him. The lighting in the parking area wasn't dim enough to disguise his drained stance. For once he wasn't being upbeat and bubbly. He seemed as tired as she was. He'd changed out of his scrubs and now wore a light-colored T-shirt that fit his muscular shoulders far too tightly for her not to notice. A pair of baggy cargo shorts and sandals finished off his outfit.

On anyone else those clothes might have looked like those of a bum, but on Ty they added to his bad-boy sex appeal. His hair was no longer tied back, like he'd worn it under his surgery cap. Instead, it looked as if he'd pushed his hands through it and let it go. He looked untamed and wild.

"Whew, this early-morning stuff isn't as easy as it used

to be in med school. Who I'm I trying to kid? It wasn't easy then." He came to stand beside her.

Did he think that she was going to act as if nothing had happened between them? "No, it wasn't." She started walking again.

"Michelle, wait."

She stopped and turned again. "Why? So you can tell me what I need to do?"

"Ooh, so the woman can carry a grudge."

"I'm not carrying a grudge! I just don't like people butting into my business."

"Maybe you just don't like people," he said in an even tone.

She stepped toward him. "I do like people."

"Then prove it."

"Prove it?" What was he talking about?

"Yeah. Say one nice thing about me."

She let out a dry chuckle.

He tilted his head and studied her. "You know, I think that's the first time I've heard you approach anything near a laugh."

"I laugh."

"When? When no one is around?" he asked, moving passed her.

"Are you trying to start an argument?"

He paused this time. "No, I was trying to give you a compliment. Maybe flirt with you a little."

"I don't want you flirting with me."

"Why not?"

She pinned him with a look. Even in the faint light she could see his wicked grin. She had no doubt that his eyes were twinkling. "Because nothing about you says you're serious about anything."

"That's not true. I'm always serious about caring for my patients."

"You know what I mean. All the nurses flock to you. I've even seen women from different departments come to the floor who have never been there before to see or hopefully be seen by Ty Smith."

"Hey, you can't fault me for that."

He was right, but she wasn't becoming one of his groupies. "Why don't you make their day by flirting with them and leave me alone?"

"Because you doth protest too much. You're far too much fun to tease. I can always count on a pretty blush and a sharp rebuttal. You challenge my mind."

"Humph." She started walking toward her car. "So you've decided I'm going to be your entertainment while you're in town. I'm not flattered."

He fell into step beside her. "The way you say it doesn't make it sound too nice. Like I'm pulling wings off butterflies. Has it ever occurred to you that I might be attracted to you?"

"No."

"No." He voice held total disbelief. "You don't think I could be attracted to you or, no, you don't think I'm attracted to you?"

"Both."

"My, you're mighty cynical for such a beautiful and intelligent woman."

She put her hands on her hips and really looked at him. "Ty, I'm no one's good-time girl. I already have enough worries, without adding you to my list."

"Don't you ever just want to have a good time?"

"I don't have time for a good time." She clicked the fob to unlock her car then opened the door.

"Hey, you never said what you like about me."

She slipped under the wheel. "Goodnight, Ty." And closed the door.

Looking into the rear-view window, she saw him saunter over to where a motorcycle was parked. He had a loose-hipped walk that belied his size. Letting him get into her head wasn't a good idea.

She stuck her key into the ignition and turned it. A clicking noise was all that happened. She tried it again. The engine refused to start.

The zoom of a motorcycle being turned off made her look into the mirror. Ty was getting off his bike and putting the kickstand down. She opened the car door. "The battery is dead."

He stepped closer. "You've had trouble with it before?"

"Yeah. It was a little slow to start when I headed here. I was going to have it seen to tomorrow."

"Well, it looks like you're going to need a ride home."

She searched for her phone. "I'll call a taxi."

"I'll give you a lift."

"I don't think so. I'll just wait here for a taxi."

"Be realistic, Michelle. How long do you think it will take for a taxi to show up at this hour? And you're sure as heck not going to sit in a dark parking lot and wait."

"I can go inside."

"Come on. Let me give you a drive home. I'll ride slowly. No fancy moves."

Still unsure, she was exhausted and the thought of having to wait another hour or longer to head home wasn't appealing. She grabbed her purse as she climbed out of the car. "Okay, but no nonsense. I saw one too many motorcycle victims when I was doing my ER rotation."

"I promise, only one wheelie."

"What?" She stepped back, planning to refuse to get on.

"Kidding. Just kidding."

* * *

Ty was pleased he hadn't had to do a more convincing job of selling Michelle on the idea of riding on his bike. Most women he'd known had seemed to be fascinated by the prospect. It was part of his mystique. For him, it was cheap and easy transportation. Apparently Michelle wasn't impressed one way or another with his air of mystery. For some reason he wished she was, but was glad she wasn't. He never dipped below the surface of his emotions and he didn't want anyone else to do it either.

He unlocked the seat compartment, pulled out a spare helmet and offered it to her. His hand remained suspended in mid-air for a moment before she took it. She made no further movement.

"You do know that you have to put it on to ride? It's the law."

She look around as if there might be a state trooper watching.

He shoved his hair back, preparing to slip on his own helmet. Michelle remained rooted to the spot as if she couldn't make up her mind whether or not this was a good idea. "Are you coming or not?" Again she scanned the parking lot like she was hoping for any other option. Taking a deep breath, she put the helmet on her head. It wouldn't go into place because of her hair.

"Here, let me help you." He lifted the helmet off her head and reached around to release her hair. He could feel her breath on his neck.

She bent her torso away from him. "What're you doing?"

"Trying to get your head into this helmet. Your hair is stopping it from going on."

"Oh."

"What did you think I was doing? Making a play for you?"

"No."

"Yes, you did." He looked her straight in the eyes, wishing the streetlights were brighter. "If and when I make a play for you, you won't need to question what I'm doing. It will be perfectly clear." With great satisfaction he watched her throat bob up and down. "Now I'm tired and I'm hungry. If you would like me to take you home you're going to have to let me help you with the helmet. Of course, I can also escort you to the lobby so you can wait for a taxi there. Either way, I'd like to get a move on."

She pulled the rubber band out of her hair and plopped the helmet down on her head.

So the ice queen responded to authority.

"I'm going to fix the chin strap now," he said in an exaggerated voice, as if speaking to a child.

"Stop making fun of me. I've never been on a motorcycle before."

She gave him such a pointed look of defiance that he wanted to take off the helmet and kiss her.

"I'm still not sure you're the one I want to take my first ride with."

He chuckled as he picked up his helmet from the handlebars. "I promise it will be a ride to remember." After slipping on his helmet, he said, "Hand me your purse. I'll put it under the seat."

Michelle did so, after only a moment of hesitation. Storing the purse and closing the seat, he then threw a leg over the bike, pushed the kickstand up and revved the engine. The bike roared to life. He looked back over his shoulder. "By the definition of ride, you have to get on first."

She lifted a leg over the seat. He had the sense that she was making every effort not to touch him. When she tottered, a hand gripped his shoulder then was gone, only to return just as quickly. He'd watched those long, delicate fingers do meticulous surgery. Now he felt their strength. What would it be like to have her want to touch him all over?

She pulled her hands away again as she settled on the bike.

"You need to move up close and hang on or you'll fall off the back."

Michelle shifted closer but acted as if she was making sure her legs didn't touch his. She held a fistful of shirt in each hand, instead of wrapping her hands around his waist.

"Ready?"

She nodded.

"Okay. Here we go." He clicked the bike into gear, let off the hand clutch and the bike moved across the lot. Less than five seconds later Michelle's arms had his waist in a death grip. Her thighs squeezed his where they met, and her face and chest were plastered to his back.

His manhood rose in response. He sucked in a breath. This had been such a bad idea on so many levels. The woman was terrified and he was turned on.

He took his hand off the handlebars long enough to pat her knee. "You're doing great."

As he turned right out of the parking lot, he realized he had no idea where she lived. He'd spent so much time trying to convince her to get on the bike that he'd forgotten to ask for directions. "Which way is your house?" he called over his shoulder.

There was no answer.

"Point in the direction I need to go."

Again he heard nothing.

"Michelle, we can't just drive around all night. You have to tell me where you live."

She lifted one finger against his stomach and pointed ahead.

"I'm going the right way?"

She nodded against his back.

It was far too late for word games. He needed directions and she seemed incapable of giving them. Just up the street was the bright sign of an all-night diner. He was hungry and because they had done surgery tonight they wouldn't be required to be at the hospital until the day after tomorrow. They had time to stop.

He pulled into the parking lot and under the glaring lights. As he eased the bike to a stop, Michelle's grip on him slackened. He missed her warm, soft breasts pressed tightly against him. As if she realized she was still holding onto him, her arms fell away and she pushed back on the seat.

"What're we doing here?"

"Getting some breakfast."

"I want to go home."

"In that case, you're going to have to tell me how to get there. Which you couldn't do on the bike. So while you give me directions, I'm going to get some eggs and bacon. Care to join me?"

Once again she looked unsure. It always caught him by surprise because she was so formidable in the OR. Maybe the overconfident woman wasn't so self-assured after all.

"I am kind of hungry."

She put one foot on the ground and grabbed his shoulder as she brought the other over. He climbed off. Michelle was already in the process of removing her helmet. When she got it off he took it from her and laid it beside his on the seat.

The diner looked like it had been around forever. It was a fifties-type place with silver siding, orange bench seats, and Formica tabletops. He loved the place already.

He held the door open for Michelle. Her hair was mussed and she still wore green scrubs but that didn't detract from her stately walk or good looks. She could have been a conquering queen by the way she held herself. What made her even more eye-catching was that it was a natural part of who she was, nothing conceited about it.

There were only a handful of people in the place but all eyes turned to her. She ignored them and scooted into the first booth she came to. Ty moved in across from her.

"I thought you might like to sit where you can see your bike."

"Good plan."

"How long have you been riding?" she asked as she picked up a plastic-covered menu.

"Since I was about sixteen."

"That young?" Her eyes widened.

"Yeah. I had to have a way to get to and from school."

She looked up over the menu. "Your parents let you have a motorcycle at that age?"

"No, my grandfather did." Whoa, she'd already gotten more personal information out of him than most people did. Usually he steered the conversation away from himself but Michelle wasn't giving him a chance to as she shot off another question.

"How did your parents feel about that?"

"They didn't care."

She looked down at the double-sided card in her hand and mumbled, "I sure would have."

"They weren't around to care." Bitterness filled his voice but, then, it always did when he spoke about his parents. Which he rarely did.

Thankfully the server approached their table. She was in her mid-forties, slightly overweight and had her thin hair tied back in a ponytail. "What you have?"

"Hi, there. I'll have the breakfast platter. Eggs over easy."

When the woman looked at her, Michelle said, "And I'd like the mile-high pancakes."

Ty smiled up at the server. "And a large pot of fresh coffee."

The woman smiled. "Coming up."

"You're amazing. That woman looked so sour when she came over to take our order and she leaves smiling because she has spoken to you."

"Why, thank you. Nothing but the power of Ty."

"The power of Ty, uh? Ty is a nickname, isn't it? I'd guess your full name is Tyrone."

Michelle was being unusually chatty. Maybe it was the late hour, maybe she was hungry or maybe it was the fact she was stuck with him. Normally he would have complained about all the personal questions but he found he didn't want to give her a reason to stop. It was good and bad. He liked her attention too much and she was uncovering his secrets.

"I was named after Tyrone, Georgia."

"Why after a town?"

"Because my parents were passing through it when my mother went into labor. You sure are full of questions."

"It's interesting. I've never known anyone named after a town. So you were born in Tyrone."

Ty hesitated a moment before he said more. He'd told maybe three other people about his birth. "No, I was born in a stand of trees beside a cotton field."

"What?"

"My parents didn't believe in going to the hospital." He put his fingers in the air to make quotation marks. "Birth is a natural process. You don't need a hospital for that."

"In this day and age I can't imagine that happening."

For Joey no doctor and no hospital, going all natural, had been a death sentence. Ty had seen to it that he was no longer associated with those ideas. "Well, it didn't just happen yesterday. I am thirty-four years old." Okay, now he'd said enough. For someone who had a difficult time building relationships at work, Michelle sure had him spilling his guts.

"You know what I mean. Medicine has advanced so far. We know so much more than we used to."

"Yeah, science has come a long way but not everyone embraces it, neither does it have all the answers." That statement made it sound like he was defending his parents, which he certainly was not.

Michelle's eyes went dark and a sheen of moisture covered them before she blinked. What had she been thinking about to bring that on?

Her eyes rose to meet his. They held a stricken look for a second before her gaze focused downward. Had he stumbled on a secret? He didn't want to look into anyone's dark closet.

To his great relief, the server returned to place Michelle's plate down in front of her then his in front of him. Now he'd make an effort to turn the conversation to something less personal and certainly more pleasant.

"Whoo, comfort food. I might think you're feeding your emotions."

"I like pancakes. Nothing special there."

He was beginning to think there were a number of things special about Michelle.

"Still an amazing amount of food for such a shapely woman."

"Shapely?"

"Don't try to act like you don't know you're a fine-looking woman."

"Thank you," she said in a humble-sounding voice.

"How do you stay in such good shape?"

"I swim laps three times a week and I have good genes. My mother…"

She put a bit of pancake in her mouth but he had the feeling she had purposely decided not to say more.

"Interesting. I took you for a gym rat. But on second thoughts that would be far too sociable for you."

'That didn't sound like a compliment. More like an insult. You don't think I can be sociable?"

"I had no intention of insulting you." This subject was more like it. Less about him and superficial. "I was just stating fact from what I've seen. And, no, I don't think you are particularly sociable."

Her eyes drifted away to watch the server pour coffee. Michelle looked up at him again. "So how do you stay in shape?"

"So you think I look good?"

"That isn't what I said. My arms were around your body just a few minutes ago. I have some idea of your physical fitness."

He knew all too well how close she'd been. How much he'd enjoyed it. His body had taken far too long to recover from the contact. The ice queen was thawing. Nicely.

"I enjoy rock climbing, wind surfing when I'm stationed close enough to the ocean, and I try to pick up a game of basketball in the local park when I can."

"Sounds like you stay busy."

"I try to. Moving from town to town can be lonely so I try to get out where people are." He forked eggs into his mouth.

She gave him a long look he couldn't quite read.

"So how did you like your first bike ride?"

"I found it exhilarating."

His lowered his chin and pierced her with a look. "I thought by the King Kong grip you had on my waist that you might be terrified."

"I was but that doesn't mean I wasn't enjoying it."

He nodded his head in fascination. "You're an intriguing woman, Dr. Ross."

"You never call me Dr. Ross."

"Yes, I do. In front of patients."

Michelle huffed. Which she did often, but he found that he liked it. "Why do you insist on calling me Michelle when you know I'd rather you didn't?"

"At first it was to aggravate you, then it was because 'Dr. Ross' sounds so stuffy in the OR and now it's because I like the feel of it crossing my lips."

Ty didn't miss her shiver or the fact that her fork came to rest a little too noisily against her plate. He'd pierced that armor she hid behind. The opposite of cold was hot. Maybe beneath that snowcap attitude was a boiling volcano of emotion ready to erupt. It would be exciting to be there when it did.

"I'd take that as praise but for the fact that the hospital Casanova said it."

"I'm no Casanova. I just consider myself a friendly person." He took a sip of his coffee.

"With all the women."

"Are you just a little jealous, Michelle?"

He made her name sound particularly sexy on purpose. Maybe he could light some fire under that snow. Her eyelids fluttered down and up again. Oh, yes, he was getting to her. But why did he want to? There were plenty of woman at the hospital who had made it clear on a number of occasions that they were more than charmed. But who did he find intriguing? Michelle.

That revelation made him sit back in his seat. He watched Michelle for a moment. She was certainly attractive enough but her standoffish ways were perturbing. He wanted to have fun and nothing about this woman said fun.

That wasn't entirely true, he was having a good time right now. Still, Michelle was definitely the wrong person to be interested in. She cried permanence and that wasn't in his plans in any form.

"I am not jealous. Why would I be?"

He gave her a thoughtful look. "I don't know. Maybe because you want me for yourself?"

She glared at him. "Now you're making things up."

Minutes later she finished the last bit of pancake and took a slip of coffee. She leaned back in the booth and yawned.

"I'd better get you home to bed," Ty said, pulling out his wallet.

"Why Doctor, do you say that to every surgeon you work with?"

His heart skipped a beat. "Why, Doctor, are you flirting with me?"

Her eyes went wide and she squared her shoulders. "I've never flirted in my life."

Ty could believe that. "Well, there's always a first time for everything. And I do believe that you were."

"It won't happen again." Her serious tone returned.

"I sure hope that isn't true. I enjoyed it. Hey, before we go, draw me a map to your house."

"I live in a condo."

"Okay, condo."

"Ma'am," Michelle called to the server, "may I have a piece of paper and borrow a pen?"

She looked back at Ty. "I usually have a notepad with me."

"I'm not surprised."

"What does that mean?"

"It means you're always prepared." His tone implied he wasn't impressed by her thoroughness.

When the server didn't immediately fulfill her request, he picked up a napkin. "Here, just use this."

"A napkin?"

"Yeah, you've never written on a napkin?

"No."

"My pockets are full of notes I've written on napkins."

"This time *I'm* not surprised."

"I guess you wouldn't expect anything different." He'd let her believe whatever she wanted. It was just as well she wasn't impressed by him. Still, it would be nice...

Ty threw a couple of tens on the table. When Michelle started to argue he said, "Don't say anything about me paying. I'm the one who wanted to stop."

Outside, beside the motorcycle again, Michelle was determined to show Ty that she could handle the bike. She picked up her helmet before he had a chance to hand it to her. Pulling it into place and snapping the strap, she waited.

His grin gave her a surge of satisfaction. After he climbed on, she joined him, not hesitating to wrap her arms around him.

"I might have to start sabotaging your car every night if I get to have you hug me."

"I'm too tired to have a pithy comeback."

He chuckled. It made a wonderful ripple of sensation against her chest. Her nipples hardened in response. The man had a sexuality that called to her on a level she'd never experienced before. Her body hummed with an urge to answer. Maybe just this once. He wouldn't be here long. For once it could be about her. But she wouldn't. That road would lead to nothing but heartache. That alone made her determined not to need a ride from him again.

"Michelle, you're home. You can let go now." Ty shook his shoulder, jiggling her. His voice held a note of humor.

Oh, no. She had dozed off against Ty's back. She was so

exhausted and he was so large, warm and comfortable she hadn't been able to keep her eyes from closing.

She jerked upright. "Uh, yeah."

"You were asleep, weren't you?"

She slid off the bike. Holding onto him as she went. She would miss not touching those powerful shoulders. "A little maybe. Thanks for the ride."

Ty put the kickstand down and began to climb off.

She removed her helmet and handed it to him.

"What're you doing?"

"Making sure you get inside safely."

"That's not necessary. I come in at all hours and have done so for years. I can take care of myself."

"Yes, ma'am. Just trying to be nice. Which one of these stately manors is yours?"

He made it sound like he wasn't impressed with the brick townhouses with the manicured shrubs. Once again she had the feeling he was scrutinizing her life and finding it lacking.

"The second on the right. Thanks again for the ride." She left him standing by the bike and headed for her front door. She pulled the key out of her scrub pants pocket, slipped it into the lock and was inside before she heard the roar of the motorcycle going down the road.

She couldn't remember the last time someone had waited outside her door to make sure she was in safely.

CHAPTER THREE

MICHELLE ROLLED OVER and picked up her phone. "Dr. Ross."

"Good afternoon, Michelle," Ty's deep-timbred voice said into her ear. Her treacherous heart leaped.

"Yes?"

"It's Ty."

"I know."

"Is that the best greeting you can give at two in the afternoon?"

"Yes."

He chuckled. "Not an afternoon person, are you?"

"Is there a problem with a patient?"

"No. I just wanted to let you know that I had Jimmy take care of your car."

"Jimmy?"

"Yeah, one of the hospital security guys. Fine fellow. He needs the extra money so I had him look at your car."

She'd worked at the hospital for years and she couldn't call a single security officer by name, but Ty knew all about one. Suddenly she felt ashamed of herself.

"Your car is running now. He says you shouldn't have any more problems. Just corroded cables."

"Uh, great. Thanks."

"You also left your purse in my bike. I've put it under the driver's seat of your car and locked it. Oh, by the way,

I had a look around and I now know your weight and how old you are."

"You did not!"

His full-bodied laugh covered her like a warm blanket from the dryer.

"I thought that might get a reaction. No, I didn't. But I did arrange for Jimmy to pick you up when you're ready. Just call Security and ask for him."

"I don't think—"

"Michelle, he needs the money. Let him have his pride."

Ty was really a good person. He saw a need and acted. She didn't say anything for a few seconds.

"Did you go back to sleep on me?"

A picture of her asleep with her head on his broad chest popped into her mind. "No," came out squeakier than she wished. "Thanks, Ty. I appreciate all you've done."

"No prob. See you soon."

Between her mother and her patients, she'd spent so much time taking care of others she forgotten just how nice it was to be taken care of. Too nice.

Four days later, Michelle was preparing to tap on the door of her patient's room when there was a burst of laughter from inside. Shawn had come through surgery well and after a short visit to CICU he was now in a room on the floor. She knocked.

A couple of deep voices could be heard then one called, "Come in."

She pushed the door open to find her patient sitting up in bed with a video-game controller in his hand. He didn't look at her. Instead, his focus remained on the bright animated characters on the TV. She glanced up to see what was happening. Every once in a while there was a white flash and a loud noise of something blowing up. Shaking her head, Michelle turned to her patient again.

Her eyes widened in disbelief. Sitting beside Shawn with another controller in his hand was Ty. She'd not seen him the last few days. With a sureness Michelle couldn't ignore, she admitted she'd missed him. Now he was shifting his body from side to side in an effort to see the TV around her.

"Dr. Ross, do you mind? I'm actually winning this time." Desperation and frustration filled his voice.

He was glad to see her too. Obviously not. She stepped to one side. Ty's actions weren't professional but from what she knew of him she would've wondered what was wrong with him if they had been.

"Thanks," Ty called to her. To Shawn he said, "You'd better move on or I'll overtake you." Ty moved his body one way and then the other as if he were the figure in the game.

Glancing at Shawn, she saw that he was making the same body movements. There was also a huge grin on his face. Michelle's heart lifted to see him enjoying himself. During the days before his surgery and those in CICU he'd been extremely depressed. He'd been so despondent that she'd worried it might affect his recovery. Ty had made the difference. For that she was grateful.

With a whoop of joy that Michelle thought might bring the nurses running the two men raised their hands over their heads.

"Once again you're the game master. Here I was helping Dr. Ross replace your heart valve and you repay me by beating the socks off me." Ty raised one hand higher and Shawn slapped it with his open palm.

Ty stood. The space in the room seemed to shrink. He was dressed in a pair of well-worn jeans and a T-shirt, with something ridiculous about "Ride a cycle and find a friend" written across his chest. He came to stand beside her.

"I'd better go and let Dr. Ross check you out. Maybe home will be on her agenda."

She smiled in agreement when Ty glanced over at her for confirmation. "It's very possible for tomorrow. Then you can get another game blaster."

Ty's laugh was deep and robust and was joined by Shawn's weaker one.

Warmth moved up her neck. Had she said something wrong?

"It's a game master." Ty said the last word carefully.

"Oh, I meant that."

Ty grinned and looked back at Shawn. "She's great with hearts but needs to get out more in the game department. You go home and rest up for our next match."

"I'll take you on any time, Ty."

Michelle liked to see that sign of feistiness. Shawn wanted to get well.

Ty smiled at Shawn. "I might not show it but I'm a poor loser. Next time you're mine, game *master*." Ty looked at her as if making a point then put out his fist. Shawn bumped it with his.

As he scooted passed her, Ty winked then went out the door. The special warmth that a man generated in a woman flared in her but just as quickly it turned into irritation. She wasn't some nurse, chasing him. She was the surgeon he worked with. How unprofessional! Suddenly all the positive thoughts she'd had about him went up in flames.

Of all the gall!

Fifteen minutes later she came out of Shawn's room pleased with her patient's progress. He would make a full recovery. Of course, he would always be a heart patient but Shawn had a chance to do and have anything a man his age wanted out of life. As she walked toward the nurses' station, she saw Ty talking to one of the staff. The woman looked at him as if he were a candy store and she loved sweets. Did every female find him fascinating?

She'd watched Ty work numerous times in surgery. He was respected professionally by both the males and females. His directives were followed without question but he could still interact on a personal level with the staff. They all seemed to like him. Was it just her that he rubbed the wrong way?

"Hey, Doc," he called as she started to pass. "Can I ask you something?"

Michelle tightened her lips for a second at the casual way he spoke to her. She was getting used to it but it still caught her off guard. No one else dared to speak to her the way he did. Her parents hadn't even called her by a nickname when she'd been growing up.

She approached him, glad the desk stood between them. He looked up at her from where he sat in a chair.

"Yes?"

"Tell me something, do you have any idea what a game master is?"

A sick, unsure feeling filled her. "Well, no."

"That's what I figured." He looked back down at the chart.

She waited but he didn't look up. His hair had fallen across his cheek so she couldn't tell if he might be looking at her. "Well?"

"Well, what?" His head rose and he considered her.

Ty picked then of all times to act serious. "Are you going to tell me what it is?" she snapped.

He grinned. "Oh, that. It's when you win at a video game. Shawn had to spend so much time taking it easy in the last few months that he's had plenty of time to get good at playing video games. He's a tough one to beat."

"I see." She didn't know if she should say the next words for fear he'd use them against her but she pressed on anyway. "You were really great with him the morning he went into surgery."

"I'm the last person he sees before he goes under. He might not have said it but he was afraid he wouldn't make it. He needed mine to be a friendly face."

She'd never thought about his job like that. "Still, I appreciate you taking so much time with him."

"Not a prob. He's a great kid who's had a lot of hard knocks."

Michelle wished she was that reassuring to her patients. She worked at not letting any emotion show. If it did, she was afraid it would overflow. She'd learned early on when her father had died the necessity of being strong. As a child it had been for her mother. In med school she'd had to be professional to survive. Now it was important that she always remain in control because her team followed her lead. Over the years it had become her demeanor, who she was. Who she had to be. She didn't know how to act any differently.

Could she be more unlike Ty if she tried?

"You're good at your job."

"Why, thank you, ma'am. I think am good at what I do too."

Why did he always manage to turn everything around so that it maddened her? "And you don't lack for an ego either," she said in a snippy tone.

"That wasn't ego talking."

"You're right. I can't fault your skill in the OR or with a patient. You have my sincerest apology for the way I acted on the day you arrived."

He presented her with a rakish grin. "Well, that was nice

and unexpected. Would you mind insulting me again so I can hear you say 'I'm sorry' one more time?"

Ooh, the man made her want to slap that smile off his face while at the same time wanting to laugh. Instead, she turned and headed down the hall.

The sound of Ty's soft merriment followed her. He knew full well he'd gotten to her.

The day was beautiful. It was Ty's non-surgery one or what he typically called his "hate paperwork" day. He finished up with the two patients on the OR schedule for the next day and headed out to make the most of what was left of the hours before dark. Using a short cut he found by going through the women's center to where he parked his bike, he was looking forward to being outside.

Sunshine streamed through the two-story-high glass windows of the building. Waiting areas with low, modern seating in front of doctors' offices occurred every fifty feet or so. Green plants were placed artfully around the areas.

He'd almost reached the exit on the other end of the building when he saw Michelle. She was sitting next to a woman who had to be her mother, the resemblance was so strong.

He pulled up short and said, "Hi, Michelle."

She looked up from a magazine she'd been leafing through. Her eyes widened and she shifted in her chair. She wasn't pleased to see him. As he approached she glanced at the woman next to her. "Hello, Ty."

The older woman beside her watched their interchange with interest, looking between the two of them. He glanced at the woman.

"Uh, Ty, this is my mother, Betty Ross." Michelle acted as if she wasn't eager to introduce him.

He stepped forward and stretched out his hand. "It's a pleasure to meet you, Mrs. Ross. I'm Ty Smith."

Michelle's mother didn't stand but placed her fragile, pale hand in his. It was cool to the touch but there was warmth in her eyes. "Hello. Do you work with my daughter?"

"I do. She's an outstanding doctor."

He didn't miss the slight color that settled on Michelle's cheeks. Wasn't she used to being praised for her work? Or was it her looks that most people commented on?

"Why, thank you. I'm proud of her. She works so hard. Too hard, I think. So are you a doctor as well?"

As unsociable as Michelle acted, her mother went to the other extreme.

"Mom." Michelle's tone said she wished she could gracefully exit from the entire conversation. "I'm sure that Ty must have been on his way somewhere."

Ty ignored her blatant effort to get rid of him. He was enjoying talking to her mother and learning a little more about Michelle. She was so close-mouthed about anything related to her personal life that he'd been surprised to see her mother was still alive. "I'm an anesthesiologist. I work in the OR with your Michelle."

He didn't miss the tightening of Michelle's lips. Making her sound like a little girl didn't please her.

"Mrs. Ross," called a nurse from the door of an office.

Michelle's head jerked toward the voice before her gaze returned to meet his. There was a look of pain in her eyes but it disappeared when she blinked. That pain he didn't believe had anything to do with him. What was going on?

"Dr. Smith, it was nice to meet you. I hope we see each other again," Michelle's mother said softly.

"It would be a pleasure."

"Come on, Mom, the nurse is waiting."

Mrs. Ross rose slightly then sat down in the chair again as if she didn't have the strength to stand on her own.

"May I help you?" Ty asked, stepping forward and offering his arm.

"Thank you. I hate being so weak."

"Hold onto my arm and I'll support you as you stand up."

"I can do that." Michelle moved to the other side of her mother.

"I don't mind. In fact, I'd be honored." Ty didn't relinquish his place.

Mrs. Ross giggled like a young girl. "Michelle, I do believe your friend is a prince charming."

Ty winked at Michelle and grinned.

Michelle groaned, and his grin grew into a smile.

"Mrs. Ross, I take that as real praise coming from you." He helped her stand.

"How would you like to come to dinner some time?" Mrs. Ross asked him.

He glanced at Michelle. She looked appalled at the idea and as she opened her mouth to speak, Ty said, "I'd love to."

"Mother!" Michelle hissed.

Mrs. Ross ignored her and asked, "Tomorrow night?"

"That would be wonderful. I look forward to it." He looked past Mrs. Ross to find a resigned look on Michelle's face. "I'll get directions from Michelle."

"Mother, the nurse is waiting," she said in an exasperated voice laced with a tiredness that sounded bone deep.

Ty watched as Michelle assisted her mother into the office. He gaze rose to the large letters above the reception window. Oncology.

That was a tough diagnosis. No wonder Michelle could be difficult at times. She had to be worried about her mother.

Ty grinned at the look on Michelle's face as she opened the door of her mother's home the next evening. He'd had a warmer welcome from his cadaver in med school. "Good evening, Michelle."

"Come in," she murmured.

"Thank you for the heartfelt welcome."

"You know this wasn't my idea." She moved as if to make sure their bodies didn't touch as he entered.

"You've made that perfectly clear. But I'm glad your mother invited me. I'm going to enjoy having a home-cooked meal. It's something I don't often get."

She looked contrite. "I'm sorry. I'm not being very gracious. Come in. My mom is in the kitchen. I normally cook for her most evenings but she insisted on doing most of the meal tonight."

She closed the door behind them and he followed her to the kitchen. Michelle's mother's home was the kind that made him think of laughter and warm fires. It was as foreign to his growing-up years as he could imagine.

His life before Joey had really become sick had been carefree. He'd been encouraged to read and question but there had been little structure. Nothing permanent in his life other than his parents and Joey. In fact, he'd known nothing of his grandparents until he'd overheard his parents talking about them when he'd been around eight.

Ty paused to looked at the pictures in the hallway of Michelle at different stages in her life, some of them including her parents. There had been no family photos like these in his life. Heck, it was hard to hang a picture on the side of a tent.

When they entered the kitchen, Mrs. Ross turned away from the stove. She looked frail but there were red spots high on her cheeks. She wiped her hands and came towards him. "Welcome, Ty, I'm so glad you could join us."

"I appreciate being asked." He glanced at Michelle. She gave him more of a smirk than a smile.

"These are for you." He handed flowers and a long thin box to the older woman.

The red of her cheeks all but glowed with her pleasure as she took them. "Why, Ty, how sweet. You didn't have to."

"I wanted to."

"Michelle, honey, why don't you put these in a vase while I see what's in this pretty box? I can't imagine."

Michelle took the flowers and went to the sink.

Mrs. Ross opened the box and pulled out a multicolored scarf. "Oh, my, how beautiful." She wrapped it around her neck.

"I thought you might like it. My mother always said a bright scarf lifts a woman's spirits."

He'd not thought of that in a long time. Not quoted his parents in years. His mother had wrapped a red scarf around her head the day they'd marched out to bury Joey.

Ty's gaze shifted away from her mother to Michelle. Her eyes glistened and she mouthed, "Thank you," and gave him a smile. It was the first full-blown one he'd ever seen from her.

His eyes widened, he blinked and returned her smile with a wink.

"Michelle, why don't you take those flowers into the living room, and you and Ty have a little talk while I finish here? I won't be long."

Michelle looked as if she'd like to have the floor swallow her. He couldn't help but grin. This might be the most entertaining evening he'd spent in a long time.

She gathered the vase and without a backward glance headed back the way they had come. He followed, admiring the sensual sway of her hips. Did she have any idea what she could do to a man? This power was stronger than any she employed as a heart surgeon. She could rule the world. His, anyway.

When they got to the living room Michelle placed the flowers on the nearest table and turned to face him. "I'm sorry about this. I couldn't be more embarrassed."

"Hey, don't be. I'm flattered. I can't say that I know of another mother who has thrown her daughter at me."

He enjoyed the blush that covered her face. Yes, the ice queen had definitely melted.

Taking a seat on the sofa, he patted the cushion next to him. "Come sit and 'talk a little'."

Michelle sank next to him more out of defeat than anything else. He appreciated seeing her a little off center. The stiff doctor in control had all but been stripped away. She was just a daughter trying to make a sick mother happy.

"So your mother has cancer."

"Yes."

"How long?"

"We've been dealing with treatments for the last six months."

"That has to have been tough. On both of you."

"It has been. I have all this medical knowledge but I can't help her. What good is it all if you can't save the people you love?"

A stab of pain filled him. What would have happened if he'd defied his parents and taken Joey for help? He knew too well what it meant to watch a loved one die. He carried the guilt daily.

"So what is the prognosis?"

"Mom seems to be doing well medically but I worry over her depression. Tonight is the first time in months that she's been this animated and energetic."

"So the way to perk her up is to see you interested in a guy?"

Michelle shifted away. "I'm not interested in you."

Ty took her hand in his and rubbed his thumb across the

top of it. He turned it over to where he could feel the whip of her pulse under the delicate skin covering her wrist. "Are you sure about that?"

She pulled her hand away. "I appreciate you making my mother happy but I don't plan to play the game any further than tonight."

Was he playing a game? No, he didn't think so. Suddenly he wanted to get to know this beautiful, complicated woman better. Careful, that idea sounded too much like getting involved. That, he wouldn't let happen. They could be friends. Have a few laughs while he was in town but that was it.

"Ever thought that I might find you interesting? Want to get to know you better?"

"No. Why would you? I'm not your type. We are too different. We barely tolerate each other."

"I think we're tolerating each other just fine now."

And they were. In fact, it had been a long time since he'd just enjoyed talking to a woman without there being any expectation on the part of either side.

Mrs. Ross stuck her head into the room. "Dinner is served."

Michelle shot to her feet as if her mother had seen them doing something she didn't want her to know about. He stood more slowly.

Michelle's heart caught and fluttered back into rhythm. Maybe there was more to Ty than she'd given him credit for. At least her mother was happier than she'd seen her in a long time. For that alone Michelle could tolerate him for an evening.

She followed her mother back into the kitchen. Michelle came to an abrupt stop, causing Ty to bump into her. His hand touched her waist briefly, steadying her.

Her mother had set her father's place for Ty.

"You okay?" he asked next to her ear. If her mother turned round now she'd think there truly was something between them. They stood so intimately close.

"Yeah."

"Ty, this is your place." Her mother indicated her father's chair.

"Thank you, ma'am," Ty said as he sat. "This looks wonderful and smells even better." Michelle sank into her chair. She watched as Ty's well-manicured hands picked up his napkin and shook it out then placed it in his lap.

His hand touching hers under the table jerked her attention to his eyes. She smiled and shook off the melancholy. He removed his hand. It was past time to let her father's place go. Maybe even other things about him. Her mother certainly needed to move on after so many years. Had they both been caught up in a void that they needed to get beyond?

"Michelle, why don't you serve Ty some roast?"

Ty picked up his plate and offered it to her. His eyes still held a concerned look. He saw things about her that others never noticed. Far too often.

She dished up the meat and her mother passed him the bowl of mashed potatoes. The two of them carried on a conversation as if they were old friends, leaving Michelle time to observe Ty.

He might be the most handsome man she'd ever seen. At first she'd thought his hair was too much but the better she got to know him the more she thought it suited him. Combed back, the ends curled around the back of his neck. Tonight he was wearing a collared shirt of tiny green plaid that made his eyes seem darker. His pants were well-pressed tan cotton twill. She couldn't fault his appearance in any way.

Even in the OR she'd started to look forward to seeing what kind of outrageous scrub cap he might wear next. She'd also noticed his original lime-colored clogs were exchangeable for bright orange ones on occasion.

"Michelle…" Her mother's note of irritation implied she must have called her name more than once.

"Why don't you clear the dishes and bring that apple pie over here? There's also ice cream in the freezer."

"Okay, how many nights of the week can I eat here?" Ty asked.

Michelle almost dropped the dishes.

Thankfully her mother just giggled, instead of telling him Monday, Wednesday and Friday.

Michelle placed the pie in the middle of the table and returned for the ice cream as Ty said, "You're a great cook, Mrs. Ross. That was some of the best food I've ever eaten."

"I love to cook. I even thought about opening a tearoom when Michelle was a small child but there never seemed to be time."

That was news to Michelle. A tearoom. Her mother hadn't cooked for herself in weeks. Michelle had thought she'd forgotten how until tonight.

"I'm sure you would've made a success of it."

"I'm too old to do that now but I do still love to go to tea."

Michelle had forgotten about that as well. Before she'd become sick her mother had gone out with her friends regularly. These days she didn't go out except when she had a doctor's appointment.

Soon after dessert Ty said he must be going. Michelle wondered if he had someplace else to be or someone else he was meeting. He didn't strike her as a home body who spent a lot of time by himself. Why she cared she didn't know, but she did.

"Michelle, why don't you see Ty to the door?"

She made an effort not to roll her eyes.

Ty graciously thanked her mother and followed Michelle out of the kitchen. She opened the front door and Ty brushed her arm as he moved his large body past hers. A tingle of heat went through her as if she had been branded. She had to stop overreacting to his slightest touch.

She stepped out onto the porch and closed the door behind them. "I'm sorry about tonight. I had no idea that she was going to put you on the spot."

"Hey, don't worry about it. I enjoyed being here. There's nothing wrong with a parent caring about their child and showing it. Your mother just wants you to be happy."

"I know, but tonight's show said that we'd stepped back thirty years or more in dating time."

"Didn't liked me being pushed at you, did you?" He chuckled.

"I was mortified."

"It was a compliment."

He really was understanding about a number of things now that she'd thought about it. "Well, I appreciate you being okay with it. My mom seemed to enjoy having you to dinner and that's something she hasn't done in a long time."

"And how about you? Did you enjoy having me?"

He made the question sound so suggestive that she felt as if her temperature had spiked. "I'm not sure what you mean."

Ty's eyes studied her for far longer than was comfortable before he said in a low, rusty voice, "I think you probably do but don't want to admit it."

It was exciting to have Ty's complete attention. He made her feel things long locked away, even those she'd never felt before. Would it really be so bad to have a fling with him? After all, he would be gone in a few weeks.

His attention was captured by something behind her. "Your mother is looking out the window. Let's not disappoint her."

His arm circled her waist, bringing her against him. Michelle didn't even try to struggle, her hands going to rest lightly on his shoulders. With her height, Ty was only a few inches taller than she was. He had a slight grin on his mouth as he looked into her eyes and brought his lips down to touch hers. Ty smelled of apples, cinnamon and coffee. Her breath slowed as his full and mobile mouth pressed firmly against hers.

Heat flowed through her blue-flame hot. When had been the last time she'd been kissed? Had any kisses ever made her feel the way this one did?

Her fingers dug into his shoulders. Ty's tightened his arm, bringing her closer. His other hand rose to circle the back of her neck. He guided her head so that he captured her mouth more fully.

Just as Michelle began to press closer he pulled away. Disappointment swamped her. She wanted more. Stumbling slightly, Ty steadied her.

"That should make your mother happy."

What? Michelle sucked in her breath. She'd experienced the kiss of her life and Ty had only done so to make her mother happy! Could she be more insulted?

She jerked out of his arms. "If I didn't care that my mother was watching, I'd slap your face."

With that, she re-entered the house, leaving Ty standing on the porch.

CHAPTER FOUR

TY'S GAZE LIFTED away from the blood-pressure monitor to Michelle. She was engrossed in watching the resident remove the cannula running to the heart-lung machine as they took their patient, a sixty-three-year-old female, off bypass in the OR.

He didn't understand her reaction two nights before when he'd kissed her. He'd made a mistake somewhere. Not usually so out of tune with a woman, Michelle's response to his kiss had thrown him. He'd thought she'd been enjoying it. He certainly had been. With her mother watching, he hadn't been able to take it as far as he wished.

The ice queen had returned, North-Pole cold this morning. She wouldn't even look at him and if she did it was to ask a question necessary to patient care only. Normally he'd have shrugged her displeasure off and moved on but Michelle had gotten to him on a level he'd never known before. He didn't like things not being right between them.

The resident tipped the heart up to get a look at the suture line on the back.

"BP dropping. Eighty over sixty. That's enough," Ty called.

The resident put the heart back in place.

"BP coming up. You guys know that makes me nervous when you do that."

Michelle and the resident weren't really listening to him. They had their heads together, looking intently into the chest of the patient.

"Where is that blood coming from?" she asked no one in particular. "What is the ACT?" she demanded, without looking at him.

"Normal range," Ty answered, letting her know that the activated clotting time was fine. Before he'd started the patient on bypass, using the heart-lung machine, he'd given her blood thinner. When the patient had come off bypass he'd had to reverse it by giving protamine.

"Do more factors need to be given?"

"No. Platelets and FFP are in range," Ty responded. He checked again. Nothing indicated fresh frozen plasma was needed.

"What does the TEG show?"

The TEG was a research tool that told him what part of the clotting cascade was deficient. "Numbers are good."

"Then we are prolene-deficient," Michelle announced.

Ty jerked his head up to look at her. More sutures were required. Her voice was higher than normal. She was rattled for some reason.

"Let's find this thing," she snapped. "We need to know if it's the suture line or a vessel."

"Pack it with sponges and see what we get."

The resident began to place sponges around the heart. Then they waited.

For the first time her eyes met Ty's. Her gaze remained long enough for him to see the terror in her eyes.

"BP?" she asked.

"Dropping slowly."

"Let's get them out," she said, referring to the sponges.

The resident removed one from behind the heart. It was bright red. "Got it."

"The arterial suture line," Michelle said, with less confidence than she usually showed . "I thought I'd put in enough stitches."

He couldn't see her eyes but her breathing had become more rapid. Ty checked the monitors to make sure all was well on his end before he looked up. This was supposed to be a straightforward bypass case, something that Michelle could do in her sleep.

Done with adding stitches, she stood, her eyes transfixed on the chest of the patient. She didn't move. Didn't say anything.

"Michelle," Ty said in a firm tone.

She blinked then turned to the resident. "Can you close?"

He nodded.

Ty could see moisture filling her eyes. Why had this case gotten to her so? He didn't miss the shock on the faces of the other team members.

Jane, her scrub nurse, asked, "Dr. Ross, are you okay?"

Michelle didn't answer as she exited the OR.

"Call the scrub desk and have Dr. Marcus come in and finish up for me," he told his nurse.

Ty was only minutes behind Michelle. He found her in the locker room, sitting on a bench. She had removed her mask and tears showed on her cheeks. Michelle looked around as if she didn't know which way to go. She wouldn't like the staff seeing her going into meltdown. He jerked his mask off and grabbed her wrist. "Come with me."

He led her out of the OR suite to the employee elevator and pushed the up button. Thankfully they didn't have to wait long for the elevator doors to open.

"Where're we going?" Good. She was coming back from that dark place.

"I'll show you."

"Ty, this isn't the time for one of your games. I just want to be left alone."

"This isn't one of my games." He was glad to see they had reached the top floor. When the doors opened he took her hand. She didn't make any attempt to refuse it. That alone told him how upset she was.

When she started to speak he said, "Hush and follow me." He circled around the elevator and pushed open the door to the roof.

"What're we doing here?"

"I always find a place to go just so I can breathe. This is my place and I think you could use it today."

"How do you get past Security?" The pragmatic Michelle had returned. That was an encouraging sign. For a second there he'd been concerned for her emotional health.

"I made a deal with Jimmy."

"Figures. Why're you doing this? You're not my new best friend," she said, pulling her hand out of his. This feistiness was better than what he'd seen in her eyes earlier.

"What happened in there?"

"Nothing. We had a bleeder. We found it. All in a day of surgery."

That statement was too flippant, coming from Michelle. "I know better. Spill. Is it your mother?"

"Why would you think that?"

"Sixty-three-year-old female. Could have died. That's who our patient is. Sound like any one you know? I don't have to be a mind-reader to get the connection."

"All brilliant deductions, Doctor. Yes. This one hit a bit too close to home," she said with disgust.

Whether or not it was the situation or her, he didn't know. He moved to where he could look out over the city, pleased she followed. If he could get her to talk, maybe he could help. He may be taking an interest in Michelle's problems, but he wouldn't be there for her for the long haul. She didn't need to come to depend on him.

When she came to stand beside him he said, "Makes you feel like the king of the mountain to be up here. As if you have some control over someone's life if not your own."

She glanced at him. "What do you know about not having control? You go through life as if it is a fun ride at a carnival."

"Take my word for it. I know it isn't. Talk to me, Michelle."

"I don't want to talk about it." She kicked at the gravel covering the top on the roof with the toe of her shoe. It reminded him of a little girl on the playground unsure if she should climb the monkey bars.

"But I think you need to. What gives?"

"What gives? Are you a hippy?"

"No, but I was raised by some hippy wannabes. But that isn't what we are here to discuss."

"What do you want to hear? I fell apart in the OR because the patient reminded me of my mother. Happy now?"

"Okay, but why?"

"Stop pushing, Ty."

"Why? Your mother is getting better."

She rounded on him. "Because I'm afraid she might die. I've already lost a father. I don't have anyone else."

She had isolated herself so completely that she had no one to turn to. "Your team has no idea your mother has been sick, do they?"

Michelle lowered her eyes and shook her head.

"You need to talk to them. When the surgeon breaks down over a patient, it unnerves the team. I knew it was serious when they all looked at you like a deer in the headlights. Not one of them blinked. They're not used to that type of emotion from you. And they had no idea where it came from."

"I didn't get the name ice queen for nothing," she retorted.

"I'm sorry. I know that must hurt."

She shrugged.

He took her by the shoulders. "You need to tell them what's going on in your life. They're your friends. They'll want to help. I want to help. Let me."

"You can't. It's not something that you can laugh off and make okay."

His hands dropped away from her. "That's a little harsh, even for you, Michelle."

She had the good grace to look contrite. "I'm sorry. That was uncalled for."

"You're upset. Why have you kept your mother's issue hidden?"

"Because I'm the surgeon, the leader. I have to be strong."

"Agreed, but you are also human. Your mother is sick. You have every right to be upset. Patients and the people you work with also need to know you are human too."

"Are you saying I'm not?"

"No, if anything I think you're too human. Feel too much. You just refuse to show it. Are *afraid* to show it."

She turned her back to him. Her shoulders slumped.

Ty wrapped his arms around her and pulled her against him. Her head rolled back to rest on his chest. "Aw, sweetheart, this too will pass. Cry it out and you'll feel better."

He might not. The more he knew about Michelle the more difficult it was going to be to leave in a few weeks. But leave he would. He always did.

Michelle sat reviewing a chart of one of her patients at the nurses' station on the floor. Her mind wasn't on what she was doing, as it should've been. Instead, it was on the last conversation she'd had with Ty. She didn't know if she would ever be able to face him again. He'd seen through her!

She'd come unglued and he'd been there to witness it. After she'd recovered from her crying jag, they'd returned to the OR suite. She'd immediately spoken to the resident about the patient. He'd informed her that woman was doing well and was comfortable in CICU.

At least today she didn't have any surgeries so she wouldn't have to face Ty just yet.

"Did you hear about Ty?" one of the nurses told another in a raised voice. "He was hit in the parking lot this morning on his way in. He's in Emergency,"

Michelle's heart dropped to her stomach. She put her hands in her lap to stop the shaking. The sudden urge to run to the ER filled her.

"Is he badly hurt?" one of the nurses asked, so Michelle didn't have to.

"I don't know. I just saw all the commotion and a motorcycle on the ground. A couple of ER staff were there. That's all I know."

Michelle bit her lip and forced herself not to make a scene by jumping up and rushing to the ER. Logging out of the computer, she tried to act as normally as possible while her heart raced. All that went through her head was wondering how badly he'd been hurt.

The emergency room wasn't a place that Michelle frequented. In fact, she had to follow the signs to find her way through the maze of hallways. When she arrived at the ER she was grateful for the lab coat that instantly identified her as a doctor and therefore gained her attention from the staff. The nurse at the desk looked up at Michelle, who asked, "Which room is Ty Smith in?"

The nurse looked at her as if she wasn't sure about Michelle's tone but checked the large chart on the wall. "Room four." She pointed down the hall.

At the door Michelle hesitated. What was she doing? What if Ty didn't want her there? She convinced herself he'd only been being kind to her mother and her and that he had no one else in town… Who was she kidding? She was worried about him.

Tapping lightly, she pushed the door open.

"Oh, my God, Ty. Are you okay?" She hurried to the stretcher.

"Hey, Michelle." He gave her a weak smile. That worried her more than anything. She'd never seen him with less than a cheerful grin.

"Don't look so scared. It looks far worse than it is."

She couldn't imagine that being true. His right arm was covered in gauze from wrist to elbow. On the other side there was a bandaged area on his upper arm and one covering his palm. His scrub pants had been cut away and there was a bandage around his knee, along with other scrapes and bruises. It looked as if his helmet had done its job. His gorgeous face didn't have a scratch on it.

"I told you motorcycles were dangerous." She touched his hand. He curled a bloody finger around one of hers then grimaced with the movement.

"I do think you mentioned that."

"Are there any bones broken?"

"Nope. A few stitches. Bruises and a possible concussion. I'm going to be out of commission for a few days, so I guess you won't have to worry about me being late."

"Not funny, Ty."

"Why, Michelle, if I didn't know better, I'd think you might care."

"Come on, Ty. You're hurt. I'd have to be heartless not to."

"It might be worth losing my bike just to get this kind of attention from you." He chuckled then winced.

There was a sharp knock at the door and a woman in scrubs with a lab coat covering them entered the room. She put out her hand and Michelle shook it. "I heard you were here, Dr. Ross. I'm Dr. Lassiter. We don't see heart surgeons down here much." She turned her attention to Ty. "In fact, this is more of the OR staff than we've seen in years. Busy morning for us. Dr. Smith, you'll be away from work for a couple of days. You'll also need help at home. Do you have anyone who can see about you?"

"I'll take care of him," Michelle said with conviction.

Ty's brows rose.

Even she was surprised by her lack of thought where that offer was concerned.

"Great. Then I'll get the paperwork started so you can take him home," Dr. Lassiter said in a pleased voice, and left.

Home! Ty would be staying at her house. Their last meeting had ended with her squalling all over him and now she was going to have him living with her. If she hadn't already been having trouble with her emotions where he was concerned, she certainly would now.

But he needed her help and she couldn't refuse. When she'd opened her mouth to say she'd care for him she'd jumped in at the deep end.

"Having second thoughts, are you?"

She met Ty's look.

"I can see it written all over your face."

He was starting to make her angry. Always thinking he could read her mind. She'd managed her feelings and had been getting along just fine until this handsome hunk of a man had come roaring into town.

She straightened her back and gave him a direct look.

"No, I was just thinking about what I needed to do to make you comfortable. I don't have guests often."

"I'd bet you haven't had a sleepover in a long time."

"You make this sound like a slumber party."

His eyes grew darker. "Slumbering with you has its appeal."

"Yeah, you look like you went five rounds with a car and you're out. I don't think you'll be chasing me around the condo. If I had to guess, sleeping is all you'll be doing for a day or so."

"That cut to the quick." He sequenced his face as if he were hurt.

"You do have some luck. It's Friday evening and we're both off this weekend."

His eyes turned serious. "I'd hate you to spend your days off seeing to me."

"Who else is going to?"

"I'll be all right by myself."

The ER doctor entered just in time to hear his remark.

"If you don't have someone with you then I'll admit you. You have a possible concussion. Someone has to be with you for at least the first twenty-four hours."

"Whoa, I don't do hospitals," Ty said.

"What? You work in a hospital." Michelle couldn't believe the distress she heard in his voice.

"But I'm not a patient."

Michelle looked at Dr. Lassiter and they both said at the same time, "Men."

"Don't worry. He's going home with me," Michelle told the other woman.

"Good. Here's his release form and instructions. You'll need to stay with him. The pain med is going to make him sleepy but you need to wake him up every couple of hours. Make him talk to you."

"Hello. I'm right here," Ty said, as if he were a little

boy trying to get his mother's attention so he could lick the cake beaters.

"You're not going to remember any of this so Dr. Ross needs to know," the ER doctor told him calmly. To Michelle she said, "I think you'll have your hands full."

Michelle was afraid of that.

Less than an hour later Michelle watched closely as Ty climbed the three steps as she opened the door to her condo.

"Wow, I never expected all this color. Like your office. This is the hidden Michelle." He looked at her. "I like it."

Michelle was sure she turned pink. His reaction pleased her. "You can admire or analyze my home later. Right now I need to get you to bed."

"Great. You say that when I'm so sore and drugged up I can't act on it."

"Come on, funny guy. I'll show you where you can stay."

She directed him down the hall to the spare room, which she'd decorated in lively colors and *avant-garde* paintings. "The bath is through there." She pointed to a smaller door to the right. "I'll let you get settled then be back to check on you. Holler if you need anything." She gathered the decorative pillows off the bed and placed them in a chair, before pulling the covers back.

Ty looked at her. "Really, Michelle, thanks for doing this. Hopefully I'll be out of your hair by tomorrow."

"Someone has to take care of you."

He chuckled. "That's my Michelle, the woman with the warm heart."

"I'm not your woman."

He headed toward the bathroom. "Maybe not yet."

Ty woke with a start. He shifted in bed and groaned. Every muscle ached and it seemed that every inch of his skin hurt. He looked around, trying to remember where he was.

The room was dim but he could make out the teal shade of the wall and the splashes of color of the pictures on it. Michelle's.

He vaguely remembered crawling between cool sheets and closing his eyes. He pushed the cover back and winced. He would have liked to have been invited over to Michelle's but he wouldn't have gone to this extreme to gain an invitation. The slide across the pavement had done a number on him. At least he'd been wearing his helmet or it would have been worse. He kicked to get unbound from the bed sheets. Despite the pain medicine he'd taken, he'd still tossed and turned. He'd appreciate some painkillers right now.

He focused on a painting of a beach scene in yellow, blue and red. Michelle's place had not just surprised him, it had been a shock. As conservative as she appeared on the outside, her home, along with her office, was filled with color. Here the furniture leaned toward ultra-modern, chrome and glass tables mixed with wooden chairs painted blue. Who would have thought Michelle was a closet color fiend? Her traditional conservative suits in pale colors hid a woman with flair.

Rolling his head to the side, his eyes widened when he saw Michelle sitting in a cushioned chair next to the bed. She was asleep.

Her hair was loose and a lock fell across one eye. She wore knit pants and a sweatshirt with striped socks on her feet. Her clothes in no way detracted from her beauty.

He'd not thought about her good looks in a number of days. Trying to keep up with her sharp wit had occupied his mind. Her house just added one more personality trait for him to contemplate. The woman was an interesting combination of contradictions. He never knew what he would get next.

Moving his neck to work out some of the soreness, he

looked around further and found the bedside clock. It was four in the morning.

"Michelle," he said hoarsely. The pain medicine had made his mouth dry. He cleared his throat and called her name again with more strength.

Her eyes opened with alarm and she jerked upwards.

"You need to go bed or you're going to be in worse shape than me from sitting in that chair."

Michelle looked at the clock. "It's time for your medicine. I'll get it."

She didn't wait for him to object before she stood and headed out of the room.

He watched her stride away. She had such an amazingly sexy walk. His eyelids drifted downwards.

A gentle but warm hand resting on his shoulder shook him.

Michelle's face was close enough that she had to have been studying his face before she'd woken him. Ty's blood heated and flowed to a part of him that had nothing to do with the accident and everything to do with being so close to Michelle.

Her hand move to touch his forehead.

"Ty, you need to sit up and take your medicine. You're running a low-grade fever."

"My head hurts."

"I'm not surprised. I bet you hit it hard when you fell."

He put his hands out on either side of his hips to push himself into a sitting position. He let out a grunt and Michelle rushed to put an arm around his waist.

He sure wished he felt well enough to really appreciate her touch.

"Let me help."

Between the two of them they managed to get him into

enough of a sitting position that he could swallow the meds with the water without it running down his face.

When Michelle didn't say anything or move away, he looked at her. Her gaze was focused on his lap. The covers had slipped down during their efforts to get him into the correct position. And had dropped indecently low. His privates remained covered but it was clear he was nude.

"You don't have any clothes on." The words were a small squeak for Michelle.

"Don't wear them to bed."

Michelle's creamy skin had turned a charming pink and her gaze remained at his waist. Under such scrutiny and obvious fascination, his manhood began to show its appreciation. He reached down and pulled the covers up above his waist.

She deserved better than a lover who couldn't give his best because his body wasn't in a good state. He groaned as he moved. What he wouldn't give for a cold bath! Maybe that would ease the roar of desire in him. He wanted Michelle with a fierceness he'd rarely known.

"In a hundred years I couldn't explain how much I hate feeling so rough right now because that type of admiration should be rewarded. Instead, I think you should make a straight line to your bedroom and lock the door."

Michelle gulped and her eyes flew to meet his gaze. Her hand shook as she offered him the rest of the glass of water. He drank it all. Some dribbled down his chin and she wiped it away.

Ty reached up and grabbed her wrist. Taking the cloth napkin out of her hand, he opened her fingers and kissed the center of her palm. "Thanks for taking care of me."

Michelle drew in a breath then let it out slowly. She nodded, picked up his medicine and left. As his eyelids drifted closed he again enjoyed the sight of the sway of her hips.

* * *

"Wake up."

Ty's eyelids flickered upwards. His eyes strained in an effort to focus on Michelle. Once again she was sitting in the chair beside his bed.

"What's your name?"

"You know my name."

"Tell me your name. I need to know you don't have a concussion."

"Ty Smith. And you are Michelle Ross. And you're not holding up any fingers."

"Funny, very funny."

"I told you to go to bed."

Her eyes didn't leave his. "Can't. I have to see about you."

"Well, I'm not going back to sleep until you lie down."

"I need to be close so I can check on you. I'm fine in this chair."

He shifted closer to the edge of the bed and patted the other side. "If you're not going to your bed then you have to share mine."

"I'm not sharing the bed with you!"

"Hey, it hurts like the devil to move. I'm not going to do anything. I'm not even capable of sitting up without a struggle. Who are you more afraid of, me or you?" He grinned at her huff of indignation. "That's what I thought. Lie down on top of the spread and pull that quilt at the end of the bed up over you. That way we both can get some sleep." He gave her his best determined look.

She stood. "Okay, if you promise to go back to sleep."

"Frankly, I'd love to kiss you all over but, much as I hate to admit it, I don't think I'd be at my best," he murmured in a gravelly voice. "So as soon as you're settled I'll go straight to sleep."

Michelle walked around the bed. She stood looking down at the space he'd offered for so long he thought she wasn't going to do as he asked. Finally, she sat down, pulled the quilt up and lay down.

"Hey, don't move around too much. It rocks the bed. Hurts," he mumbled as he closed his eyes.

She went so still she gave a new meaning to the saying "as stiff as a board" but at least she'd get some decent sleep. He liked knowing she was near far too much.

CHAPTER FIVE

MICHELLE CARESSED THE smooth, heated silk beneath her hand. Mmm. It felt wonderful. She liked fine sheets and pillow cases but this one was extra special. She rubbed her cheek against it. Perfect.

Her eyes opened, to be captured by green ones that didn't blink. The pain that had fogged Ty's eyes the night before had disappeared, to be replaced by desire that was crystal clear.

She tingled with want. Her fingers flexed against the skin of Ty's waist and her cheek rested on his upper arm. Michelle wanted to groan but clapped her mouth closed. Hadn't she already embarrassed herself enough?

With a jerk, she sat up. Glancing at Ty, she found his gaze still on her. Why didn't he say something? Defuse the tension, as thick as ice, between them? He'd always made jokes. Where was one when she needed it?

"I'll, uh, get your medicine."

"Michelle?"

She stood and pushed her clothes back into place.

"Yes?"

"I couldn't think of a nicer way to wake up."

She shoved her hair back, hoping it was going into some semblance of order. "I bet you say that to all the women."

His look intensified, bored into hers. "I do not."

Heat flared in her. It felt good to be considered special by this man. "I'll get you something to eat."

"I'd rather have you," he said softly as she went through the door.

Michelle headed straight to her room and into the bathroom. She looked in the mirror. Her face was flushed as if she were a teenage girl who'd received her first kiss. And Ty hadn't even tried!

She'd been the one caressing his chest. The one who had rolled towards him. How could her body have betrayed her like that?

But it had been an extremely pleasant feeling to have Ty look at her with desire. What if she took him up on his interest? Would it be so bad to let go for a while? They were both adults…

All those romantic thoughts amounted to nothing. He was only interested because she'd all but thrown herself at him in her sleep. He'd made it clear the other night that he'd only kissed her for the benefit of her mother.

Enough of that. Ty had been injured and still needed care. Starting with something to eat. Heck, she'd been so caught up in her attraction to him she'd not even asked him how he was feeling. He managed to get her to forget everything but how he made her feel.

She washed her face and pulled a brush through her hair.

In the kitchen, she started the coffeemaker and pulled out eggs, bacon, cheese and bread. She was in the process of putting together an omelet when Ty entered the room.

All he wore was the bottoms to a scrub set. He'd been given a new pair in the ER to come home in as a leg had been cut out of his other ones. In fact, that's all he had to wear. Her hand shook as she picked up the whisk to whip the eggs. She beat them far too vigorously in an effort not to stare.

Had Little Red Riding Hood felt this unsure when she'd faced the wolf? That was a foolish thought. She was a grown woman and a doctor who saw people undressed regularly. For heaven's sake, she was acting like a silly schoolgirl seeing her first naked chest. The problem was that it wasn't bare chests that got to her, it was Ty's in particular and it being in her kitchen. Few she'd seen before were as muscular or well defined as Ty's.

"How're you feeling?" she croaked.

He gingerly put a hip on a bar stool. "I'm stiff. I needed to move around a bit."

"Well, don't start thinking you're well enough to do as you please."

"I promise to be a model patient," he said with a weak smile.

"You can start being that by taking your meds and eating all your breakfast. I'll have it ready in a minute."

She put her back to him. Placing a pan on the eye of the stove, she turned it on to heat. She didn't have to look at Ty to know that he was watching her. Every fiber in her body was aware of his appraisal. The hair on her arms stood on end.

Minutes later, she placed a plate with a cheese omelet, bacon and toast in front of Ty.

He inhaled deeply. "This smells and looks wonderful." He cut into the eggs and forked them into his mouth. "Just wish it took less effort to eat."

"Would you like me to feed you?" Michelle asked.

He twisted his lip up in disgust. "I'm in bad enough shape without having the humiliation of being fed like a baby. Hey, you do know that a way to a man's heart is through his stomach?"

What would it be like to have Ty's heart? To wake up every morning touching him? Being touched?

She returned to cooking her food in the hope that Ty might think the heat in her cheeks was coming from the stove. "I've heard that but I'm only interested in getting you well enough that you can make you own breakfast," she said over her shoulder.

"Hey, I don't take up that much room."

Yes, he did. He filled every room he was in as far as she was concerned.

They ate in silence until Michelle said, "I'll need to take a look at those stitches as you ran a fever last night."

"I figured as much. I hate to ask it but I think the bandage on my knee needs some attention as well. It has bled through."

"As soon as we're done here I'll see about getting you cleaned up and then you can get back into bed. You look as if you're fading fast."

"I'll have to admit I'm not feeling as energetic as I'd like to be. Thanks for the food. I'm going to wash before you see about my bandages."

She put her plate in the sink then picked up Ty's and did the same. "I'll straighten up and be there in a few minutes."

Killing as much time as she could to make sure Ty was out of the bathroom, she knocked lightly on the door to his bedroom fifteen minutes later.

"Michelle, could you help me?" Ty called from the direction of the bathroom.

She didn't think twice before she hurried towards his voice. "Are you all right? What have you done?"

Ty stood near the tub with the shower curtain pulled back. A towel was wrapped around his waist.

"What're you doing? You can't get in the tub with those bandages on."

"I wasn't going to get in the tub. I sponged off the best I could and I was just going to wet my hair so I could wash it. But I decided that wasn't such a good idea. Could you help me?"

Michelle smiled. He sounded pitiful. "Why didn't you ask me sooner?"

"I don't know. Somehow it doesn't sound too macho to ask a woman to wash your hair."

She laughed genuinely this time. "Turn the water off."

He did as he was told then looked at her questioningly.

"Put your pants back on. Customers don't get a wash and dry in my beauty shop dressed in a towel. Meet me in the kitchen."

Ty dropped the towel to the floor and struggled into his scrub pants again. Barefoot, he padded to the kitchen. It hurt just to walk but he knew he'd feel better if he was at least clean. Michelle stood by the sink with towels and a bottle of shampoo at hand.

"So did you work your way through school in a beauty shop?" he asked.

"No, but my mother used to wash my hair like this all the time. You have enough that it needs to be done this way."

"Are you complaining about the length of my hair?" he asked in as indignant a tone as he could muster.

"No. I've never seen more beautiful hair."

Her sharp intake of breath told him she hadn't meant to say that. He grinned. Thankfully that didn't cause any pain. "Why, thank you, ma'am. I always hated it. Too curly, like a girl's."

"I know more than one girl who wished she had hair like yours." Michelle suddenly turned businesslike and folded up a towel lengthways and placed it on the counter in front of the sink. She turned on the faucet.

"Now you're starting to embarrass me. Let's get on with

this." He glanced at her. Had she said she didn't think that was possible?

After testing the water with her hand, Michelle said, "Lean over the sink. Put your chest against the counter." She pulled out the hand sprayer. "You might want to close your eyes."

He leaned forward from the waist and felt every muscle in his body. He moaned.

"I'm sorry. You must be very sore. I'll make this as quick as I can."

Warm water hit his head and Michelle's fingers ran along his scalp, fanning out and moving through his hair.

"Turn your head the other way," Michelle said in a soft voice that sounded as wonderful as the spray felt.

When the water stopped he groaned.

"Are you in pain?"

"No. Not if I don't move. I moaned because that felt so good."

She laughed quietly. "I used to complain too when Mother turned off the water."

He started to stand.

She placed a hand between his shoulder blades. "Stay where you are."

The heat of it was like a brand on his skin. Her fingertips trailed away.

He looked at the sink drain and waited. The top of what had to be the shampoo popped then there was a squirting sound.

"Here." She handed him a small towel. "I don't want to get any soap in your eyes so hold it over your face."

Seconds later her fingers begin tunneling through his hair. Slowly her fingertips massaged their way across his scalp. She applied pressure and he sighed with pleasure as she worked her way up and over the crown of his head.

Coming back down, she took extra time at the base of his neck in an almost erotic movement of her fingers.

"Mmm, that feels good."

She giggled lightly and scrubbed with more force, using the ends of her fingers.

Ty closed his eyes and enjoyed the sensation, forgetting about any pain. The pressure ended. "Hey, don't stop now. That feels so great."

She chuckled. He moved as if to stand and she said, "Be still or you'll get soap everywhere."

A second later spray, warmer than before, hit the top of his head and flowed downwards.

Michelle's fingers returned to moving gently through his hair as she removed the suds. Far too soon, she turned off the water. "Stay still. I'm not done yet."

A towel flapped over his head and she began to gently rub his hair dry. She was as thorough and precise at hair washing as she was in the OR.

He shifted and looked her direction. One of her breasts was within an inch of his lips. His mouth went dry.

"Stop moving."

Had she caught him?

"Turn your head."

Disappointment filled him at losing such a delightful view. Adulation replaced his regret when both breasts were pressed firmly against his shoulder as she leaned over to get to the top of his head. Grateful to be on the receiving end of all this attention, Ty hated to see it end. He'd had no idea how pleasurable it was to have someone wash his hair. Especially if it was Michelle.

"You can straighten up now."

Ty did so but far too stiffly. Did he look as pitiful as he felt? He shook his head, throwing fine droplets of water around him.

"Hey, you're getting me wet," she squealed.

Ty looked at Michelle and smiled. His gaze dropped. Her shirt was plastered against her body, leaving nothing to his imagination. "It looks like you're wet already."

She looked down. Instantly she brought the towel in her hand up to cover her chest. "I'll go and change."

"You don't have to on my account," he called as she headed down the hall.

Michelle closed the door of her bedroom and leaned back against it. Had she lost her mind?

First she'd installed Ty in her home. Then she'd let him insist she sleep beside him and then she'd felt sorry for him and washed his hair. What was going to be next? Would he wiggle his finger and she would jump into bed with him?

She'd crossed that large black line of control she'd had over her life. Ty had ridden in and her brain had turned to mush. Grabbing a dry shirt out of her chest of drawers, she dragged off the wet one she wore and pulled on a dry one.

The glow in Ty's eyes had created an unfamiliar heat deep in her that felt so right. It had started a fire in her center that flowed out, ripple after ripple and made her feel alive. The man had a way of unlocking emotions she'd put away. Had her wanting things better left alone.

Taking a deep breath, she opened the door and went back into the kitchen. Ty was no longer there. Retracing her steps down the hall, she found the door to his room wide open. Ty lay on the bed sound asleep. What little activity he'd done had worn him out. He looked like a small boy, lying on his stomach, his face relaxed. It was a handsome face, all slants and planes. A golden tan covered his back. He was a man who spent time outdoors. The desire to touch him almost overwhelmed her. She wanted to caress that expanse of skin. Instead, she pulled the blanket she'd used during the night over him.

A lock of Ty's still damp hair had fallen over his forehead. Against her better judgment, but unable to resist, she pushed it back into place.

He shifted in his sleep, moaning as he did. Her heart went out to him. She wanted to take his aches away. He was so beat up that he couldn't even get into a hot bath to ease the soreness. Moving again, Ty wrapped his arms around a pillow and pulled it to his chest.

Michelle couldn't remember ever being jealous of an inanimate object before. She wished she could curl up next to his gorgeous body. But she couldn't.

Ty found Michelle sitting in the corner of the sofa in her living area. This room was off the kitchen but he'd not been in it before. Decorated in cheerful hues, like the rest of her place, the room also had a cozier feel. Quilted throws hung off the backs of the chairs and the lighting came from lamps instead of the harsher overhead lighting. Books lined one wall and the TV took a less prominent spot in the corner. She had it turned on and was watching an action movie that was about five years old. Even in her movie choices she continued to surprise him.

The sun was setting. Her face glowed in the last of the light filtering in from the window on the far wall. It was the type of light that a photographer dreamt of having when taking a picture of a subject. Michelle looked angelic. Ty couldn't help but admire her. She was pure beauty.

Michelle must have felt his eyes on her because she looked over the back of the sofa at him.

"Hey." He came further into the room.

"Hey, yourself. How are you feeling?" She twisted further towards him.

"Much better."

"Good."

He moved around the sofa. "Will you help me with this?" He held out his scrub shirt. "I can't seem to get it on by myself."

She stood and took it from him. Gathering the material up around the neck, she said, "Lean over."

He did so and she slipped the material over his head. Lifting his arms, she helped slide the shirt on and down. Her heat warmed him but not once did she touch him. He had no doubt that had been intentional. What was she scared of? There was something there between them, didn't she feel it too?

Michelle returned to the same spot on the sofa. He took the other end.

"You hungry? I didn't even wake you for lunch," she finally said.

"Yeah. I could eat."

She hopped up as if she was looking for an excuse to get away from him. "I'll fix you something."

He grabbed her wrist with his uninjured hand. She stopped and looked down at him. He pulled her down gently, this time closer to him. "You know what I'd really like to have?"

Michelle's eyes widened and she shook her head.

"A meat-lover's pizza. Why don't I buy you dinner?"

She pulled her hand from his. Her look of relief was almost laughable. "Did you think I was going to say something else?"

"No. No, I didn't. I'll call for the pizza. While we're waiting I'll give those bandages a look. You went to sleep so fast that I didn't have a chance to change them and I hated to wake you."

"I buy dinner if you want me to let you look at my stitches." He raised a challenging brow.

"You make it sound like I want to look at a tattoo on your butt."

He laughed. "Wouldn't you like to see it?"

Michelle rewarded him with an appalled look before she stood. "I'll call the pizza delivery place and get the supplies so I can give your arm and knee a look."

Ty listened as Michelle spoke into the phone and rattled around in the kitchen. It seemed like forever since he'd heard those sounds of domestic tranquility. It hadn't happened since he'd lived with his grandparents. His grandmother had made the same noises while his grandfather had sat in the den, reading the paper. They were the sounds of a home.

Bitter-sweet memories filled him. His grandparents had been both surprised and perplexed to see a teenager they'd barely known existed standing at their door. Despite that, they'd invited him in with open arms. It had been the first time he'd ever slept in the same place for over three months. The only time he'd known true stability.

They'd been so old when he'd arrived that he'd not only taken care of himself but often times them too. Somehow doing so had seemed to ease the pain he'd felt at not doing more for Joey. When they'd died within months of each other while he'd been in medical school he'd been devastated. What little foundation there had been in his world had crumbled. The last time he'd heard from his parents had been over three years ago. Who knew where they were now?

Michelle, returning with her hands full of supplies, interrupted his morose thoughts. "Interesting. A surgeon who is prepared," he said as she laid gauze, tape, and surgical scissors on the low table in front of them.

"It's just the usual first-aid type of stuff. Nothing special. Everyone has them."

"I don't."

She met his gaze. "And that would be because you don't stay in one place long enough to have a real home."

Michelle couldn't have made a more accurate shot if she'd punched him in a boxing match. She was right. He didn't, and he wanted it that way. Saw to it that he remained uninvolved.

"Remind me to stop by the drug store and buy a first-aid kit. How does that sound?"

"Smart. Now, let's have a look at your stitches first then I'll redo the gauze on your hand and knee before putting antibacterial ointment on those scrapes."

Michelle carefully cut the gauze and removed the pieces from his arm. She had a tender touch. A mother's touch. That was a completely random thought. If she ever became a mother it wouldn't involve him.

"All looks well. I'm going to just put a four-by-four over it but you're going to have to promise to keep it dry. No hair-washing on your own."

"Yes, ma'am. I'll let you do all my hair-washing."

She looked up at him with serious crystal-blue eyes. "You know making fun of the person who's taking care of you really isn't very smart. They might do something that hurts."

"I might be worried if it was someone else but I don't think I have a truly mean bone in your body. Under that armor of designer clothes, sexy shoes and all-business demeanor you're a softy. You've made a major mistake, Dr. Ross. You've let your guard down where I'm concerned."

Her pupils enlarged and she bit her upper lip. He could almost see the cogs turning in her brain. She looked so endearing and mystified he came close to leaning over and kissing her. She blinked and met his gaze again. The realization she'd been caught darkened her eyes.

Ty placed his hand over one of hers. "Hey, it's not the end of the world. I won't tell anyone, I promise."

She pursed her lips and that old resolve returned to her eyes. "Now you really are making fun of me. Let me see that hand."

He offered his bandaged hand. She took the same care with it as she had with the other but this time unwrapped it slowly. The last bit of gauze stuck to his raw skin. He winced.

Her head jerked up, eyes full of sympathy. She pressed her lips tightly together as she continued to work. When she pulled the last fragment free she said, "Oh, Ty, I'm so sorry. That has to hurt."

He looked at the red, angry area of his palm, which no longer had the top two layers of skin, then back at her. Michelle's eyes were luminous, heavy with tears. The woman did heart surgery and she was crying over him losing skin.

"Hey, don't cry, Michelle, ma belle. I'm okay." He brushed her cheek lightly with his uninjured hand.

She didn't say anything or look at him. Instead she picked up the ointment and started spreading it gently over his wound. Done, she covered it again. She didn't speak and neither did he.

After she'd rewrapped the gauze she said, "Hold this." He placed his fingertip where she indicated. Pulling a piece of tape off a roll, she secured the gauze.

"For me to rebandage your knee you're going to need to take off your pants and I need more gauze. While I'm gone, pull them down and make yourself decent using this blanket. I'll be right back."

"It's been a long time since a woman told me to pull

down my pants." He chuckled at the snort she gave as she left the room.

Michelle soon returned. "Put your heel on the table."

He did so and she started to work on removing the bandage, all business.

"You know, you have gorgeous hair," he said.

She gave him a quelling look.

"So you don't like to be complimented."

Her fingers continued to work with the same efficiency she did in the OR. "I didn't say that."

"Then you do like to be complimented."

She gave him a pointed look. "What I do know is that I'm used to my patients being sedated and I like it that way."

He laughed so hard he had to hold his sides because the pain was so great. "You are too much, Michelle."

"Would you be still and let me finish this?" Her lips quivered in her effort not to smile.

Minutes later she announced, "Good. There's no redness around the stitches." She began wrapping the new gauze into place.

Finished with the knee, she turned her back and let him pull his pants back up. Together they applied ointment to his other lacerations. Done, she gathered supplies. "I'm sorry I can't do something more for those bruises. They have to hurt."

"Maybe kiss them and make them better," he quipped.

"My mother isn't around." The words were as crisp as the leaves on the ground in fall.

He narrowed his eyes. "What does that have to do with it?"

"The only reason we would kiss is to make her happy."

Grabbing her, he jerked her against him. His hurt hand smarted but he didn't care. "I couldn't kiss you like I wanted to with your mother watching but I sure as hell can now."

He ran his fingers into her hair and, holding a mass of the sunny threads in his hand, he brought his mouth down to hers. Michelle would know this one was for her and not her mother.

Before Michelle could catch her breath, Ty's mouth seared hers. His tongue broke the seal of her lips and entered. He didn't ask permission but took. He demanded her attention, her acceptance. She held onto his shoulders, the only stable thing in her spinning world of pure pleasure.

Could she feel more alive? Need more? She was on fire.

Ty's tongue swept, demanded and conquered. His strong arms pulled her tighter until she leaned against him, almost sitting in his lap. Her fingers bit into the muscles of his forearm in an effort to find control.

It felt so good to be against him.

He pulled his mouth away just far enough to say, "Let go, Michelle. Experience it."

The dam burst on her control. She wrapped her arms around his neck and brought her mouth to his again. This time he didn't have to ask for entrance—she was there waiting with a welcome. She took all he gave and returned it. Blazing need pooled heavy and low in her. She writhed against him, pressing her breasts against his chest.

When he tried to pull away she moaned in resistance. She moved her hands up through his hair and directed his mouth to hers. His deep chuckle ripped through her as well as him, they were so close. Yet they weren't close enough. Time stood still as he took over the kiss.

The doorbell rang.

Ty's hands came down to rest on her waist. He gently pushed her away. "I do believe I might have created a monster."

Michelle stiffened and looked away, embarrassed and

angry at the same time. Could she have acted more desperate? Humiliated herself more?

The doorbell sounded again.

Ty placed a finger under her chin and lifted it so that she had to look into his eyes. "Hey, I'm not complaining. Desire is the most perfect form of flattery. And I'm definitely flattered."

She gave him a wry smile.

He dropped a quick kiss on her lips. "I'll get the pizza."

She and Ty decided to eat on the floor in the living room and watch a movie. They found that they were both big fans of action adventure films. She would never have guessed when he'd come into her OR that day that she would have ever had anything in common with Ty. He continued to dumbfound her. By just riding into town he'd tipped her ordered world sideways. Somehow he'd added an excitement to it that she hadn't even known had been missing.

With the movie credits rolling, she pulled herself up off the floor and started to gather the plates and pizza box.

"Do you always have to clean up? Have everything just so?"

She looked down to where Ty still sat with his back against the sofa.

"Leave it. You'd be amazed at how freeing it is. Bet you can't do it."

She dropped the empty box onto the table with a thud and turned to walk away. "Goodnight."

"I didn't mean to make you mad." He sounded truly apologetic.

"It does get old when you're always making snide remarks about how I live, dress, act."

"Hey…" Ty made an effort to stand and groaned in the process.

Unable to help herself, Michelle rushed to him. "What's wrong?"

"I'm just stiff from sitting so long. How about giving me a hand?" He reached his hand towards her.

If she touched him again, what would happen? She'd made a point to keep distance between them as they'd watched the movie she'd still been acutely aware of him the entire time. Particularly after their hot unforgettable kiss earlier. Fear controlled her. She was afraid she could go into his arms far too easily, into his bed. And why shouldn't she? He'd be gone soon. She'd be able to return to her settled life. But could she keep her heart uninvolved? She knew what losing someone did to a person. Would it be worth it?

"It isn't a commitment for life. I just need a tug up."

The man was perceptive. He didn't miss much about her or people in general. That was a trait to be admired.

"Come on, Michelle, ma belle," Ty sang, "live a little. Help a man out."

His grin, as always, was infectious.

Michelle put out her hand and his firm, large one encircled hers. It was emblematic of what he was doing to her life. Blanketing it, binding her more securely to him.

She stepped back on one foot and pulled. Ty, in a lithe movement that made her suspect that he might have been faking his aches and pains, came to his feet. As he moved upwards she leaned further back. When she started to stumble his grip became stronger. He pulled her forward against his solid body, his arm circled her waist and held her firmly in place.

Ty's eyes captured and held her attention. His mouth hovered inches from hers. She wanted to lean forward and touch them with her own, feel them pressed against hers again. Swallowing, she said, "You made up needing help."

"Truthfully, I didn't but it worked out well anyway."

His mouth lowered, taking hers gently, testing. This time he was asking.

Her cellphone sitting on the table rang and rattled against the wood.

"You're not on call. It'll keep," Ty whispered against her ear, before he kissed the sweet spot behind it.

She wanted to do as he'd asked but she couldn't throw away ingrained habits so easily, despite being on the road to heaven.

"I can't." She stepped away and Ty let her go.

"I know. It's who you are."

Michelle picked up the cellphone and answered. She listened, suddenly feeling sick. "I'll be right there."

Tears hit her cheeks before she could get them under control.

Ty put his hands on her shoulders. "What's wrong?"

"My mom's in the hospital. She collapsed. Her neighbor found her. I forgot to call," she said frankly.

"Because of me."

Michelle didn't answer. "I have to go." She headed towards her room for her shoes.

"I'm going with you."

She stopped and looked at Ty. "No, you need to stay here and rest. You look like a postcard for a hospital stay yourself. Being black and blue."

"If I were a man with less self-esteem I might be devastated by that comment. I'm going with you."

"You don't—"

"I said I'm going."

She'd been alone with her mother's illness for so long that she couldn't imagine what it would be like to have someone along for support. It sounded nice, really nice. "Okay, but I don't know how long I'll be."

"It doesn't matter. I'll stay as long as you do."

"If you start hurting you're getting a taxi back here. I don't need two people in the hospital to care for."

"Yes, ma'am."

She knew that tone well by now. Ty would do as he pleased, no matter what she said.

"Michelle."

She looked at him. "Yes."

"Don't think what was happening here is over."

Heat zipped through her, carrying anxiety, apprehension and the sweet thrill of anticipation. Ty wanted her. Not only now but later.

CHAPTER SIX

TY WAS GLAD to see Mrs. Ross settled in a room and comfortable. Her blood count had dipped, making her feel lightheaded and causing her to fall. With a blood transfusion and a couple of days' stay in the hospital, she'd be home again.

Michelle had stress written all over her face. Was this the same self-assured woman Ty was beginning to know so well? Her mother's illness was taking its toll. Her breakdown in the OR and the over-the-top fear she'd experienced when she'd been called about her mother said her emotions were tissue-paper thin. She'd been carrying the load of worry by herself for far too long.

At least he was here for her now. He hadn't been for Joey. That pure, raw panic in Michelle's eyes had reached deep in him, to the place where he didn't want to return.

Ty looked at the mother and daughter as they spoke quietly. Where it had once been a strong woman and a weaker one, now all Ty saw was two fragile women who loved each other. Even though he wasn't completely comfortable with how involved in Michelle's life he had become he would support her to the best of his ability until it was time for him to leave.

"You two need to go home. I'm all right. The nurses will take good care of me tonight," Mrs. Ross said, looking past Michelle to where he sat.

"Mother, I don't want to leave you in here alone," Michelle said.

In a stronger voice Mrs. Ross said, "Ty, please see that Michelle gets home safely. She's tired and you don't look much better. You shouldn't have come anyway with all those injuries." She looked back at her daughter. "I'll go to sleep as soon as you are both gone."

"Mom—"

"No argument. Ty, take care of her."

"Yes, ma'am." He went to stand beside Michelle's chair. "Come on. We'll come back first thing in the morning." He took her elbow with his uninjured hand and urged her to stand.

Michelle leaned over and kissed her mother. "I'll see you in the morning."

"I'll be here." Her mother gave her a weak smile. "Thanks, Ty."

He nodded. In the parking lot he said, "Let me have your keys. You're too done in to drive."

"You drive a motorcycle." Michelle yawned wide and long.

"I assure you I remember how to drive a car."

Michelle handed over the keys without further argument. Ty helped her into the passenger side of the car and closed the door. She was dead on her feet. He'd had induced sleep the night before while she'd been up checking on him every hour or so. He didn't remember every time she had, but as conscientious as she was he knew she'd done it. If he didn't miss his guess he'd say she'd not slept any today either.

As a surgeon part of her job was to have the stamina to work long hours but that wasn't when you were emotionally involved. Worry over her mother had drained her.

Before he'd pulled out of the lot, Michelle's head was bobbing. "Put your head on my shoulder."

She shook her head. "You're bruised."

"I'm a big boy, I can handle it."

She didn't fight him or argue further. Leaning her head against him, she was resting peacefully seconds later. There was something right about having her under his care. It made him think of what-ifs. But he didn't do long term. Didn't stay in one place. Guilt ate at him. He'd let Joey down. Would end up letting Michelle down also.

It was better not to get involved. But on some level wasn't he already?

Michelle woke to Ty calling her name. What a wonderful way to come out of sleep.

"We're home. I wouldn't have woken you and just carried you into the house but my hand and arm…"

"Hey, it's the thought that counts. I can walk."

"Thanks for letting my ego down easy."

She went in ahead of him. "I'll get your medicine."

Ty stepped to the kitchen counter to stand beside her. He took the prescription bottle out of her hand and put it down. He cupped her cheek with his good hand. "I can take care of myself. You've looked after everyone but yourself today. Go and get into bed."

Michelle blinked slowly with a drowsy look that made him think of tangled sheets and her beneath him. She had no idea of the power she was gaining over him. Thankfully she didn't argue, which told him just how worn out she was.

"Goodnight," she mumbled as she walked off.

Ty groaned. He needed to take something that would make him sleep because every fiber in him wanted to follow right behind her and straight into her bed. But he wouldn't take the medicine. He wanted to be alert if Michelle needed him during the night.

After securing the condo for the night, he headed down

the hall towards his room. As he was entering, a sound of glass breaking came from Michelle's room.

Ty went to her door, which was slightly open. "Michelle, is everything all right?"

A muffle sound was all the response he received.

He nudged the door wider. "Michelle, are you hurt?"

"I...need your help," came from the direction of what had to be the bathroom. Ty stalked across the room and didn't hesitate to enter the bathroom.

Tears ran down Michelle's face. She sat on the edge of the tub with a towel haphazardly wrapped around her, leaving more skin exposed than covered. If she hadn't looked so distraught he would have tugged on that towel and finished what they had started earlier in the evening.

Instead, he saw shattered glass surrounding her feet and some type of pink-colored liquid on the floor. Michelle held her hand in her lap. A finger dripped blood.

"I don't know what's wrong with me," she sobbed.

Ty's heart contracted. An emotionally brittle Michelle tore at his soul.

Still wearing his shoes, he stepped further into the bathroom and snatched a hand towel off a hook. Lifting Michelle's injured hand, he wrapped the towel around it. He ignored his injuries that screamed against the pressure as he scooped her up into his arms.

She didn't resist, leaning her head on his shoulder. So frayed, she didn't comment on his wounds either.

He laid her on the bed. "Stay put. I'll get something for that finger."

She rolled away from him and pulled her knees up to her chest. The towel around her body slipped upwards, barely covering her bottom. Ty turned away and made his way to the kitchen to find the first-aid supplies she'd used on him earlier in the day. Locating them in a small drawer, he took out what he thought he'd need. By the amount of blood he'd seen, it looked as if she might need stitches.

Returning to her room, he found Michelle still curled on the bed. She looked so lost and pitiful. This was no longer the self-assured, in-control, sharp-tongued woman he knew from the OR. Michelle had morphed into a scared, exhausted and heartbroken daughter with an ill mother. The ice queen had turned human.

His chest tightened. All he wanted to do was to gather her up and hold her tight, reassuring her that all would be well. But if he did, could he stop there?

She needed someone to care for her. To help her carry her burdens. To stand beside her when she required help. Could he be that person? His past said no. But he was here now. He would take care of her while he was here.

Ty sat on the edge of the bed. "Michelle, you're going to have to roll over and let me see your finger. We need to get it covered or you'll get blood all over the bedspread." He reached out to touch her shoulder but only let it hover, unable to trust himself if he came in contact with the creamy skin. He rested his hand on the bed. "Come on, ma belle, let me see your finger."

Michelle rolled but remained in the same fetal position. She flopped her hand out into his lap. Ty undid the towel and was pleased to see that the cut wasn't as extensive as he'd expected. Using the wet cloth he'd brought from the kitchen, he cleaned the blood away. A sticking-plaster would do.

She watched him work with blank eyes. She didn't even wince when he touched the cut with the cloth. Her detachment worried him. Had she become so despondent that she'd given up?

As he finished applying the dressing he smiled at her and said, "You know, at this rate the two of us aren't going to generate much trust in our patients. We both look like accidents waiting to happen."

He was pleased to see a slight smile form on her lips. He liked it. She didn't do it often enough.

"I'm going to clean up the mess in the bathroom. While I'm doing that why don't you put on a nightgown and get into bed? You'll feel better after a good night's rest."

Not waiting for her answer, he took the first-aid supplies back to the kitchen and found the broom and dustpan. When he returned Michelle was asleep but still covered in only the towel and lying on top of the spread.

Putting the broom and dustpan in the bathroom, he came back and pulled the spread away on the opposite side of the bed from Michelle. Circling around to her side again, he lifted her. She snuggled against him, warm and perfect. She was very appealing with her hair disheveled and so much smooth skin showing. Most troubling of all was that she smelled wonderful. Like springtime flowers and rain.

Ty placed her on the sheet and gently pulled the towel from her with a growl of remorse and a straining of his manhood. Reminding himself that at this time she was more patient than lover, he resisted the urge to linger and look his fill. With a jerk of the covers he pulled the top sheet and spread up over Michelle's shoulders.

After turning the bedside table lamp on and the overhead light off, he headed to the bathroom to clean up. Minutes later he had what he assumed was bath oil removed from the floor. The smell was strong but it reminded him of the sleeping woman who so tempted him in the bed just a few feet away. With a sharp note to keep his mind on the job, he went back to sweeping.

This clean-up job was the most domestic thing he'd done in years. In fact, the last few days had been most unusual. Eating in a kitchen. Sleeping in a real home. Being a part of someone's life. For once in a long time he wished for more. These types of thoughts wouldn't lead to anything positive. He'd already learned more than once that he couldn't take a chance on having those feelings. It was too easy for it all to be gone. It wasn't worth the pain.

Replacing the broom and dustpan, he threw the towels he'd used to clean up the oil into the washer. He'd check on Michelle and head to bed.

Unable to resist touching her and making the excuse that she might have a fever, he pushed a ribbon of hair away from her face. He was pleased to find that her skin was cool. Satisfied she wasn't sick but unsatisfied where his body was concerned, he reached over and turned out the lamp.

"Ty."

"Yes, ma belle?"

"Would you hold me?" The words came out as if she was bone weary.

He stood shock still. Could he? Could he not?

"I'm so cold inside."

He'd hold her until she went back to sleep. Surely he could muster that much self-control over his basic instincts and help her through this time. But she was naked.

Breathing deeply and kicking off his shoes, he slid under the covers and onto his side. He ran his unbandaged arm under her neck and the other circled her waist. This time he was grateful that a bandage covered most of his hand. If he been able to feel her skin against his palm there would have been no way to control his desires. Michelle snuggled up against him and with a deep sigh stilled. He gritted his teeth and tried to think about taking a bath in ice water. Seconds later her even breathing told him she was asleep again.

Would she even know she'd asked him into her bed tomorrow? Or what he'd suffered to be here?

His fingertips brushed her skin. It felt warm and silky smooth. He wanted to explore more of her. With a groan, he shifted. Even the loose pants of his scrubs felt tight. With great effort he pushed the fact that she was naked out of his mind, or at least tried to. It was impossible. His body throbbed with lust, despite his best efforts to convince it otherwise.

Ty rubbed his cheek against her soft hair. Breathing in the floral scent of her bath oil, which was as classy as Michelle, he looked off into the dark. He begged for sleep to ease the agony, confident it would never come. The night would be a long one.

Michelle shifted to find a wall of warmth preventing her from totally rolling over. She snuggled closer, her face padded against the musk of heated skin. Wanting more, she put an arm over it and aligned herself.

"Michelle. Stop."

A dark rumble above her head jerked her to reality. She held her breath.

"Let go, Michelle, so I can move."

She didn't. She didn't want to. Didn't want Ty to move.

Ty felt so good against her. She wanted more. All of him. Her hand rested partly on material and partly on skin. She nudged what had to be his scrub shirt upwards until her hand found heated skin.

"Mmm." Her fingertips flowed over the skin, feeling it ripple.

A groan of deep agony warned, "Michelle, wake up."

"I don't want to. This is a nice dream," she mumbled as she traced the line of his last rib. "It feels good. I want to feel good."

The rush of air being forcefully sucked in came from above. "If you keep that up it won't be a dream but reality."

"Okay," she said, pushing the material further out of the way.

He winced.

Had she lost her mind? She was coming on to a man who had been in an accident. He was hurt, sore. She had reached a new low in the need department. But what would be so wrong with them making each other feel good for just a little while? Ty wanted her. He'd made that clear.

Looking up, she found his heavy-lidded eyes focused on her.

"I'm sorry. I'm hurting you." She moved away.

"Hey, come back here. This is the kind of pain I like." His voice was a low gravel tone laced with desire that made her nerve endings sing.

Running her hand further under his shirt, she trailed the flat of her hand across the contours of his chest, following every dip and curve. He didn't move, letting her explore to her heart's content. The palm of her hand caressed and came to rest low on his belly. She leaned over and kissed the spot where her hand had been.

Ty hissed in response, "Michelle, if you go much further there'll be no stopping."

"I'm not a child. I know what I'm doing. Yes. I want this. I want to feel good, alive."

Ty's hands gripped her under her arms and pulled her up until his lips almost touched hers. "Aw, ma belle, I'm just the man for the job."

His mouth took hers in a sweeping kiss, like none she'd ever experienced. His tongue demanded entrance and she gave it. He savored and devoured, then turned playful again.

Her breasts tingled, tightened as her nipples hardened, anticipating Ty's touch.

His hands roamed with complete freedom along her sides and over her bare bottom. He lifted her, bringing her closer. She felt the ridge of his arousal against her stomach. A giddy feeling rippled through her. She'd made Ty want her in the most elemental way. The man who charmed all the women and could have anyone wanted her. *Her.*

Michelle pushed at his shirt again. She wore no clothes but he was still dressed. She wanted her skin against his. Wanted all of him. Wanted, needed to be touched, tasted and be taken. Whatever it took to forget her responsibilities. To live for herself for once.

"Off." He let her go and she rolled away. He raised his chest inches from the mattress and she helped him remove his shirt.

His arms circled her again and her breasts came to rest against his chest. She shifted, trying to get closer. His heat and need flowed through her. With a grunt that reminded her that he was hurt, he rolled her onto her back.

"Ty, you're hurt—"

"Shut up," he said softly. His mouth captured hers. Slowly, far too slowly his hands moved towards her breasts. They ached for his touch. Her nipples beaded, rose and awaited his consideration.

One hand came to lie wide and heavy on her middle. He made small tantalizing circles along her skin, which sent ripples of desire dancing through her. She sucked in a breath, held it as his fingertips worked magic.

This was living. Something she'd put on hold for far too long. And even if it was just for tonight, she would grasp this feeling with both hands.

Ty finally cupped a straining breast and her hips flexed. He lifted the weight of her breast and ran a fingertip around the tip. She throbbed in her center, burned with need. She opened her eyes to find Ty watching her. His eyes had turned the dark green of a forest in summer. They bored into hers.

He continued to tease her breast as he whispered, "There's nothing icy about you. You are pure molten lava for me. Ma belle."

His mouth dipped to favor a nipple.

Her hips came off the bed and her eyes closed as she sailed away on a tide of pure pleasure.

His mouth released her. When he pulled away she let out a sound of disappointment, begging for more. If he didn't touch her…

Ty didn't disappoint. Moving to the other breast, he took it into his mouth. He tormented and teased by circling his tongue around her pebbled tip. She throbbed with a craving that only Ty could satisfy. His attention brought white-hot heat to where she wanted him most.

His lips came back to hers, before departing again to leave small kisses along her jaw line. He pushed her hair away and kissed the sweet dip behind her ear. She shivered and brought her legs up to circle his hips.

Ty broke her grip and shimmied down her body, leaving wet kisses as he went. She clawed at his shoulders to stop him.

"Oh, no, here you don't run the show. We share. Right now it's my turn," Ty growled.

"I want—"

"I know you do. I do too. But not yet. I must enjoy you some more."

Ty kissed her belly, orbited her bellybutton with his tongue. She flinched and groaned.

"So responsive. So hot for me," Ty rasped, his voice rich with approval.

He continued to place kisses over her skin, across the ridge of her hip bones and lower. Michelle's fingers found his hair and played with it, letting it fall between her fingers. Watching as a curl caressed her fingertip. It was as wonderful as she had imagined it to be.

One of Ty's hands found her calf and slowly slid up to her knee. His finger caressed the underside until she could stand it no longer and pulled way.

The small rumble in his chest said that had been his plan. She opened for him and he pressed his advantage. His talented and capable fingers traveled along the length of the inside of her thigh, teased and moved down to her knee again.

Michelle whimpered with disappointment. She wasn't going to be able to take much more. Then his fingers started their slow, excruciatingly magnificent travel upwards once more. He did it again and again, each time stopping just a little closer to her begging center.

Her hands clawed at the sheets. She'd become nothing but a mass of wonton, beseeching need. He was driving her beyond reason.

Finally, Ty's finger touched her center and her hips arched off the bed.

"Easy. Soon. Very soon." His finger entered her waiting heat and she came unglued, bursting with release. His body covered hers and their lips met. "That was a beautiful thing to behold, ma belle, but we're not finished."

Ty pushed up and away from her as if any pain or soreness he might have felt was forgotten. He headed out the door as if on a mission. Michelle curled into the bed and enjoyed the lovely waves of pleasure that Ty had left behind. Seconds later, he returned with a packet of protection. She watched as he peeled out of his pants and underwear at the same time.

There was nothing bashful about this man as he stood proudly before her, all wild hair, expansive chest, flat stomach, slim hips and strong thighs. The most obvious was his desire for her standing tall and ready. Michelle couldn't take her eyes off him. He was the Greek god of her dreams.

Ty took care of protecting them. The bed dipped as he rejoined her. "There's no going back from here, Michelle. You say the word and I'll leave," he said quietly but with meaning.

She wrapped her arms around his neck and pulled him to her. He lowered and surrounded her. With a sigh, she accepted his weight. For once she wasn't afraid to be out of control. To have someone take the lead.

He kissed her deep and long before his hands found her breasts and gave them the attention they longed for. He shifted so that she cradled him between her legs. His manhood rested at her entrance.

"Look at me," he growled. "I want to see that passion you try so hard to hide when I enter you."

Her eyes flickered up to meet his. As if he could stand it no longer, he buried himself deep in her. Ty leaned down and breathed into her ear, "Heaven, ma belle."

He pulled back then pushed forward again. Michelle flexed to meet him, taking him completely. Ty increased the pace. She joined him. As they moved faster, she climbed higher. Reaching her peak, she exploded into beautiful waves of perfect bliss. With the sound of her name drifting off his lips and a final thrust, Ty found his completion. His weight covered her but she offered no complaint.

Some time later, Michelle lay with her head on Ty's stomach as he played with her hair. She lifted his hand with the bandage and kissed each fingertip. "You are right. We are a pair."

"How's that?"

"You're all banged up and even I have an injury. We won't inspire much confidence as doctors." She held up her finger and giggled. She couldn't remember the last time she'd truly giggled. Ty brought that out in her. She felt wonderful.

"I'll kiss yours if you'll kiss mine."

She looked up at him. He had a wicked grin on his face.

"That sounds like a fine idea. I get to go first." She rolled over and placed a kiss just below his waist and moved downwards. She fully expected to have another mind-blowing, body-sedating and deliciously satisfying experience this time around as well.

Ty woke to the afternoon sun shining into the room. Michelle's leg lay over one of his. Even in her sleep she tried to dominate. Earlier, he'd let her and had more than enjoyed it. Her hand rested on one of his shoulders and she had a handful of his hair intertwined in her fingers. Her head had found a bed in the crook of the other shoulder.

He was sore and stiff from the motorcycle accident and the events of the night before had not improved that but he wouldn't have missed having the responsive and tender Michelle in his arms for anything. It felt right to have her there. As if she belonged. It had been a long time since anyone had belonged to him.

They'd slept, made love and slept again. Michelle had gotten up long enough to call and check on her mother. After receiving a favorable report, she'd returned to him. Their lovemaking had been slow and gentle the next time as if they'd both wanted it to be special.

Michelle stirred beside him and he hugged her close. It was nice, really nice. Could he do this every day? Looking down at her face, he wished he could. The question was did he know how? He had no experience at staying in one place or having someone depend on him.

His heart thumped hard against his chest. What was happening? This feeling was foreign to him. He'd no intention of caring, didn't want to take the chance. Had fought it for years. Was he falling for Michelle? Had it already happened?

She twisted in his arms and her hand rubbed his cheek. "You need a shave."

"You weren't complaining about it a while ago."

"I guess I wasn't," she said softly. "Ty, I want to thank you."

What? The world as he knew it had made a one-eighty turn and she was thanking him for sex. Had he been used? He sure felt like it.

"I appreciate…this…all you've done," she went on, oblivious to the fact she was stabbing him in the heart.

Ty sat up. "Hell, Michelle, that wasn't sympathy sex. There's more than that between us. I know you want people to believe you're a cold fish, but I know better."

He disentangled himself from her, pushed the sheet away and stood.

Michelle opened her mouth as if to speak.

"Stop there, Michelle. You've already said enough."

She sat up, pulling the sheet over her breasts. "Where's this coming from? You don't take anything seriously. You're planning to leave soon."

"Sure I do. I was serious last night. Plenty serious about you."

"You can't be, we don't even have anything in common."

"It sure seemed like we had plenty in common last night and a number of times after that."

"Relationships are made up of more than sex."

"So all that has happened between us you sum up as just being sex?"

She gasped.

"Exactly. It does sound cold and one-sided."

He snatched up his clothes and headed for the other bedroom. After calling a taxi, he washed up the best he could and was waiting on the curb when his ride arrived.

CHAPTER SEVEN

THE NEXT WEEK was the longest and most difficult of any Michelle had experience since her father had passed away. She'd never felt more alone.

Her mother had been released from the hospital and was doing well. She asked about Ty often but Michelle dodged her questions. How could she tell her mother what had happen between her and Ty?

Work was the worst. She saw Ty but then really didn't. To her great surprise he was no longer assigned to her OR. They might pass at the scrub sink or at the nurses' station but they had become strangers. For two people to have shared such closeness, they were a world apart now.

She would never have thought she would miss Ty so much. He'd gotten under her skin. Had become part of her life in such a short time.

"Dr. Ross, is everything okay with you?" Jane, her surgical nurse, asked after one of their cases.

"Yes, why?" She didn't dare admit that she was pining for Ty.

"You just haven't been yourself the last week or so. I'm… concerned about you."

Michelle stopped what she was doing and looked at Jane. "You've never asked me anything personal before so why now?"

"I don't know. You seemed to have changed somehow. Like you're giving me a chance to ask." She hesitated then said, "I know what's said about you but I also know you care about the patients above all else, even to your own detriment. I see it in the way you worry over them. Don't let what some of the nurses say get to you. There are those of us who know differently."

Michelle was speechless. She and Jane had worked together for years and this was the first time Michelle had ever heard anything like this from her. "Thank you, Jane. That means a lot to me."

The woman gave Michelle a reassuring smile.

A few days later, Michelle overheard a group of the nurses talking about going to Buster's to hear the surgeons' band play.

Taking a breath, she asked, "Do you mind...uh...if I join you?"

The shock on the nurses' faces would have been comical if not for the fact it was so sad that she had chosen to be so remote that she received that type of reaction.

Jane stepped forward. "We'll save you a place at the table."

The other nurses murmured their agreement.

"Thank you. I'd like that." She gave them all a sincere smile as they headed toward the locker room.

"Jane," Michelle said.

The nurse stopped and turned back to Michelle with a questioning look on her face.

"May I ask you something?"

"Sure."

"I saw the looks on the others' faces just now. Have I really been that bad?"

"Yeah, I guess you have. You're a great surgeon but not

very personable." Jane reached out and placed a hand on Michelle's arm. "But I think that's changing."

Michelle gave her a weak smile. "Thanks, Jane."

She gave Michelle a reassuring smile. "I'll see you this evening."

A couple of hours later Michelle groaned when she looked at the growing pile of clothing on her bed. Since when did she have such an issue with dressing? She'd always laid out her outfit for the next day, had everything organized. She looked at the rows of suits and dresses hanging in the closet in perfect order. For some reason she wanted to shake things up a bit. Wanted to live a little differently. Wanted Ty's attention again.

She'd hurt his feelings unintentionally. Their time together had been earth-shattering for her. If she let herself care he'd break her heart, she had no doubt about that. Nothing about Ty said permanence. No stability. She had to have that. There was her mother to consider. Her job. Even if she wanted to she couldn't pick up and follow him if he asked her to, which he hadn't. Her practical side couldn't help but remember that he was only here for a few more weeks.

Right now he wouldn't even have a conversation with her. Their time in bed together had been wonderful, but she found she yearned for their discussions. His sharp wit when they disagreed. His smiles, making her laugh, getting her to have a different perspective on things. She missed their friendship.

Wow. They'd had a friendship. She'd not had a real friend in years. Someone who knew what was going on in her life. She'd actually confided in Ty. That was something she'd even had difficulty doing with her mother.

Maybe tonight he'd speak to her. See that she was trying to say she was sorry, attempting to make a change. Maybe they could get back on a better footing. What she wanted was for them to at least be friends.

Running out of time, she settled on a pair of designer jeans. She'd not worn them for months and was pleased to discover they fit perfectly. After adding a red short-sleeved shirt and red patent heels, she was pleased with the effect. When was the last time she'd spent this much time fussing over what she wore? She usually did it with confidence and very little thought. Had she ever dressed to get the attention of a man before? She took longer than usual with her make-up and hair. After adding some swinging earrings and jingly bracelets, she was ready. She looked into the mirror and smiled. Surely Ty would notice her.

With an unfamiliar nervous flutter in her belly, she picked up her keys and headed out the door. By the time she reached Buster's much of her confidence had waned. She drove an extra trip around the block in an effort to fortify herself.

What if Jane and the others didn't talk to her? What if she had to sit at a table alone? Worse, what if Ty was there with a date?

For heaven's sake, when had she become so insecure? When Ty had shown up.

She was a well-respected heart surgeon in a large metropolitan hospital. She'd been taking care of herself, her mother and patients for years, so why was she having such a difficult time going into a public place and having a drink? Because she was scared.

She pulled into the first parking spot open. Enough of that.

Entering Buster's, her eyes needed to adjust to the dim lighting. She stood to the side of the doorway, pushing away the urge to turn and run. Just as she'd made up her mind to do so, Jane appeared beside her.

"Hey, Dr. Ross. I'm glad you came. We have a table right up front. Been saving you a seat."

"Hi Thanks." Michelle followed Jane through the crowd to the table.

Six other OR nurses Michelle recognized were already there.

"Hey, everyone. Dr. Ross made it," Jane announced.

Each said hi and gave Michelle unsure smiles. They were obviously uncomfortable about sharing their table with the ice queen. She'd have to work on changing that. "Hello. Please call me Michelle."

That request brought on jaw-dropping looks from almost everyone. Jane took one of the vacant chairs and Michelle squeezed into another. The serving girl wearing short shorts and a tight T-shirt came by and asked for their drink order.

Michelle looked around but didn't see Ty. Lauren, one of the nurses sitting on the other side of her, leaned over and said, "I've been wanting to ask you where you buy your clothes."

A ripple of pleasure went through Michelle at the unexpected question. The others around the table leaned in closer to hear her answer. She smiled at them all. "I shop at a number of places. But I really like this particular boutique over in Winston-Salem."

"You'll have to give us directions. You always look so put together."

"Thank you." She gave them a bright smile.

"Maybe we could plan a girls' day out and you could show us where it is," Jane suggested.

Girls' day? That sounded kind of nice. "Sure," Michelle said.

"Then let's plan it for some time soon," the nurse across the table said.

Michelle smiled. "Okay."

The band started filing onto the tiny stage area in the back of the room and to the right of them. Michelle was acquainted with all the band members but the one who had her complete attention was Ty.

He wore his usual jeans and T-shirt that she'd come to recognize as his favorite clothing, even though she'd only seen him briefly and even then in scrubs in the last few weeks. His attire tonight suited him. Even in dress, they were opposites.

Ty stood to the side of the leader of the band and focused on tuning his guitar. Minutes later the band broke into their first song. It was an upbeat rock-and-roll number that everyone was familiar with. The crowd went wild.

They moved from that song right into the next. The band was quite good. Ty had a real flair for the dramatic on the guitar, which wasn't unexpected. His playing was an extension of his personality. The crowd showed their appreciation a number of times and most of the women couldn't keep their eyes off him.

The band was well into the third number when Ty scanned the crowd. Michelle saw the instant he became aware of her. His gaze had gone past her and quickly returned. His look didn't waver from where she sat. She smiled. Good. He'd been shocked to see her. For once, he was the one off balance.

For a moment his fingers hesitated on the strings of the guitar. Seconds later his attention was forced to return to the number he played. During the rest of the set, his eyes continued to drift her direction.

After one of the times Ty had stared at her, she glanced at Jane to find her watching her. Jane leaned over and said into Michelle's ear, "Ty sure is interested in someone at our table."

She shrugged. "I guess so."

* * *

Michelle made her way to the restroom during the band's break. Exiting the restroom, she stopped short when she saw Ty standing with his back against the wall, hands in his pockets and one foot over the other. He gave her a level look.

"Slumming tonight, Michelle?"

Her heart constricted. She might have deserved the shot but that didn't mean she liked hearing it. "You invited me. Remember?"

"That was weeks ago."

She shrugged a shoulder. "So I was a little late showing up." He wasn't going to make this easy. "The band is good. You're good."

He lips tightened and he nodded, not taking his eyes off her, as if he was having to plan his response.

She waited, not sure what would happen next or even what she wanted.

"Why are you here, Michelle?"

Apparently he wanted her to spell it out.

A woman came down the hall heading in their direction. Michelle glanced at her, unsure about baring her heart in front of a stranger.

"Come with me." Ty grabbed her hand and pull her further down the hall.

"Where're we going?"

He paused and pinned her with a look. "For once, just let me lead."

They stopped in front of a door. He knocked. There was no answer so he opened it, pulled her in. It was an office. A lone small lamp burn on the desk. Ty closed the door behind them.

"I'll ask it again. Why're you here, Michelle?"

"Don't you know?"

"Maybe. But I want you to tell me."

She took a deep breath. Ty's gaze slipped down to her chest and quickly returned to her eyes. At least he still found her desirable. That was a positive sign.

"I'm sorry I hurt you. I didn't mean to. Please forgive me."

Ty stood looking at her long enough that she feared he would reject her.

"I shouldn't let you off so easily." Suddenly he closed the few steps that were between them. He pressed her against the back of the door with his body while his hands burrowed though her loose hair. His lips swooped down to capture hers.

With a moan she circled his waist with her arms and pulled him closer. Ty didn't have to request entrance into her mouth, she offered it. Michelle grabbed the whirling and unfurling sensations flowing through her and hung on for the ride, having no idea how much she'd missed Ty until that moment.

"Mmm," she moaned.

"Missed me, did you?" Ty said as he left kisses on her nose and eyes.

"Maybe a little."

He chuckled and pressed his hips into her. "I missed you just a little too, Michelle, ma belle."

Ty lips took hers again, but this time the kiss was more restrained, making her beg for more.

There was a knock at the door. "Hey, Ty, you in there? We're on in five."

"I'll be right there," Ty called, then leaned his forehead against hers.

The sound of their panting filled the small area.

"I've got to step away from you right now or I won't be presentable in public."

It was empowering to know she had such an effect on Ty. It was an intoxicating feeling.

He stepped back, letting his hands caress her cheeks as he did. He moved to stand beside the desk well out of her touching distance. Her hands itched to have him close again.

His eyes started at the top of her head and moved slowly down her to stop at her shoes. "You sure look incredibly sexy tonight. I particularly love those hot red shoes. I hope all that effort was for my benefit."

"Could be I came to see one of the other band members play."

He growled. "Even if you did, you'll be leaving with me."

Was he jealous? "Nice to know that your ego hasn't deflated any over the last few weeks."

"You might be surprised how easy it is to damage my ego."

Michelle's heart skipped a beat. Was she really that important to him?

"I'll leave with whoever I wish."

In two quick steps Ty had her in his arms again. "I don't think so," he said before his lips met hers. When he pulled away his mouth hovered just above hers. "I'll tell you what, you promise I'm the only person you'll leave with and I'll buy you a burger after the last set. Maybe tell you which table Buster dedicated to your father."

Her eyes widened. "What?"

"You heard me. We'll talk about it over that burger." He gave her a quick kiss. "Now I've got to go."

Michelle moved so Ty could open the door. He allowed her to leave ahead of him. As they walked down the hall, Jane approached them. She looked from Michelle to Ty and back again. A large grin formed on her face. "Hello, Ty, Michelle."

"Hey, Jane," Ty said as they passed her.

"Ty," Jane called above the sounds of the band warming up.

"Yeah?"

"You might want to wipe that red lipstick off before you go on stage."

Michelle had no doubt that her face had turned the same color as her lips.

He grinned and rubbed the back of his hand across his lips. "Thanks, Jane. Michelle attacked me."

Michelle held her head high and kept moving, grateful for the low light. For once she didn't care who knew her business. Ty was at least speaking to her.

Ty had hardly been able to believe his eyes when he'd seen Michelle in the audience. He'd done a true double-take. He hadn't had to wonder if she'd come to see him—it was as good as written all over her face. Her eyes were for him only.

He'd worked his way to her table after the first set to find her not there. Without asking, Jane had pointed him in the direction of the restroom. He'd tried to look casual as he'd waited for Michelle to come out, but his insides had been churning. Thinking of little else but wanting Michelle and remembering those extraordinary hours they'd spent together had made the last two weeks apart horrible.

He wanted her to regret treating what had been the hottest night of passion he'd ever experienced as if he'd been there only to help her through a bad time. But to be fair, he hadn't led her to believe that their relationship would be anything but a casual thing, only lasting until he left. He hadn't changed his mind. But at least this way she wouldn't expect something more, something he couldn't give.

When Michelle had finally emerged from the ladies room he'd wavered between relief and insecurity. Would she be glad to see him?

He'd meant to be cool, to act as if her being there hadn't affected him. It had worked for a little while before he'd had to touch her. And what had he done? Attacked her like a teen in heat. He grinned. She'd seemed to enjoy it. It had been almost painful to leave her with her lips swollen from his kisses and a flame of desire glowing in her eyes to return to the stage.

Now he was trying to focus on his music despite his attention continually returning to Michelle. Her eyes were always there to meet his. She had a slight smile on her face, which pleased him. Beautiful any time, Michelle was radiant when she smiled. Something she was doing more often now. She deserved to be happy.

The band finished their final number and said goodnight. Ty put up his guitar and shook hands with the other members. He searched the area where Michelle had been sitting and found her no longer there. After a moment of panic, he located her waiting near an empty booth across the room. With an excited skip to his heart he grinned and joined her.

"I saw this one open and thought I should get it before someone else did." She returned his smile.

"Great. You have a seat. I'll go to the bar and order those burgers. What would you like to drink?"

"A soda would be fine," she said as she slid into one of the bench seats.

Ty laid his guitar case on the other bench and made his way across the room. He hurriedly placed their order, worried that Michelle might change her mind and leave. Had he ever felt so insecure about a woman before?

Returning to the table, he said to Michelle, "Scoot over. Emily is taking up all the room on the other side."

She wrinkled up her forehead. "Emily?"

"Yeah. My guitar."

She moved further into the booth. "You named your guitar."

"Sure. Doesn't everybody?" He slipped in beside her, moving close enough that her thigh met his from hip to knee. If he could get away with it, he'd say forget the burgers and let's go home but was afraid he'd scare her off. He'd already come on too strong.

"I don't know. I don't play a guitar."

"Maybe I'll teach you someday." He picked up her hand and began caressing each finger. "With these long fingers I bet you could make lovely music."

She gently pulled her hand away. "Who knows? I might just take you up on that offer some time. Now, tell me what you were saying about a table here being named for my father."

"See that booth over there." He pointed across the room. "There's a little gold plaque on the table with your daddy's name on it."

"How do you know?"

"I was in here the other day and happened to sit at that booth. When I read the plaque I knew the Ross had to be yours." She looked as if she wanted to push him out of the way and go and have a look.

"I had no idea."

"I figured you didn't," he said.

"Why didn't you tell me sooner?"

"I don't know, maybe you pretty much told me that

you had used me and didn't plan to have any more to do with me."

She had the good grace to appear ashamed. "I'm sorry. I hadn't meant to imply that."

By the expression on her face, he believed she was. "I can't really blame you. I've never given you any indication that I wanted more."

Her eyes grew wide and she looked at him expectantly. "Do you?"

Ty tightened his lips and shook his head slightly. "No. I'll be leaving in three weeks. That's how it has to be."

She gave him a resigned look of understanding and looked away.

He needed to get them back on an even footing again, change the subject. "Hey, when that couple leaves we'll have a look."

One of the barmaids brought their meals and refilled their drinks before she turned to another table.

"I can't eat all this!" Michelle exclaimed. "This burger is bigger than I remember."

"I sure can. I'm starving," Ty said, picking up his burger from beside a pile of French fries.

Minutes later, with half his burger gone and Michelle well into hers, he said, "So tell me about your father."

He smiled as she wiped her mouth daintily. She was all lady, even in a bar and grill.

She finished a fry. "Well, he was an accountant with one of the banks here in town."

Ty looked at her. "That's what he did for a living. Tell me about him."

Her eyes held a solemn look. She blinked and leaned back into the corner of the booth. As if the words were water pouring out of a pitcher, she said, "His name was Alan William Ross. He played basketball in high school, he liked to fish, and loved to laugh. Fried chicken was his favorite Sunday meal. He wore suits when he went to work and refused to wear one on the weekend. He went with me to the mall one Saturday afternoon but he didn't come home with me."

"What happened?"

"He died of a heart attack at forty-two years old."

"I'm sorry."

"I am too." She looked around the room. "I miss him every day. He brought me here the Saturday he died."

"No wonder you haven't been back. It must have been tough to come tonight."

Michelle's look met his. "It was. In more ways than one."

"I'm glad you did."

"I am too."

Michelle straightened again, bringing her leg back into contact with his. Where it belonged. They ate in silence for a while. Ty enjoyed sharing a meal with someone, especially when it was Michelle. He was starting to discover that the loner life didn't have as much appeal has it once had.

"Now it's your turn," she said, eating her burger with more gusto than she had before. "You know about my family. How about yours?"

The last bite of his burger lodged in his throat. He forced it down. This wasn't where he'd been planning to go when he'd asked about Michelle's father. His parents, his past were things better left alone.

"I don't think you want to know about them." With a relief that knew no bounds, he watched as the couple that had been sitting in the booth they'd been waiting for left. "If you're done, we can go and look at that plaque now."

"Yes, I'd like that."

Ty watched as Michelle ran her index finger over the

gold-colored plaque on the worn wooden table. "Alan Ross sat here."

"Ty." She looked at him and said, "Thank you for this. I'll have to tell my mother." She slipped her hand into his.

He squeezed it. "How is she?"

"Doing better than she has in months. She's no worse for wear after her stay in the hospital. She's even starting to get out more. Maybe she has turned the corner."

"I sure hope so. Are you ready to go?"

"Yes."

"Do you mind giving me a ride home? My motorcycle is still in the shop."

"Oh, I can't believe I've forgotten to ask about your injuries. You don't seem to be favoring them anymore."

"They are all better. My palm is still tender but that's no big deal." He put his hand out to show her.

"When did you have the stitches taken out of your knee?"

"I took them out early last week."

"Figures," Michelle said with a curl of her lips.

"If you want to give them some TLC, be my guest."

"Do they need it?"

"No, but I do love getting attention from you. Especially if you're washing my hair," he said with a grin.

She lifted her shoulders and let them drop. "Maybe if you're on your best behavior…"

"How about that ride, then?"

Michelle smiled. "I believe I can give a stranded man a ride home."

The question was whether she would be willing to come in when they got to his place.

Michelle pulled the car into the parking space that Ty indicated. The apartment complex was as nondescript as any she'd ever seen.

Would Ty invite her in? Did she want him to? Would she go if he did? She'd been trying to answer those questions with every mile she'd driven.

"Thanks for the ride." Ty opened the door and maneuvered his large body out of the compact car. Going to the passenger door, he opened it, leaned in and retrieved his guitar.

Her stomach dropped. He wasn't going to ask her in. She watched as he started to walk away. Blinking, she put the car into reverse then pushed it back into park. Perhaps she should reach for what she wanted. She rolled her window down.

"Hey, you have any coffee?"

"Yeah. Want some?"

"Yes."

She joined him on the sidewalk and they strolled towards the building. They entered the open stairs area and climbed to the second floor. She followed Ty to the third door. He put his guitar down and slipped his hand into his pocket. "I was wondering how long it would take you to get up the nerve to ask if you could come in," Ty said with a grin before he pulled a ring of keys out of his pocket and placed one in the lock.

Had he been playing her? Was he so sure of her he knew she didn't want to go home? "What made you think that?"

"I don't know." He pushed the door open with his foot. "Maybe the way you looked at me while I was playing tonight."

"I didn't look at you in any way."

He chuckled while picking up his guitar and stepping inside. She followed him. He closed the door behind her. The only light was the one burning over the kitchen sink.

"Yeah, you did. Like you could eat me up."

"I did not."

"You did. Just like I'm going to do to you."

Michelle had no idea when or where he put down his guitar. All she knew was that Ty's arms held her tightly and his mouth had found hers. Her arms circled his neck. He eased the pressure and found a different angle so that his mouth more completely took hers. This time the passion between them soared. She shuddered against him. Her blood hummed with the heat that Ty generated deep in her. Tingling all over, her heart tap danced to the driving need he created. He pulled away. She groaned in complaint.

"I thought you wanted coffee," Ty said.

She cupped his cheek and brought his lips towards hers. "I don't even like coffee."

He looked at her with twinkling eyes. "Why Dr. Ross, if you're not interested in my coffee then what do you want?"

"You." Her lips found his.

Michelle woke to the smell of coffee and bright sun filling the window. She had slept well into the morning, a luxury she rarely allowed herself. Instantly she knew Ty wasn't near. The comfort and security she felt when he was around was missing.

She found his T-shirt on the floor, where she had dropped it after pulling it off him the night before. Slipping it over her head, she tugged it down. She inhaled deeply. His scent surrounded her. She had it bad for the man. Could Ty possibly feel the same way about her?

She padded barefoot out of the bedroom in search of him. As he'd taken her to his bed during the night, she'd not noticed much about his apartment. Out of the fog of desire she had only seen that it was furnished with the necessities only. There was nothing personal in it outside of Ty's clothes and guitar. Nothing permanent. Just like Ty.

For once she refused to dwell on the past or the future and live in the now.

She found Ty with his hip against the counter, drinking a cup of coffee. He wore nothing but his jeans. She'd never seen a sexier man on billboard or TV. When he saw her a smile slowly creased his face. The smile that was for her alone. Her stomach fluttered. Her ego was going to be a big as Ty's if he kept looking at her that way. She'd been wanton enough last night.

"Hey," she said softly, suddenly feeling shy.

"Hey, yourself, ma belle." He lifted his cup.

"Why do you call me ma belle?"

He chuckle softly. "Haven't you ever heard the old Beatles' song, *'Michelle'*? It reminds me of you. Pretty." His finger caressed her cheek. She leaned into his touch, liking the idea of belonging to him.

"Would you like a cup of coffee, ma belle?"

She shook her head.

"No, that's right, you don't drink coffee." He put the cup down and looked in the refrigerator. "Bottled water?"

She took the bottle. "Thanks. You travel pretty light."

"Yeah, not much room on a bike." He grinned.

"That's a fine-looking coffeemaker, though. Carry that on your bike?"

"Naw, but I request a good one to be supplied by the house service wherever I stay. Hey, how about we go to the beach for the day?"

She looked at him. "I can't do that."

"Why not?"

"That's hours away. I need to check on my patients. See about my mother."

"We can stop by the hospital on our way out of town and you can call and check on your mother. Come on, Michelle, for once in your life do something spontaneous."

A slow grin formed on her lips. "Okay." His look of surprise made her laugh.

"You'll go?" he asked, eyebrows raised.

"Yes. I'll go. Sounds like fun. How's that for spontaneous?"

"Perfect." He reached over and pulled her close for a kiss.

"Let me get a quick shower first. We'll need to stop by my place also," she said.

"I need a shower too. How about I join you? That way it'll take us less time."

She ruined the serious look she'd manufactured by breaking out in a smile. "I doubt that. I think you're hoping I'll wash your hair."

Ty gave her his best wolfish grin. "Among other things."

She gave him a look suggesting she would enjoy the "other things" as much as he would.

CHAPTER EIGHT

MICHELLE HAD TO admit that there was a feeling of freedom that came with saying yes to a spur-of-the-moment idea.

Her shower—okay their shower—had taken longer than she'd planned but it had been the nicest and most rewarding one she'd ever taken. She'd agreed to wash Ty's hair and in return he'd washed all of her. Afterwards they dressed and prepared to leave.

"I'm not riding two hours to the beach on your motorcycle," Michelle announced as she slipped on her shoes.

"My motorcycle isn't out of the shop yet. So you can cool your righteous indignation. I've arranged for a rental. I've gotten tired of bumming a ride. In fact, could you drop me off at the rental place? They've got my replacement in."

"Okay," Michelle said as Ty settled into the passenger side of her car after placing his guitar in the back. She liked that about him. Ty wasn't one of those men who thought he should always drive just because he was the male. He was comfortable with who he was.

"While I see about the car you'll have time to check in on your mom and call the hospital," Ty suggested.

He knew her so well. She needed to let her mother know she'd be out of town for the day.

Ty climbed out of the car with a wave of his hand and a "See you in a few" at the car rental place.

At home Michelle made her calls. She discovered that her mother had made arrangements to spend the afternoon having tea with a couple of friends at a local luxury hotel.

"You enjoy your day, honey," her mother said after Michelle had shared her plans.

Her mother had been acting more like her old self after her recent hospital stay. She'd even begun cooking again. A couple of nights during the last few weeks Michelle hadn't even stopped by to see her, at her mother's insistence. The awful thing about it was that it had been during the same weeks she hadn't seen Ty. The nights had been impossibly long.

She'd just finished talking to her mother when Ty knocked on the door and she let him in. He looked irresistible. She had to grin. He was hers for the time being.

"What?"

"Oh, nothing," she said, moving further back into her condo.

"How's your mother?"

"Amazingly well. She's going out to tea with some friends."

"I told you she'd be fine." His deep voice sounded like warm molasses.

"Yes, you did. It must be wonderful being a know-it-all." She turned and grinned at him.

He stepped closer giving her a gentle kiss on the lips. "You know, it's nice to see you smiling."

Michelle kissed him back. "You know, I'm really looking forward to spending the day with you. Hey, I need to get us some towels." In her room, she looked for her beach bag. It had been so long since she'd spent a day at the seashore she had to search for the bag. Locating it, she stuffed it with towels, sunscreen and a hat for herself before returning to the living room.

"I didn't know it took such a large bag for a bikini," Ty commented with a grin from where he lounged on the sofa.

"You're such a funny man, Dr. Smith."

"I don't find the thought of you in a bikini funny at all." His eyes took on a predatory look.

Warmth flowed through her. All it took from Ty was one special expression for desire to flame within her.

"Come on, we'd better go if we're going to get some beach time in. We'll take my car," Ty announced, reaching for the overstuffed bag she held.

"I was going to suggest we take my car."

He huffed. "It has all the trappings of the family van. If you're going to the beach you need to be in a beachy car. I have just the auto."

Ty had her curiosity aroused now. "What did you rent?"

"You'll see, but it's something that'll suit us both. Let's go. I need to grab my guitar out of your car."

Michelle preceded him out the door. They walked to the parking area, stopped at her car then Ty led her towards a black convertible sports car.

"You rented this! Why am I'm not surprised?" Michelle yelped.

"Yeah, I thought it might be the best of both worlds. Wind in the face for me and secure enough for the safety-conscious in you."

"You rented it with me in mind?"

"I did."

"But you weren't speaking to me."

"Yeah, but I was hoping you'd come round."

"Why did you think that might happen?"

Ty opened the trunk and placed the bag, guitar and his towel there. He turned to her. "Because I think we are good together. That you wouldn't want to waste what time we have together. I hoped you might come around."

So he hadn't been holding a grudge against her. Instead, he'd just waited for her to figure her feelings out.

"Come on." He shook the keys at her. "You want to drive?"

Michelle quirked her lips and took them from him. "You know, I believe I do."

She climbed in and secured her safety belt. With a chuckle he slid into the passenger side. She glared at him.

"What?" he finally asked with a raised brow.

"Buckle up."

With a playful look of disgust he jerked the belt across his waist and clicked it into place. "I'm ready when you are."

With a grin she cranked the car. Michelle maneuvered through the light weekend traffic and out onto the interstate. Applying gas, she appreciated the well-built fast car as they sped down the road.

"I had no idea you were such a speed lover," Ty said over the noise of the wind around them as they hit the open road.

She glanced over at him. "That's because you don't know as much about me as you think you do."

Ty reached over and placed a hand on her bare knee below her shorts. "I know most of the important stuff." He teased her skin with his thumb.

She pushed his hand away. "Don't distract the driver."

"Do I distract you?" he asked with a smirk.

"Too much," she responded without thinking. And he did.

It was nearing lunchtime when they arrived at the beach.

"Would you like to sit down somewhere to eat or would you rather grab a sandwich and eat on the beach?" Ty asked as they cruised along the shore road.

"A sandwich would be wonderful beside the water." Michelle stopped at a traffic light. While they waited she raised her face to the sky. "I'm so glad you talked me into this. Just having the sun on my face feels wonderful."

Ty took one of her hands and squeezed it. "You look magnificent." Ty reached over and kissed her.

The honking of the car behind them jerked them apart. They laughed and Michelle pulled away. A swirl of joy went through her. She'd just gotten caught necking at a red light. Had she ever done something so foolish? She smiled. This feeling was what it meant to be happy. Something that had been missing in her life for far too long.

"Pull in here." Ty indicated a deli that sat just off the road. She parked. Ty opened the door and said, "I'll run in and get everything we need. You just enjoy the sun. I'll be right back."

She watched as he walked away with his self-assured gait. He held the door for a woman and two children exiting the building. Ty smiled at them and said something that made them grin in return. Ty made people feel good. He made her feel special.

By the time Ty returned, she'd moved to the passenger seat.

"Hey, you're not going to drive any more?"

"I thought it was time for you to chauffeur me around for a while. I want to see the sights. I haven't been here since I was a girl. I can't see everything if I have to pay attention to my driving."

"Well, as long as I get a tip for my trouble."

"You have something in mind?" She gave him her best somber look.

"I do. But I don't think out in public is the right place."

She enjoyed sharing comments and secrets that were special just between the two of them. Ty was not only her lover but her friend.

"I know the perfect stretch of beach for us so you rubberneck to your heart's content."

"Have you been here often?" Michelle asked as she looked out at the ocean beside the road.

"Yes."

"Did you work in a hospital near here?"

"Not exactly," he said flatly.

Was he being evasive on purpose? "Is it some secret?"

"Michelle, just leave it alone."

She turned to look at him. His eyes remained on the road ahead. A muscle jumped in his jaw it was so tightly clenched. "Why did you bring me here if you don't like it?"

"I do like it. I just hate some of the memories."

Michelle understood that. She asked nothing further.

Minutes later, Ty pulled into a subdivision of six small beach cottages and then into the drive of one of them.

"What're you doing? You can't just park here," Michelle stated, looking at the storybook place in front of them.

"I'm not. I know the guy who owns this place."

Michelle studied the small but immaculate house. "Oh. Nice. Very nice."

"I thought you might like it."

"Come on, I'll show you around," Ty said pleasantly, as if his earlier mood had completely disappeared. They climbed the stairs to the white-painted rail porch. He placed a key in the lock of the bright blue door.

"You have your own key?"

"Yeah, I stay here sometimes between jobs."

"You don't own a place anywhere?"

"Nope. Never have."

Michelle was surprised. She couldn't imagine going through life being little more than a vagabond. They might be on the same page in bed but their book of life was entirely different.

Ty pushed the door open and let her enter ahead of him. The room they stepped into took her breath away. Windows covered the back of the house and beyond lay the white sandy beach and crystal blue ocean. The furnishings were done in nautical colors. It was a shiny and light room while at the same time a place of comfort. Michelle loved it immediately. "This is wonderful. It's just the kind of place I'd love to have for a hideout on days off."

Ty chuckled. "Come on, I'll show you the rest of the cottage. I think you'll like it too."

The house had three bedrooms. The two small bedrooms shared a bath. They were brightly decorated also. The master bedroom faced the ocean. There were ceiling-to-floor windows and glass doors that opened onto the deck that covered the length of the house along the back. It was as meticulously decorated as the rest of the place.

"It's perfect!" Michelle exclaimed. "You may have to force me to go home."

"You can stay as long as you like. Let's go to the beach. I'm ready for a swim. Why don't you change while I put our lunch in a cooler and get a couple of folding chairs?" Ty said, as he headed out the bedroom door.

Half an hour later Ty found them a spot in the sand. There were few people sharing the area with them as the beach was mostly used by the owners of the cottages. Occasionally people walked by along the ocean edge. Ty placed the two chairs side by side and put an umbrella up between them.

He had changed into swimming trunks that were navy blue with a yellow stripe running down each thigh and wore no shirt. He'd pulled on a baseball cap that controlled his hair but left his irresistible curls gathered along the back of his neck. Dark glasses covered his eyes. He could have been a lifeguard with all his tanned, honed muscles and good looks. She couldn't take her eyes off him.

He didn't even look in her direction when he said in a hoarse voice, "You know, if you don't stop looking at me like that I'm going to forget about spending time on the beach and take you back inside to the nearest bed."

Warmth that had nothing to do with the temperature filled her. "I wasn't looking at you."

He flipped up his glasses and gave her a direct look. "Yes, you were," he said with amusement in his voice.

"Are you calling me a liar?"

"If the shoe fits," he quipped as he adjusted his chair closer to hers and sat. "You can maybe make it up to me by going for a swim with me."

Michelle pulled the large T-shirt she was using for a beach covering off. She'd not worn a bikini, as Ty had requested, but she did feel like she looked good in the aqua one-piece. His low whistle didn't disappoint.

"I think you might look far sexier in that than in a two-piece. It makes me imagine all that beautiful creamy skin beneath." He threw his hat into the chair and grabbed her hand, pulling her towards the waves. "Let's go. I need to cool off."

They ran into the water hand in hand, laughing as it splashed against their chests. When a larger wave came toward them, Ty lifted her up to prevent her from being swamped. He let her slide down his wet slick body and stole a kiss.

Ty swam with strong, sure strokes through the surf, dove under and returned to where she trod water. He surfaced with a splash and shook his head, sending salt water into her face.

Michelle retaliated by shoving a handful of water in his direction.

"So you want to play that game," Ty said, his face a mask

of mock evil, before he sent water her way. She shot some more back and war was on. Finally Ty plunged under the water, wrapped his arms around her waist and pulled her under. She came up sputtering and him laughing. Michelle turned her back to him as if she was mad.

Ty moved closer. "Hey, I didn't mean to make you—"

Michelle rounded on him and propelled two handfuls of water into his face.

"You sneak." He grabbed her around the waist again, pulled up and fell into the next wave.

This time when they came up, Ty didn't let go. Instead, his lips found hers. He requested entrance to her mouth and she gladly opened it. Her arms circled his neck and her legs looped his waist. He tasted of salt and life. When Ty broke the contact Michelle didn't immediately let go. His hands moved to cup her bottom under the water. She looked into his stunning eyes that so confidently returned her look and knew she was hopelessly in love. The pure, clear and forever kind of love.

Fear filled her. She let go of him and pushed away. "I'm worn out. I could use some sun time."

Ty didn't argue. He took her hand and helped her stand as the tide washed the sand beneath their feet away. Had she ever had more fun being with someone? But he wouldn't be there much longer. Her heart would break when he left. She slipped and his strong arms supported her, not unlike the way he had done over the last few weeks. He'd been there when she'd needed someone. It had become so easy to depend on him.

She plopped into her chair and he followed suit after picking up his hat. Ty shifted the umbrella so that most of their bodies were in the shade.

"We're both going to need some sunscreen," he said, pushing his wet hair back and pulling on his hat.

Michelle dug through her bag and came out with a bottle.

She squirted a blob into Ty's outstretched hand. Planning to do the same in her own, it was forgotten when she got caught up in watching Ty apply the lotion across his chest.

"Hey, you'd better get that sunscreen on. With your fair skin you'll be red in no time."

Michelle refocused, burying a shard of hurt deep down, and started spreading the liquid over her skin. She glanced at Ty again, this time noticing how he pulled his hat low to shade his eyes. "I've been meaning to ask you where you get those ridiculous surgical caps you wear all the time. They're certainly not the usual ones offered in the supply magazines."

"You don't like them?"

"They suit you."

"That was a nice dodging of the question. They're made by the sister of a guy I worked with over in Virginia. His niece has cancer. A group makes and sells them as a way to raise awareness and make some money for his niece's treatments."

Michelle's mother was the one with cancer and Ty was doing more to speed the need for research than she was. "I see."

He reached over and squeezed her hand. "I didn't mean to make you feel bad."

"I'm fine," she murmured, and closed her eyes.

A few minutes later she turned her head and opened one eye to find Ty with his eyes closed and breathing deeply. She shut hers and joined him in sleep with a soul-deep rightness that came with knowing he was near.

Ty woke to find Michelle still resting beside him. She looked peaceful, content for the first time since he'd met her. He'd not allowed her much sleep the night before. It had been so good to have her in his arms again.

She'd amazed him on the drive over with the aggressiveness and confidence she'd shown as she'd driven. He hadn't been sure she'd like the sports car, worried that she'd consider it frivolous and unsafe. Instead, she'd embraced it. He normally liked to do all the driving but he had to admit he found it nice to just sit back and enjoy the ride. Michelle took advantage of the limits of the car without overstepping the bounds of the law.

His stomach growled. It had been a long time since their rushed drive through breakfast.

"Is that you making all that noise over there?"

He rolled his head towards Michelle. Her eyes were still closed but there was a hint of a smile at the corners of her lips.

"As a matter of fact it is, smartypants."

She opened her eyes and grinned. "I'm hungry too."

"Then I'd say it's time for some food." He pulled the cooler toward him. Opening it, he removed a clear plastic-wrapped sandwich and handed it to her. "Ham and cheese on wheat or if you prefer it ham and provolone on a Kaiser."

"Ham and cheese on wheat sounds great."

He handed her the sandwich along with a small bag of chips and a can of drink. Then chose his own. They ate in silence for a few minutes.

"Ty?"

"Hmm?" he said around a bite of sandwich.

"Will you tell me why you got so upset earlier about me asking about you staying here?"

The food stuck in his throat. He had to force it down in a gulp. He should have known she'd ask. Michelle wasn't the type to pretend a problem didn't exist. "My family lived here during the summer sometimes." He heard her shift but he focused on the waves hitting the beach.

"So what was bad about that?"

"When I say lived here, I mean in a tent under a pier or in a vacant house.'

"Why? Did your father lose his job?"

Ty chuckled, the sound dry and bitter. "I've never known my father to have a job in the traditional sense of the word."

He'd told few people about his parents. In fact, he'd found it easier when he'd been in college and med school just to say they had died. But it felt good to be telling Michelle the truth. Saying it, having it out in the open was cleansing. Also he was sure the information wouldn't go beyond Michelle. Even if it did, did it matter any more?

"Something like that. My dad took seasonal jobs and occasionally my mother would also."

"So you've never live in a house of your own?"

"Not really. I stayed with my grandparents for a couple of years while I was finishing high school and after that there were dorms and a mattress on the floor, whatever I could find."

"I didn't know people still lived like that."

"You'd be surprised by the number of people that live their whole life as transients," Ty said as he watched a seagull work himself closer for some food.

"Do your parents still move from place to place?"

This was harder than he'd thought it would be. "I guess. I've not seen them in seven years. They showed up when my grandfather died. I don't know how anyone got in touch with them but there they were."

"You don't get along?" she asked in a low voice.

"It's not so much that we don't get along as it is that we don't share the same beliefs." Even though he answered Michelle's questions he still wasn't being as forthcoming as he could be, but he needed to say it and she needed to hear it.

"As in religion?"

"No, it's more that they don't believe in traditional medicine and I'm a doctor. They are not impressed."

"I'm sorry."

"Hey, it really doesn't matter."

"I think by your tone of voice that it does matter. It would matter to me. What my mother thinks is important to me." She said nothing for a few minutes. "So you decided at sixteen that you would become a doctor and went to live with your grandparents?"

"Something like that," he murmured.

"What're you not telling me?"

Michelle had gotten to know him so well, but he couldn't tell her about Joey. Couldn't admit that he'd let his brother die. "Nothing."

"Yes, there is. I can hear it in your voice."

His heart constricted and he let out a heavy breath. What would she think when he told her? How could she not think less of him? Be disappointed. "You won't let it go until you hear the whole sordid story, will you? If you must know, I had a younger brother. Joey had asthma. My parents thought it would get better with rubs and warm weather. After a while he got worse. My parents wouldn't take him to the doctor. Even though I thought they should I didn't say anything. Didn't make them take him. I was there when he drew his last wheezing breath. Now you know it all."

For a long time all he heard was the lap of the waves against the sand and the scream of seagulls and relived the pain.

Michelle's hand came to rest on top of his, which lay on the chair arm. She stroked his fingers until he spread his so that hers weaved between his. For once in his life he felt as if someone understood his broken heart.

"I'm sorry. Truly sorry."

Ty turned his hand and took hers in his. "I am too."

They sat for a long time, neither of them saying a word. There was healing to just having Michelle's touch.

"You're getting burnt," Ty said. "Let's go in."

Michelle didn't feel like she was but she didn't question him. She put their leftover stuff from lunch into the cooler. Ty stood and helped her to her feet. She reached for the chair.

"Leave it. We'll get them later." He picked up the cooler and took her hand as they walked back to the house.

While passing through the kitchen, he placed the cooler on the island. He led Michelle into the master bathroom. She didn't ask any questions, seeming to understand that he didn't want to talk. He turned on the shower and guided Michelle under it. She didn't say anything as he stripped her suit off and then his own as they rinsed. Turning off the water, he snatched a towel from the rack and dried Michelle's hair then her body.

"There's a robe in that closet," he said, indicating a small door with his chin. He flipped the towel over his shoulder and pulled it across his back. Michelle put on a robe and handed him the other. He shrugged into his and followed her into the bedroom. She opened the door, letting in the breeze, and stood on the threshold. Pushing her damp hair away from her face, she looked out towards the ocean.

Ty came to stand behind her, wrapped his arms around her waist and pulled her back against him. There was something about holding Michelle that made the sadness of his childhood disappear. That made him think that, with her, happiness might be possible.

They watched as a spring storm darkened the sky and slowly rolled towards them. As the first drop of rain hit the deck, Ty stepped backwards, taking Michelle along with him. He kept moving until the bed hit him behind the knees.

Letting go of her long enough to remove her robe and his, he pulled the covers back. Slowly they sank to the bed.

Hours later Michelle lay awake curled in Ty's arms, looking out at the ocean. His breath brushed her cheek each time he exhaled.

Their lovemaking had been extraordinary. The passion had been powerful, searing and exquisite. Ty had taken his time to bring her close to the pinnacle and had then held her there, only to let her slide down to send her upwards again. She had never felt more worshiped, cherished, as if he was making sure that she had no doubt who was loving her. Had he intended to brand her with his mark, ruining her for anyone else?

Still he whispered nothing about the future.

A few minutes later he woke up. She felt his lips on her shoulder and his length pressed against her bottom. "I have no strength where you are concerned," he uttered in a rough, sleep-laden voice.

She smiled. There was nothing like being wanted. It was a perfect moment and she sought to capture it and never let it go but she had her heart to consider. It would burst as sure as a glass shattering on the floor but she had to know. Had to prepare.

"Ty."

"Mmm."

"What're we doing?"

He kissed her earlobe. "You mean you don't know?" His fingers trailed along the curve of her hip.

She rolled over to face him. "I mean us. Where does this go?"

His eyes flickered with something she couldn't put a name to before he grinned.

"Ma belle, can't we just have some fun together while I'm here? Enjoy each other. See where that leads."

She already had an idea of where things would go. She'd be left behind to stitch up her gaping wounds while he rode off into the sunset on his motorcycle. But she couldn't resist him. She'd learned that life was too short not to grab happiness when she could. Right now she wanted to seize that with Ty. Live a little. No, live a lot. "I guess so."

He kissed her and made her forget about everything but the moment.

Some time later Ty said, "Why don't we stay here tonight? My case is the late one and yours is too. We could drive back early in the morning. We could eat fresh seafood and enjoy the sunset. What do you think?"

Why not? She'd decided to live some and today she was going to do that. "Sure. That sounds like fun. But we'll have to be on the road early."

"Sure thing." He had such a boyish grin on his face she was glad she'd agreed to stay. He gave her a kiss on the lips before he got out of bed. "I'll get what we need if you want to stay here and call your mother."

He knew her far too well. "That would be nice. I'd like to check in with her and the hospital."

CHAPTER NINE

TY LAY IN bed with Michelle curled against him. He lightly stroked her bare hip as she slept. The last few weeks had been wonderful. The best he could remember.

They had spent every minute together outside work. A number of times they had shared dinner with Michelle's mother at her house. The more often he sat in the cozy kitchen with the mother and daughter over a hot home-cooked meal the more those old feelings of the need to belong pulled at him.

Michelle had even joined him at Buster's when the band had played one weekend. There had been a number of curious eyes as they'd entered the bar but soon Michelle had joined the other staff members and blended in as if she had always been one of them. The two of them had even returned to the beach cottage for an entire weekend.

Michelle continued to give generously in her lovemaking and he'd rewarded her in return. The days had been nothing but pure bliss as far as he was concerned. Better than he deserved. But the nagging thought persisted that it couldn't last. He wasn't the guy to depend on, to trust when the going got tough. Michelle needed someone strong and sure who could be there for her no matter what came her way. She deserved that much.

"Hey, sleepyhead." He jiggled Michelle lightly.

"Hi, there," she muttered into his shoulder, which she was currently using as a pillow. He liked the fact she had to touch him when she slept. He found he liked a number of things about Michelle. If he had been a different man, he could be comfortable with her forever.

He'd sworn he wouldn't allow himself to develop those feelings. He couldn't let Michelle know how much he cared. It would only hurt her more when he left. Who was he trying to kid? It was going to be the hardest thing he'd ever done to leave her. But they both knew the deal. Michelle had made her choice. He'd been nothing but up front with her.

Once during the past weeks she'd asked, "Have you thought about maybe taking a permanent job somewhere?"

"Not really."

"What if one came open here? Would you consider staying?"

He'd kissed her and that had been the end of the conversation. She'd hinted a few additional times that she hoped he'd remain longer and he'd never made a comment one way or the other. He was dodging her questions, not wanting to take the joy out of their time together. Neither of them seemed to want to push a discussion about the future but it was racing towards them like a car at the Daytona 500 and it wouldn't be waved off.

"Ma belle, you know that Schwartz will be back in a week."

"I heard," she mumbled as she kissed the ridge of his jaw. Her hand crept lower on his middle. Her lips moved towards his mouth and that was the end of the conversation again. Maybe he'd resist longer next time.

Some time later they were sitting on the couch in Michelle's living room when she said, "I thought you were going to teach me how to play the guitar."

"Did I say that?" He hesitated.

She twisted toward him. "Yeah, you did. How about showing me now?"

On some level Ty wished he'd never mentioned it. The last time he'd agreed to teach anyone to play had been when Joey had asked. He'd just learned his first chord when he'd started getting so weak it had been difficult for him to practice. Still, Michelle gave Ty such an imploring look that he couldn't bring himself to turn her down.

"Get Emily and I'll show you a few chords," he said.

She uncrossed her legs. "I don't know how I feel about fetching another woman for you."

"Jealous, are you?" Ty quipped with a smile. After he'd chiseled through that thick cover of seriousness Michelle had built around herself, he'd found below a sense of humor waiting to see the light of day.

She gave him a smirk and headed out of the room.

With encouragement, Michelle had been willing to try something new more than once in the last few weeks. They'd gone indoor rock climbing. She'd agreed to go on a short afternoon ride with him on his motorcycle after it had been repaired. Now she was asking him to teach her how to play the guitar. It was as if she was trying to get caught up on all the things she'd missed out on since her father had died.

Michelle returned with his guitar. He stood and took the case from her.

"Have a seat." He laid the case on the low table in front of the couch and removed the instrument then came to sit beside her. Strumming the strings a couple of times and tuning it, he offered it to Michelle.

"Now, hold it this way." He placed the guitar across her thigh and showed her where to place her hand along the neck. He moved in close, their thighs touching, and put an arm around her until he could reach the strings. The other hand he placed over hers holding the neck. "Now, place your fingertips here and here, and hold the strings down. With your thumb…" he indicated the one over the base of the guitar "…strum."

Michelle did as he instructed then put her hand in the air and shook it. "That hurts."

Ty's heart constricted, forming a knot of pain in the middle of his chest. Those had been Joey's exact words and actions the first time he'd run his finger over the taut wires. It had been so long since Ty had let himself think about Joey, really remember the hurt and desperation and bone-deep guilt that had been part of his life for so long. Why was it now festering to the surface with such persistence?

"What're you thinking?" Michelle asked softly.

"Nothing," he murmured, making a slight shift away from her.

"I can tell by the look on your face that something is bothering you."

She always seemed to be able to do that. Every time he drifted into negative memories she was able to read his mood. No other woman had ever done that before. He'd never let anyone close enough that they could. Michelle had slipped past those barriers he'd carefully built and maintained like they never existed. He'd let her see things no one else had been privy to.

He looked at her. Michelle's eyes had a resolute but uncertain look, as if she feared what he might say. "I was starting to teach Joey to play when he died. He thought it hurt when he strummed too."

Michelle's eyes clouded over. "We don't have to do this."

"No, I want to. Joey would want me to show you how to play."

She gave him a reassuring smile. "Then I'll do my best."

Ty returned her smile. "Let's try it one more time."

The thoughts of teaching Joey had become a bitter-sweet memory. He had Michelle to thank for that.

The next afternoon the clerk called, "Dr. Ross," as Michelle went by the OR central desk. "Dr. Marshall left a message that he'd like to speak to you when you have a minute."

Michelle smiled and said, "Thanks for letting me know, Roger."

The man's eyes widened a second before he smiled. "You're welcome."

Roger had looked as if he was surprised that she knew his name. Had she really been so aloof? She'd noticed that after they had gone to Buster's that there had been more camaraderie in the OR among her team. They had been good together before but now they were seamless as they worked. She had to admit that it made for better patient care. Why hadn't she realized that sooner?

Michelle knocked on Dr. Marshall's door and heard him call, "Enter."

She'd not been in his office since she'd gone to complain about Ty the first day he'd been at the hospital. That seemed like a lifetime ago. Now she'd give anything for him to stay. She'd mentioned him leaving and he had too but they'd never really discussed it. Maybe if she ignored it, it wouldn't happen.

Ty cared about her. She felt it every time he looked at her, touched her or spoke to her. When they made love the feeling was more powerful than any other time. But did he care for her the way she did him? The one thing that she was sure of was that she loved him.

She stepped through the doorway into Marshall's office.

Dr. Marshall waved her closer. "I just wanted to run something by you before I make a decision."

Michelle sat in one of the two chairs in front of his desk. "What's going on?"

Dr. Marshall pulled off his silver rimmed glasses and rubbed his eyes. "Well, to start with, Schwartz isn't returning. He's decided to continue working with the foreign aid group. He's going to take the director's position. So I'm in the market for another anesthesiologist."

"Have you thought about asking Ty Smith?"

"He turned me down, even though he's great by all measures."

Michelle sucked in a breath and held it. Feeling lightheaded, she grasped the arm of the chair until the skin across her fingers turned white. She was bleeding emotionally. Her chest felt as if it was caving in on her.

Breathe. Breathe!

Heat swamped her and her lunch threatened to return. She squeezed her arms around her waist. Ty couldn't have made it clearer that he didn't love her. He'd been offered a way to stay with her and he'd refused it. And not even told her about it.

Pain so searing that it burned as hot as lava settled in her chest. She'd hurt when her father had died. She had been worried sick when her mother had been diagnosed with cancer but nothing compared to this torment.

Dr. Marshall continued, "I was wondering if you have any suggestions about who you might like to work with?"

"I'm sorry, I need to go."

"Michelle, are you feeling okay?" Dr. Marshall asked, his forehead wrinkling.

"I'm fine." She'd never been further from fine. "I'll think about it and get back to you."

Michelle didn't wait for additional questions. She bolted for the door before she broke out in sobs. Finding the nearest private restroom, she locked herself in and let the tears flow. A quarter of an hour later she stood before the mirror, looking at her puffy eyes.

What a fool she'd been. She'd let herself hope that perhaps she and Ty were building something permanent, special. It had all been one-sided. She'd been Ty's female distraction while he'd been in town.

That wasn't true. He'd been up front. He'd not once said that he was going to stay. It had all been her, wishing.

Well, it was all over now.

She stood straighter and pushed her hair into some kind of order. This too she would get through. She'd survived other devastating events in her life and she'd live through this one eventually. Ty not loving her wouldn't break her. It was time to call it quits between them and move on. She might as well start accepting it.

After dabbing a water-cooled paper towel around her eyes, she opened the door and headed towards her office. Thankfully her day was over. She picked up her purse and made her way out of the hospital.

Where was Michelle? Ty had looked in the OR, on the floor and had finally gone to her office. She was nowhere to be found. They didn't check in with each other but he didn't usually have this much trouble finding her. He finally punched in her number on his cellphone.

"Hey, where are you?" he asked when she answered.

"I'm at home," she said in a dead voice.

What was going on? Had she heard? "I thought we had plans to try out that diner over on 60th Street tonight?"

"I'm tired. You go on without me."

"Why don't I get us a to-go plate and bring it by?"

"No, thanks. Look, Ty, I just want to be alone tonight."

What wasn't she saying? Knowing how stubborn Michelle could be, he wasn't going to get it out of her over the phone. "Okay. See ya."

Less than an hour later Ty stood in front of Michelle's door. He knocked and moments later Michelle opened it. She was dressed in one of his T-shirts, a worn pair of sweat pants and a bulky sweater. Nothing about her appeared like the well put-together professional she'd worked so hard to appear for so many years. Something was wrong, badly wrong.

"What're you doing here?" she snapped.

"Well, thanks for the warm welcome." He lifted the two white takeout boxes. "I brought you dinner."

"I told you that I didn't want any."

"And I thought you said that just so you didn't have to see me and I'd like to know why." He was making an effort to sound glib while inside he was tied in knots with worry that she knew the truth. He only had a little more time with Michelle and he wanted it to be happy. Her attitude implied that his wish might not be granted.

Michelle put her hands on her hips, her sweater falling open to hang loose. She wasn't wearing a bra and her nipples pushed against the thin fabric of the T-shirt. As he watched, they pebbled. In her mind she might be mad at him but her body was still responding. She must have noticed his gaze because she pulled the sweater tight around her and crossed her arms over her chest.

Ty followed Michelle's gaze as she glanced at the older couple walking in their direction on the sidewalk in front of her condo. Their faces showed interest in what was happening between him and Michelle.

She turned back to him and hissed, "Come in. I don't want to have this conversation in front of my neighbors."

Stepping back, she allowed him to enter, followed and then closed the door behind her. Ty continued on into the kitchen, setting the boxes down on the closest counter. He turned to find Michelle standing behind him in what could only be described as a warrior's stance.

"When were you going to tell me?" she demanded, her look boring into his.

"Tell you what?"

"That you were offered a job at the hospital," she all but shouted at him.

"I didn't think it mattered. You knew I planned to leave. I've tried a number of times to discuss it with you but you didn't want to talk about it."

She had the good grace to look away. "So when do you plan to call ahead for a coffee-maker, pack up your boxes and get on your bike?"

"Day after tomorrow."

She gasped, her face going pale. Her next words came out in a strangled voice. "That soon."

"Yeah." The word drifted off as if he hated to say it. His heart constricted in agony. He was hurting her. Just as he'd hoped he wouldn't do. He hadn't expected the depth of pain he'd feel knowing he had to leave her. That she wouldn't be a part of his life but he couldn't stay. That was for her sake. He was no good for anyone.

She stood back and studied him. "You are more like your parents than you think." There was a note of censure in her voice.

"I'm nothing like them," he said sharply.

"Think about it, Ty. You don't stay in one place. You're always running. You don't even really own anything."

"Don't you get it? If I stayed I'd end up failing you. I found that out a long time ago. I'd let you down. I did that once and I refuse to let it happen again."

"How do you know? You've never stayed in one place

long enough to see what you're capable of. You won't know until you try."

"I know," he said, with a surety as immovable as the Appalachian Mountains as he backed away from her.

She shook her head sadly. "You carry so much guilt over Joey. You were a kid. You couldn't have done more for him."

He made an aggressive step in Michelle's direction and bared his teeth as he spat the words. "I could have made my parents take him to a doctor. The hospital. I could have taken him myself. I could have asked someone for help." He bit the ugly words out. "You don't know anything about me. What makes you think I wouldn't let the same thing happen to you?" He pointed his finger at her. "I'm not good enough for you."

Michelle stood her ground proudly through his tirade. For that he had to admire her. A lesser person would have been frightened.

"I would never have taken you for a coward," she said with a tone of regret. As if she'd had a revelation, she continued in an even voice, "You're afraid to commit. You're making excuses not to. You're not afraid you'll not be here if I need you. You're afraid that you might get hurt if you are. You're running because you *do* care." She narrowed her eyes and gave him an earnest look. "Don't you ever get tired of running from the past?" She waved a hand around. "It'll never stop following you."

What did she want him to admit? That, yes, it followed him everywhere, never left him? He looked at her for a long moment. "You talk about me being a coward. Have you told your team how sick your mother has been? Have you confided to anyone outside of me in years? Hey, maybe that's the way you want it. You knew I'd be leaving so it would be easy to tell me. You wouldn't have to invest yourself in anyone. You are still mourning your father. Still trying to be the perfect little girl. Where has that got you? No friends, no life. No happiness."

She put her hands on her hips and glared at him. "You have some nerve…"

"Hey, you believe you have all the answers? I'm thinking that maybe you need to realize a few things also. Realize that you can't control everything. Your mother's cancer. Whether I leave or not. All you can control is you and your life. And you decided to close off people years ago."

Michelle's mouth drew into a thin line and her eyes widened as a stricken look covered her face. She blinked and cleared her throat before she said in a subdued voice, "That all may be true but that still doesn't change the fact that you are still trying to deal with not standing up to your parents. Not insisting they take Joey to a doctor. You went into medicine to help and that's all well and good.

"But you run around from one place to another like the masked hero doctor. Spreading your brand of medicine and happiness as a shield against dealing with your past. You didn't leave your parents' lifestyle behind, you just ran away from them. And the pain. No matter how great a doctor you have become, it can't bring Joey back. All you can do is live well and honor him. That much I have learned in the last few weeks."

Her words hurt. Cut to the quick. The strong, clear-minded and confident Michelle had returned with a vengeance and pinned him to the wall. "I care about you, Michelle, I do. That's why I have to go. I don't want to watch as disappointment fills your eyes."

"That's the biggest bunch of bull I've ever heard. You don't know what it's really like to care about someone. Not since you were sixteen have you stuck around long enough to find out. You're not fooling anyone but yourself. And

I'm not sure that you're doing a good job of that either. You don't care enough about me to stay and try to build a real relationship. You're taking the easy way out. Never getting emotionally involved."

He glared at her but she didn't slow down. "Maybe we're not that different after all. But I do know one thing, I want a man who will be beside me through thick and thin. You're right, you probably aren't that person."

A stabbing pain tore through Ty's gut with those words. Michelle had given up on him, had decided he wasn't worth the trouble.

"Well, I guess everything that needs to be said has been. Goodbye, Michelle." He headed for the front door, the take-out boxes forgotten, the food gone cold just like his heart.

CHAPTER TEN

TY PULLED THE motorcycle to a stop near the campsite. He'd been on the road for weeks and had covered five states in search of his parents. Traveling from one to another, he checked locations they'd frequented as a family years earlier. Each spot he visited held good and bad memories.

When he'd left Raleigh and Michelle, he gone to his next assignment, which lasted only two weeks, sure that he would move on as if nothing had happened. Michelle would forget him in time and he would remember her as a pleasant interlude during a work assignment. But that couldn't have been further from the truth. He missed Michelle with a pain so consuming that it was almost tangible. At work, he remembered the intensity of her eyes snapping at him over her mask. On his motorcycle it was her thighs pressed tightly to his as he turned a curve. The worst was when he played his guitar. She'd ruined the joy for him. Michelle was in his blood.

Trying to outdistance the growing grief that roiled in him, he'd not accepted the next anesthesiologist position offered. Instead, he'd decided to take some time off and travel. He'd ridden his bike far and fast, trying to clear his head and hopefully his heart of Michelle. That hadn't happened. If anything, he'd become more miserable. He was constantly fighting thoughts of what Michelle would think about the places he was seeing, wishing she was there to share them. The worst was that he worried she might move on and no longer give him any thought.

After another aimless day he had fallen into bed. Sleep had eluded him. In the early hours of the morning he'd given up and seen the situation for what it was. He was hopelessly in love. It was time to face the truth and do something about it. But he had to face the past before he could ask Michelle to share his future. If he was going to do that, he had to find his parents. The thought of doing so made his stomach contract but it still had to be done. Now he was parked at a camp in central Florida. He'd been told his parents were there.

Placing his helmet on the seat of his bike, Ty walked across a grassy area towards the mobile campers parked under the trees. As he approached, a man in ill-fitting clothes came out to meet him.

"Can I help you?" the man said in a gruff voice that held a note of suspicion.

It was part of the lifestyle to be distrustful of any outsiders. Ty found it ironic that for years he'd been an outsider. The one new to the hospital, the staff, the OR team. In those places more times than not he'd been welcomed.

"I'm looking for George and Miranda Lifeisgood. I was told they might be here." His parents had changed their last names long ago. They'd said they'd had left their old life behind and their last names as well. To his knowledge they had never legally married. Smith was his mother's parents' surname and Ty had taken it when he'd move in with them.

"Who's looking for them?" the man asked, glancing over his shoulder.

Had he been signaling to someone? "I'm their son."

"Son?" he asked, as if he didn't believe Ty. "Didn't know they had one."

"Are they here?" Ty asked with a note of frustration. The woman in the last camp he'd visited had been sure his parents were traveling with this group. Ty started to step around the man when another one came out from among the campers and headed in his direction.

There was something familiar about the man's walk. He wore clothes similar to those of the first man but this one had the bearing of a leader as he stalked across the ground. His curly dark hair was streaked with gray and hung freely around his shoulders. As he came closer Ty knew without a doubt that it was his father. He was an older version of what Ty saw when he looked in the mirror.

Ty's heart beat faster. All of a sudden he had the urge to turn and leave but he had to face his demons and that meant talking to his parents.

"George," Ty said. He had never been allowed to call his parents by anything other than their first names.

"Ty? Is that you?" his father asked, coming to a halt just out of touching distance.

Ty nodded. "Yes."

"What brought you here?"

So much for the warm family welcome. He hadn't expected more but it would have been nice. In reality he'd not treated them much better at his grandfather's funeral. "I wanted to see how you and Miranda are."

His father looked at him so long without saying anything that Ty feared he would reject him.

"Come, your mother will be glad to see you." His father turned and walked off, not waiting to see if Ty followed.

Ty stayed a few steps behind his father as they weaved in and out between campers that had seen better days. Children ran around barefoot and elderly women sat huddled together, speaking softly, as they passed. Where Ty had

once been an insider he was now very much the outsider.
They finally reached a camper that was set a little off from
the camp.

His father's deep voice called, "Miranda, come out here."

Ty's heart thumped harder against his ribs. He would've
known his mother instantly. She had aged but done so
gently. Her long wavy hair reached the middle of her back
and was controlled by a red bandana. Dressed in a flowing multicolored shirt that reminded Ty of Michelle's
bright home, shorts and wearing rope thongs on her feet,
his mother looked like the quintessential beachcomber.

"What's going on?" she called, stepping out of the camper
door and coming down the steps. She looked in his direction
and said in a breathy voice of pleasure, "Ty."

"Hello, Miranda." Ty held his breath. Would she turn
him away? His mother stared at him for a moment as if she
couldn't believe that he was truly there. She wasn't the only
one. Finally, she opened her arms and Ty walked into them.

"I didn't think I'd ever see you again," she whispered.

"I know."

She pushed him back to arm's length and studied him as
if she were a fortune teller getting a reading. "You're well,
I see, and here for answers."

Ty nodded. He and his mother had always been in tune
with each other.

"Then come, sit and let us hear your problem."

His mother welcomed him as if nothing had happened.
Was it that easy? Ty glanced at his father. He was moving
folding chairs around so that they faced each other. His
father hadn't been as friendly as his mother but he hadn't
turned Ty away either. Obviously it had been he who had
held the grudge, not his parents.

They all took seats.

"First tell us how you have been," his mother said.

Ty gave them the short version of his life but didn't mention Michelle. He felt that if he put his plans into words it might jinx them. They were too important to take that chance.

"How have you both been?" Ty looked from his mother to his father.

"We are well," George said.

His father had always been one for few words and apparently that hadn't changed.

His father's face turned serious. "So, Tyrone, tell us why you are here."

Ty didn't miss the implication that he wouldn't have come unless he wanted something. Did they really have no idea what burden he carried?

"I want to talk about Joey."

His mother flinched. His father reached over and took her hand.

Ty forged ahead. "I want to know why you wouldn't take him to a doctor."

"Because it is not our way," his father stated firmly.

So the answer hadn't changed.

"Joey could have lived if he'd only had medicine." Ty worked to keep his voice even.

"We had no money for doctors or medicine," his mother said in a wistful voice. Had she begged his father to help Joey?

"There are programs. We could have gotten him care. I should have gone for help."

His father let go of his mother's hand and sat straighter. He looked directly at Ty. "We did what we could for Joey. It was meant to be."

"Did you know that I feel responsible for Joey's death?"

"Why would you feel that way, Ty?" His mother sounded truly mystified.

"Because I should have made you do something to help him."

"We did all we could," his mother said.

Ty let out a sound of desperation. Nothing was different. Except that his parents had moved on. He was the one who was stuck in the past. "Would you have let me take him to the hospital?"

"No," both his parents said at the same time.

The mountain-sized guilt that he had been carrying around slipped slowly off him. They wouldn't have listened to him even if he'd insisted that Joey see a doctor. They were so set in their beliefs that they wouldn't have allowed him to take Joey.

"We take care of ourselves. We'll not let others tell us what we need to do," his father stated.

His father referred to the government. His parents didn't vote, didn't pay taxes so they didn't exist. They wanted to keep it that way. No matter the cost.

Ty stayed a while longer and they talked about the past. Before Ty left he had his parents agree to keep in touch. They would at least drop a postcard in the mail to let him know where they were from time to time. As they got older he could check on them, use his skills as a doctor to help them when they wouldn't seek it elsewhere.

No matter what Michelle thought, his life was very different from that of his parents. He shared some traits but in other ways he was thousands of miles away from them. Sadly, he and his parents would never be close but they were still his parents. He'd try to leave his guilt behind and build a future free of blame.

Michelle knocked on the door of her most recent patient's room. Mr. Jordon was a seventy-year-old man who would be in her OR for triple by-pass surgery first thing the next morning. She gently pushed the door open. Her patient lay propped up in his bed and appeared to be asleep. A white-headed woman about the same age as the man sat beside him, holding his hand.

Michelle rounded the bed to stand beside the woman. "I'm Dr. Ross."

"I'm Martha Jordon. Richard's wife."

"I won't wake Mr. Jordon. He needs to rest. I was just checking to see if he or you have any questions about the surgery."

"What're his chances?" Mrs. Jordon seemed to be forcing the question out.

"I won't lie. The surgery is an intensive one but we do them here all the time."

Mrs. Jordon glanced at her husband and when she looked back her eyes were glassy with moisture. "Richard is all I have." She sniffled. "We couldn't have children. So he's everything to me." A tear dropped to her milk-white cheek. "I had cancer three years ago and he nursed me through the horrible chemo. I can't lose him now."

Michelle's heart broke for the woman. She knew what it meant to be alone. That deep endless void that nothing or anyone else could fill except for the person missing. Glancing around, she found a spare chair and brought it alongside Mrs. Jordan's. Sinking down on it, Michelle took the older woman's hand and held it. For a long moment they sat, saying nothing. Human touch was enough.

Finally Michelle said, "Mr. Jordon is strong. He should be fine. You need to take care of yourself. He'll need you when he gets out of here."

Mrs. Jordon gave her a weak smile. "I'll be there for him."

Michelle gave the fragile hand in hers a gentle squeeze.

"I know you will." She stood. "Now, I want you to go home soon and get some rest. The nurses will take excellent care of Mr. Jordon overnight and I'll be in to see you both in the morning."

"Thank you, Dr. Ross. You've been very sweet."

Sweet? Michelle couldn't remember anyone ever calling her sweet. Determined, a good surgeon, self-reliant, but sweet? She kind of liked having that adjective assigned to her. "Goodnight."

Mrs. Jordon gave her a small nod and turned her attention back to her husband.

Michelle left and went to the nurses' desk. "Who's Mr. Jordon's nurse tonight?"

The other nurses looked everywhere but at her before one said, "I am, ma'am."

Michelle smiled at the young nurse and watched as she noticeably relaxed. "I'd like you to call social work and see if they have a volunteer who could sit through surgery with Mrs. Jordon. She has no one else and she shouldn't be alone."

By the time Michelle finished making her request everyone at the desk was looking her direction.

"Yes, ma'am. I'll see to it. If there is no one, I'll come in. It's my day off. They're such a lovely old couple."

Michelle smiled and glanced back toward Mr. Jordon's room. "Yes, they are. Thank you…"

"Becky."

"Thank you, Becky."

Michelle walked down the hall to her next patient. She'd never done anything like holding a family member's hand before and had certainly never thought of who sat with them during surgery. It felt good to focus on helping someone else instead of her misery. Ty would have been surprised and pleased if he'd seen her. More than that, she was proud of herself. Ty may have left but he'd been a blessing in her life, encouraging her to break out of her shell and show that she cared. For that, she'd always be grateful to him.

She still needed to take one more step.

The next morning she entered the OR. Her team stood ready to go to work. They all looked at her expectantly. Instead of her usual "Are we ready to begin?" she said, "I'd like to tell all of you something."

Almost in unison their brows rose.

"I know I've been a bit rigid and at times difficult to work with." There was no argument. She really hadn't expected there to be one. "My mother has been fighting a difficult battle with cancer and I've been preoccupied with her care and prognosis. I've been deathly afraid that I might lose her."

Murmurs of concern greeted her that were so heart felt that Michelle regretted she'd kept her mother's illness a secret for so long.

"My mother had cancer a couple of years ago and is doing great now," said one person.

"My niece had it as a child. She had her first baby six weeks ago," commented one of the scrub nurses.

"My father has it now," said another.

"I'm sorry to hear that," Michelle offered.

"How's your mother doing?" the nurse at the end of the table asked.

"Very well. We're getting good reports but the fight isn't over."

Jane, who stood at her right elbow, said, "I'm here if you ever need to talk."

"Thanks, I may take you up on that some time." With a lightness in her heart she'd not felt in a long time, Michelle meant it.

"Now, we need to get Mr. Jordon patched up. He has a wife that's waiting for him to get better."

Everyone took their positions and waited for her to take the lead.

"Mark, why don't you put on some of the rock and roll you like playing before I get in here?" Michelle said in a teasing tone.

"Yes, ma'am."

When all looks settled on her, she raised her brows and said, "Are we ready to begin?"

Hours later, Michelle walked into the surgery waiting room. Mrs. Jordon looked haggard but glad to see her. She took a seat next to the older woman and took her hand. "Mr. Jordon came through the surgery well and he's doing fine. You can see him as soon as they get him settled in CICU. That will take a few minutes."

"Thank you, Dr. Ross."

Michelle let go of the older woman's hand and stood. Smiling down at Mrs. Jordon, she said, "You're welcome. He should be home and under your care in less than a week."

"That sounds wonderful." Mrs. Jordon looked over at the woman sitting two seats over and back to Michelle. "I understand you are the one to thank for Robin being here."

Robin must be the volunteer in the traditional hospital volunteer jacket.

"I just thought you might like a little company," Michelle said. "I'll see you tomorrow. Please get some rest. We all know what bad patients men can be," Michelle said, and smiled.

It felt good to know that she'd not only done her best for Mr. Jordon but for his wife as well. Ty had told her that if she'd just let others in that she'd no longer need him. He'd been wrong. She'd started letting people in but she still needed him just as much as she ever had. Would the ache ever ease?

The blazing hot days of summer were in full swing as Michelle pushed her way into the OR for the last time that afternoon. The last weeks had been difficult ones as she'd adjusted to Ty's absence. There had been no phone calls, emails or letters. Nothing. It hurt but he was a free spirit and she'd expected nothing less. But it would have been nice…

It hadn't been easy, still wasn't if she allowed herself too much time to think. She'd strived day by day to move on. She'd shared a shopping trip with a couple of the nurses who'd asked her about where to buy clothes. It had been enjoyable and they'd planned to do it again soon. She wouldn't exactly call her interaction with the nurses friendship but she was making a step in the right direction. It was a slow process, learning to open up, but she was making an effort.

Her mother was still seeing her doctors regularly and all the reports were good. Michelle continued to be pleased with her mother's efforts to recover. She went out more, spent time with her friends and otherwise required less of Michelle's time. The downside was that it gave Michelle even more time to wonder where Ty was and what he was doing, which left her gloomy. Thankfully her days were busy.

"Hey, everyone, are we ready to go? Whose turn is it to pick the music?" Michelle asked as she walked toward the surgery table.

Silence hung over the room for a second before Jane said, "I think it's yours."

"Then how about some of the classics?" Michelle took her place and looked toward the head of the table. "Are we rea—?"

Her heart stopped, jerked into motion again and kicked into warp speed.

The sparkling green eyes that held steady over the mask of the person in the anesthesiologist's chair she knew so well. They were the last thing she saw before she went to bed at night. They were the ones that burned warm and caring in her dreams. The ones she wouldn't mistake for anyone else's. The ones she had looked for every time she'd entered the OR but had never expected to see.

Ty.

His gaze held steady. Waiting. Questioning. Asking.

Her breath came in soft, short gasps.

Someone cleared their throat, making her remember to blink.

Ty's eyelids lowered too but when they came up again his eyes held that infamous twinkle. Her heart zipped faster. If she'd paid closer attention, she would have known sooner that it was Ty. He wore a hot pink scrub cap with gray elephants on it. Who else would wear a scrub cap like that? She knew all too well what his thick, wondrously curly hair felt like in her hands. The perfect touch of it running through her fingers.

Glancing at the others in the room, she could see that they were watching her closely for a reaction to Ty being there. This time it wasn't in uncertainty but in anticipation.

"I'm ready. By the way, I like your taste in music," Ty remarked with a hint of humor in his voice.

How like Ty to joke when her nerves were tied in a knot. What was he doing here? Why hadn't he told her he was coming?

"I've been led to believe that music soothes the savage beast," she said in a dry tone.

He chuckled behind his mask.

How could she be expected to do her job with him sharing the OR? How long would he stay this time?

Michelle took a deep breath and let it out slowly. She was a professional and she had a surgery to perform. Thankfully it wasn't a difficult one. Maybe this was the case she should let her resident take the lead on.

Ty glanced at Michelle more than once but she never returned his look. It was as if she was making a point not to acknowledge that he was there. Did that mean she wanted nothing to do with him? Or did it mean that she was so aware of him that she was afraid she might be distracted? He hoped with every fiber in his being that it was the latter.

Ty had questioned whether or not to agree to be in the OR without letting Michelle know first. He'd been assigned the case and there had been no time to speak to her. Michelle was a consummate professional and would always put her patients' care first. If he'd thought anything less he wouldn't have taken the case.

Thankfully the surgery wasn't a long one. As soon as the resident finished closing, Michelle was out the door.

Ty had to stay with the patient until he was settled in CICU. Then he'd go in search of Michelle. He would have to hunt for her. She'd been shocked to see him and she would have gone somewhere to regroup before she could face him. He hoped that when he found her she'd still want to have something to do with him.

After checking on the floor for her, he then went back to CICU. He was told that she'd come and gone. He called her but she didn't answer. Was she so mad at him that she would refuse to speak to him? A fist of worry squeezed his heart. Had he missed his chance?

Determined to make Michelle hear him out, he circled around by her office to see if she was there. If not, he'd go to her house and then her mother's if necessary. He tapped lightly on the partially open door to Michelle's office then pushed it wide.

She sat behind her desk, removing the wrapper from a chocolate cake roll. Her hand shook slightly as she worked. Maybe she wasn't completely unaffected by his return after all.

"Hiding from me?" he asked.

She pinned him with a narrow look. "No. And I didn't say come in."

"No, you didn't but I wasn't sure you'd invite me in if I'd asked."

"What're you doing here, Ty? I thought you were long gone."

"Disappointed to see me?" Michelle had slipped her armor on again. She was covering up her feelings and he wouldn't let her push him away but she'd make him work for it.

"I don't care one way or another," she said in a perfect tone of dismissal.

He stepped closer and studied the contents of the trash can. Looking at her, he grinned. "I think you might. What's that, your fifth cake?"

She threw the cake she held into the garbage. "How many cake rolls I eat is none of your business."

"I think the number might have something to do with me being back and that makes it my business. At least, I hope it does." He moved around the desk, propped his hip on the corner and looked at her.

She squirmed in her chair and didn't meet his gaze. "How long are you here for this time?"

He couldn't help but tease her. "You're not glad to see me?"

Lurching upwards, she stood and glared at him. "Oh, for heaven's sake. I've not heard a word from you in weeks.

Now you show up expecting me to greet you with open arms. What do you want?"

"You."

Michelle's heart thudded against her chest as her blood zoomed through her veins. Had she heard Ty right? "What do you mean?"

"Come on, Michelle, you're an intelligent woman. You know what I mean." He grinned. Reaching out, he placed his hands lightly on her hips and tugged her closer.

She resisted slightly but Ty increased the pressure until his arms encircled her waist. She laid her hands on his shoulders and arched back so that she could see his face. "You can't just waltz in here and act as if nothing has happened. What I want to know is how long you plan to stay. I can't deal with you always leaving."

He leaned forward, bringing his lips inches from hers. "Why not?"

"Because." It was killing her not to lean forward and meet his lips with hers.

His mouth continued to hover a hair's breadth from hers. "Maybe because you love me?"

"I don't love you."

"Well, that's too bad. Because I love you."

She floated on a cloud of pure bliss at the possibility of those words being true. Did she believe him? She so wanted to. Pulling her shoulders back so she could look into his eyes, she asked, "Really?"

Ty grinned. "Really." His expressive eyes reflected the truth of the statement. "Now, with that cleared up, I'm dying for a kiss. I've missed you, ma belle."

One of Ty's hands moved to cup the back of her neck. He brought his mouth to hers. She leaned into him and wrapped her arms around his neck, meeting Ty's kiss with one of her own. He nipped at her bottom lip and she opened for him. He wasted no time claiming her. His tongue dipped and parried, requesting her submission. Michelle willingly gave him everything. How she had longed for his touch. She moved closer, running her fingers through his hair, wanting all of him.

The sound of someone clearing their throat made them jerk apart. Ty made a rude remark under his breath and stood.

"Excuse me, Dr. Ross," the social worker said, looking embarrassed. "I did knock. More than once, and the door was open. I need your signature on this order before the patient can be discharged."

Heat warmed Michelle's face. She'd been caught passionately kissing a staff member and she didn't care. She straightened her bright blue sweater and reached out to take the paper the woman offered. Ty made a discreet move to stand behind her chair.

Michelle provided her signature with a flourish and gave the woman a wry smile. The social worker left quickly, without looking back. Michelle giggled.

Ty chuckled and came around the chair to stand beside her. "You got caught necking in the hospital."

"That news should be all over the building in less than five minutes."

"Do you care?" Ty asked with concern in his voice.

She smiled and stepped closer to him. "Not really."

Ty studied her. "You have changed."

"How's that?" she asked with a secret smile on her lips.

"There was a time when you wouldn't have wanted anyone to know your business. And look at the way you're dressed. By the way, that blue is very becoming on you."

She grinned at him. "Thank you, you silver-tongued devil. I have made some changes. Or at least I've been trying to. It's hard. I did tell my team about my mother. They deserved to know. I'm just sorry I didn't do it sooner. I had no idea so many of them have been affected by cancer. They have been very supportive."

"Is this the place where I'm not supposed to say I told you so?"

"It must be hard to be right all the time," she retorted.

"It is." Ty pulled her to him, taking her lips in a sizzling kiss. "That's not the only thing hard about me." His hand cupped her butt, bringing her against his length so that his manhood stood rigid between them.

"I think it's time we find some place private." He gave her a quick kiss.

"I'd like that."

"Get your purse," Ty growled.

She pulled it out of a drawer then he took her hand and led her out of the office.

"Where're we going?" Michelle asked in a breathless voice when they reached her car.

"Your place. I don't have one yet. I'll follow you."

Ty didn't wait for her answer before he stalked off in the direction of the motorcycle parking area. As she drove, Michelle glanced back at Ty, who followed her closely. Was he playing her again? It was one thing to want her, it was another to be around for the long haul. She'd made some changes in her life but the idea of having a special someone forever hadn't altered. Pulling into her spot in front of her condo, she saw Ty take the closest empty one to hers. She'd hardly stepped out of her car before he stood beside her.

He pulled her close, giving her a blistering kiss that was far too brief. "I've missed you. Got to have you."

She grinned. "I'm glad to see you too."

Ty took her hand and they walked to her door. As she unlocked it he said, "I plan to show you just how much."

Heat pooled low in her. She wanted him too.

They entered and Ty kicked the door closed with his heel. He gathered Michelle into his arms before she could put her purse down.

"I need you," he said in a raspy voice, "so much it hurts." His lips came down to claim hers in a soul-searching kiss. His hands roamed her body as if he was remembering every slope and turn. He pushed at her clothes, the tips of his fingers finding the sensitive skin beneath her camisole.

Michelle was on fire. All she wanted was to be bare beneath him. Their clothes littered the floor as they slowly walked toward, stumbled to and fell onto her bed.

"You deserve more than a fast tumble but I can't wait to have you," Ty said, his breath hot against her cheek. "I've already waited too long."

The low rumble of his desire-filled voice increased her need. Michelle opened her legs for him. His manhood came to rest strong and ready at her entrance.

Ty's gaze found and held hers. "I love you," he said as he pushed into her wet, waiting warmth.

"And I love you." She encircled his hips with her legs and welcomed him to where he belonged. Ecstasy enveloped her. She'd found her safe haven once more.

Ty reveled in the feel of Michelle's warm, luscious body nestled beside his. This moment, this woman were what had been missing from his life. He planned never to leave her.

"I think I'd like you to make love to me again really soon." She ran a hand over his chest, causing his skin to ripple in reaction.

He chuckled and caught her hand under one of his. "I think we need to talk first."

Michelle twisted so she could meet his look. "Since when are you the practical one?"

"Since it's time that I was."

She sat up, pulling the sheet with her, covering her breasts. Disappointment filled him. She had such lovely breasts. It was probably just as well. He needed to keep his wits about him. Pushing into a sitting position and reclining against a pillow, he faced her.

Her eyes turned thoughtful. "What changed your mind?"

"I found out real soon that life wasn't the same without you. I decided pretty quickly that I wanted you in it and if I wanted that I had to face my past, accept some things about it and myself." He paused and looked away for a second. "I went to see my parents."

Michelle leaned forward. "Oh, Ty, that must have been hard."

"It was, but it wasn't as difficult as I feared it might be. That's one of the reasons that it took me so long to get back here. I had to hunt for them. I rode from one end of the east coast to the other before I found someone who said they'd seen them recently." He crossed his arms over his chest. "My parents haven't changed. Aren't going to. They would've done the same for Joey today as they did back then. They wouldn't have let me take him to a doctor. I'm learning to accept that."

Michelle's hand cupped his cheek. "I know it won't bring Joey back but you make a difference in others' lives every time you step into the OR. You've made a difference in my life."

He kissed her palm. "Thank you for that."

She sat back and began playing with the hem of the sheet, no longer looking at him. "How long are you staying this time?" She glanced at him from under lowered eyelids, worry creasing her brow.

He ran a finger across her forehead, smoothing the furrows. "No time soon, ma belle. In fact, today was my first day as a full-time employee of Raleigh Medical."

Her eyes went wide. "Really?"

"Yes, really. I called Marshall when I decided you were right about me always running. I've decided I need to make a change in my life too. The job was still open and I accepted."

"Why didn't he say something to me?"

"I asked him not to."

She smiled. "So you'll be assigned to my OR regularly? If you are, you'd better show up on time."

"I think I've learned my lesson about that. But I'm not sure that I'll be assigned to your cases."

"Why not?"

He grinned at her perplexed look. "I don't know if Marshall will assign a husband to a wife's OR cases." He watched with joy and growing hope as uncertainty, amazement and then understanding moved across Michelle's face. "Will you marry me?"

She squealed and wrapped her arms around his neck. He kissed her with all the love he had in his heart.

Seconds later she pulled away. "Are you sure? You've moved around all your life. I don't want to be the reason you're unhappy."

"Ma belle, I've never been surer of anything. I've learned the hard way that you're what I want. I need to be where you are to be happy."

"You think you can live a conventional life?"

"I've already made a start. I bought the cottage from my friend. Well, he's more like my business associate. I'm a silent partner in Doctors to Go. Anyway, nothing screams stability like a mortgage."

Michelle observed him closely. "I'd say that's a start in the right direction. But I want you to be sure." She paused a moment. "Hey, why didn't you tell me you owned part of a business?"

He grinned. "Maybe I thought you might be a gold digger. Maybe I just didn't want to admit I was more of a conformist than I let on."

She leaned over and kissed him. "I don't think you'll ever be anything but unorthodox in a number of areas of your life, and I kind of like that about you."

"Really? I promise to conform enough to drive a minivan if you'll just have me and maybe a couple of my children."

"I'll have you any way I can get you. And I'd love to have your children."

"So," he raised a brow, "that's a yes?"

"Oh, that's a wonderfully perfect yes." Michelle sealed the promise with a kiss.

* * * * *

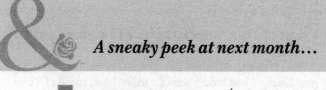

Doctors, romance, passion and drama—in the city that never sleeps

0113/03/MB44

Work hard, play harder...

Welcome to the Gold Coast, where hearts are broken as quickly as they are healed. Featuring some of the rising stars of the medical world, this new four-book series dives headfirst into Surfer's Paradise.

Available as a bundle at
www.millsandboon.co.uk/medical

Join the Mills & Boon Book Club

Subscribe to **Medical** today for 3, 6 or 12 months and you could **save over £40!**

We'll also treat you to these fabulous extras:

- FREE L'Occitane gift set worth £10

- FREE home delivery

- Rewards scheme, exclusive offers…and much more!

Subscribe now and save over £40
www.millsandboon.co.uk/subscribeme